Aristotle and the Secrets of Life

Margaret Doody is John and Barbara Glynn Family Professor of Literature at the University of Notre Dame. She is the author of a number of books including *The True Story of the Novel* and *Aristotle Detective*. She is also writing a book on Venice.

Magaret Anne Doody

Aristotle
and the
Secrets of Life

Ἀριστοτέλης καὶ Στέφανος
An Aristotle and Stephanos Novel

arrow books

Published by Arrow Books in 2004

1 3 5 7 9 10 8 6 4 2

Copyright © Margaret Doody 2003

Margaret Doody has asserted her right under the Copyright, Designs and
Patents Act 1988 to be identified as the author of this work

First published in the United Kingdom in 2003 by Century

Arrow Books
The Random House Group Limited
20 Vauxhall Bridge Road, London SW1V 2SA

Random House Australia (Pty) Limited
20 Alfred Street, Milsons Point, Sydney,
New South Wales 2061, Australia

Random House New Zealand Limited
18 Poland Road, Glenfield,
Auckland 10, New Zealand

Random House (Pty) Limited
Endulini, 5a Jubilee Road, Parktown 2193, South Africa

The Random House Group Limited Reg No. 954009

www.randomhouse.co.uk

A CIP catalogue record for this book
is available from the British Library

Papers used by Random House
are natural, recyclable products made from wood grown in
sustainable forests. The manufacturing processes conform to
the environmental regulations of the country of origin

ISBN 0 09 943557 8

Typeset by SX Composing DTP, Rayleigh, Essex
Printed and bound in Great Britain by
Bookmarque, Croydon, Surrey

This novel is gratefully dedicated
to
BEPPE BENVENUTO, 'the resurrection-man',
and to
ROSALIA COCI, 'la tradutrice incomparabile'

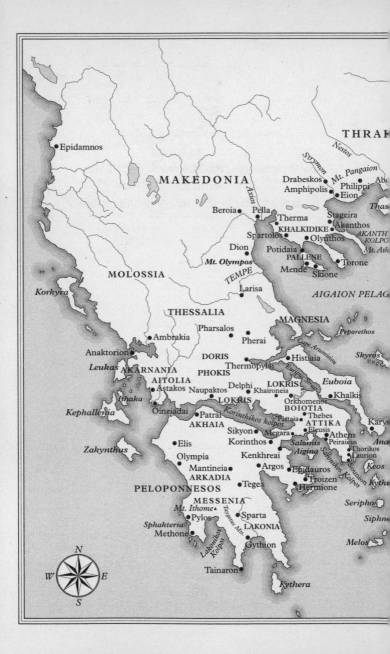

List of Characters

FAMILY CIRCLES AND CONNECTIONS OF ARISTOTLE AND STEPHANOS

Aristotle son of Nikomakhos: philosopher of Athens, age 54

Pythias daughter of Hermias of Atarneos: Aristotle's wife

Pythias the younger: daughter of Aristotle, a child nearly 6 years old

Herpyllis: slavewoman who takes care of young Pythias

Phokon: Aristotle's senior male slave, efficient and responsible

Olympos: Aristotle's second male slave

Kallisthenes: Aristotle's nephew, Alexander's historian

Stephanos son of Nikiarkhos: Athenian citizen of good will, nearly 26 years old; trying to better his prospects and get married

Eunike daughter of Diogeiton: Stephanos' mother, one of

the tribe of Erektheus

Theodoros: Stephanos' younger brother, not yet 10 years old

Philemon: Stephanos' cousin, age 25; a veteran

Smikrenes: irascible farmer of Eleusis area, Stephanos' prospective father-in-law

Philomela daughter of Smikrenes: Stephanos' bride-to-be, age 15

Geta: slave of Smikrenes, Philomela's old nurse

Philonike: estranged wife of Smikrenes, mother of Philomela, a bee-keeper living in Hymettos

Philokleia: mother of Philonike and grandmother of Philomela, managing family farm in Hymettos

Dropides: second husband of Philokleia, step-father of Philonike, a man of invalid habits

Philokles: brother of Philonike and uncle of Philomela; inheritor of estate in Hymettos, but now travelling in the eastern islands

Mika: elderly slavewoman of household at Hymettos

SCHOLARS AND STUDENTS OF THE LYKEION

Theophrastos: scholar, age 40, with a strong interest in plants; Aristotle's right-hand man

Eudemos of Rhodos: witty and urbane scholar, near Theophrastos' age

Demetrios of Phaleron: young scholar, extraordinarily handsome

Hipparkhos of Argos: serious scholar in his late 20s, looks like a horse

Arkhandros of Lampsakos: serious scholar in his 30s, very pale

Mikon: student, age 14, who takes an interest in the Lykeion's research projects

Parmenion son of Arkhebios: grandson (illegitimate line) of Alexander's great general Parmenion, age 14. A young student whose strange mental state causes concern

CITIZENS OF ATHENS AND THEIR ASSOCIATES

Megakles: important Athenian citizen with a sun-burnt bald spot and an earnest manner

Thrasymakhos: important Athenian with some claim to be an orator; father of Mikon

Apollonios: sturdy and patriotic citizen who resents Makedonian rule

Theosophoroas: middle-aged citizen of sardonic temper, with no great love for Stephanos

Epikrates: rich little citizen, cheated in a deal with an Egyptian perfumer

Hypereides: orator and statesman, age 61; antipathetic to Makedonians; helpful to Epikrates in his law case

Antigone: freedwoman, successful whore of Athens, owner of a brothel; involved in a lawsuit with Epikrates

Euphorbos: young man of good family, a humorist and game-player

Kallias: rich citizen, fond of his pets; owns a monkey

Eurymedon: of the tribe of Eumolpidai, a guardian of the cult of Demeter who takes his religious charge seriously

Gorgias son of Lysippos: dramatic citizen in his early twenties, son of a rich silversmith

PERSONS ENCOUNTERED ON THE JOURNEY AND IN THE EAST

Aiskhines: Athenian captain of small fast ship *Eudaimonia*

Hermippos of Laurion: traveller; engaged at home in silver business, owner of an ore washery and smelting furnace

Widow: Hermippos' daughter, mother of child Philokleia

Philokleia: Hermippos' little asthmatic granddaughter, age 7

Miltiades: cheerful merchant of marble

Philokhoros: traveller of distinction who seems to dote on his slave

Sosios: slave to Philokhoros

Doris: crippled slavewoman with little dog

Kardaka: mistress of Doris

Magistrate of Delos

Lysis: manager of brothel 'Naumakhia' in Mykonos

A marble merchant of Paros

Aristodamos: gentleman of Naxos with ties to Delos; an old friend of Aristotle

Nikias: Koan captain of small fast ship the *Niké*

Koriskos: son of an old acquaintance of Aristotle, on an embassy to Alexander

Iatrokles: surgeon of Kos and descendant of Asklepios; an old acquaintance of Aristotle

Kleumedes: Iatrokles' partner, a physician of Kos and descendant of Asklepios

Oromedon son of Daliokles: important citizen of Kos, old friend of Aristotle

Peleus: practical army man, used to organising convoys

Diophantos: officer in charge of a platoon in Lykia

Menestor: Theban captive, age nearly 17; a slave
   working for officers of the army in Asia
Harpalos: Alexander's treasurer, former student of
   Aristotle
Pythonike: beautiful Athenian mistress of Harpalos, who
   accompanies him to Asia
Nanno of Kalymnos: beautiful and rich lady of the
   islands, formerly mistress to a Makedonian general

Various travellers, sailors and soldiers

CONTENTS

Speak to me, O Muse, and open my mouth that true and good things may come from my lips. Let me tell aright this history of plunder and evil, pain and captivity and wandering over the wide sea.

Thanks be to Asklepios that I was healed of my wound. May all the blessings of Hygieia flow through me and mine, now and always. With all honour to Asklepios the divine Physician, to Paieon, ever-hymned in realms above, and to Lord Apollo.

PART I
PARTS OF ANIMALS

I

The Sanctuary of Asklepios

It was still dark as we moved cautiously along the narrow way at the side of the steep Akropolis, towards the southern slope. Four men, two of whom were slaves carrying a litter, and one unseen woman, enclosed in the box they bore along.

'Be careful!' exclaimed the older man sharply, as one of the slaves nearly missed his footing on the invisible path. A few belated owls still hooted around the temple above us. Straining our eyes against darkness we searched for the shrine. Wings flapped. One of the cocks I held was struggling to fly, as if to escape his death or else to hasten towards his appointed end. It was hard holding on to the birds with their wiry feet and claws and writhing necks, especially as I could not see them. I could feel one of them digging into my hand, even though we had bound their beaks for the journey.

The shrine at last was before us, a dark shape mysteriously solid in the no-dimension of night. We waited, at the head of a little line of suppliants, in the summer morning, the strange time just before dawn. The sky grew less dark. Birds chirped. Then along the eastern horizon as along the edges of a cut a redness bled along the eastern sky. The first rays struck the temple door, and the door opened. We pilgrims and suppliants joined the priests and their attendants in singing the morning hymn:

> 'Awaken Paieon Asklepios
> Awaken and hear thy hymn!'

Aristotle and the slave assisted the woman out of her cramped container. She stood there, leaning against her husband, a thin woman, but evidently pregnant, and heavily veiled. We moved together towards the altar-place. Somewhere near us were the snakes in the sacred pits, but I could not see them. I unbound the cocks; Aristotle and the slaves assisted the attendants in taking them to the altar. They flapped and crowed, announcing the dawn just as the attendant advanced upon them with a thin sharp knife. Their 'coco-ricoo!' was cut short. A splash of blood dabbled the marble stone and the bright confident feathers. The light moved in a rosy ray streaming over the altar, making a glimmer in the blood and in the sightless eyes of the severed heads, floppy under their red combs.

We stood in prayer and supplication in an enclosure lit by a little altar fire and by the fresh dawn light. A sweet summer morning breeze came through the open door.

The priest-physician asked 'What is troubling you?' and Aristotle answered.

'My wife has been troubled by mild fever and want of

appetite. Often she cannot keep food down when she does eat.'

'Is she pregnant?' the priest asked quickly. 'Lady, I insist that you must answer for yourself. Who are you? What is your name?'

'Pythias, wife of Aristotle of Athens.'

'Are you pregnant?'

'I am.'

'You know,' the priest said addressing both of them, 'that Asklepios has no remedy for pregnancy, as it is a natural matter, and we do not treat it. And you should know that no child is to be born within the precincts consecrated to Asklepios.'

'But,' Aristotle argued, 'my wife's troubles are other than just those of pregnancy itself. I am a physician's son and I know. She has feverishness, she trembles. Describe your symptoms,' he added, turning to Pythias, who answered in a voice low and pleasant, with more than a little touch of foreign inflection:

'Hot and then cold. Trembling in the limbs. Some weakness in the eyes that comes and goes. And trouble with my stomach and some soreness in the side. It is not like my former childbearing.'

'You have borne children before?'

'Two stillborn, one who lived a year and died of a disease, and one a little girl who lives now.'

'And you, sir.' The priest turned to Aristotle. 'Describe your own afflictions.'

'Pain in the leg – sciatic trouble. Stiffness and pain in the thigh and leg.'

'Any others?' He looked at me, I shook my head. I was there as a supporter of Aristotle, literally. I stood at his left side ready for him to lean on if need be. Aristotle was supporting Pythias. On her other side stood Aristotle's kinsman Theophrastos.

The priest-physician and our party went on into the proper prayers. I gazed around the inner precincts with eyes increasingly cleansed by the growing light. There were many good images. Asklepios the little child, the newborn babe – surrounded by soft flames or light rays. Asklepios the Beloved, the Great Healer. This is a really good statue of the healer seated on a throne with snakes like wheels standing out in relief along the sides of the chair. Asklepios holds his staff with the snake entwined around it. His long curly hair and luxuriant curling beard make him look slightly foreign, like a Phoenician. His face is noble, the eyes wonderfully carved and deeply set. They look off into the distance with a suggestion of suffering and hope – yet these eyes seem also to look at you, with a look of great compassion. Behind the healer there is a large votive relief showing Asklepios with his sons, the two physicians, one Machaon the surgeon and the other Podaleirios, a treater of internal ills. And a good tall image of his daughter Hygieia. One may hope not to need Asklepios' sons, but everyone wants his daughter, who is Health itself.

At that moment we were all together there in that tight little sanctuary, close to the healer – Aristotle and Pythias, myself, Theophrastos. Together, alive and safe. The light glided in and struck the wall, so that I could now see clearly the thank-offering images hung upon it. Some of these were crudely carved sticks, others elaborately polished wood with fine carving. Not a few were in silver that made a pleasant glitter in the sunbeams. One bronze image of a full-sized big toe glistened with polish, and was adorned with a miniature garland. A leg, a hand, an eye, a penis. Here, a shield showed gratitude for delivery from war. There, part of a ship carved in marble – a sign of someone saved from shipwreck, or recovered from physical damage wrought by a shipwreck. Garlands of real hair fluffed out on pictured wooded heads, images of children made well. All gave assurance of the power of the divine Physician, and the strength of healing of the dark earth, the sacred springs, and the serpent who comes from the depths.

We departed from the sanctuary, Pythias leaning on her husband, after the priest-physician gave some instructions, which seemed to involve chiefly change of diet and sitting in a warm place in the sunlight. Pythias had to be helped carefully into the litter. We set off again, Aristotle limping a little from the sciatic trouble. It was especially irritating to someone as active and restless as he – his group have been called 'the Peripatetics' because he liked lecturing while walking about. He preferred in general to be in motion. I wasn't worried that Aristotle would be permanently crippled. The philosopher was still surprisingly active for a man of his age, even if he suffered intermittently from sciatic complaint, especially after he was careless or forgetful enough to sit very long on a damp marble bench. As for Pythias, she would soon be delivered of her trouble and Aristotle would have the son he long had wished for. The priest-physician had been right, perhaps, to be a little alarmed about the risk of a birth within the shrine, as is forbidden absolutely in the holy place, for Pythias was evidently near her time.

Aristotle himself seemed relieved and expansive.

'I have so seldom been here,' he said, 'but Pythias wished to come. I would have liked us to go to the Asklepion in Peiraieus, which is in some ways finer than this one, and I think has better priests. And many associations too – you remember it in Aristophanes' *Ploutos?* But that is too far for her to travel, while it was quite practicable for us to come here. She will be easier in her mind.'

'What did they prescribe?' I asked, more from a sort of politeness than real curiosity.

'The usual sort of thing, you know. Hydromel when she can keep nothing else down, for the honey-and-water mixture will quench thirst and supply food for the baby. Liquids are good. Eggs, too. Sitting in the sunshine – fortunately we have a courtyard where she can do that. They consider it partly an eye problem. When she recovers she is to offer at the shrine an image of an eye – as for me, I should donate the image of a leg. I shall have them done in silver I think, and we will sacrifice a pig. By the time we have the images made, we shall have our baby – our boy, as I hope and believe.'

'At least,' I said, 'you have already sacrificed a cock. In advance.'

'"A cock for Asklepios." Sokrates' last words – as I know you will recall. The cock cries at dawn, so this is an offering for day, for light and life itself. When we are born we see daylight, enjoy the gift of our first dawning. In sacrificing a cock we give thanks for the new day.'

'But Sokrates said that just before he died,' I objected. '*He* didn't get a new day. They were putting him to death at the time.'

'Sokrates must have meant in thanksgiving for the new

day, even though it was to be his last. But more truly, I suppose, he meant an offering of thanksgiving for the whole of his life, for the gift of birth. For being permitted to exist and to have a human life in the world. To live is a wonderful thing! When we get back to the Lykeion, let us look up Plato's account in his wonderful book.'

We had left the Akropolis and skirted the Agora, already beginning to fill with the morning crowds, as we made for the city gate. Although they now had the benefit of daylight, the bearers of Pythia's litter had a hard time in threading through some of the narrow streets with their burden. Men hammering metal or making chairs seemed determined to carry out their work on the footway, making the path difficult. Children ran up to us to try to sell us things. One of them, a little fellow wrapped in a cloak with a thick hood, was most persistent, poking some shabby herbs at us. At length Aristotle took the faded fennel and tossed him a coin: 'just to get rid of him,' as he explained.

'That child doesn't look very healthy,' I said. 'He probably has some illness if he is so wrapped up and hooded when it is nearly midsummer.'

Indeed, the day was growing warm already, though midsummer was some twenty days away. Outside the city, harvests were ripening, or had already been gathered. Hay had been cut. Sweet roses bloomed briefly and you could smell flowers even in Athens, where you cannot see the gardens that flourish behind house walls.

It would have been a relatively short journey to return to my own house; the way back to Aristotle's house was slightly further, long enough for slaves with a burden. (Not that Pythia was heavy – far from it – but the litter itself was an awkward object.) Aristotle lived outside the city gates, in the opposite direction from Plato's Akademeia, which was likewise outside the city gates. Aristotle lived in an eastern region, well watered by the Ilissos river and shaded with plane trees – a lovely area, though at that time quite noisy with the building of the new Stadium. His celebrated school was in the precinct named for Apollo Lykeios, the god of wolves – who, curiously, also keeps wolves away. Aristotle's school was referred to as 'the Lykeion', just like the nearby gymnasium at which the young men did their military service training. He took private students, and had special scholars working with him, but the area was a place of open groves and free discussion; the Lykeion neighbourhood was a gathering-place for philosophers and philosophy-seekers. Most of Aristotle's celebrated lectures were public in the good old fashion. The area had always been full of young men, so it was a good place to garner those who wanted to engage in intellectual conversation.

Aristotle had to rent accommodation for his family and his school. The law of Athens prohibited aliens, even a resident alien, a *metoikos* like Aristotle, from owning any property. Thus, even though he had been Plato's best – and probably favourite – student, Plato could not bequeath the Akademeia to him. Aristotle had left Athens for a long time after the death of Plato. When he came back, married to this foreign woman, he rented his own residence in the Lykeion area. He had sunk some of his personal money in the place, adding on and creating outbuildings. His needs included an inordinate amount of space for books. Any major changes had to be approved by the city, and of course his improvements represented a loss, as he could not sell the place to another, nor legally bequeath it to his heirs.

When we arrived at the Lykeion, Aristotle was visibly anxious to see that Pythias was immediately settled in their home. 'She is tired and needs to rest,' he said.

'Herpyllis will look after me,' said a muffled voice from within the litter.

'Olympos and Phokon will help us and put the litter away,' Aristotle planned. 'So, Theophrastos, why don't you take Stephanos into our Thinkery and introduce him? Treat him to one of our modest meals? I shall join you later.'

The slaves set the litter down and helped their mistress out of it. Very gently Aristotle took her hand, and then put his arm around her. The two went up the shallow flight of garden steps to the house door. I heard her say 'I am so glad Herpyllis is here now. You need not come in if you have your visitor.'

'Of course I shall see you in, my darling,' said Aristotle in a tone I had never heard him use before.

Theophrastos took charge of me and conveyed me a different way to the school's main buildings. I knew the Lykeion well – I had studied there myself for all too short a time, attracted by Aristotle's reputation and then by his intellect, until my father's business dealing grew so entangled and his means so straitened that I had had to leave. Shortly after that, my father died, and my family was plunged in chaos. I was by no means one of the best students at the Lykeion and the lack of my presence cannot have been any blow to Aristotle. But I turned to my old teacher later. After the death of my father, when my cousin was accused of murder and our family was besieged by difficulties, I came to ask Aristotle for help, though I had no claim upon him. I had turned up at his house, seeking advice, one day in the early autumn, nearly three years before this morning's visit to the Asklepion. I had reason to be glad I did so, for the philosopher's generous intellect and practical activity saved our family from disaster. Aristotle and I had recently been involved in another curious crime, when we had pursued an abducted heiress to Delphi in the spring of this same year whose summer warmth we were now enjoying.

Despite my growing friendship with Aristotle, however, I was by no means familiar with the Lykeion in its present state. Changes had been wrought since my time, as Theophrastos pointed out to me.

'We had to add more space – we extended the book room, simply because we had so many books. That's not counting the ones that Aristotle keeps in his own house.' I nodded, for I had seen him at home in his personal room with its surprising quantity of books. 'We have a special compartment for keeping especially valuable rolls dry and clean,' Theophrastos went on. 'Aristotle calls it "the book-pantry". And he designed this room.'

We were entering a long room – about twice the length I remembered. The upper half of each wall was now lined with shelves and compartments for book-rolls. The room smelt sweetly of the wood; it struck me that these boards, obviously of very good quality, must have been a costly importation, since wood is extremely scarce in Athens. In the lower middle of the wall below the book compartments and at waist height was a wide shelf running around the whole room, making a sort of universal work space. The light came in from windows high up under the roof, to keep rain out.

'Aristotle calls this room "the book kitchen". We write here as well as read. He designed those windows and had shades of linen made, so the sun doesn't fall directly on the rolls when they are open, and fade them,' Theophrastos explained. I could see that on the side of the room which the sun struck the windows were covered with strips of cloth.

'And now we have so many plants and specimens sent by Kallisthenes we are housing them in a special plant room.' He turned towards the door. 'Oh, here's Demetrios.'

A young man of most striking and unusual beauty came into view. This Demetrios was tall and well-shaped, with an admirable – nay, perfect – nose; his hair, worn rather long, was a sunny colour even in this pleasantly shady room. 'Demetrios of Phaleron,' Theophrastos introduced us. 'Stephanos of Kydathenion.' I wondered fleetingly why Theophrastos introduced us by naming the deme rather than by father's name; such a beautiful young man must have an eminent father. Demetrios nodded kindly to me. Although he could not have been much more than twenty years of age, the aristocratic youth seemed possessed of great aplomb.

'Demetrios has done most of these wonderful drawings,' Theophrastos explained. 'Demetrios, do move those shades a moment so Stephanos can see better.'

I now realised that against one wall, resting on the very furthest reach of the wide shelf, there were a series of drawings and diagrams. This was certainly not like the usual picture gallery! No Daphnes or Andromedas. They were the oddest things. Here was a picture devoted to an animal's leg, its parts labelled. There was a womb, and a scrotum with the testes – the central figures without any bodies attached. One picture was full of various spiny fish, with crustaceans displayed in a strip at the lower edge.

'Exceedingly well done,' I exclaimed politely, looking at these uncouth images of squid and sea-urchins. 'You have a variety of ingredients in your "book-kitchen".'

Demetrios of Phaleron laughed. 'You must not think,' he assured me, 'that Aristotle thinks it denigrating for us to refer to his "pantry" and his "kitchen". He claims the centre of the body is a kind of kitchen or furnace. The stomach is always busy cooking, and the heart too, kindling and sustaining the natural heat, without which the soul cannot function. And the nourishment –'

'Is transmitted to the rest of the body,' continued Theophrastos. '"Where every part continues the work and cooks with its own heat",' the two chorused, evidently repeating well-known phrases and opinions of the master. A curly-haired youth came into the room, attracted by their amusement.

'Ah, here's Mikon. Stephanos, son of Nikiarkhos. Mikon, son of Thrasymakhos.' The merry little fellow of some fourteen summers came confidently up to us. That he was well-born I could have deduced from the fact that Theophrastos made such a formal introduction of this child. 'Mikon has made unusual progress. And he has assisted in creating the pictures – he has done much of the shading and coloration.'

'Impressive,' I agreed. 'What are the pictures for?'

'They're going to go into books,' Mikon exclaimed.

'And be read by *everybody!*

'When they are finished,' Demetrios explained. 'That is the idea – they will be copied into the books on animals that Aristotle has been working on.'

'And then,' added Mikon, 'there are all the new plants to examine.'

'Yes,' said Demetrios. 'Let us show you, Stephanos. Aristotle's nephew Kallisthenes, who travels with Alexander, has sent us new plants from Asia.'

'I should like to see them,' I said politely. I knew from Aristotle's talk of Kallisthenes that he held this nephew in high regard. So did Alexander of Makedon. Kallisthenes, as an outstanding scholar and writer, had been chosen by Alexander to accompany him to Asia. Aristotle's nephew was now travelling with Alexander and his army in order to write the official history of the Great War with Persia that was taking place. Or *had* taken place. As Alexander now held Persepolis and Babylon, it only remained to find and kill King Darius of Persia. But I hadn't quite realised that Kallisthenes was still a kind of partner in Aristotle's own labours, providing him with a steady supply of Asian materials for his natural studies.

We went from this 'book kitchen' to the next room through a short corridor with a door at each end. I presumed efforts had been made to shut off the room of living specimens so that the damp and smell should not pervade the book room. In various places on the wall and hanging from hooks in the ceiling were innumerable (so it seemed) roots and branches. One bush had ruffled rosy bloom upon it – most attractive, with an interesting smell. But many of the plants seemed dull, dry and withered.

'It is hard to keep them,' said Demetrios, following my

gaze. 'Kallisthenes packs them cleverly in damp moss and so on, but they do suffer. And Athens' air is probably saltier than these upland plants are used to.'

Some animal skeletons also hung from the ceiling (I thought I recognised a dog). In tall thick pottery containers pieces of animals floated. On a large work-table were scattered drawings of the plants and a number of writing tablets, some covered with information.

'This is our "back kitchen" or "slaughterhouse",' explained Demetrios. 'Nowadays we tend to call it "the plant room". But we are mainly interested in animals.'

'Who is writing?' I asked, looking at the tablets.

'We all do. We design a description on the wax tablet,' explained Demetrios. 'Then we discuss it – and if we agree upon it, someone copies it out into the big book that is the draft of our eventual catalogue. Here's Hipparkhos of Argos. He can explain some things better than I can, especially the animals.'

Hipparkhos was a big eager-looking man with a long face and long sensible nose.

'And do you work on horses?' I enquired. As this man's name means 'master of horses' – really, Master of Horse, describing a cavalry leader – I thought this pleasantry rather clever. I might not have thought of it had Hipparkhos not looked so like a horse himself. But he frowned at my frivolous question, looking like a horse in perplexity.

'We have no great variety of horses here. The common horse is a well-known quadruped. Could we obtain a different sort of horse from Asia, of course we should like that. Aristotle is looking for a variety of animal kinds. I'm working with Eudemos here in writing descriptions.'

'Stephanos, son of Nikiarkhos of Athens.' Theophrastos' tone moved to extreme formality, so I guessed almost before I saw him that this newcomer was very well born. 'Eudemos of Rhodos.'

Eudemos was tall, with dark curling hair; he was much more handsome than one expects in a scholar, though not as statuesque as young Demetrios. Eudemos acknowledged me with aristocratic ease. Without unnecessary change of facial expression he murmured some conventional expressions of his pleasure. 'And Arkhandros of Lampsakos.' Arkhandros was pale, like a root vegetable kept too long in a cellar, and his black hair only emphasised his pallor.

'These scholars,' Theophrastos explained, 'all assist in the great undertaking. They are Aristotle's chief – er –'

'You may call us assistants,' said Eudemos politely. 'Along with Theophrastos here, the scholar on whom the master most relies. We are Aristotle's cooks. We cut up animals and plants.'

'But it is more than that,' exclaimed young Mikon. 'We are going to produce a rational plan of all the things that are – so everything that is will be known.'

'*All* that is! That is too tall an order.' Aristotle had come up behind us. 'But we are trying to explore the universe of Nature, and to create rational categories for living beings.'

'Without the appropriate categories, thinking cannot happen,' added Arkhandros, probably quoting or paraphrasing something he had heard from Aristotle himself.

'You see what great steps we are taking in our journey towards knowledge, Stephanos,' Aristotle said to me.

'This is something I have been working on since I was a young man – after I left Plato's Akademeia – but it was not possible to complete it when I was working on my own. Now I have these able assistants and scholars' – he waved a comprehensive hand – 'to aid me, so we proceed apace. As Herodotos wrote his gigantic enquiry into the whole nature and development of the war between Persians and Greeks, so I am writing a full account of the animals. Here we observe and write down all the differences between them that allow us to set them into different classes. We observe the wonderful order which is everywhere in the cosmos, though sometimes seeming too small – or too large – for us to see.'

I murmured politely, but I felt somewhat repelled by the musty earthy odour of the plant roots, and even more by the meaty contents of the pots.

'It seems strange for a philosopher to be concerned with animals,' I remarked.

'But why? As we are, as Plato suggests, featherless bipeds, we should have respect for the animals. We study Art – why not Nature, so much greater than the arts? We must not pout because flesh or blood or spines or beaks or organs are distasteful – we can leave childish exclamations of disgust to children. The question is, how can we discuss a world which we do not know? We live in ignorance, and our descriptions are partial and irregular. The same with calendars – you know that I have been interested in collecting accounts of the Olympian and Pythian Games, and so on. Not because I am peculiarly concerned with athletic events, but because these lists give us measurements of time – year after year. Eventually – soon – we can construct a regular world calendar, with all events set on a line of time, giving us a uniform picture of temporal reality without which history – the study of mankind – isn't possible.'

I felt a bit alarmed at this notion. 'I like Athenian time,' I said.

'Well, let us say that in Athenian time and Lykeion time we call it "time to eat". Stay to take food with us,' said Aristotle. 'I shall eat with the scholars and pupils today, as Pythias is very fatigued and needs to lie down. Fortunately she has Herpyllis with her. A real treasure! – a household slave from my mother's family in Euboia. She's an accomplished nurse, and good with children. Pythias thinks the world of her. I encouraged Pythias to lie down as I really don't like the swelling in her ankles,' he added. I was embarrassed by being made the recipient of such intimate information. But Aristotle had no close relative of his own nearby (except perhaps for Theophrastos, whose exact degree of kinship remained undefined), and I supposed he needed to share these family details with someone.

'Mikon, do you call the others into the Refectory,' Eudemos commanded. 'Tell them the meal is ready now.' Mikon departed eagerly.

'I should add that it is a very humble meal,' said Aristotle. 'We don't drink wine when we are working in the middle of the day. Very Pythagorean, our repast. I promise you, we'll see to it that you are not served anything in those pots!'

We departed from the room of specimens and went into a long room, an indoor lecture hall, where the slaves had set up plank tables on trestles. Stools were placed along the edge. It was a simple arrangement for a simple meal.

The little band of young students filed in, led by Mikon. They were healthy and sun-tanned, laughing and talking, their din only a little repressed by the presence of Aristotle and the senior scholars. Their presence and chatter added a note of cheer. But one among them seemed sad and withdrawn, and stared down at his plate without consuming anything.

'How do you like our arrangement?' Aristotle asked me. I was seated in the position of honour, on his right, a post usually, I imagined, reserved for Eudemos or Theophrastos. 'Very much as it was in your day, I recall. We often eat out of doors now the weather is so fine, but it is easier and quicker for the slaves to set everything up here when there are a number of persons.'

'And your slaves have had a wearisome slow errand to the Akropolis already. How did your visit to the shrine of Asklepios go, O Aristotle?' enquired Demetrios.

'Oh – well, just as those things always do,' said Aristotle. I thought he wasn't best pleased that his personal life should be the subject of general conversation in these surroundings. 'Do you know,' he added with a more general glance around, 'I am myself supposedly descended from Asklepios, through his son Machaon?'

'Then you should be a surgeon and slice things open,' said Hipparkhos. 'By the way, how are we going to deal with all our specimens now that it is so warm? Will they survive the hot weather?'

'The weather has become most agreeable, hasn't it?' remarked Eudemos, who was on Aristotle's left. 'The month of Skiraphorion is delightful – especially as it has only antique and unimportant festivals. The Skira itself, for one. Quite charming. The procession of the priestess of Athena, the priest of Poseidon and the priest of the Sun all tramping out on the west road under a white canopy. And the best of it is, nobody knows what it means.'

'This is also the month of the Dipolieia,' remarked Theophrastos. 'The festival of Zeus Polieus, guardian of the city.'

'And the biggest sacrifice of the Dipolieia is the Buphonia. The time of the ox-slaying has come again! An Athenian custom. We ought to go.'

'Perhaps,' said Aristotle, 'we can make up a party to see the murder of the ox. Would you come, Stephanos? It is probably a long while since you saw the Bouphonia.'

'Thank you,' I said politely.

Changing the topic, I asked Aristotle, idly enough, about the pale, unsociable pupil. 'Who is the young fellow who seems so sad?'

'He? You may actually have heard of him before, Theophrastos told me about him when you and I were coming back from Delphi in the early spring. Young Parmenion there was in a bad way. He gets very tearful and sad, often for no reason. And sometimes he has outbursts. He seemed better in the late spring, though I know he now has a real cause for concern, as he is worried about where his father is. But his troubles seem to be largely in his own mind, and I fear they now increase again.

'Perhaps, Theophrastos –' to this gentleman, who was seated on my right – 'you can tell us more of the condition of young Parmenion.'

'Bad and getting worse,' said Theophrastos. 'I thought his bad mood was lifting, but now I fear it may be seriously deteriorating. We should really take him home,

I fear. He's too young to send on his own.'

'He is the grandson of the great general Parmenion, isn't he? Strange in one of such descent – if on the wrong side of the blanket – to show such weakness of mind,' said Hipparkhos. 'But as for taking him home – might be dangerous. Things are still disturbed in the East.'

'We might have army protection. Certainly his whole family, including his father, is friendly to the royal house. Above all, great Parmenion, once chief Companion of King Philip and now Alexander's second-in-command,' said Theophrastos, in his precise manner. Theophrastos always loved to get facts in order. 'It is true that this boy's father was not a *legitimate* son of the great general, but he has always been treated quite as one of the family.'

'The boy was allowed to be named after his grandfather,' observed Hipparkhos.

'Quite so. And Parmenion's legitimate son Philotas, a brilliant general in his own right and one of the Companions of Alexander, is very fond of this nephew. The lad has reason to hope for favour and assistance – but we still are not quite sure where to find his father, Arkhebios. As a Makedonian soldier, he serves in Alexander's army. At one time he was in the island of Rhodos, helping with the pacification. There is a possibility he has been moved to Kos.'

'Well, you or Eudemos might take a trip eastward,' said Aristotle jovially. 'Eudemos might like to go – he comes from Rhodos, after all. A pity that we cannot do anything for the boy here. Perhaps a visit to a really good centre of medicine would help. Kos itself might help him.'

Dismissing that subject, he turned back to me.

'Well what do you think of our Lykeion now?' he asked.

'Grown since your time, hasn't it?'

'It has,' I acknowledged. I didn't quite like thinking of 'my time' as a long way off.

'Our book collection is considerable now. Fortunately, Theophrastos loves the books – taking care of them, I mean. He never lets them get dusty, nor the tabs get out of place. He sees to it that everything goes back to its correct location. As you see, we have attracted many excellent scholars to work with us. Eudemos comes from a very distinguished family in Rhodos, but he has spent his time here working, with his hands as well as his mind, on Asian plants. As he is from that region he has a familiarity that others might not. Though I myself had spent time on the Asian coast at Assos and in Lesbos. I came to know the coastal region of Asia pretty well, years ago. It was there I first seriously began studying animals, looking at the life of the shores, observing the rays and squid and crustaceans.'

'So, you are going to try to describe everything that lives?'

'That is what we would *like* to do – but it is too ambitious! Yet it is possible to work with such a multitude of kinds that what we say will be right. All men – even scholars – have lived hitherto with insufficient categories – even an entirely insufficient idea of what a category is. And truly we need to investigate systematically. We study the particulars.'

'Aristotle thinks,' said Demetrios, 'that there is a kind of art in Nature – even in the small things.'

'Assuredly, yes. Nothing is unimportant. Consider what Herakleitos said on the privy: "Come in; there are gods even here." There is a beauty in the intricacy of bodies – of living bodies. For the body is no mere shape – not just a "form" as the vulgar and even some who are educated think of forms – but a point of development and of activity. Nature is a dynamic specialist. She prefers to make each organ perfect to serve one purpose. Not a cheap worker like the humble smith who for utility makes you a brass lampstand-and-meat-spit in one! Think of what we have seen of the vessels that carry the blood –'

'Though these are very difficult to observe,' said Demetrios seriously. 'It is hard to peer into the inner secrets of nature. We can cut an animal open, of course – but then the life is gone even as we observe it, and the blood gushes away.'

'We have found,' said Hipparkhos, 'that for observation it is sometimes better to starve the animal so that the blood vessels stand out sharply. But of course we do not succeed in seeing all the blood vessels, even in that manner.'

'But what we do discern is very regular and beautifully ordered,' said Aristotle. 'Like the rills and channels in a well-arranged and well-watered garden, where the skilled gardener has created a main channel and then conducted many little rivulets out from it.'

'That's the kind of comparison Theophrastos loves,' remarked Eudemos. 'I'm not sure he didn't first suggest it. Theophrastos loves gardens.'

Aristotle ignored this, being caught up in his subject.

'At the same time, mere particulars do not form the categories themselves. Of course not! And our *catalogue* is not what we shall publish. That is just a beginning. Without method, without thought, all one has is mere lists. I could make a list of the times I pare my fingernails, and it would be quite true – and quite useless unless I had some end in view. The end in view is not just knowledge of the world around us, but also a real understanding of what life is. Life in this world of coming-to-be and passing away. Our subject is nothing less than Life itself.'

He quite took my breath away with the expanse of his topic.

'Of first importance,' said Aristotle, warming to his theme, 'is the inherent power of the intellect which leads it to perceive or divine – in some ways one might even say to generate – order. The intellect knows order as a participant in the divine Mind in the universe. Thus we have already within us the power to perceive and speak of categories. The *idea* is not created by molluscs and trees.'

'Oh, quite, yes,' I agreed, indistinctly, as I was chewing on a tough piece of bread at the time. I was not certain that I was going to grasp all this.

'The body exists for its perfection, which is the soul, the capacity to move and beget and so on. It is absurd to think, as some do, that the soul is "in the body" as a sailor is "in a boat". The soul is the form the body seeks. Intellect is primary. But the lively intelligence using the organs of the body perceives the world. The understanding needs an assemblage of particulars – to *chew* on, if I may use such an analogy.' His eyes twinkled as I hastily tried to swallow the bread I had been doggedly masticating.

'We need the details, the living particulars. It is possible to obtain an understanding of the world by working with it, using the senses to examine particulars. As long as one has a *method*. It is the mind that must analyse – otherwise you're just left with a curious list, as I say. We want to establish the attributes, so we can treat together animals that are connected by their attributes. And in analysing living things, the productions of nature, we look not for history but for causes. In Nature the causes are ends, not beginnings. Always remember, *Nature creates for the future.* In theoretical sciences, or in study of objects of human art, we start with what already is. We think backwards, about a history. A new statue has a kind of being, but no future, only a past. It lacks the signs of life. A puppy has a future. In study of natural things we are always looking at what is *going to be.* In embryos of all kinds, including eggs, the beating heart, the sovereign organ, is formed first for the work it *will* do. A human embryo has hands because it will be a man who will use them.'

The others had become quiet, in order to listen to Aristotle's animated speech.

'So,' Eudemos said when Aristotle fell silent. 'By taking thought, and through a process of complete and regular observation — not piecemeal nor whimsical — we will arrive through particulars at general truths.'

'Yes,' added Hipparkhos. 'And you see the advantage. We will truly know what species are. So when a new animal is discovered — Pop! It goes into its correct category as soon as it appears.'

'This world itself manifesting an order at once wonderfully complex and beautifully simple,' added Aristotle. He did not seem daunted by the amount of work that must remain to be done. His eyes sparkled. Though the meal had been as he promised, Pythagorean, of only vegetables, bread, fruit and water, yet beholding his enthusiasm one would think he had drunk a noble wine.

'I am grateful to all my fellow-scholars here for their

tireless work and wonderful insight,' Aristotle added. 'Together we can carry knowledge forward.'

'It seems an odd thing, in a way,' I said. 'Philosophy – isn't it supposed to deal with Truth, and the Good, or how to behave oneself – that sort of thing?'

'Ahh!' Aristotle expanded. 'Philosophy is a love of all truth. Truth in the universe, right now, right here. Indeed, it is great and most sweet to contemplate Truth and the Good. But who is it who contemplates? An ignorant person or the reverse? The mind is open to the world, and opens that world. The good philosopher examines his physical and his human world.'

'Then, it is not a few Philosopher-Kings we need,' Demetrios observed, 'but many true philosophers among the citizens.'

'Yes, indeed. And it is proper to educate the young into a wide and true knowledge so they go into the world and create better societies, better states. You know, the philosopher should be a man who is prompt to aid his fellow men, who mingles with others and wants to help. It is a poor philosopher who remains deaf to a cry for help. And with a higher, more rational and more benevolent form of state, a political life that is full and thoughtful and harmonious, men will be able to touch all about them – in a world not obscure or unknown to them. Such an educated man will do more than exist. He will fully live a life and not exist merely, like a plant or rock – or even as a badger.'

'Aristotle says,' Hipparkhos chimed in, 'that many men live in a blur and need to *see*.'

'Thus it is,' said Aristotle, 'that in our work lie seeds of a better life for men to come. I truly believe, Stephanos, that the full study of philosophy is of benefit to all humankind.'

He beamed at me, at the young pupils, and at the table of attentive scholars around him, his friends and associates in the great endeavour. I have often thought subsequently of that day, when the Lykeion seemed a sanctuary full of life for Aristotle, of thought and joyful plans, before sorrow and even despair had touched the life of the Master.

II

Murdering an Ox

The expedition to see the ox-slaying, as suggested by Eudemos, did truly come to pass. Aristotle's slave brought me a written invitation to join the Lykeion party. I decided to go, and also to take my little brother Theodoros with me as a treat. We all met on the slope of the Akropolis before the great Temple of Virgin Athena. Theodoros frisked and capered about me in excitement. There were people enough, but not huge crowds. I could avoid persons I did not want to meet, such as the grave citizen Theosophoros who had taken such a decided part against our family during our earlier troubles. I saw this man in the distance, looking quite as vinegary as ever.

Aristotle, as I had expected, was surrounded by his little cohort. 'I think you know everybody by now,' he said. And I did. Hipparkhos with his noble equine nose; Demetrios of Phaleron with his striking beauty and affable manner. Eudemos, so handsome, talkative and easy-mannered, nobody could miss, and I even recollected pale Arkhandros. They had in charge the little group of students, including doleful Parmenion and Mikon the cheerful. After I introduced Theodoros and gave him temporarily into the older boys' care, we all moved off together to the nearby precinct of Zeus Protector of the City.

Mikon was useful in clearing others out of our path and pushing us along so we could stay together. This caused some grumbling, not to say altercation.

'Mind what you're doing, young fellow,' said one citizen, while a more peppery one remarked, 'If you dig into me again like that, boy, I'll have your hide!' Theophrastos had to apologise for Mikon's zeal.

Such apologies were not directed to the more raffish of the crowd. A group of town youths from the poorer neighbourhoods began to call out abusive remarks, of the sort that indicate that one loves one's mother too much. This slowed our progress a little, as our boys were only too quick to reply, even though Eudemos remonstrated, telling them this was not gentle behaviour. One of the town boys, a powerful, strong-shouldered lad, challenged Mikon to fight him. When Eudemos restrained our young scholar, the town boy hooted and cavorted in triumph. He turned his fingers into horns above his head and charged at us.

'I'm a bull!' he bellowed. 'A bull! And you're cows. Sorry shit-tail cows! *Cow!*' he roared again at Mikon.

'You'll be sorry,' said furious Mikon. 'My father is Thrasymakhos. He's a very important man. *He*'ll make you sorry.'

'"My father is Thrassus,"' the boy mimicked in the deliberate mistake of crude satire. 'I tell you, boy, your papa is a cow. Not an important cow – just a cow! Boo!'

The thick-necked boy rushed at us several times, stamping his feet and bellowing. Then he changed his game, and hopped along waving an imaginary sword in the air.

'To me, men! Sound the war-cry! Clear away this chaff – ho! I'm Alexander. Yah-boo! I can beat the lot of you! *I'll* set you right, you pale Medes and Persians!'

The bull-faced boy strutted beside us for a bit, imitating our walk, while his rude companions cheered him on. Then he made another fearful lunge, crying out, 'I am Alexander the ruler of Athens! I'm the king of all of you – cowards! Yah!'

He exhibited to Mikon and the timorous Parmenion a fearful face, distorting his mouth widely over his teeth like a grinning satyr mask and making his eyes bulge alarmingly, as if they would depart from their sockets. Parmenion blenched, while Mikon and his best friend Dorkon tried to break from restraint and start hitting. Our own pupils (including Theodoros for the nonce) began yelling too, as loudly as the common herd of youths who opposed them, and I did not like Theodoros to hear what they said. (Although as my younger brother went to school he would doubtless hear everything in his time.)

'Our lads, being well-born, should not fight this scabby lot,' said Eudemos loudly, 'but there seems no reason why we should not discipline these unruly youths.'

'No, indeed,' said Hipparkhos, even more loudly. 'A good switch would do the trick, I think.'

'Or a good strong cane,' agreed Eudemos. 'You need our medicine, children?' He started towards them. The bull-like boy and his friends made off, sufficiently prompted by further strong suggestions regarding the medicinal use and practical efficacy of canes and switches. Of course the men could not carry out these threats as the louts, however vulgar and ill-behaved, were presumably the sons of citizens. It is a serious offence to commit an outrage against a citizen or citizen's child by clutching or beating him, unless (like a schoolmaster) one has the parent's consent. At least, with the boys sent off, the valiant Mikon could be released from his elders' restraining hands. We continued on our way and approached the scene of the morning's ritual action.

'How old is this ceremony exactly?' Demetrios asked Aristotle.

'Well, you know *The Clouds* of Aristophanes – we should read that play this afternoon with the boys, I think. The rite was certainly old by Aristophanes' time. In that play you remember, young Pheidippides, a member of the younger generation who believes he is so much wiser than his father Strepsiades, despises older people and good advice. Such a view is encouraged by Wrong Reasoning, who jeers at the old ways. Wrong Reasoning refers to "these archaic things like the Dipolieia and brooches made of cicadas, Kedeides' obscene dances and the Bouphonia." Nowadays we wouldn't wear brooches made of cicadas, but the Bouphonia survives.'

'And so do some obscene dances,' observed Eudemos.

'It's starting!' cried Theodoros. The acolytes were placing sacred wheat and barley on the stone altar.

Now a little procession of oxen, four or five, were led into the sacred space. They looked used and tired, long beyond their first youth. If a plough-ox has to be sacrificed it makes more sense to use one near the end of

its time. Led or urged by their keepers, and followed by
two hooded priests of Zeus, the beasts went round about
the altar, as they had to do until one of their number
should choose to be sacrificed. At last one ox lost its fear,
lifted its heavy head and scented the food. It extended its
thick meek neck above the altar stone, and started to eat
the grain. That was the sign. A hooded priest approached,
as the happy ox was still eating. A long string of saliva
dripped from its mouth. The hooded priest lifted a bronze
axe – and struck. He struck well, a single blow. The beast
fell at once, with one bellowing moan that became its
expiring breath. It lay lifeless.

'Now is the interesting part,' whispered Aristotle.

The priest who had struck the blow then fled away. (A
path had been cleared, so spectators would not impede the
ritual flight.) The axe was taken by the other attendant,
who pronounced upon the case:

'I declare we must search for the doer of this
murder. And the axe that has committed the murder
must be tried.'

We followed the priest and acolytes and officials
away from the sanctuary of Zeus, filing into the
precinct of the Prytaneion Court. The axe was held
up for inquest in a ritual trial for killing:

'Whose is the axe?'

'It is the axe of the man who struck the mortal
blow.'

'Where is the man who slew?'

'He is being sought for.'

'Is this surely the axe that struck the fateful
blow?'

'It is, assuredly.'

'How do you know?'

'I saw the deed done with my own eyes. I picked up the implement from beside the body.'

'Then by the power of this court and the law of this city Athens and the right of the murdered I condemn this axe. This implement has no more a right to abide here, and must leave Athens for ever. I condemn it to be thrown into the sea and be no more seen. Let no murdering object remain in our city.'

The axe was then borne away for the sentence to be immediately executed.

Of course, the same sort of trial would have taken place in the Prytaneion had any inanimate object killed a person. Even if an object (like a dropped pot or windblown tile) kills a man by accident, it must have a court sit on its case and be judged and thrown out of the city. Whatever has killed a man is contaminated. Not long before, a man had been slaughtered by a blow struck with a mallet, and the wooden implement had been sentenced in the same way as this axe. What makes the Bouphonia extraordinary is that the 'murder' is only of a plough-ox. Yet the killing (which is really committed by the whole city) is treated as a private and abominable murder.

'It makes no sense,' said Demetrios. 'Entertaining, however, if meaningless.'

'Not meaningless, no. It must seem odd to anybody now, I think,' said Aristotle. 'For we now consider *murder* as the deliberate killing of one intelligent being – a human – by another intelligent being – human also. This custom makes us realise that we did not always see it thus. The ritual supposedly comes from the reign of King Erekhtheus, in the dawn of time, just as Athens began to come into being. The best explanation I have hit upon is that the Bouphonia commemorates the moment when human beings decided not only to tame animals but to kill them – to breed them for killing and eating. But perhaps something like the rite existed even earlier, to commemorate with sorrow the fateful decision that man has the right to kill any animals for human food.'

'And we still feel guilt for that,' said Theophrastos. 'That is why I want our boys to see the Bouphonia, to make them aware of what we do. For we treat our animals as household mates and friends, and then they are killed off by us and eaten. We have – most of us – self-restraint enough to keep our hands from murder. But we lay violent hands on innocent animals, even those who do us other service, like the ox that ploughs and helps us to get the good grain from the earth. Thus I think the Pythagoreans are most right, or at least most consistent, who bar the eating of meat.'

'Let's go back and see the ox now,' suggested Mikon. We returned to the original site of the 'murder'. The ox had been stripped of its hide and the corpse or carcass was now on a huge spit over a fire. People crowded around, especially those from the poorer districts, eagerly awaiting their feast. The smell of roast meat began to drift over the Akropolis. The ox hide, cleverly and quickly stripped off the carcass, with the head still attached, was being rapidly stuffed with hay and straw. As his meat roasted, the beast began to reappear in this imitation – his height, his shape, but not his motion, cleverly reproduced.

'There,' said Aristotle. 'I could not have created a better example. It perfectly illustrates the difference between form as living entity and form as mere shape. "Form" in the sense of "shape" is not enough – *this* is not the ox. It is a simulacrum of life but lacks the signs of living. Mere shape does not make life.'

'What does make life?' I asked idly. 'Not just in the case of this ox, but in general. Why is something dead or not?'

Aristotle laughed. 'There you have the mystery of life, Stephanos. But we certainly know that a statue – or a corpse – is not a man. Living form requires function and motion. Life is activity realised in material.'

The new 'ox', lacking in signs of life but standing up, was hitched, inertly obedient, to a plough. As if the events of the day were but a game for it and it could go back to work as it had yesterday.

'There's Papa!' Mikon waved at a tall, dignified gentleman who stood with a small group of his friends. They were obviously important personages, with their retinue of slaves behind them. These friends of Mikon's papa unfortunately included the grave citizen Theosophoros of the acid wit, a man whom I knew and did not like. But there was also the much younger and more genially witty Euphorbos, whom I did not know, but thought I should like. Thrasymakhos, the papa of Mikon, a well-born man with a noble and severe countenance, was known to me by sight. He had held some public offices, and had made a couple of well-received speeches, giving him a claim to the title of orator. This man was of one of the oldest Athenian families, although he was also related to the foreign orator Thrasymakhos of Khalkedon who figures in Plato's dialogues. This distinguished Athenian, leaving his acquaintance for a moment, courteously came towards us.

'Good day, Aristotle. I see you are taking good care of my little curly-head troublemaker here. Is this a holiday? Or are you at work?'

'Both. We study the ritual and its history.'

'And we're going to read *The Clouds* today, too, Hipparkhos says,' added Mikon.

Thrasymakhos did not comment on the suitability of Aristophanes' satiric critique of Sokrates and his educational system as reading matter for the young, but responded with simple approbation:

'Good. Good. Yes, I like to see the true ancient Athenian customs like our Bouphonia preserved. Now, who are all these? Theophrastos I know, but am I correct in thinking that I do not know all these masters who work in your school?'

Aristotle, explaining that I was simply a friend, introduced his group: Eudemos of Rhodos, Demetrios of Phaleron, and the rest. Thrasymakhos, with ostentatious affability, condescended to introduce us to his friends. He was about to begin with Euphorbos (because he was the best born, or perhaps the most impatient) but Aristotle cut him off by saying, 'Of course I know my own former student!' and Euphorbos, laughing, said at the same moment, 'Of course I know my own old teacher!'

'Dear master, how are you?' Euphorbos said, embracing Aristotle affectionately. 'It has been too long a while. And how do you get on at the Lykeion? Is it politics now or animals that occupy your time?'

Euphorbos when smiling affectionately at Aristotle was certainly a most appealing sight. He was slightly lanky but well-proportioned, a man a year or two above my own age, but with a litheness and a happy countenance that ensured his appearing constantly youthful. Euphorbos had the brown hair in hyacinth-tight curls that appeals to painters and sculptors, and that aristocratic bearing that always takes the eye.

'Have you been enjoying the proceedings?' he enquired, turning to the rest of us. 'It is like a drama, or a parody of one, is it not?' There was a twinkle in his eye. 'The poor old ox! Like a sad old wronged husband. I seem to hear Klytaimnestra saying "Fetch me the axe!"'

I warmed to Euphorbos, witty and merry and fond of literary reference – as I am myself. Perhaps, it occurred to me, he had picked up that habit of quotation and mock-quotation from Aristotle.

'But I chatter too much,' Euphorbos apologised, 'when I ought to be introducing the wise Theosophoros and the distinguished Megakles of Athens and other admirers and friends of Thrasymakhos, to this learned company.'

Thrasymakhos' other companions were undoubtedly middle-aged, but they were a distinguished set; our group looked rather pale and weedy in comparison. Theosophoros at least deigned to acknowledge the introduction to myself. 'Stephanos is already known to me,' he said, indicating that a little such knowledge went a long way.

'And this is Megakles of Athens,' Thrasymakhos continued. Megakles had short hair, greying slightly and a really impressive bald spot in the middle of his head. The bald spot was beginning to redden in the early summer sun. Despite this unwanted blush, Megakles was distinguished in appearance and extremely well dressed in a finely woven khiton. He greeted us all in a noble manner, courteous, assured and unsmiling. (A gentleman among inferiors has no need to smile.)

'It gives me great satisfaction to make your personal acquaintance. I have heard so much of you as you have become famous, O Aristotle of Stageira, and go among us. It is very important work that you do. Educating our Athenian young people is a great privilege and a mighty responsibility.'

'It is so – I feel it!' Aristotle was in earnest. 'What could be more important than the citizens of the future?'

With such happy banalities we passed a few minutes. Then Thrasymakhos, patting Mikon's curly head, asked if he could take him out for the afternoon, promising to return him by evening. Father and son went off surrounded by their attentive slaves. Our little group separated, and we of the Lykeion party began to prepare to go home. Aristotle did not enforce Pythagorean doctrines, however, for he allowed such of the boys and their teachers who wished to do so to partake of the roast meat in the square before setting off. Theodoros certainly was not backward in coming in for his share.

And that was the day – a pleasant one it seems, a day of a harmless amusement combined with instruction. We had all thought more about an old Athenian custom. The weather was fine and Athens looked beautiful. We had perhaps made some new acquaintance – not least Theodoros, who was very taken with the boys at the school, old and wise as they seemed to him at his age of nearly ten years.

But that occasion did not really end so pleasantly. On the

morrow we heard that a boy had been killed. The killing had happened down at the coast and not in the city of Athens itself, which was something of a relief. Still, he was an Athenian. It became clear that the victim was the boy who had insulted us and made faces, shouting 'I am Alexander!' This false Alexander, the bull-faced boy, had been killed with a strange implement. An antique bronze axe had been found by the body. Suspicion rested on the axe that had killed the poor ox. Aristotle was soon called in to help with enquiries. He had the priests questioned. They were certainly responsible for throwing the axe into the sea as commanded by the ritual trial. But it appeared that of late the custom had arisen of not *quite* throwing the axe away. That is, it would be thrown into the shallows, whence it would be recovered after a few days.

'It's a valuable antique axe,' one of the priests said, in tears. 'We couldn't afford to lose it. It's not as if it really killed a person! And we use it only once a year. When it has been in the sea a certain time it is considered cleansed, and we bring it back.'

As it turned out, the priests and their attendants had actually and literally thrown the axe into the sea. But in truth they deposited it with a gentle throw from a boat into the shallows in a position well marked by them. The priests had used the same part of the coast for several years, so anybody with sufficient curiosity to study what they did with the object might readily find it. But how had the lethal thing come back on land and committed a killing? Some among the common people spoke ghoulishly of a demon arising from the water, dripping axe in hand ... But as the crime was ingeniously recon-structed, it was speculated that some youths unknown, presumably young persons of the poorer sort living in that area by the sea, had 'rescued' the axe and played with it, probably imitating the ox-slaying and fatally killing the bull-like boy.

As this boy's parents were poor they could not hope for handsome compensation, especially if the doers of the deed were likewise poor. So they could not pursue the matter. They accepted some money as a gift from the city, although Athens denied official responsibility. No youths came forward to confess to the crime. The axe was tried again – for real murder this time. And on this occasion too it was sentenced to be thrown into the depths of the sea, though this time the sentence was carried out vigorously with many persons watching. But the murderer – or perpetrator of accidental manslaughter, perhaps – whoever he might be, remained untried and unknown.

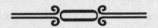

III

Meeting a Monkey

My thoughts turned much on my own future. A most important matter was my marital union, which would define much of my life afterwards. At one time I had hoped to marry into some exalted family, taking Kharmia daughter of Kallimakhos to wife, but, as things had turned out, I was now betrothed to the daughter of one Smikrenes, who farmed his own land near the westward road by Eleusis. Smikrenes was an Athenian citizen but by no means exalted, nor was his temper the best – indeed, his ill temper was known throughout his own district. But I had done him a slight kindness and he had softened to me. I had actually met his daughter, so strange and untoward are the things that happen when we travel, although of course the pretence should be kept up that I had not seen her, lest her reputation be scarred. Philomela daughter of Smikrenes was comely and sweet voiced, well-bred and good of heart, and marriage no longer seemed the difficult and heavy task it had once appeared.

I had discussed marriage with Smikrenes when Aristotle and I were returning from Delphi earlier in the spring. Smikrenes and I had begun the long process of debating about the dowry, though nothing was seriously settled then. Messages had gone between us since that time. True, I was still young for marriage, according to Athenian custom and practice, for the right age was around thirty and I would be not quite twenty-six. But marriage was one of the few immediate ways of assisting the condition of our family by association with another citizen family and another landholder. Now it was high time for me to show myself to Smikrenes again, and I wanted to look like a serious man. I took a slave with me, and a donkey, with a little pile of presents.

'Well, who'd ha' thought as you would turn up after all,' was Smikrenes' first observation to me, not over-agreeable.

'But of course,' I said as heartily as I could. I tried to look cool and manly and well-born, though it had been a hot sweaty journey. I was glad to find that the odorous dung-heap before the door had been somewhat reduced, evidently by Smikrenes' use in energetic cultivation. 'Surely, O Smikrenes, you and I should become better acquainted.'

'Maybe, maybe,' he said, in dubious tones. 'I've got a lot of work on at present.'

'Let me help,' I said eagerly. 'And my slave also can assist you.'

'I dunno's I want people picking about my business.

You'd likely to do it all wrong,' he said. 'But things is going well – on the whole. Some excellent little piglings are a-fattening a treat, and we have a new calf. Take a look.'

Smikrenes was pleased to have someone to show his farm to. It was undeniably in excellent condition, although some assistance with the labour would be a good idea. I was inwardly debating how to bring this up tactfully when we went to the house.

'We can sit outside, since the weather's so peaceful,' suggested Smikrenes. 'Mebbe Philomela will have set us out some grub. Not that her cooking is anything much – I'm most ashamed to set before company such stuff as she turns out, but it's the best we can do.'

I recognised this as a figure of modesty, and a high point of tact and company manners, so I countered by praising the oat cakes and the cabbage-leaf rolls and the cheeses, and the sweet cakes obviously prepared for the occasion. The old serving-woman brought them to us. I could sense Philomela herself behind the door to the kitchen, and I hoped to get a glimpse of her. I already knew that she was lovely, with grey-green eyes and brown hair with an acorn sheen. When she is my wife, I thought, she will not be such a drudge. But of course I did not say this to Smikrenes. He was eager to start in on our bargaining.

'Well, I suppose you rash young man will want to wed in Gamelion, like everyone else, though trudging through them roads in winter's not going to be much pleasure for us. Indeed, I don't know as I can make it . . .'

'O sir, you must come – my household would be dishonoured for ever if you did not. A bride must be taken into her husband's family house with all her relatives present. And we can make a fine procession as the bride is taken from her home to ours.'

'Fine processions simply cost money for gimcracks and trash, as you will discover before you're much older. And it's sure to rain! All that finery thrown away. And Philomela will catch cold into the bargain. Maybe it will go on her chest, with a fine chill to boot, and you'll have the pleasure and expense of burying her instead of bedding her. Oh dear, it's a sad thing, to see my only daughter – my only living child – go to her grave before me!'

'These are too-sad thoughts,' I expostulated gently. 'My family will be so happy to see her. They will treat her with great care, I promise you.'

'Well, but I'll ha' lost her, and that's a tough bone to gnaw. And here I have to find a dowry and lose a worker. Who's going to help me with this farm all on my ownsome?'

'I have some ideas about that,' I said. 'Let me give you a slave to help with the work. I can do that I think at the time of the wedding – and –'

'Slaves!' He spat on the ground. 'I want someone who's family, a real citizen, someone who takes an interest. I don't know what the gods were thinking on to keep me without sons – what a curse that is! And another curse is that savage wife of mine who left me in the lurch.'

'*Who* is she – and *where* is she?' I asked bluntly, though I had long been ruminating about how to put these two important questions. 'I take it she is alive?'

'My wife? May she wander the shore of Styx for a long while and lack a penny for her passage when her time comes! My wife is alive and flourishing. Least when I last heard.'

'I was told that this woman – I don't know her name or parentage – left you and went to live with her first husband's son.' (I did not add that my sole informant on these matters was a little boy who had been visiting in Smikrenes' neighbourhood at the time when I first met the irascible farmer.)

'I don't know how these lies get about. Her name is Philonike, and she is the daughter of Philonikos of Hymettos. Well-born man with a goodish estate. True, she had been married afore, but not for long, her first husband dying at sea. She had no children by that marriage. She was still young enough when we wed, about seventeen, and I was more than thirty-five. My wife Philonike gave me a daughter, Philomela there' – with a gesture to the pantry door – 'and then had a stillborn nothing, and then gave birth to a son. But the son died soon after, just a baby, never got his *khoes*.'

I nodded. Children are given a special celebration upon reaching their third year. At the Spring festival, the Anthesterion, each receives the present of an ornamented *khoes*, a cup to commemorate the fact that the child is viable and may now truly be considered a person. Philomela's lost brother had died, like so many, in the fog of infancy.

'In no wise uncommon, infants dying so much as they do,' Smikrenes agreed with my unspoken thoughts. 'But Philonike took on terrible, and then went silent and wouldn't speak nor eat – a useless lump. So her papa come for her and took her to their home "for a while" they said, "until she gets well again". I guess she ain't never considered herself proper well, for she never came back. Though that papa's dead now, she still stays in their house.'

'But –' I exclaimed. 'You could divorce her and take another wife! Then you could have more children –'

'Well, I know. Nearly done so at one time,' he agreed. 'When I was young and lively and stupid enough to do it all again. I ain't a-going to wed no more, don't you fear. Her papa had no right to take her off home, as she had borne a living child by me. So I could have taken him to court and asked for her back. Never heard that she slept with any other man, though. I s'pose I always thought she would come home again. One sunny day, thinks I, I'll get a letter saying "I'm a-comin' in three days' time, with a box of new clothes – Love, Philonike." But no message, not of that sort. It was main foolish of me to marry out my own deme like that. If she'd ha' been a neighbour's child, she'd been more get-at-able.'

There was much in this story to think about, not least the unpleasant possibility that the woman was mad and that madness ran in the family. On the other hand, not to wish to live with Smikrenes was in itself no certain sign of insanity. At least the woman wasn't divorced – I don't think I could bring myself to wed the daughter of a divorced mother. True, Philonike had behaved very ill. But perhaps her unaccountable behaviour was the fault of her parents – and a lack of persistence, not to say a lack of emotion, on the part of her husband. It was certainly hard on Philomela to have been deserted in that manner. Perhaps, however, she had been lucky on the whole not to have been given a stepmother.

'I should come by and have a look at your own holding,'

said Smikrenes. 'Don't mean your town house, but your farm.'

'Yes, certainly,' I said. 'We have some excellent olive groves. Some of the rest of it is a bit run down perhaps. We need to repair a few of the outbuildings. Two aged servants, Dametas my steward and Tamia his wife, look after it. They are faithful, and careful. But I am afraid that they are really far too old now, very shaky, and I must find someone else – though I have to provide a home for them, of course, and they will still do what they can.'

'Running down, going to rack and ruin – that's the way with farms. If you don't keep up with your holding, soon you're nowhere. Oh, well, s'pose you was too young and ignorant to do much when your papa died. And at least there is real Athenian land. That's the main thing. But there is another man-child, isn't there?'

'Yes. My little brother Theodoros. I am not the only inheritor and he must always have a good provision made for him,' I explained. It was well to be clear on such points. Theodoros would always have a claim on the family estate. 'I hope he won't have to worry about these things the way I have had to do. He is *much* younger. Just a child.'

'Ah, well, the more boys the better. Another pair of hands to help out, too.' Smikrenes did not seem displeased. 'Probably better for my daughter in the long run, if anything should happen to you, as she got no brothers by me, see? But . . .' he added in a thoughtful tone, staring into the distance, 'Philomela and her children has always got to be provided for, and well provided for.'

'Certainly!' I exclaimed.

'I'd like it if we could work it out so's that *her* children get my holding, whatever else happens. And if your little brother gets part interest in your estate, and you was dead, then he and Philly could share the house in Athens. I mean, he could rent out part, and give her the proceeds, or live in the house altogether and pay her for her half.'

'I'll think about that,' I said cautiously. 'It sounds right that your grandchildren should inherit your land. For immediate expenses, I can bring to the marriage straight away some money from the sale of our surplus oil this last year – for sheets and some new furniture and a wedding feast. I believe I can safely promise food and clothes for Philomela and her children.'

'Well, my daughter and her young will not want for clothes while *I'm* alive, whatever *you* do about it, that's certain. And – I don't like to set a sum right today you understand, but I think I can promise a fair amount in money down as dowry. But I want the proper security for it.'

'Of course,' I agreed. '*Apotimema* is a regular thing. I can make over part of the land of the same value as the dowry.'

'So – and it must be part of the land that isn't hereditary and inalienable, but readily saleable. Then if you die or divorce her, or she dies and leaves children, we've got security. Always like security. That's why I'd better take a look at your property before I come down too handsome. Make sure you have something right to offer. Not taking some pathetic stony yard and calling it a field, mind you that!'

Dealing with my future father-in-law was trying to my

temper, but I swallowed and looked as amicable as I could.

'Pity it is,' said Smikrenes, following his own train of thought. 'Pity that she cannot get hold on her mother's money. They still owed me somewhat, in dowry. Then they had the gall to insist that they didn't, as she had turned back on their hands – although she was *not* divorced, like I told you. And that family is warm. Some of their funds ought to go to Philomela. It's a tidy holding in Hymettos, and my wife's father was doing very well. Now this man – Philomela's grandpapa on her own mother's side – *he's* dropped off his perch. She did ought to have a share of what he left. There is money in them Hymettos folk, sure as eggs.'

'But why haven't you requested her inheritance?' I asked in some surprise.

'Well, I thought of going up to them to demand it but never could find the time. I don't trouble much about the city.'

'But surely,' I exclaimed, 'as a citizen you go to the Ekklesia.'

'Well, on occasion. But I ask you, is it reasonable to expect men farming their own land to leave off work every ten days and walk so many stadia into the city and out again just to hear a lot of well-dressed citizens holding forth? Even when it's a great orator like Demades or Demosthenes or Hypereides, I get tired of it sooner than quick. True, we're paid a bit now for attending, but it's still not worth it. And the city so dusty and noisy. Full of carts and rubbish!'

I was rather taken aback by this description, but I had to admit I hadn't thought before of the burden of citizenship on the countryfolk.

'As for the law,' continued Smikrenes. 'Jury service is bad enough. But you don't want to get tied up with legal disputes, for that leads straight to hiring rhetoricians – and days and *days* lost in Athens argufying around the courts. Not for me! And sometimes it does a man's reputation no good, nor his family's neither. Just telling the whole city your troubles. Still, you're a young man and you've been educated a lot. All talk and no digging with the likes of you. So maybe you'd come off better than me if you tackled them. But don't be rash.'

'I certainly ought to try,' I agreed. 'Where should I go?'

'My wife Philonike's living where her papa lived, out by Hymettos on the west slope. Her papa's gone, like I told you, but another man come along and got married to her ma, and took to living there too, just as if he owned the place! Mind you, he can't really own it, this step-pa, for Philonike has a brother. Philokles, his name is. But I don't rightly recollect where he is now, or what he's doing. Haven't seen him since I don't know when.'

This was news indeed. If Philomela's mother had a brother, then this man, Philomela's uncle, was a person of the first importance. Governor of his own family, he stood in an almost parental relation to his sister Philonike, Philomela's mother and thus in a way to Philomela herself. This man Philokles should certainly be informed as soon as possible of the planned marriage. He might prove disagreeable, and resistant to letting any of the money he was sitting on go out of the family to his niece. Yet both law and custom held him to some obligations. I should certainly try to meet him.

Meanwhile, I made arrangements with Smikrenes for him to come to our farm. At some time soon he should also visit us at our house in the city, so he could see it and meet my brother.

'Still much business ahead,' Smikrenes agreed. 'But I dare say now we can have the formal betrothal come Boedromion? End of the summer. I should be able to announce the exact amount of the dowry, and by then we'll both have got things straight. No obstacle then to the wedding.'

This seemed fair enough. At the formal *engye* the girl's father would hand his daughter over to me, giving her to my protection, and, as is customary among families of better quality, he would announce at the same time the amount of dowry. After this public and formal acknowledgement we couldn't go back on the contract. To start the autumn with this clarification seemed a good idea, and the wedding details could all be arranged with plenty of time. I still had to make sure that my mother came round to the idea. True, I was planning to marry the daughter of a citizen of Athens, born in an Athenian deme. That much was in favour of the match. Mother would be disappointed, however, that I wasn't marrying the daughter of one of our wealthiest citizens living in one of the grander areas of the city of Athens. But as I looked out over the peaceful summer countryside, I felt there were compensations – and the more when I caught a fleeting glimpse of Philomela's hair and cheek behind the door.

Matters did not move much forwarder at that time, although I stayed at Smikrenes' house for two days. The gifts were graciously received. I had not forgotten even Geta, the old serving-woman and Philomela's former nurse, for such females can be very useful. At last I set off for home, my beast of burden much lighter, if not my heart. I let the donkey have a holiday, while we walked, I and my slave. This servant was good with animals, and the donkey meekly trotted along beside him. It was some compensation for the man's general dullness and the lack of deftness of hand. He had lost part of a finger; fortunately, there was nothing wrong with his legs, and he did well on errands.

As we came back to Athens I sent this fellow back to the farm with the beast, and proceeded on my own to the Agora. It was the later afternoon, when the sun is less overbearing and people come out to see what is to be seen. It was still hot, however, and dusty, the sort of day when dogs lounge about the public buildings looking for a cool marble floor on which to flop, finding congenial resting-places in the middle of an elegant stoa or on the steps of a temple. I had come idly enough to look for news, but the smell of one of the little cookshops attracted my attention, and I allowed myself to take something to eat. I was leaning over the stall, musing still on my own affairs, but the liveliness of the throng and then the heat of a conversation just behind my back forced me to move beyond my own thoughts.

'The taxation is enough to kill us!' So one white-haired citizen was grumbling to his friend, a little wizened man who seemed to agree, but a third citizen, a sturdy bald man, took up the argument.

'Nay, for the taxation is the way of making our city strong again. Through it we have won new walls and new battleships. If you wouldn't be under the yoke of Makedon, pay taxes gladly. That's all Athens does – we sat out the war this spring and let Antipater crush the Spartans.'

It was at this point that I really looked at the group, wondering at this boldness when there might be emissaries of Antipater or other Makedonian sympathisers (not to say spies) in the vicinity.

'Hush, Apollonios! Preposterous! No one ever paid taxes *gladly*,' said the little wizened man with a quiff of dark hair like the plumage of a bird. 'But pay 'em we shall. In hope to make Athens great and feared again.'

'Remember how much wealth and treasure Alexander has,' said outspoken Apollonios. 'The wealth of Persepolis! Now we hear he has set fire to Persepolis, and stored all his wealth together in Babylon.'

'All this fuss, and the need for high taxes – all this is brought upon us by the ridiculous desires of a family that calls itself "royal",' said the little man with the dark quiff. 'A barbarous family from outlandish Makedonia. Why, at one time there was a question whether men of Makedonia could participate in the Olympic Games. I say they are not really Greeks, at all, no matter how much they may strut.'

'Oh, but they are *so* Greek,' laughed another man, joining the group. I recognised Euphorbos, the lanky and merry, Aristotle's former student, who had greeted him so warmly at the ox-slaying.

'How do you make that out?'

'They must be – they work so hard at being Greek,' explained Euphorbos. 'Our Alexander,' he continued, 'ran about the walls of Troy, to imitate Akhilleus conquering Hektor. Is not that touching? Alexander endeavours to be so *very* Greek – he carries the works of Homer about with him in a box. He out-Hellenes Helen. Poor Alex, clutching his box so as not to lose his culture.'

'You are in the right of it, Euphorbos, if you are saying

he is no Attic man,' said the bald citizen. 'Let Athens reassert herself. I say, revive the Athenian League. With the wealth of the liberated islands and cities, we could support our rule and protect our settlers. If there is to be an empire, let it be of Athens, not of Makedon. Athenians have no kings. Let the young man from Makedon go back to Pella and call himself as "royal"as he pleases on his own dunghill.'

'Disgusting, the way these foreigners are taking over our city,' said a younger citizen who joined the group in the wake of Euphorbos. I recognised this newcomer too, a solemn man with a kind of priestly presence. Eurymedon, with his slender build and a face as beautiful as a sculpted mask. Tall Eurymedon with his great large eyes and straight nose. His bearing was that of an aristocrat, but his face, distinguished, sensitive, stiff and serious, looked more like the visage one would imagine for a tragic poet – though as far as I knew he wasn't one. Eurymedon was a man of much importance, a member of one of the oldest clans, the Eumolpidai. The descendants of Eumolpus guard the temple and rites of Demeter and Persephone at Eleusis. No one can participate in the Mysteries without a Eumolpid as a sponsor, and the priests of Demeter come from that clan. Some of the Eumolpidai are very religious – but by no means all of them.

'It is right, what you say,' said Eurymedon, in his clear precise voice. 'These men of Makedon who call themselves "royal" are fairly common stuff, even when well-intentioned. They encourage the presence of other foreigners, and weaken our customs and religion, and our political life. We Athenians should resist their insidious ways. Is this not so, Hypereides?'

I turned about at this question, for the man coming up to the group was celebrated.

Hypereides the famous orator was quite old at this time, being over sixty years of age, though so active he seemed younger. Moralists say much sex can injure the health and bring on old age, as well as ruining one's fortune, but Hypereides maintained both health and fortune, despite the notorious fact that (after his wife died) he kept three beautiful mistresses at once. He was impressive, if not sweet of countenance. (For all that, women seemed to like him more than well enough.) Hypereides could always be spotted in a crowd; he was tall and his long face with the long-lobed ears (like the handles of an ornate jug) appeared above the heads of other men.

In youth, Hypereides had studied with Plato. At first he had just written other people's speeches for them, but then he became famous as a pleader and even orator. He had stood against the Makedonian party and had prosecuted their supporters in court, or defended anti-Makedonian sympathisers. Hypereides was not bitter and peppery like Demosthenes, however, but a sunny, happy-tempered man who won people over – in court and out of it – by his easy manner and liking for a good quip.

'Well, isn't it true, Hypereides, as Eurymedon says?' asked the bald man. 'We need to cast off the yoke of Makedon in our thoughts and actions alike.'

'It's late for that,' said Euphorbos, speaking seriously to Hypereides. 'Athens has been crushed – Demades was right, when he said Athens lost an eye when Thebes was destroyed. King Agis and his Spartans have fought with glory, and Agis died a hero on the battlefield. We did nothing but sit in our houses and talk about the weather. Athens cowers to the godlike rulers of Makedon.'

'Nay,' said Hypereides. 'These rulers are but mortal men. You notice that despite the honours paid to King Philip, and the new fashion of calling him "immortal", he is but a complete corpse after all. I tell you, that no tyrant once felled ever rose from the dead, while many a city apparently destroyed has returned again to its old strength.'

'But how to resist as good patriotic Athenians?' asked the bald man. 'You, Hypereides, urged us to free and arm the slaves and the foreign residents! But that would have been clean against the constitution. We need to find our own modes of resisting. As we freed ourselves from tyrant rule in days gone by. See Harmodios and Aristogeiton show us the way!'

The bald patriot gestured towards the famous statue group. Of course you could not really see it from where we stood, because the skeletal structure of the new temple of Apollo Patroös (at last being rebuilt) was in the way. The celebrated two bronze statues commemorated the two heroic youths who (generations ago) had assassinated a tyrant. The bronzed youth Harmodios points his sword to stab the tyrant while Aristogeiton, older and stronger, holds his sword above his head ready to smite the tyrant's head off. It is a very pleasing set of statues – all the more because the sculptor hasn't bothered reproducing the man who is just about to be killed, so you don't have to feel anything for him.

'If we look at the statues,' commented Euphorbos, 'we should remember we are still looking at copies. The Persians stole the real ones. But now Alexander is going to send us the original statues back from Persepolis. Is that not thoughtful of him! I find that very pleasing – not every tyrant will support the opposition in that manner, to be sure.'

Euphorbos ran his fingers through his hair and took on a different expression, a ridiculous mask of conceit and self-importance.

'"Gentlemen of Athens, I Alexander, the Great, the wonder of the Hellenes" – he thinks of himself this way, you know – "the universally extolled, the marvel among youth, offer you – offer you freely, for no extra charge – an object lesson: First kill your tyrant – if you can get at him!"'

'Euphorbos, you can never be serious,' remonstrated the bald citizen.

Euphorbos shrugged, and produced from his sleeve a pair of gold knucklebones. 'Serious is as serious does. Let us give up politics and play at knucklebones, where at least some can win. Do you wager for a throw?' The gold 'bones' spun up in the air and shone in the hot sunlight.

'We got rid of tyrants before and we can do so again!' Apollonios was heated. 'And get rid of those who take bribes from Makedonia to betray their country!'

'Gently, Apollonios,' entreated Hypereides. 'No violence, I beg of you. Gentlemen, you should really guard your speech with more care. As for bribe-taking of any sort, the Ekklesia and all good citizens are against it, as they have ever been.'

'But, Hypereides,' said Eurymedon, 'we must take note. Athens is being choked not just by men of Makedon but by foreign persons of all kinds. It is bad enough that she should be tossed in the stew of all sorts of Greek states, that new League that Philip cooked up for his own advantage. But see how we are being flooded with Kyrenians, Phoenicians and the like – as well as beggars who drift here from the newly reconquered lands in Asia.'

'And traders – Phoenicians. Egyptian trash!' The little dark-quiffed man spat angrily. 'Get rid of them all, Hypereides, I say!'

'Cannot be done,' said Euphorbos. '*You* know that, Epikrates. Many Athenians are fond of Egyptian perfumes, is that not so? Have we none of us carried a sweet-smelling gift to a mistress? Or' – turning to Epikrates – 'to a choice boy, slave or free?'

'But I shall have justice,' said the little man called Epikrates, turning purple in the face. 'I shall have *justice!* Hypereides is helping me against that filthy Egyptian and the whore he set on to tempt me! To the rubbish heap with all the riff-raff! So say I.'

'Are you addressing *me*, gentlemen?' Another man had come up to the group. Unlike the serious knot of political speakers, he seemed light-hearted and jaunty. 'Are *we* riff-raff?'

I turned and saw his reason for his using the plural, for this newcomer was not alone. He held on his shoulder a monkey, and not a small one. He took hold of the monkey's paw and waved it at the group. 'Are *we* riff-raff?' He spoke in a high affected voice to imitate the monkey's imagined speech. 'I say, all of you are riff-raffy – some of you niff a bit, my word you do!'

As the monkey was at that moment screwing up his face the words matched the action quite well. The beast grabbed a piece of fruit from the master's bag and started to chew it, dripping juice.

'What an enormous and ill-bred animal!' exclaimed someone who had come up beside me at the food-stall. It was Theophrastos. 'Greetings, Stephanos,' he added. 'I am glad to come upon you, for I should speak with you –'

Theophrastos was interrupted by the monkey, which spat a large piece of wet pulpy fruit straight at his head. Its owner laughed. Hastily Theophrastos wiped his head with the edge of his cloak, which was at once stained by fruit juice. Despite the hubris shown by his animal, and the misfortune sustained by Theophrastos, the monkey-owner seemed unperturbed. He was a pleasant fellow to look at, his head well barbered, his teeth white and clean, and his cloak and ring of the best. At this moment, his well-barbered hair was being drizzled upon by monkey spit. The animal hopped up and down on his shoulders: it was certainly the cynosure of all eyes. Having got our attention, the monkey then displayed all its parts with what seemed conscious pride.

'I congratulate you, Kallias. I don't believe I have ever seen a larger one,' said Theophrastos drily.

'Ahh,' laughed the man Kallias, stroking his pet. 'You don't get many like this. It comes from far away, beyond Egypt. Black men bring them to Egypt, even to the new city Alexander is building, and there you can buy them.'

'Or your factor can,' said Epikrates sourly. 'I had forgotten, Kallias, how much business you do with the shipping, to Egypt and elsewhere. One of the kind who send honey from Hymettos to Egypt, and bring Persian stuffs to Athens.'

'There are good markets, now,' said the monkey-owner. 'Even better once the liberated cities of Lydia and Ionia have settled down. A great deal of trade. People abroad will pay well for all sorts of things. Dogs, for instance. You wouldn't believe how well dogs do. Spartan hounds are in demand. And hounds of Melita – I mean not my own deme, but the island.'

'Melita – not even Greek! An island crawling with Phoenicians and traders from Karthago!'

'But it breeds good little hounds. Fine-boned, thin and small. That's why I called mine "Little Twig". She'd sit on my lap. Some of you know my favourite dog – or rather bitch – from Melita –'

'And how is *she*, I beg to know?' asked Euphorbos politely. As he spoke, he played with his knucklebones, keeping the glittering gold pair hopping around the back of his hand without even looking at them. 'One should always enquire solicitously after the health of one's friends' bitches.'

'Alas! Poor Little Twig! I must be sad while I remember her. She died the other day. We have had her buried with pomp. A grave in the garden. I myself have designed a nice little tombstone for her. You must come and see it. It says

"A fond farewell.
Her master commends to the shades
his Little Twig.
A small piece of Melita lies here."'

'Very touching.'

'When you do a thing, you certainly do it well,' said Apollonios. 'Didn't you recently make an offering in the Asklepion, for your great toe? Never seen better bronze, or a more detailed likeness of a toe.'

'A poor thing, but all my own,' laughed the monkey-man. His monkey suddenly got up and jumped from his shoulders to the pavement, where it sported itself like a satyr, waving its long penis around and about. A little crowd had collected, offering shouts of laughter and encouragement.

'Watch out, Euphorbos, guard your backside – he's attracted to your rear entry!'

'How much do you pay him, Kallias, to do your job at home?'

'Hey, the brothel's nearby! Bid this little gentleman hasten there directly. He's got more to give the girls than most of their customers.'

'Come, Theseus.' Kallias the owner of the beast gave a shake to its little gold chain – was it really all solid gold? – and began to walk across the Agora. Theseus the monkey resisted by lying down, but the chain necessitated his being hauled along after his urgent master. The animal had one last revenge. As the creature got to its feet, it made water copiously and splashed as many as it could – including the crowd who deemed themselves spectators and were caught unawares. The cursings and scramblings that followed seemed to satisfy the beast immensely. Then the monkey moved smartly away, trotting behind his master with many grimaces.

'What a terrible beast!' exclaimed Theophrastos. 'Kallias' family were once great aristocrats and generals, and look what he has come to – a man who prides himself on dogs and monkeys!'

'Well, he is happier than the other men around him,' I responded. 'Anyway, many in that family have been rich and – to say the least – jolly. Wasn't one of Kallias' ancestors noted for extravagance? Before he became a general. Wasn't he even accused of sacrilege?'

'Sacrilege? Who speaks of sacrilege?' It was the grave citizen Theosophoros whom I had tried to avoid on the day of the ox-murder. I had reason to believe he did not think well of me, and was surprised when he addressed me formally, ignoring Theophrastos. 'Good day, Stephanos, son of Nikiarkhos.' I returned his greeting, hoping he would pass on.

'*Sacrilege* – dread word. We must all be wary of the slightest approach to it,' Theosophoros continued. 'Our safety depends upon constant avoidance of such offence. You, O Stephanos, mingle with philosophers, who are not always immune to such a charge. Philosophers should be humble. Megakles, let me make you known to Stephanos son of Nikiarkhos. Stephanos, be known to Megakles.'

I bowed and murmured that I was happy to see him again. Of course I already knew this man Megakles, who had been introduced to Aristotle by Mikon's father at the Bouphonia. Unsmiling Megakles with the greying hair and the large bald spot ripened to a deeper rose in the sun of midsummer. Seeing this important acquaintance, Euphorbos strolled up to join us.

'Nowadays,' proceeded Theosophoros, 'we must all be extremely careful to avoid *sacrilege*. We must all be careful, for instance, not to say any word against a great man, now departed.' He glanced significantly towards the statue of Philip of Makedon placed in the Agora by the Athenians after our defeat at Khaironia. 'An honorary citizen of Athens, no less! What can one do but admire?'

'Killed by a man he tried to bugger once too often, but now proclaimed divine and immortal.'

'Hush, Euphorbos,' said Megakles indulgently. 'Cease

your jesting when it isn't prudent. Be glad at least we know *some* people of good Athenian name. Yours, Stephanos, is an excellent name, let us introduce you —'

At Megakles' insistence I was hurried over the short distance to the little cluster of men whose talk I had too visibly overheard. The great man introduced me with stiff formality to Eurymedon and the others. I felt embarrassed, as my hands and mouth were greasy with sausage. I also could not avoid introducing Theophrastos to Theosophoros and likewise to Megakles, who really ought to have recognised him. Theophrastos certainly had no reason to be glad of the encounter at this moment, when not only his clothes but also his countenance bore traces of the monkey's fruit. His oblong face had become flushed; never graceful, he was at present decidedly awkward. Speaking in his usual very precise manner, Theophrastos resisted Megakles' cool entreaty that he join them, and moved off into the market-place. I felt it necessary to stay and talk civilly to these friends, who were recovering after the confusion brought about by the advent of Kallias and his monkey.

'Did you see that truly *dreadful* animal?' asked Eurymedon. 'Someone should tell Kallias that the monkey tricks of his are not seemly in the Agora.'

'Whatever he may do with his monkey at home,' added Euphorbos.

'The beast might do well in the City Council,' added Theosophoros drily. 'There are members of the Boulé who act with as much sense and dignity as Kallias' energetic and too-well-endowed companion.'

'So this is Stephanos of Athens,' said short Epikrates, his quiff standing up on end, perhaps from taking fright at the monkey. 'I have heard of you. I trust your cousin has quite recovered from his brush with the law?'

'The two of you hiding under cheese in a cart, so I hear,' Apollonios interjected.

'Isn't it wonderful what strange stories get about in Athens?' I wasn't going to be drawn into a tedious and slightly embarrassing tale. 'But Epikrates, I hope rumour is wrong in saying that you have some legal vexation at present?'

'The world knows it!' said Epikrates with venom. 'Against that stinking Athenogenes the perfumer. Hypereides is going to assist me.'

'I was just going to suggest,' I said mildly, 'that Aristotle might be able to help you.'

'That,' said Megakles heavily, 'is extremely disrespectful to our good Hypereides. Not all of us hang upon Aristotle's sleeve, begging him to help us out of scrapes.'

There was a pause. I felt myself blush. It is true I had intended a mild insult, but hadn't intended to be called on it.

'I beg pardon, and meant no offence,' I said meekly. 'I was merely concerned for the peace of mind of Epikrates –'

'I certainly am not offended' said Hypereides heartily. 'We all know the brilliance of Aristotle – and his influence. Certainly, Epikrates and I have no reason to be ungrateful for any good thoughts or assistance.'

'Well, this is the case,' said Epikrates. 'Here's Athenogenes the Egyptian perfumer had a slave boy I wanted, but he got a woman to – to persuade me to buy the boy's father and brother too. Buying three slaves – expensive. Forty minai! *And* I was to be responsible for any debts incurred by these slaves.'

'Athenogenes was certainly ingenious,' interpolated Hypereides. 'He not only sold him three slaves (with that unjust debt clause attached), but also got him to sign an agreement to take one of the perfume businesses. Athenogenes wrote an agreement in which he said he gave Epikrates one of the perfume shops, "to set against any debts".'

'That's what he told me – that the shop would pay any debts of the slaves! But that scented Egyptian was a great liar! The confounded perfumery business that he made over to me in "compensation" proved riddled with debts – at least five talents' worth. Five talents!'

'You see?' said stern Apollonios. '*This* is the result of allowing all these foreigners into Athens. That Egyptian perfumer is just the type of these migrants who come in and try to take over. He even has the gall to call himself "Athenogenes", as if being merely *born* in Athens, dropped here by his trashy dam – as if that littering here gave him any kind of claim. These vermin are ruining our great city! None of us will be able to lead the life of citizens if this continues.'

'That is one of the gravest consequences of Alexander's advances,' agreed Theosophoros. 'These riff-raff from other places, coming like locusts. Jumped-up freedmen and all sorts who think they can get rich. Poor Epikrates. They stink of civet but they wouldn't care if they stank of shit, as long as silver and gold goes into their boxes.'

'And little innocents like Epikrates being ruined! Taken in by a good Athenian whore as well. It is a wonder I do not weep in thinking of it!' Euphorbos pretended to wipe tears from his eyes.

'It is important,' said Apollonios, 'that some of us stand

up against these pernicious new ways. We need not be lost. Athens is strong and can be stronger. Stephanos, young men like yourself should take an active part in the new movement to restore and fortify Athens – not only her citadels and walls, her temples and her ships, but her spirit.'

'And,' added Eurymedon, 'those who take such an active part can count on the reward of the approval of good men.' Eurymedon always seemed to speak in a liturgical voice. Probably he already took some role in the religious rituals at Eleusis. 'And who knows the will of the gods?' he added. 'The Makedonian man is plunging further eastward, ever onward. Who knows what the gods have in store? He might be lost there – which of course we would all regret,' he added drily.

'You, O Stephanos, are young and single,' said Theosophoros. '*You* might be interested to note that some rich and patriotic citizens of Athens possess daughters who are not humpbacked or one-eyed.'

'Whenever I do marry,' I said carefully, 'it will most certainly be to the daughter of a man and citizen who is descended from generations of Athenian citizens and landowners. On that I am determined.'

'Good fellow,' said Megakles, his bald spot blooming rosily in the afternoon sun. 'We know you take an interest in philosophy – as we all do. Particularly my friend Thrasymakhos, whose ancestor was so well acquainted with Plato. But just the same, we don't want to get carried away, do we? Remember, the enchantments of philosophy may mislead unwary men into sacrilege. Any disrespect to the gods now, any deviation from established and safe customs, creates holes in the wall, so to speak, through which evil can enter.'

'True. Sacrilege is a very bad thing,' I assented. 'But I am still concerned as how to help Epikrates in this dispute with the perfumer. For poor Epikrates must have lost a great deal of money.'

'Which we shall try to recover,' said Hypereides, with a graceful smile. 'Epikrates and I should discuss the case.' He detached Epikrates from the group, and the two went off together, little Epikrates trying to match his step to that of tall, confident Hypereides.

'Humph!' said Apollonios. 'Epikrates deserves what he got, entertaining himself with the slave boy and the woman. Farting around a brothel and dripping sentiment over a boy. Just asking that smelly Egyptian bastard to diddle him!'

'Hypereides is almost too good-natured,' said Eurymedon. 'Epikrates probably should not take up his valuable time.'

'One cannot but agree,' said Euphorbos, making his face stiff and matching his tones to the solemn ones of the Eleusinian. 'For lo, brethren, all things must be in proportion. Why should the ox worry over the sorrows of the gnat?'

'Ah, but consider,' said Theosophoros, 'Epikrates is a good citizen and his money can be useful to the cause. If that money can be recovered from that unsweet seller of sweet oils. Is that not so, Stephanos? It is worth while, is it not, to defend ourselves through use of the law?'

'Certainly it must be,' I said, disdaining to derive any personal application from this remark. 'Or else we would not have laws. I beg your forgiveness, gentlemen, for it has been a great privilege to meet you, but I must, unfortunately, depart at this time.'

And at last I got away from them. I had not turned two corners on my way home when I found the fruit-spattered Theophrastos lingering by the way.

'You said you had something to say to me,' I said. 'What did you want to talk with me about?'

'Aristotle,' Theophrastos said simply. 'I wanted you to go and see him. He is well – in himself. But he is worried about Pythias, who has not been well. I think he would take pleasure in your presence. But not to bring him hints from such as those,' he added bitterly. 'He should not be bothered just now. Come and see him as a friend, Stephanos.'

'Tell Aristotle I shall come to see him tomorrow.'

IV

Sweetness and Bees

Taking Theophrastos' suggestion seriously, I went next day to see Aristotle. It occurred to me that a discussion of Epikrates' case might provide a good pretext for a visit. I did not want Aristotle to think I was officiously hovering, or presuming on my own position, since I was neither an equal friend nor a blood relation. Aristotle was at home, instead of in the Lykeion where I had expected to find him.

'We'll sit inside in my room if you don't mind,' he said. 'I know it is a trifle warm. It would be nicer to sit outside, but I should like Pythias to be able to use the garden freely if she is disposed to walk, or sit in the sun.'

'How is your wife?' I asked.

He sighed. 'Not well. I'm afraid this pregnancy is proving difficult. I have always held – I have written – that pregnant women should not give themselves over to idleness or be forced to rest, but should take regular and sufficient exercise. That's why I have said that it would be good to have a number of shrines to the goddesses of childbirth – Hera, and Leto for instance – so that pregnant women could walk to them. And a woman bearing a child should eat nourishing food – she does not require a slender diet. But Pythias finds it trying now to walk any distance. I urged her to seek out the shrine of Demeter – she has a special devotion to Demeter – but she says she cannot go so far. And she eats scarcely at all. I have been keeping her company as much as possible. Sometimes I read to her. I haven't been working as much at the Lykeion as I had planned during this period. Ah well, I do have able assistants.'

'Yes, you are lucky there – Theophrastos and Hipparkhos and the rest.'

'Once this difficult time is over – and Pythias is nearly at the end – we shall both be much better. And the baby, too. It will be able to benefit from summer weather and grow strong and hardy.'

He sighed a little as he spoke. Aristotle looked paler than I was used to seeing him – certainly in summer. I noticed how his hair, which used to make me think of a fire spirit, had drifted towards grey, or run into dull sandy shades. It was disheartening to feel his brightness a little dimmed. He seemed preoccupied.

'What is the news, Stephanos? I get about so little at the moment. How do things fare with you?'

I was unwilling to trouble him with the patriotic and anti-Makedonian sentiments I had heard uttered the day before. I recollected and told him a suitable version of the conversation about Harmodios and Aristogeiton, and about the promised return of the original statues as a gift from Alexander.

'And at least,' I said, 'they will be better works of art than the copies. And a good thing to remind us of our patriotism and Athenian history. Though some people will apply it to Alexander's own case.'

Aristotle made a face. 'It is really not a very simple or very nice story, that of Harmodios and Aristogeiton. People forget the truth and say "they killed the tyrant". But they did *not*. The real tyrant at the time was Hippias, and it was too difficult to kill him. So those two killed Hippias' brother, just as he was innocently lining up the pageant wagons and marchers for the Panathenia procession. Surely an innocent and even laudable and pious occupation! Some say Aristogeiton was anxious to kill this man anyway, because the tyrant's brother had developed a love-longing for Aristogeiton's own beloved Harmodios. Who knows? But, you see, they *didn't* kill a tyrant. Harmodios himself was killed straight away when the guards arrived, and Aristogeiton lived to be tortured – long enough to wish that he had died when Harmodios did. Worst of all, Hippias became more suspicious and cruel, and clamped down on Athens in a way he had not done before. So, what was accomplished by this act of heroic violence?'

I was surprised at this deflating view. It was a standard school theme that as we were against tyrants we should be for Aristogeiton and young Harmodios. Glad of the chance to change the subject, I turned to my own affairs, and offered a summary of my conversation with Smikrenes.

'It is a lucky thing for my future father-in-law,' I commented, 'that I am basically honest and not litigious. His conduct in the past indicates how frightened he is of anything to do with the city, or legal action of any kind. He did not even reclaim his wife! Now I must try to search for her, in the Hymettos region.'

'You certainly should do so,' said Aristotle. 'For two reasons. First, and most important, you should not marry the daughter without knowing more of the nature and conduct of the mother. You cannot in propriety talk with her yourself, naturally, but be sure to ask some shrewd questions of whatever male relatives you encounter. If you suspect that she is not sane, do *not* marry the daughter. If you suspect that she is unchaste, do not marry the daughter. Second, it is important to establish for the sake of your children whether there should be any benefit to them from such an alliance, especially if there is an inheritance. Much can be done there. For example, make sure that this woman's deceased father left a legitimate will. You know, if he was influenced by his wife in making the will, that testament can be declared null. It might be of benefit to you if a will were set aside.'

'Strange, in some ways,' I mused. 'It seems so natural for a man's own wife to be consulted. In devising a will that affects their children.'

'No – no, Stephanos, the law is right. After all, strictly speaking, the children are not hers but his. It is the *father* of the child who supplies all the life-material, the identity. What the children are is already present in the father's seed. The mother simply gives the embryo house-room. She lets it lodge with her, as it were, nourishes the growing infant in her womb for nine months. Woman is matter, but form is male. Matter is supplied by the mother, but form comes from the father. Therefore, the care of children is perfectly the husband's prerogative.

Moreover, a woman, if she were allowed to have influence, would be sadly likely to be under control of her own family – especially her own brothers – and they could use her to defraud the rightful heirs. Hence, to make a will under the influence of a wife is reckoned the same as making a will under durance or some other coercion. When you look into it, you find the law quite sound.'

'Well, here is a case I have heard of that might appeal to you. There is a little man called Epikrates who must go to law. He was probably influenced and persuaded by a prostitute, who helped him to be swindled by an ingenious Egyptian myrrh-merchant.'

I hastened to regale him with the story (in so far as I knew it) of Epikrates and the Egyptian perfumer. As I expected, Aristotle was highly entertained.

'There must be something more to this story,' he said. 'Epikrates doesn't count for much – except that he is so rich! And thus important in Athens. Truly, I should like to do a favour for Hypereides himself. It would not be impolitic to oblige him.' I was relieved to feel that, as usual, Aristotle was many steps ahead of me and quite aware of the political situation. There seemed all the less reason for rehearsing the utterances of Megakles, Apollonios and Eurymedon.

'Sir, there is someone to see you,' said the slave who had been keeping the main door.

'Well, Phokon, have you let whoever-it-is in? Who is it? I presume, from your tone as well as from your words, you take our visitor to be someone who is no gentleman.'

'Sir,' said the slave, smiling a little, 'it is certainly no *gentleman*. But what to call her in gentlemen's ears I cannot rightly tell.'

'That is, you know all too well.' While the slave endeavoured to suppress a laugh, a slender female form appeared behind him. This was patently not a gentleman, and ladies do not call at gentlemen's houses. As we tried to get a clear view of the visitor, our noses were saluted with Eastern gales of teasing sweetness.

'Well, this is clearly no female quacksalver trying to get at my wife! Nor some fake priestess of Demeter, the goddess whom my wife loves. It would be hard to deny Pythias, for I love her as much as she loves Demeter. But no,' Aristotle continued, gazing at the female person who had now moved to the threshold and stood in front of the hapless porter. 'I see this is unlikely to be a priestess or medicine-woman. Let her fully enter the room and announce her own name.'

The woman obediently and gracefully came into the room. The book-lined apartment seemed an incongruous setting for this apparition. She was tall for a female, and slender, but very well-shaped. Her hair, a great deal of which was on display beneath an attractive green cloth flung over her head, was the most peculiar colour, both dark and fair, with twisty points of a reddish hue. Her eyes were outlined in some dark stuff in what I now thought of as the Egyptian manner (but with much more subtlety than I had seen on the face of the Egyptian prostitute I had met in the brothel in Kirrha). Gold bracelets circled both wrists, and a little chain of gold ran about her waist. This woman's gown was of a white linen so fine it must have been Egyptian, and on her finely-shaped feet were carefully wrought sandals of green leather, with the straps like leaves and tendrils curling over her feet. It was odd to think of those sandals plodding the dusty road to

Aristotle's house. The woman herself was beautifully cool, not a drop of sweat nor a hair out of place, though it was a summer afternoon. She was as slender and elegant as a young palm tree swaying in the wind in the sanctuary at Delos.

'Well, well,' said Aristotle, as we both surveyed this sweet apparition with admiration and interest. 'Let us know your name.'

'Sir,' said the woman. 'I am Antigone of Athens.'

'Antigone of Athens! Well, there's a change. The most famous woman of that name was Antigone of Thebes – perhaps you know of her. Oidipous' daughter.'

'Sir,' said the woman, 'I come to you for help. For I have much trouble!' With a graceful movement and a kind of swoop like a well-bred heron she came across the room and sank to her knees, then extended one hand imploringly to touch Aristotle's right knee. He drew it back, but had to extend his own hand to raise her – a touching tableau.

'Please,' he said, patting her head, 'it is too hot for a lot of kneeling and getting up again. Why don't you sit down somewhere and tell us – me and my friend – a plain tale?'

'As you are so good as to hear me,' said the woman, humbly. She sat herself down on a footstool, like a white dove coming tremblingly to rest.

'If you haven't heard of me before, you may soon,' she began, in a particularly sweet voice. 'I am Antigone, and I can say no more for myself than that I am a freedwoman and the daughter of a freedwoman, and I am a harlot of Athens, as my mother was too. I work independently. Well, that is, I did, until I set up my own establishment, and I now have two girls working for me.'

'A rise to success, in short,' said Aristotle.

'It seemed so until recently. For one of my clients was this man Epikrates, who was a regular customer, although he liked boys as well as girls. He wanted to get a boy belonging to an Egyptian perfume-seller, Athenogenes. The slave he wanted was the younger son of a slave called Midas, a good worker and of some value to Athenogenes.'

'Did Epikrates want to set the boy free?' asked Aristotle.

'Dear me, I don't know. I don't remember that he said so, but he may have done. Sometimes men say a great many things. Anyway, Epikrates eventually complained to me that Athenogenes would not sell the boy on whom he had set his heart. He asked *me* to negotiate with Athenogenes, and I did. I so softened Athenogenes that he said he would sell all three – Midas and both of his sons – for forty minai.'

'Did you tell Epikrates to hasten to clap up the bargain?'

'I must honestly say that I did tell Epikrates to act quickly. For I was not sure how long Athenogenes would hold one mind. But I had no more to do with the affair. Epikrates feels ill-used by the perfume man. Now *they* – Epikrates and his friends, I mean – are dragging me into it.'

'How well did you know Athenogenes? Were you partners?'

'No – no. He had been a client of mine, and I bought some perfumes and unguents – and medicines too – from him. Naturally, he saw I was a good customer. The girls need oils and sweet scents for their work. He let me have a discount, because he knew my house would do a regular business in that way. But that is all.'

'Did you get money from Epikrates?'

'Yes.'

'How much?'

'About two hundred and fifty drakhmai.'

'And this was specifically a commission for your aid in persuading the Egyptian merchant to do as Epikrates wished?'

'Well, yes – a commission. He paid me other money for . . . for my regular services.' She flushed charmingly, like the first clouds of dawn, and then began to weep, silently, the tears welling into her eyes and starting down her lovely cheek, without any howls or sniffs. The material with which she had outlined her eyes remained admirably steadfast at its post. 'O sirs, I am in great trouble – for what can a poor woman do when accused by the rich and great?'

'*You* don't seem in any particular danger,' said Aristotle cautiously. 'This is not a *criminal* case. I don't see how it can be made out to be anything more than a civil disagreement, if there were no more to it than a legal matter between two gentlemen.'

'No, indeed. Epikrates signed a contract –'

'Ah, it is only legal if there *were* a contract – a written contract. But how do you know there really was a contract? Did you actually see one?'

'Oh, yes, sir, indeed. I saw it and Epikrates was in his right mind and knowingly signed it. He set his name in full, not just his mark.'

'Ah. That seems satisfactory. Well, all that Epikrates can really ask for in law is some of his money back. He cannot succeed in a *criminal* prosecution. He can probably get a favourable hearing for his demand not to bear the burden of the debts that came with the perfumery business foisted on him along with the slaves. Tell your friend Athenogenes that making such a bargain with concealed debts in it is a mean trick, and if he persists in such things he is likely to get into serious trouble in Athens. As for you – you can only be in trouble to the extent that you were involved. But, as it isn't a criminal case, and you are a freedwoman, you need have no fear for your skin. The law case may affect your business, if you are asked (though it is unlikely that this would be demanded) to help restore some of the money. And you said your business is very small, only two harlots employed as well as yourself? In that case, Stephanos, you need not apply, for their house is sure to be too busy.'

'Oh, sir.' The courtesan gathered herself together and stood up gracefully. 'If you or your young friend should wish to come to my house you would be well entertained, I dare avow. Actually I do have three girls at command now – but you could always get the very best.'

She looked at both of us, coyness mingling with a certain scepticism or just deprecation. Although as I looked at her longer I saw she was not in her first youth, she still seemed magnificent. With her curling tendrils and green-leaf sandals she was a female manifestation of Dionysos.

'Farewell,' said Aristotle, rising courteously. 'The porter will see you out.'

'Allow me,' I said. I had the pleasure of handing her to the main door, feeling the silken skin of her soft hand and the shape of her arm through the soft material of her clothing. I also had the satisfaction to my curiosity of seeing her stepping into a little one-ass cart and being driven away by her slave. So, after all, she had not had to walk dusty roads in those wonderful green-tendrilled sandals.

At the departure of this new Antigone, Aristotle turned to me.

'Did you see, Stephanos?' he asked, with some of his old eager animation. 'That woman gave herself away! She herself *did* see the contract – therefore she *was* a party to the whole thing. I can almost guarantee that this charming Antigone is a secret – or not-so-secret – partner of the perfume-seller Athenogenes. I will get hold of Hypereides and tell him as much. I shall also suggest that Epikrates make as his excuse in the law case the statement that he was besotted by this woman – carried away with love for her! Let him say "Eros working together with a woman is much too powerful for male nature, and can overthrow any man." Thus Epikrates can say he did what Antigone asked without knowing entirely what he did. It would be better, by the way, for Epikrates if he could declare that he wished to free the boy he spent the money on.'

'I suppose,' I agreed, 'that it would look a little more noble and a good deal less crass.'

'Precisely. But I shall tell Hypereides to produce this Antigone herself before the jury. Let Epikrates say he was besotted with love – and *then* let her be produced in the flesh. She would have a terrific effect. Just imagine *her* in a courtroom! Men would readily believe that Epikrates was carried away by love-desire – intoxicated, in the manner of men. They would thus find his stupidity much more forgivable. If that last will and testament is wrong which has been made by a man under the influence of his wife, how much more wrong is that contract which has been made under the undue and omnipotent influence of a powerful courtesan.'

'Do you think that is altogether fair to her?' I asked. 'She came to you as a suppliant, after all.'

'But *why* did she come? Probably to see if she could get something out of the pro-Makedonians, since Hypereides and the anti-Makedonians are against her. But this beautiful whore is *not* honest. She knew too much about that contract. And she must have received more from Epikrates than the two hundred and fifty drakhs. For she has recently bought another girl for her establishment, and that costs a handsome sum. Especially as this madam evidently is in the fine *hetaira* line, and must go in for elegance and good conversation, perhaps offering a little music as well. Upon my word, Stephanos, I hope your youthful heart – or loins – may not be overset by this vision! Antigone, indeed. Well, the original Antigone was persistent too, I'll say that.'

I *was* affected by the vision of this Antigone (and by her scent, and the touch of her hand), though I was wise enough not to go to her house. Actually, my body still yearned after the Egyptian Tita (seen only once and never enjoyed by me) in the rocky little harbour under the cliffs of Delphi. I did go to a good brothel that night, and was glad I did. I finished the evening by drinking a great deal, to the sound of flutes; I got home late (or early) and slept a deep healthy sleep.

The next morning I set out in pursuit of my future wife's

mother – or, rather, her relatives. By this time I had gained a little further light on the subject of the whereabouts of her family's settlement on the lower slopes of Hymettos. Philomela's stepfather, whose name was Dropides, dwelled there, on the property of his wife's first husband – a strange enough arrangement. I started off early, before sun-up, so as not to become tired by walking the whole distance in the heat of the day. But it took me a while to get out of the city, and the sun was advancing as I made my way beyond the city walls towards purple Hymettos, the range of marble hills protecting Athens on the south-east side.

The countryside was in a festival of summer, fields laughing under the light. Reapers were taking in the harvest in golden armfuls. In the small gardens that ran beside or behind the humbler houses, women could be seen tending the vegetables. I walked with pleasure even as the day warmed. I went through a field whose crop had recently been harvested; the field was lying idle and placid in the early sun that caused its stubble to shine and gleam like radiant precious things. In the middle of the field was a little closed house, obviously the property of a phratry, and holding their holy objects until the next celebratory occasion.

The land began to rise, and I was walking into hill country, following the pine trees beside the River Ilissos as that stream sped swiftly (less swiftly now, in high summer) downward from its source in Hymettos to give water and life to Athens. The fountain whence Ilissos flows is sacred to Aphrodite, and supposed to remedy sterility in the man or woman who drinks from it. The family that I was looking for lived not far from the source of the river, in the uplands, but on a flat part with some arable land, a miniature plain set in the side of the mountain. As I moved upwards following the river, trees offered welcome shade. Dragonflies sported on the surface of the water. The air was everywhere clear and grateful to the sense – not just to the smell, but to the sense of breathing in itself.

I thought I was drawing near as I moved out again from the shade of trees and saw a wider space. Across from me I could see a woman walking through this space. She walked with such grace and dignity that she looked like a princess or priestess of old time. Alone, momentarily, in the landscape, she moved with purpose across it, towards some objects that I could not clearly descry. I could hear the hum of insects in the still air.

To the left I now saw the small farmhouse and outbuildings, crouched in a fold of the ground so as to make best use of the flat and tillable lands. I went up to the door and knocked. All this while I was greeted by the furious barking of the yard dog, who was, however, firmly tied to a projection on one of the outbuildings and could not leap at my throat. At last I was answered by an elderly slavewoman, who shuffled along and peered at me shortsightedly. Whatever this family's wealth, they did not waste money on the purchase and upkeep of impressive servants.

'Who's that, Mika?' a querulous voice said from the inner room. I started to explain but was cut short. 'Don't stand maundering but come in,' said the voice and I came.

The inner room was agreeable enough in shape and size, but not as agreeable as it might be made. It was full of litter. I don't mean just crowded with many things, as one might say that sometimes Aristotle's room seemed to be full of books, open and closed and tumbled about for reference, or that a woman's room is full of her sewing and fabric and loom and so on. It was full of things that are not useful and that nobody would ever want. There were piles of crockery, most of it cracked or chipped, and pieces of furniture that had died or given up from bad usage or old age.

Dropides – for this must be the master of the house – sat in a chair softened with cushions and draped with various fabrics. He was sipping something out of a thick pottery cup. My advent did not disturb him. He looked at me and went on drinking, if in a well-bred and delicate fashion. It was an awkward moment, for I was speaking after a fashion to my fiancée's grandfather, or the substitute for that patriarch. An elder, and the head of a house.

'Sir,' I began formally, 'I ask your pardon for this intrusion, and beg to explain my reason for coming to you. I am Stephanos son of Nikiarkhos of Athens. Through great good fortune I have become acquainted with Smikrenes of Eleusis and I wish to marry his daughter, whose name I am told is Philomela.' I spoke thus formally to avoid giving the vulgar offence of being over-familiar; it is usually very rude to refer by name to the female members of a man's family. I took a deep breath and continued:

'To this plan Smikrenes agrees, but I would earnestly wish to consult the girl's mother's relatives likewise. Smikrenes' daughter is the child of your wife's daughter.'

'Not *my* daughter,' Dropides interjected. He was evidently not ill-educated, for he spoke better than did Smikrenes, for instance, but his low voice lacked colour and emphasis. Neither my arrival nor my statement seemed to have excited him.

'This I know. But you stand in relation to Philonike daughter of Philokles in place of her father, as you are her stepfather and natural guardian.'

'She doesn't need much guarding. I leave all that to my wife. My wife's outside now, seeing to the reaping. She works with and directs the men. But she can be fetched. Mika, fetch Philokleia.'

The blear-eyed old woman shuffled off at his bidding. He took another sip. This strangely indolent man did not look truly old, though he acted elderly. He must be, I thought, a good ten or twelve years younger than Hypereides (possibly more). Yet one couldn't imagine him striding though the Agora or indeed anywhere else. Dropides seemed to live like a woman, letting his wife act in the manly way.

'Indeed,' I said, nonplussed. 'Pray do not put your household to trouble on my account.'

He caught my surprise.

'I am an invalid, I fear, sir – a confirmed invalid.' He coughed gently. 'Philokleia my wife has a couple of years over me, but she's spry and wiry. I am not so young as I was. Why, you say yourself I'm a *grandfather*, as it were, to Philomela. Philonike my stepdaughter is no chick – she's five-and-thirty, if a day. And now Philonike's daughter has taken a maggot to be married! I find it best to let others do anything that needs doing. Why shorten life?'

He quietly adjusted a sheepskin, one of the many mats or rugs that hung about his chair.

'I keep my shoulders and knees warm, and try to

maintain an even body heat,' he explained. I thought he must truly be ill to wish for any coverings or soft fabrics on a day that was so warm. Though in this room, evidently thick-walled, it was not unbearably hot so much as too stuffy. The many extra objects, the cracked chairs and wormy tables, seemed to exhale their dust as they decayed, even while we were speaking.

Mika returned, her low grumbling voice addressing someone else, a woman who answered more sharply.

'Ah, there's Philokleia now!' Dropides smiled. 'If she stands in the room just off here – with only a curtain between us – then she can answer any questions you want, without you seeing her or anything improper.'

I was glad to assent, and Philokleia took up her stand as she was bid behind the curtain. Her obedience, however, had its limits, for she remonstrated with the head of the house.

'You had best left me alone, husband, for we were getting on so quick with the grain, and me being gone will slow everything. Whatever can be the matter, that you summon me in on a working day? It will be too hot to go on soon, and the men will insist on food and a nap, so part of the morning will have been clean wasted.'

'I humbly beg your pardon, sir,' I said. It seemed best for the proprieties to maintain the fiction that I addressed the master of the house, and that his wife addressed him also. 'Please, O Dropides, convey my apologies to your wife. I would not disturb you or her on any light occasion. But I am wishful to wed Smikrenes' daughter Philomela, the child of your wife's own daughter.'

'Ha,' snorted the woman behind the curtain. 'So Philonike's brat is of marrying age? Doesn't time fly.' It was odd to think that I had just heard the voice of Philomela's grandmother.

'Please tell your wife,' I directed Dropides, 'what I am saying to you, that I would like to know that Philomela's marriage was approved by her kindred on the mother's side. And of course I wish to know' – this was the pith of the matter – 'whether Philomela's mother Philonike still has a brother living, for his approval of course should be asked. As well as yours, sir,' I added carefully.

'Mine?' said Dropides. 'Oh, *mine* doesn't count, I'm just a step-relation. I don't know as I have ever heard of you. Wife, have you ever heard of this man Stephanos?'

'No, never,' said the woman. 'Smikrenes I know. We should really call in my daughter, for she's the person this most concerns. Mika, fetch Philonike.'

Mika, muttering under her breath, went out into the heat again. I did not want to slacken in my questioning; I felt the important point about the brother had been passed over. I was aware, however, that I might appear as a most unwelcome claimant upon the family's wealth.

'If you please, sir,' I said, still addressing my remarks formally to Dropides, despite the fact that the family supply of knowledge and energy evidently – even in his own opinion – belonged to his wife. 'What can you tell me about Philomela's uncle on her mother's side, the brother of Philonike? Your stepson?'

'Not much of a son,' said Dropides. He took a long sip from his pot. 'A headstrong youth, little apt to listen to his elders, to my way of thinking. Foolish, very foolish.'

'Humph!' said Philokleia. 'He's a good boy, my Philokles. Just because he thinks to better himself, *you* think he's a fool.'

She certainly spoke of her son in the present tense, I noted, so she was reasonably sure he was still alive.

'Where is he?' I asked. 'And why,' I demanded with conscious daring, 'have you kept Philonike at home all this time? Away from her lawful husband?'

'Hah!' said the woman behind the curtain. '*Keep* her! She's not been a prisoner here, I can tell you.'

'Surely not,' said Dropides, roused with some energy in his tone. 'It was her own father brought her back, after she had lost her child —'

'She was all dazed-like at that time,' interjected Philokleia.

'So it was his doing that she was here,' said Dropides. 'Nothing to do with me. I wasn't going to chase her out of house and home, that's all. If her husband wanted her, why didn't he come and get her? Isn't that so, wife?'

'Right!' said Philokleia, in a triumphant tone. '*If* old Smikrenes wanted the girl, he should have said so and gone to some trouble about it. But Philonike was happy here, you see — it's her home. She loves the hills and heights, the plane trees and the river, and the smell of thyme and the heather. Everything's too flat down in that area around about Eleusis, she said — no life in it.'

'And she's good with the bees,' said Dropides. 'Some say women shouldn't look after bees, but she does it beautifully. And with my Philokleia having enough to attend to with the farm, she found it hard to keep the bees as well —'

'Well, that's a truth,' said Philokleia, in a resigned tone. I thought she had not intended to mention this talent of her daughter's, which made the couple seem more self-interested in retaining her. 'Philonike looks after bees —

quite wonderful – makes her own hives. She don't seem to get stung like some others do. It's a sign that the bees choose her, you see. She loves her bees, she certainly does –'

Mika came in again; there were more sounds, and a low conversation. A tall figure came swiftly into the next room – and I realised that this was my mysterious woman who walked like a princess. The beekeeper. The objects she had been moving towards were her beehouses.

'Well, Philonike,' said Philokleia. 'Here we've been talking of your beekeeping, and how good you are at it – to a young man who wants to marry your daughter Philomela. Seemingly with your husband Smikrenes' permission. What do you think of that, eh?'

'Marry? My little Philomela – marry?' This was a beautiful voice though it spoke in agitated tones. The tall and shapely woman came close to the curtain. I could see her eyes glimmering through the fabric.

'Sir, assure your wife and daughter that Philomela is in good health and of marriageable age and is a beautiful girl – her father says,' I added hastily. I must not let on that I had actually seen the girl herself. 'I pray you, Dropides, ask your stepdaughter to go and see Philomela, to assure herself that the girl is well, and also that she is happy with this arrangement.'

'Ahh,' said the tall woman. 'I should so love to see her! But – I don't think that is possible – if I went, *he* would keep me and I don't want to go back. I'd be afraid even to go to the wedding.'

'Oh, but you must come to the wedding,' I said impulsively, addressing her directly through the curtain that divided us, though this was not proper. 'Your mother and stepfather too, and then all will be well. And you must see your daughter – if you care about her at all –'

She laughed without humour. 'Care? She was the only reason I hesitated to leave – knowing I would give her up. The hardest thing in my life – after losing the other baby, that is.'

'Please, good lady, see your daughter, and consent to this wedding,' I said. 'I am respectable, if not very rich, I am born of a good family, and I am in good health, with some prospects. You must see that I owe it to any children Philomela and I may have – the gods be willing – that I should also undertake this marriage with the consent of Philomela's uncle, your brother.'

'And I suppose,' said grandmother Philokleia in her sharper tones, 'you will be wanting to know if there is any money in it for you?'

'Yes,' I said. 'Frankly, I need to know whether there was or is any disposition for Philomela, and thus for her children-to-be, following the death of her father, your husband. Your first husband, I mean.'

There was a short silence. I heard the women whisper. Dropides closed his eyes and seemed to meditate. Philonike said something like 'We shall have to tell him!' And Philonike's mother spoke again.

'This is the way of it. Of course there must be a formal accounting of this with someone who can attest to your standing and character. But if matters have gone this far, we should say "Yes." There *is* some portion of inheritance under the will of my late first husband, Philomela's grandfather. He left a portion of the land – not ancestral land, of course – and some money for her. Naturally, this is in the care of his son Philokles.'

'And *where* is Philokles?' I enquired. This was surely the important question.

'Ah, well. That's a point. Philokles has gone East. The boy thought while I – and Dropides of course – managed things here, he would be better off going to one of the islands and seeing if he couldn't find a new settlement there, now that everything in the East has opened up with Alexander chasing the Persians away. We heard from him once – he is in one of those islands – one with a lot of wind, and snakes, he says, which you don't expect on islands.'

'Rhodos, mother.'

'Yes, Rhodos – sounds like roses, whether it's rosy or not. Of course he may have gone to the mainland by now, or to one of the other islands, Kos, maybe, as that is so healthy, he says. But he was intending to plant a small farm and open up a business on Rhodos.'

'So –' said Dropides, opening up his eyes again. 'You would have to chase after him out there, young master, for we don't rightly know where to address him. If you can't find him, nothing can be done. He'll come home when ready, no doubt. But there's a lot of stirring work going on in the East now, a man could pick up a fortune –'

'Humph!' Philokleia snorted. 'There's enough to be made here, if people would only attend to their work. My girl Philonike, like I said, is wonderful with the bees.'

'And so you have Hymettos honey,' I said with approbation.

'Yes,' Philonike herself replied. 'We have Hymettos honey – the best in the world. And our hives are in a lovely place, with sufficient shelter. The bees are happy, so they make the best honey. Let me give you a little pot to take home with you.'

'You might as well take it while you can,' said Dropides. 'Philonike does wonderful honey – it's so excellent that we have been able to sell some. Nowadays there's a big trade in it. It's valued, you see, for cooking and medicine both. So we are thinking of opening up the farm to more beehives, since there's real money in it.'

I thought to myself that any opening up and improving the produce would be done by the women without any active assistance from Dropides.

'That is excellent,' I exclaimed. 'Such a happy farm as you have – in such a lovely place!'

'It *is* nice,' said Dropides, looking about his stuffy room with great complacency. 'A man likes to have all his things about him. We are very well set up here – want for nothing – lots of pots. Lots of tables. And the best honey. Wheat and barley too. Also a few grape vines, mostly good for vinegar. Not much wine, but excellent vinegar. Take a drink yourself, young sir, of cool water from Ilissos' fountain, with a dash of our vinegar in it. Very good for the health in summertime, that is. I take it myself, though sometimes I have to have a dash of wine instead – the vinegar sitting ill on my stomach. But have some water and vinegar – with just a whisper of honey, if you like. Honey is always good for the throat and the bowels.'

Mika brought me the drink of vinegar and water, which I drank unsweetened; it was delicious. This had been a favourite drink of my childhood in hot summers, but the water here was certainly superior, and the vinegar lived up to Dropides' account.

'Mika,' said Philokleia, 'take our guest out to the storehouse and give him a pot of honey on his way out.'

At this hint I made my farewells and went obediently with Mika. To my surprise tall Philonike came too – not exactly with me, but as a shadow flitting behind. I supposed that she wanted to make sure her hives and honey stores were not molested. There were rows of hives, pottery jars lying on their sides, or cunning hutches of old tree trunks. As we approached the area, a warm buzz filled the air. The storehouse was built into the ground, and Mika lowered herself into the coolness and brought back a jar. The scent of honey wafted everywhere, and the bees started to come towards us. The door to the storehouse was swiftly closed.

'How wonderful the bees are,' said Philonike. 'They know exactly what they are doing. Humans make war, but bees make honey.'

'Don't bees sometimes make war, too?' I asked. 'We get our honey from their greed – and then we are greedy ourselves.'

'And then such as I come and fill the hives with smoke, and destroy their golden cities,' she added.

There was a silence, while the bees hummed about us. Philonike broke the silence at last.

'Please, sir, find some way of conveying my warm greetings to my daughter,' she said. 'I will do everything reasonable for her – except go back to live with Smikrenes.'

'You are not divorced?'

'No – no. I have never been unfaithful. Just – not there.'

'Was he cruel to you?' I asked, audaciously.

'Oh no. Not according to his lights. It was just a disagreeable way to live. I like the hills, and the bees, and the smell of thyme. I am happy enough. And I think my brother will be all right. Philokles always comes well out of everything, no matter how difficult or dangerous. If you find him, you will like him. And of course I think that you and my daughter Philomela should have your share of my father's estate. Whether Dropides thinks so or not is no concern of mine. Farewell.'

After this unorthodox speech to a man not related to her, the strange woman who moved like a king's daughter walked swiftly away. I plodded back to Athens, with the honey pot, getting warmer and warmer, in my hand.

V

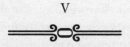

Odour of Blood

I pondered long on the meeting with Philomela's mother and her grandmother, and thought much about the farm at Hymettos. It really belonged to Philomela's missing uncle, the man who had gone off to Rhodos or somewhere. That estate did not belong at all to Dropides, though he was certainly in the place of the male head of house – if only in his supine way. Such a man can make great mischief, like Aigisthos who took over Agamemnon's house and his wife, with Klytaimnestra's connivance. But there was no adultery in this case, and Dropides did not seem like an Aigisthos. I hoped his stepson would not be a vengeful and resentful Orestes – I had really had enough of Orestes on a former occasion.

If only Philomela got some share of the wealth of the farm! Even a little would eke out the slender living which I had to offer. I needed to search out her mother's brother Philokles, the man who had so unkindly removed himself from Athens to seek his fortune elsewhere. Who knew when he would return? As long as the farm in Hymettos was running smoothly, as long as his mother was alive (and as long as the irritating Dropides made his home there), he might well feel no need to come back. Therefore, in order to come to any arrangement with him (at least with any celerity), it appeared I might have to take a long journey to the eastern islands – further than I had ever before thought of travelling. The notion seemed madness when it first came into my thoughts. But as I turned the matter over inwardly, it appeared less implausible. Before I married, I needed to get the money arrangements straight. But the journey itself was formidable to my mind. For one thing, it would mean travelling by ship, living on the water, the dangerous element to which (aside from short swims) I had never yet entrusted myself.

I tried to see Aristotle in order to consult him on the question, but when I arrived at his house he was engaged with another visitor, so private talk was not to be expected. I recognised the small man with a quiff of unruly dark hair and bandy legs – not at all a sightly personage, though he wore good clothes and behaved like a man of consequence. At my entry this other visitor did not even turn around, much less rise from his chair, where he was perched with a ruffled air like an offended bird. A bird of ill omen I later thought him, though perhaps that is not fair.

'Stephanos. This is Epikrates, whom I think you know, the friend of Hypereides.'

I certainly knew him, the little man who had tried to buy the boy from the Egyptian Athenogenes and who had been inveigled by that Egyptian perfume-seller into taking over a business with nothing but debts. The last time I had called on Aristotle we had the memorable interview with another character in the same case, the beautiful Antigone of the Dionysiac green sandals. I smiled inwardly. Whatever this Epikrates had been up to, he had nothing to do with Dionysos.

Epikrates smiled sourly. 'All Athens knows of my misfortune,' he said drily. 'Hypereides suggested that I come and consult with Aristotle regarding the conduct of the case – though of course Hypereides will take charge of it.'

'And you could have no better counsellor for a courtroom,' said Aristotle heartily. 'I believe that you can force some financial restitution from the perfume-seller – if not from the *hetaira*. I think you would be well advised to leave her alone – treat her as a witness, merely.'

'Her!' exclaimed Epikrates. He jumped off his chair and stood up in the irritation of his anger. 'That whore – that flame-haired piece of trash! I would like to have the hide off both of them – her and that sweet stinking foreign bastard. They should both be flayed in the market-place!'

Having pronounced this doom, Epikrates sat down again, his hair standing straight up on his head in the agitation of the moment. This fellow was palpably willing me to depart so that he could continue the discussion with Aristotle. There was no chance of private conversation, so I left. At least, I reflected, Aristotle was making some friends – or non-hostile acquaintance – among the men who hated the rule of Makedon, men like Hypereides and his circle. Harmony between Aristotle and these patriots should conduce both to the philosopher's tranquillity and to that of the city. I had, of course, no real opportunity to ask after the health of Pythias on that occasion; a man cannot be expected to discuss his wife while meeting with men over business.

It was only two days later that I called at the Lykeion, to consult with Eudemos or Arkhandros about the best ways of journeying to the places where Philomela's uncle Philokles might be found. These scholars were from abroad; Eudemos was from Rhodos itself. They would know the best routes and also how a voyager might get in touch with people in such places as the Ionian and Karian Islands near the coast of Asia. I should certainly need some letters of introduction if I went chasing through the seas to these far-off islands. Thus it was that I was seated in the 'book kitchen' of the Lykeion in the early morning, waiting for Eudemos in the company of Theophrastos and Demetrios, when a slave came running in:

'O, sirs – Theophrastos, sir! The mistress' time has come this morning and it's getting worse. Master says please to come, and I'm to go for another doctor.'

'Yes, go!' said Theophrastos. 'I shall come to your master at once.' He turned to me. 'Perhaps you had better come too, Stephanos.'

'I don't want to intrude at such time –' I said.

'The Master likes you,' Theophrastos answered simply. I followed him out of the Lykeion's academic rooms and into Aristotle's own house. The house had a frightened hurried air; slaves were whispering in corners, and female slaves were speaking in an agitated manner, and running to and fro with cloths and basins. Everything in this house was usually so well ordered, but this time it did not seem so.

Aristotle was in his lovely book-lined room. The last

time I had seen him, consulting with and reassuring the wretched Epikrates, he had seemed as he always did – lively and jovial, quick-minded, like the sun at his zenith, shining from mid-heaven on the grateful earth, looking with approbation alike on men, animals and plants. I was not prepared for seeing him so agitated, so pale. He kept running his fingers through his hair.

'Sit with me, Stephanos. Please stay. I will go to Pythias from time to time, but a man is often in the way – the women feel this. I am a doctor too! But I do not know that I am the best doctor in this occasion. I have sent for another who has more experience with women's ills than I have.'

I looked about the room for aid but nobody else was about. There was a beautiful water jar, and also a graceful wine-pourer on a little table in the corner, with an array of cups, preparations either for the long wait or for the celebration. 'Have some wine,' I suggested, but Aristotle rejected it with a gesture. So I poured out some water, and persuaded him to sit down and drink it. He looked as if he had had very little sleep. I suggested he lie down, but he shook his head vehemently.

'Not until this is over! This is no time for sleeping. If only I knew more – about what might be done to ease the passage of this child. The birth of little Pythias was nothing like this.'

'These things have their own time and manner,' I said to comfort him. I did not know in the least what I was talking about. 'I have never before been in a house where a woman was giving birth,' I admitted. Yet suddenly I was struck by a hazy impression of blood and confusion, of someone crying behind closed doors, of noise of some kind, of presence and absence. Of heavy silence, like a room furnished with only a stone at its centre. And bloody cloths. Yet this could hardly be a recollection. I was at school all day when my mother gave birth to Theodoros.

Suddenly a woman's cry came through the walls. It ripped through the air and seemed to tear everything into shreds. It was much worse than the cries and screeches of tragedy – so real, you knew it must be torn out of the body by the power of pain. Aristotle clenched his hands. I could see the sweat on his forehead.

'Pray the gods that may be because she is near the end of it,' I said. 'Maybe the baby is coming out right now.' Aristotle did not reply. We sat in silence.

The terrible cry was repeated. Aristotle rushed to the door. 'I cannot stand this! I must go to her!' He disappeared into the private apartments whence issued that awful sound.

I did not like to leave him, so I stayed where I was. I felt queasy and tried to think of something else. But there came another terrific cry, so harsh, so edged that I felt the house walls might cleave under it, as under a giant's sword. Then there was a silence or subdued murmur, and more trampling of feet in the passageway. Somewhere in the house I sensed the presence of blood, a scent of it wafting through the rooms and tainting the air. Yet, after all, I reminded myself, every house in Athens saw a childbirth from time to time, and women were doing this every day . . .

There was another cry or shout, but much fainter: the harsh edge and the vibrant pulsation had gone out of it. More murmuring, and other voices raised – someone's voice spoke the words 'Zeus Saviour' loudly and entreatingly. I sprang up from my chair as if I too had to join in the prayers. A long lull was followed by a subdued cry, and then the wretched sound of sobbing. Then, almost like a formal chorus, came the regular ululation in women's traditional manner. The hairs on the back of my neck stood up.

Someone was sobbing while coming down the passage to Aristotle's room. The door opened. Theophrastos entered first; he was almost guiding Aristotle, as if the Master were the blind prophet Tireseias, or Oidipous travelling to Kolonos with Antigone pulling him along. Aristotle indeed walked like one to whom sight was of no use. His eyes were wet, though he did not weep and cry out. He was very pale.

'She's dead,' he said, in a quiet and toneless voice. 'Pythias – my beloved wife – is dead.'

'And the baby?' I asked tactlessly.

Aristotle's face screwed up as if he found the words difficult to create and push out.

'The baby is dead. It was born dead. It must have been dead for a while. O Stephanos!' he turned to me and leaned against me for a moment, as if he were fragile. 'So much for my hopes! How could I have been stupid enough to let this happen? And what will I do without her? She was my beloved, the dearest and the best!'

I patted his shoulder awkwardly. 'I am sad for your loss,' I said awkwardly, trying to remember the right words for these occasions. 'You were a good husband to her, I am sure. And you have your philosophy to console you.'

'Oh yes. Philosophy.' Aristotle started to laugh.

'Stop that!' said Theophrastos, shaking him. I was surprised to see him treat Aristotle so brutally.

'Had he not better sit and take some wine?' I asked.

'Yes, that's probably the best thing,' said Theophrastos.

'But I cannot just sit here as if nothing had happened.' Aristotle moved restlessly about, his eyes flickering around the room, but still as if he did not see what was before him. 'I should do something for her . . .'

'You cannot do anything,' I pointed out. 'The women will do all that has to be done. And Theophrastos and Demetrios and I will invite people to the funeral.'

'The funeral should be soon,' said Theophrastos. I knew what he meant. The smell of a certain corruption, the dead baby and whatever else had secretly gone dead inside Pythias before she died, seemed to seep through the house already. Washing and unguents would stem that tide, but not for ever. The house needed to be rid of that corpse, or corpses.

I poured out wine for Aristotle from the jar on the table, and this time he obediently sat down and drank it. 'I shall probably get drunk from a few sips and pass out,' he warned us. Both Theophrastos and I thought this sounded like the best plan for the moment. I was almost stunned myself by the naked intensity of his grief, and yet somewhat surprised to see the Master so overthrown merely by the death of a woman.

He groaned. 'Why was I such a fool? Why did I let this happen?'

'It is madness to reproach yourself,' I said. 'This was none of your doing, it has nothing to do with you –'

'Oh yes, Stephanos. It has. My philosophy – as you call it – is a torture to me. For I should not have let this happen. I should have known that something was wrong – known long before. I should have put a stop to this pregnancy. Had we done so early enough, she would have been well. You cannot keep me from reproaching myself, because I *did* know better.'

We let him babble on, and plied him with drink until he sank into an uneasy doze and we put him (still uncleansed from his contact with death) into a bed that we ordered the slave make up in the book room. The marital bedchamber would not be habitable for a long while. Indeed, the whole house seemed to hold a heavy miasma, an odour of triumphant death that would not budge. Once Aristotle was lying down I left, truly thankful to be out of the house.

On the day after the death, I went early to visit Smikrenes. It seemed only proper to discuss with him the new possibility of my roaming to the eastern islands in search of Smikrenes' brother-in-law Philokles. This sole uncle of my bride-to-be evidently had the correct information about the inheritance of Philomela's mother, and he was the only person who could legally agree to give us access to it. Smikrenes was almost cheerful at the prospect of an influx of wealth, but soon inclined to his more natural gloom.

'Them people always makes things sound better than they are,' he warned me. 'It's not as if they was rushing to give you anything now, when they might do. I remember Philokles — always dashing here, dashing there, very impatient. I don't know as I'd want to deal with him.'

'Well, we have to deal with him.' I was really thinking that Smikrenes should have dealt with him long ago. 'No one who lives at the Hymettos farm at the moment has full legal control,' I pointed out. 'The woman's second husband does not have inheritance rights, and is not the true governor of the place or the inheritance. And the women — your wife and mother-in-law — cannot act legally, though their work is causing the estate to prosper. Philokles seems to be well off, given that this estate must be his inheritance. If there is a part share for your wife and her child, we might well be able to combine to create a business with the honey alone which would bring an increase of wealth. And any immediate settlement in property, cattle or cash would assist myself and Philomela immensely at the beginning of a marriage.'

'I see that well enough,' he said. 'Strange, ain't it. Here I am, near the coast – and you in the city – and Philonike's family in the hills. We'll make a *trittys* by ourselves, our family, once you unite with it.'

I laughed at his little joke, likening us to one of the units created in order that different areas of Athens should feel united. Each deme belonged to a 'threesome' or 'trinity', an association of each region of the town within the walls with a region near the sea and a region in the hill country. Of course in the real political arrangement, Hymettos still counted as in the town of Athens; it was the region beyond that counted as the 'country beyond the hills'. My future father-in-law, however, was pleased at his wit, and my response to his jest made him more kindly disposed to me. I thought it best to bring up at that time the subject of money for immediate use.

'If somebody doesn't find Philokles and pin him down,' I said, 'he may not be back in Athens for years – if ever. He might get rich in a new colony and decide to stay. Or he may die in the islands and nobody hear of it for years. So the proper course for all our benefit would seem for me to go to the East and seek him. But that is an investment of money as well as of time, and I have very little of the former thing, though I have some time.'

'I have to say, I shouldn't want to go dashing about the world,' said Smikrenes. 'All very well for people with nothing better to do. Dangerous, though. I'm happy where I am. Still, I dare say as it's my wife's money we're looking for, you're right. And I will put something into the venture.' He sighed heavily, and I knew it would be hard for him to part with money. But at least the plan was beginning to form, and before I left Smikrenes' home I had encouraged him to name a sum that, if not munificent, would make my journey possible.

This was not a day of pleasure but a business day. I caught a glimpse of Philomela, but was not trying to do so. Before yesterday I had begun to look forward to marriage, thinking of the pleasure of the bed, the regularity of life, and the increased respect from other men – even though I was full young for marriage. I had thought of giving Philomela more rest and some treats. I had even begun to imagine, idly, some children to result from our union: a little boy and a little girl, vague figures who played happily about a rather hazy garden within my mind. But the events of yesterday made marriage taste like blood and sweat. New fears accompanied the idea of the new responsibility. After all, if Philomela remained on her father's farm in her present condition, a tranquil if hard-working virgin, she would not have to challenge death in that ruthless form which had conquered Pythias. I did not like to think of Philomela uttering such cries as I had heard. The gods can surely wring from us our dearest possessions.

I left Smikrenes' farm while it was still night, in order to get back to Athens in time for the funeral next day. When I arrived in the city, it was just at the break of dawn, the time when the working slaves and some citizens begin to be up and doing. As I was on one of the streets approaching the Agora, I encountered two respectable men talking together. I recognised one of them: sardonic Theosophoros, who had thought fit officiously to befriend me in the Agora a few days previously. The other man, much younger, was my acquaintance Gorgias. He lived nearby, in the grand house that had belonged to his father, Lysippos, a wealthy silversmith now far away.

'It is certainly an outrage,' said Theosophoros. 'What can it mean? But possibly it is a kind of accident – some young louts at play.'

'What is the trouble, gentlemen?' I enquired, coming up to them.

Gorgias appeared pale and agitated, but it had long been my impression (because of the circumstances of our first meeting) that he was always pale and agitated. That was his usual style. Such a judgement was somewhat unfair, as Gorgias laboured under extreme difficulties at our first acquaintance.

'Another curse has fallen on my house,' he announced tragically. The tragical seemed Gorgias' natural mode.

'What curse?'

'This morning I found a dead dog at our gate.'

'So?' I said unsympathetically. 'Dogs die all the time. Why not at your gate or mine?'

'It was a *killed* dog.' He shuddered. 'Come and see, Stephanos. I have not moved it – I was going to report it to the prytany. Whoever committed this vile action has made my herm impure!'

With these cryptic words he led us back to his (or rather his father's) house, the handsome mansion built in the old days and purchased by a wealthy silver merchant who had been able to make improvements. I had been there twice before last spring, once for a dinner and shortly after that to help when Gorgias' cousin was mysteriously abducted and Aristotle was called in to consult about the matter. This fine house of course had a well-made herm. Every house in Athens has a herm in front of it, a pillar usually of stone, sometimes of bronze, with a male genital carving and a head on the top. Sometimes the penis is just sketched in and sometimes it is quite elaborate, with a carving of the balls and the rod. The herm marks the sacred boundary of the house, wards off evil, and protects the household with the energy of divine fertilising power. Since this is a representation of a deity, commonly said to be Hermes, who protects the house and gives it fertility and abiding life, any shame to a herm is an act of sacrilege.

When we got to the silversmith's house we could see clearly enough what he meant. The top of his herm was obscured by a very large, very dead dog. The unfortunate animal had been sliced open the length of the body. A deep cut or trench ran along in its underside from the throat through the belly to the genital area, so all its inner secrets were exposed. Entrails dangled everywhere. The genitals (it was decidedly a male dog) had been partly cut loose, left dangling in obscene parody of the genital marking upon the sacred pillar. Flies had begun to work on the bloody mess.

'You see?' said Gorgias. I had to admit he had a right to look pale. 'I should report this. It is not only an insult to me, but a sacrilege!'

'I do see that,' I admitted.

'*Anyone* can see that,' sniffed Theosophoros. 'Perhaps not boyish play, after all. Who could have done this, Gorgias? And why? Don't you think this insult must have been meant for your father – and your deceased uncle – rather than for you?'

Gorgias' voice took on an edge of dangerous self-control as he replied, 'As to what men of barbarous mind or childish louts may think I am not able to say.'

'Quite so,' I agreed. 'I suppose you had better report this to the authorities, Gorgias, and then deal with the household pollution after your slaves have carted the corpse of this dog away.'

'Certainly I am not going to bury it on my property,' said Gorgias. 'But I don't want my mother to hear of it – she is very unwell this summer. So the sooner I go about the business – and the more quietly – the better. I was wondering about asking Aristotle –'

'Please leave Aristotle alone,' I said bluntly. 'Have you not heard? His wife is dead and he buries her today.'

'Ah, yes,' said Theosophoros. 'Unlucky to contaminate a funeral by conversing about funeral of a dead dog.'

His words reminded me that I should wash and change and get rid of the pollution acquired in the vicinity of the dead animal. I was covered with dust and needed to wash anyway, and there was little time to lose. With a few reassuring words to Gorgias I slipped away.

When I arrived at Aristotle's house, after a proper interval for ablution, I realised that the funeral would of course be small, as it was only for a woman. Many of the teachers in the Lykeion were there, and some of the students. A few friends of Aristotle's came. If the little baby who had died while still hidden in the womb had lived to taste the air, and been held in his father's arms and given a name, then – even if it had lived but an hour – a son of the house would have died, and the number who came to the funeral would have been much greater.

Decorously we accompanied to the Kerameikos the corpse – or rather, corpses – of the woman who had once lived and the infant who had never truly been alive. Aristotle, clad in one black garment, walked slowly after the bier. The bier was also attended by a group of wailing women (their lament kept within bounds, as recent laws frowned on great exhibition of grief). I thought the woman who led the troop of female mourners must have been Herpyllis, the favourite slave of Pythias, who had come from her old home to assist her mistress through childbirth; really, as it proved, to help her through her last days. Men looked serious, the women clustered together, faces veiled. The schoolboys fidgeted a little. One of these boys looked about him vacantly, as if wondering what he was doing there. He yawned and sighed. Parmenion, the young man of disturbed mind.

The body was placed in the deep earth, and Aristotle scattered upon it a few valuables – a cup, a necklace, a ring with gems, earrings flashing brightly one last time in the light as they dropped out of the living world. Aristotle was still pale but in complete command of himself, like a man and a philosopher.

We went together back to his house, where we stood about in the courtyard; we all needed a ritual wash by now before entering a house, or we might pollute it with the funeral proximity to a corpse. The senior scholars stood about the bereaved Aristotle, taking the place of relatives, and the boys formed a kind of silent chorus as we were moved to commiserate with him in careful words. The gentlemen, or most of them, departed, but I lingered.

'O Aristotle,' I said. 'This is a hard day for you. It makes me sad to see you.'

'It is hard,' he said. 'And now the funeral is over. My wife is gone – gone absolutely! It seems so strange. The house will feel empty. But at least now, Stephanos, I am going to design the most marvellous monument to her. I know someone who will make it up quickly for me. Pythias shall not long lie in an unmarked grave. And what words and images can do to commemorate her I shall cause to be done.' His hand flickered as if he were already at his writing stylus, designing the monument in accord with his imagining.

I could feel that he was consoling himself with having something else he was going to do for Pythias. It seemed sad to think of him spending time designing a tombstone – he who could so readily write books for all mankind to read.

VI

Parts of Animals

The dead dog left in front of Gorgias' house had been partly erased from my mind, as the funeral of Pythias supplanted it in my attention. I must stress that the episode of the dead dog was the first of the outrages – at least as far as anyone acknowledged. And that first outrage came *before* the affair of the monument – a fact about which it seems important to be clear. As for the indignity inflicted upon young Gorgias, it appeared obvious to me at first that (as Gorgias himself suspected) this was a personal insult, the work of some enemy to his family. Most likely it had to do with a grievance against his father or his uncle. Or it might have been merely the work of someone who felt anger over the family's dealings in silver. Gorgias himself was always ready to see things in terms of a tragic destiny. The idea of a malign fate hanging over the prosperous family of silversmiths was, after a fashion, not unpleasing. If they were the peculiar target of the gods, then the rest of us were free from harm.

But that this was not the right explanation became apparent in the days following the funeral of Pythias. The next outrage affected my old acquaintance, most unbeloved by me, the prosperous Eutikleides. In the past, this man had taken a leading part in trying to fasten great harm to our family in connection with a notorious murder. As this attempt was defeated, he was never in very good humour with myself, but he had made his position more secure with the government, and also with the people (by pious acts and large donations). By this time, he had recovered his station among the citizens; the fact that he was of a leading family, one of the tribe of the Etioboutadai, did not injure his chances. Lykourgos, himself a member of the Etioboutadai, had been promoting the cause of Eutikleides and his worthiness to lead an embassy. But now this eminent citizen received fame for a different reason.

'Eutikleides finds a dead donkey,' chortled the citizens and their hangers-on in the Agora.

'Eutikleides is a dead ass,' the commonplace wits giggled.

'Not entirely true, for this was not an entire ass. Matter of fact,' said one wiseacre, 'strictly speaking, it was *not* "a dead ass" that Eutikleides found on his herm. Not the whole animal. It was the rear part only of the beast which graced his frontage.'

'Eutikleides is an ass's arse!' So burst out the obscener wits, chalking the statement on walls for remembrance. Eutikleides became intimately associated in such scrawls with the rear end of a useful working animal.

If there were a certain enjoyment of the discomfiture of sour-faced Eutikleides, it did not endure. Unease took the place of merriment as more and more citizens awoke to find the body parts of animals polluting their herm, gateway or door. The front half of Eutikleides' donkey (minus the head) turned up – very dead – in front of the door of another much poorer citizen, and the head of the donkey (presumably it *was* the same animal), very maggoty by this time, at last came to light too, set up at the entry of a prominent and likeable man.

Smaller families of lesser importance received smaller portions of animals: a portion of a body of a weasel, or a very dead rat. One got a boar's pizzle, another the leg of a goat. These, like the majority of the segmented animals, had died a natural death, and were too well aged to be used for eating. The goat, for instance, had probably slipped and died amid the rocks and been found a good while after. So the victims of the prank or insult did not have even the consolation of a meat meal. The thing was always ugly and noxious to the senses. Amusement and vexation turned to alarm as houses were polluted and families shamed.

'This is a terrible thing!' said one citizen, speaking to friends in the Agora. 'We must take it up in the Boulé! The Council should not rest until we know who is doing these things.'

'These are dreadful outrages,' another agreed. 'They augur very ill for Athens.'

'Another Alkibiades has come upon us!' lamented a third. 'This is like the Mutilation of the Herms – an insult to religion and a threat to the state!'

Everyone shuddered at the recollection of the Mutilation of the Herms, a terrible if mysterious episode in our history. Of course, nobody actually recollected it –

though perhaps in Attika there were one or two ancient dodderers who had been alive (or at least born) at the time. But we had all heard about it. Long ago the brilliant young aristocrat Alkibiades, protégé of great Perikles and friend of Sokrates, had (so it was alleged) led a group of youths in seriously damaging or even destroying many of the herms of Athens, lopping off the virile members, and chopping off or severely defacing the heads. Thus they insulted religion and so were said to be trying to subvert the constitution of the city. The beautiful herms standing outside public buildings in the Agora, antiques with ancient carved heads, were severely damaged, in a horrid desecration of a sacred area. Shortly after this mysterious outbreak of destruction, Alkibiades led the Expedition to Sikilia (ill-fated as that was), and refused to come back to stand trial when it was determined he had a case to answer regarding the Mutilation of the Herms as well as another piece of blasphemy, an enacted parody (so it was alleged) of the sacred – and secret – rites of Eleusis.

Alkibiades' irreligious behaviour threatened the well-being of Athens. But instead of coming to defend himself at a trial, he went over to the enemy and fought for Sparta. Later, after he saved the Athenians at Samos, he was rewarded: not only allowed to return but given a command. But thereafter, unpopular following a defeat, he fled again, took the side of the Persians, and died in Phrygia. Alkibiades, handsome, lovable and intelligent, proved to be a brilliant traitor. This puzzling man had no loyalty to anybody but himself. But we did not have such flamboyant aristocrats nowadays, surely. And whoever did this was getting his – or their – hands very dirty with blood and putrescence and disgusting substances, not just chipping at stone as Alkibiades and his gang must have done.

I should have liked to discuss the question with Aristotle, and to consider with him too the case of Alkibiades, but it was obviously a mistake to intrude upon his grief. Patently, this was the right time to put my own wits to work, to see if I could make any sense of this disturbing pattern of impious insult. Was it a horrible joke? I remembered that Theosophoros had first suggested to Gorgias that the deposit of dead dog with which he had been favoured was a prank of young people. That comforting explanation twitched a recollection of another incident – the death of the vaunting bull-faced boy. This sturdy son of a fisherman had been killed after the Bouphonia, with the ritual weapon used in the ox-killing. It was suggested in the lawcourt that the death of this boy was a prank that went wrong, a killing brought about by foolish play among loutish youths unknown. But how many such dangerous youths could there be in Athens?

At least these latest outrages did not involve the death of a person. The beings killed and cut up were all animals. Why animals? Well, I reasoned, if you want to pollute a place with blood, animal-killing is cheaper, easier and less risky than homicide. And the person – or more likely persons – committing these outrages apparently found it more convenient to use on most occasions animals already dead, rather than working at a fresh slaughter each time. I reasoned, looking at the evidence, that care was evidently taken by the delinquent and bloody prankster not to *steal* animals. The theft of someone's beast would entail severe legal penalties, and there was the risk that an

identifiable animal could point to the identity of the
animal-killer. Normally – if the word can be used of such
an abnormal activity – these unknown and sinister louts
preferred parts of animals taken from a defunct creature.
Beasts of any value for food or labour, domesticated
animals which might figure in criminal indictment, had
been all too evidently dead already of natural causes
before being cut up and used. Only common dogs, and
vermin such as rats and weasels and so on, appeared
freshly and bloodily killed. The parts of animals seemed to
signify not only pollution but also mortality. A reminder
of mortal nature, a mocking recall of death? Was it only
that? Or did this exhibition hold a further message – a
menace?

After much reflection, I made a list of the persons who
had received these bloody tokens, starting with Gorgias
and Eutikleides. Of course, I realised as I worked on my
list that I could not affirm that I or anyone else really
knew of *all* cases. Probably some people who had been
thus visited managed to keep their own secret. Looking
closely, however, at the list of names I knew of, it became
clear to me that they had one thing in common. All who
had been so unpleasantly visited were known to be
supporters of – or salient beneficiaries of – Makedonian
rule.

This was worrying. I could clearly see that I myself
might be placed among that number. In a mad moment, I
even wondered if Lykourgos himself were engaged
behind the scenes in doing this nasty deed in order to
unsettle his opponents. But I rejected that notion –
Lykourgos, so staunch for national unity, for order and
prosperity,   would   find   such   tactics   and   bloody

manifestations deeply repulsive. The Council and the government in general were obviously trying not to make too much fuss over these outrages. I could see the point in not setting a panic a-going. But, even if it were merely the work of young louts in sad want of a good whipping, there was something very disturbing about this reeking joke. Its unpredictability was part of its power. Some days there would be nothing, then on another day there might be two such bloody or putrefying manifestations of the flesh.

I went to see Aristotle, to condole with him and not to consult him about these bloody appearances. It seemed better not to mention to a man in such mourning the disturbing and unpleasant symptoms of hubris affecting the city at large. In order to be soothing I deliberately bored him with talking about my own life, my planned marriage, my wife's relatives. I explained about the bees and the possibly profitable sale of honey. Aristotle awakened mentally a little when I mentioned the bees.

'I studied bees at one time, extensively,' he remembered. 'Complicated little creatures. There are several kinds. Each hive has a leader twice as large as the gold worker bee. Some call these "kings" and others "mothers" of the swarm. The present month is their best season for honey-making and also for laying the best and strongest larvae. They make no honey before the rising of the Pleiades. If your taste is acute – like my own – you can tell at once if honey is made from thyme in flower. I dare say you are right about an increasing demand for Hymettos honey. But how are you going to get your hands into it? – to use a sticky metaphor.'

I explained again about the absent Philokles and then

told him my tentative plans for a journey to the eastern islands. He was mildly interested.

'It will be a great distance to go,' he said. 'You had better ask Eudemos of Rhodos to make you some kind of map. And he can tell you about Rhodos, perhaps draw a plan of that island.'

I agreed, though in fact I had already thought of all this and had conversed with Eudemos and others at the Lykeion about the journey and my destination.

'You must come tomorrow,' said Aristotle. 'For the monument. I hope my monument will be finished. I told them I would come tomorrow to see it. They've been working day and night to oblige me. It will be so beautiful!'

When I returned on the morrow, Aristotle was unusually brisk and more cheerful than he had been since the death of his wife. He led me to a place not very distant from the Kerameikos, where the stone carvers had been working on the monument. We crossed a dry yard, the ground covered with stone chips, small pieces of marble and mica that hurt to walk upon and glinted in the sun. We passed on into a shed, dark until the light was cast upon it through the open door. The mason was there, doing his best not to grin proudly as he and his assistants gestured towards the far wall. I suspected that they had got up a drama to please Aristotle in creating an effect, for at the beginning the monument was nowhere visible. Something occupied the far wall, however, something that took a great deal of space – something with a cloth thrown over it. With a flourish, at a signal from Aristotle, the mason twitched off the cloth.

Sliding out from under the folds of coarse drapery was

a lady – first her head and a shoulder, then the
magnificent proportions of her, complete to her sandalled
feet. It was a lovely woman sculpted in high relief, as if she
had left the world of earth to become newly embodied in
a different kind of flesh. She was seated, within the
conventional shrine square. Before her was a bearded
man, with his face averted, shielding his face with his
cloak; the man nevertheless let his grief be known in the
tension and droop of his body. The two were touching
hands, in a sweet but dignified version of the classic
farewell scene. The lady, in all her gentleness, even with
her touch of sadness, seemed full of life and glory. She was
beautifully painted, her robe in blue with an edging of red
and touches of gold. With the hand that was not in her
husband's she was holding a golden sheaf of wheat. Her
sculpted head, though the back was partly covered with a
transparent veil, yet revealed her dark hair touched with
reddish-brown, and the slight circlet of gold that crowned
that head turned slightly towards us as if in enquiry or
pity. Her eyes were painted lifelike, deep brown pupil
surrounded by clearest white. She shed a beneficent gaze
upon the dull dark shed. The monument sustained the
radiant glow of fine marble, and the touches of gold made
it sing. I gazed on this effigy of Pythias – whom I had
never seen or known – and thought she looked like
Demeter herself. So might Demeter look, the goddess
mother who had known bereavement, comforting a
mortal with grace and graciousness. Pythias herself, but
not herself.

'There!' said Aristotle. 'Pythias had a special reverence
for Demeter. Hence the wheat. She is reflected in
Demeter, and Demeter in her.' He said nothing, I noted,

about the mourning man, himself in shaded effigy. 'The stone is the best Pentelic marble,' he continued. 'And there – see, on the stone, the writing –' Aristotle moved me closer, so I could read the inscription upon the monument. It was large enough to offer much space for lettering. In the fine white marble the letters were clearly chiselled and easy to read:

PYTHIAS
Daughter of Hermias of Atarneos
Wife of Aristotle
Sweetest and Best
Eminent for Virtue, Renowned for Piety,
and the Intellect that reaches to heaven
Given to all good works
Much loved.
Let her memory be ever honoured in Athens where
she lived and died.
Dearest, farewell.
Offered by her Husband, Ari

'It's not finished yet,' said the mason apologetically, 'but it should be done by tomorrow morning. We've only to finish the name "Aristotle" as you see and put in "son of Nikomakhos" as you directed.'

'If "Nikomakhos" wasn't such a long name,' put in his foreman (rather impudently I thought), 'we could have had it done tonight, for certain. Good we had a monument in preparation that someone else dropped out of paying for – we couldn't never have done it this quick otherwise.'

'How do you like the inscription, Stephanos?' asked Aristotle. 'It is not as long as I could have made it, but it expresses something, do you not think so?'

'Oh, yes,' I said.

'The day after tomorrow,' said Aristotle, 'we shall put it up. This monument will be some consolation to me; I think I shall often go to the Kerameikos to see it. I have asked a few friends to come while the tombstone is put in place. I should like you to be there, Stephanos.'

I agreed. Pythias had gone. Her tomb said so. I believed that once Aristotle had put up the tombstone he would feel better. Surely now his life would reassume its normal shape. I was very wrong about that.

'Pythias will not go unmarked,' said Aristotle, with a long sigh. We went off to our respective houses. A thunderstorm had gathered, offering unusual refreshment in the heat, and I was soon drenched.

The ground was still wet when I arose the next morning before dawn, awakened unusually early. Perhaps, so I later thought, some sound or movement had disturbed my sleep. I went outside, to see if our drains had worked properly; I was a trifle worried about our roof and water-spouts. Thus, thankfully, I arose early and was the only member of our household to find the abominable present someone had left for us. I didn't really see the dreadful gift at first. When I came out I heard footsteps and went to the front of the house to peer over the gate. I was just in time to see a couple of men (slaves, judging by their scant attire and bare feet) running down the street. They turned a corner, but before they vanished into the morning's dusk I caught a glimpse of the larger and slower of the two, and thought he looked slightly familiar. One of the slaves attending on Thrasymakhos – or had it been Megakles? – when we met these gentlemen at the

Bouphonia. Perhaps – perhaps not. I could not be certain, they were a dim flash before the eye. Then I turned back to the house frontage and saw our herm.

The herm was there, our herm of modest sandy stone with its carved head which I knew so well, blurred by age, its face and beard, like its virile member, slightly crumbling. It stood where it had always done. But it now had acquired a new part. The head of a horse had been jammed on top of it. It was as if our herm had metamorphosed into an animal – also, oddly, as if the herm had playfully decided to wear a grotesque hat, or put on a mask as at a play in the theatre.

The horse's head smelt of decay but most of the flesh was still upon it. One eye was partly eaten away, by maggots or by birds. The other eye remained, as I could see by the silvery light of the pre-dawn sky. This good eye had been forced to stay wide open; someone had stuck the eyelid permanently back to the head with a pin. The dead horse winked at me in a giant leer. The big teeth of the animal, ridged and dirty white, distinctly showed in its open mouth. As I looked into that mouth, I saw a long yellow worm begin to crawl forward along the tongue. I nearly puked on the spot. But this was no time to indulge my inner feelings. I had to get rid of the thing. Conquering my repulsion, I took the dead object in both hands. I rushed to the shelter of the back premises, within our walls – at least the neighbours should not see this. Even at this early hour, a cloud of flies went with me, a buzzing halo around that horrid head.

It took me a while in my haste to find the implements I needed, but I did eventually get a spade and some other tools, and dug vigorously in an obscure part of the yard, making as deep a hole as I could to put the rotting head in. I never liked horses, and I liked this one less than any as I sent it to its rest. Once the earth had covered it I would (I hoped) lose my aureole of flies which troubled, buzzed, and bit. For the first time I was glad that our old house-dog had died, a few days before, even if near the end he was so feeble that he might not have been able to dig up the grave. The site of this interment was soon just a rough place in the yard. I threw a pile of brush on the spot, as if it had fallen there accidentally, the sort of thing that people always intend to remove but don't really bother with.

I worked stealthily, for I did not wish to awaken even our slaves. The kind of work I was doing is certainly a job for slaves, but the inconvenience of employing them struck me forcibly. I wished no being capable of speech to know about this. If I had owned a parrot I would not have let it know. I still had much work to do privately. Once I had disposed of the head, I had to go back with some water and deal with our poor desecrated herm. At least the putrescence, and the accompanying stink of dead horse, though nauseous, left no such indelible stain as the streams of blood that had flowed from Gorgias' dead dog.

I purified myself then with hasty ablutions and prayers, and I did not feel pure until I had got rid of the clothes I had been wearing while carrying the horse's head. Fortunately, all I had on was a well-worn old tunic. But if I been wearing my best fine-woven himation, I should have had to do the same. I threw my tunic away, burying it in the yard where the contents of the chamberpots were thrown, and was content to enter the house naked. The burial place of the tunic was not far from that of the horse

– or, rather, the piece of horse vouchsafed to me.

I do not mind admitting that I was conscious of fear the whole time. Not of apprehension of the task. Though it was revolting to handle that putrescent filth, which filled me with nausea. What I felt beneath the disgust was a far deeper fear – of the underlying message, the significance of this baleful thing. A curse had come upon my own house. I felt in all my instincts that this sign was deeply malignant, and that not only my house but my family was not safe.

VII

The Monument

When the day had fully awakened and the family (kept in blessed ignorance) were stirring, I considered going to visit Smikrenes in Eleusis. I decided, however, that I had no time for the journey, as I had agreed to attend the setting-up of Aristotle's monument, and must keep my promise. But a plan had begun to form in my mind, and I did not wish to delay. Instead of walking to Eleusis deme, I wrote a careful letter to Smikrenes. I first debated with myself whether he were literate enough to receive an epistle, but remembering that he had thought he might receive a letter from his estranged wife, I concluded he was up to the perusal of a simple message. I hoped so. I presumed Philomela had never learned her letters, but most people think it best for a wife to be illiterate. An illiterate father-in-law might prove an inconvenience. Epistles themselves are an inconvenience, as somebody else may read them, and I certainly did not wish to blurt everything out to Smikrenes, let alone to someone who (by

chance or malice) might peruse my written message. I had
to be clear yet obscure, eloquent yet plain. Eventually it
was written to my satisfaction and I sent the message with
the slave who knew the way to Smikrenes' house. The
slave was quite unable to read – most satisfactory.

The next day – a day engraved for ever on my memory –
I went to see the monument to Aristotle's wife put up over
her grave. I had not been looking forward to assisting at
this tiresome and melancholy ceremony. It seemed to me
a waste of a morning. Now, especially, while my own
anxieties mounted and when my new plan was maturing,
it was irritating to be summoned to this distraction. Yet
the monument was evidently of great importance to
Aristotle, and if my presence there would console and
support him, I could not stay away.

I dressed myself in serious apparel, and walked out to
the Lykeion, where I found Aristotle similarly arrayed,
in company with some of his close associates –
Theophrastos, of course, but also Eudemos and
Hipparkhos and the rest. The whole body of young
students did not accompany us, but a few of the older
youths came, noticeable among them the strange lad
Parmenion. I could see that Hipparkhos and young Mikon
were both keeping a close eye on him, and thought
perhaps the untoward youth had been allowed out on this
expedition chiefly as a way of exercising some control
over him, as well as of guiding a mind that tended to
wander. We moved together through the city gate
towards the Kerameikos where Pythias, lying now
unnamed in that great cemetery, would henceforth be
proudly known. We did not stop at the mason's shed.

What we wanted would be brought to us.

The Kerameikos was still and drowsy in the hot day. The common whores, male and female, who haunt the area for their nightwork, and perform their favours behind the tombs, had disappeared at the arrival of the clear summer light. The River Eridanos which runs through the famous cemetery, such a respectable river in wintertime, had dwindled to a trickling sluggish brook. Dragonflies hovered above the stream and moved through the rushes at its brink. On the dry paths, our feet sent up puffs of dust.

When we got to the grave site, only a few of Aristotle's friends in the city were present, Gorgias among them. I was surprised to see Epikrates, but assumed that he must have made this gesture of respect out of gratitude to Aristotle. We made a little knot, a miniature crowd.

Then there was a creaking and straining of a wooden wagon, drawn by two oxen, and the masons came into view, as dramatically as they could manage, as if organised for a procession. They were evidently determined to make a good production of this task. Attendant slaves marched at the side of the cart. With difficulty and straining the men, slave and free, drew the large stone down over the ox-cart, its back ingeniously constructed to drop down and make a ramp. Still masked in its drapery, the monument moved along in a stately manner. With crowbars and ropes, and a good number of exclamations, the men moved the stone into position. I saw that a digging had been made in the earth, an oblong hole preparing the place to receive its stone.

The ground was bare over the grave – any dampness caused by the rainstorm had long vanished. Little whorls of dry dust spun around the site, and drifted over our feet and sandals. When the monument was finally dropped into position, a cloud of dust arose.

'You know, sir,' said the chief mason, addressing Aristotle, 'that it's early days, as I said before, to put a stone up – you want to let the grave settle. We're likely going to have to come back and reposition it later when the ground's sunk better. Stones like this does much better when what's beneath them has shaken down more solid.'

'Just so,' said Aristotle. 'As often as necessary. I do not wish the grave to go unmarked any longer.'

The monument was adjusted and earth shored around it. We could see tantalising glimpses of stone as the cloth swung about it. Sweating heavily and muttering imprecations (though they were trying to restrain themselves out of respect to that sad and serious spot of earth), the men finally placed the monument to their satisfaction, and removed the ropes that steadied it. We all kept watching steadily – all except the odd young man Parmenion, who stared vacantly up at the sky and yawned.

'Now!' said Aristotle. The mason twitched off the covering. The marble monument and the beautiful statue gleamed in the light. The bearded man averting his face continued to bid farewell to the seated lady, so splendid in her attire with its touches of crimson and gold, her blue robe matching the serene blue sky against which she glowed. She gazed partly at the man saying farewell to her, and partly on the thin sheaf of yellow corn she held in her hand. Yet in some way she appeared to be looking upon us as well, with a divine pity, from under dark hair. She seemed as one untainted and free, offering us the sheaf of wheat she carried as a gift of consolation. There was a little puff of exclamation from the watchers. 'Beautiful!' 'What splendid work!'

'Her name is no longer unknown or her grave unmarked,' said Aristotle. And indeed the name PYTHIAS was very clear and distinct. The monument dignified the site. A bird flew over it, its gentle shadow gliding along the marble as if with a secret promise of renewed life and motion.

'It is lovely,' I said sincerely.

'This stone worker is an artist,' said Gorgias.

'It is very good,' said Eudemos, squinting and gazing critically as if regarding an object of art in a great house or a temple. 'It vies with the grand monuments of the older times.'

The monument indeed did very well among these other monuments of Athens, though some of the tombs of past centuries in the Kerameikos are extraordinarily impressive, wrought by first-rate Athenian sculptors. Near us was another gravestone from the time shortly after the era of Perikles, a large marble monument to a virtuous Athenian wife, the lady shown seated, with a maid handing her jewellery box to her.

'I shall often come to see it,' said Aristotle, rather dreamily, looking at the Demeter figure on his monument. 'It is good enough even for Pythias.'

'The lettering is excellent,' said Hipparkhos. 'Very clear.' It was. The mason had finished the work and now the full name 'Aristotle son of Nikomakhos' could easily be read.

'It is certainly *clear*,' said Epikrates.

As he said these words, Hypereides came striding

towards us. This big confident man, the man to whom smiling came as easily as his rhetoric, came up to Aristotle with a grave face of commiseration. The sun shone rosily through his jug-handle ears.

'My dear friend Aristotle,' he said, 'I compassionate you on your loss. These are hard days.'

'Yes, they are. Thank you,' said Aristotle.

'So – this is the monument,' said Hypereides thoughtfully.

'Yes,' said Aristotle again. Speaking not like a great philosopher but as simply as any other man, he added, 'It is a nice monument, isn't it?'

'Ahh – h.' Hypereides sighed. 'My dear Aristotle, that is what I have come to talk with you about. It won't do you know, my dear sir, this won't do at all.'

'I beg your pardon?' said Aristotle.

Hypereides raised his hand, like an orator calling for silence. This was evidently a prearranged sign. Three men came up whom I had not noticed before that morning. 'You know these gentlemen, I believe,' Hypereides continued.

'Megakles of Athens – I believe you are known to Aristotle?'

I recognised Megakles at once, of course. He was the man with the large rosy bald spot whom I had first encountered on the day of the killing of the ox. This important gentleman I had also seen in the Agora on the day of the monkey. Megakles' growing bald spot had darkened to the colour of wood as the summer advanced. But he was just as dignified and unsmiling now as on those other two occasions. Megakles inclined his head towards Aristotle, but made no further acknowledgement. On this occasion, unlike that of our meeting in the Agora, he took no notice of me. Hypereides went on with the introductions.

'And Eurymedon – Athenian of the deme of Eleusis. Eurymedon, you must know Aristotle, is one of the Eumolpidai, and thus most discerningly jealous of the honour of Demeter and her daughter.'

I had already recognised pious Eurymedon with his face like a sculptured mask.

'And Euphorbos,' continued Hypereides. Lanky, curly-haired Euphorbos bowed his head. Usually his face was animated, but today he was unusually quiet and grave. Naturally, out of respect for his former teacher, as well as for the dead and the proprieties of the occasion. But what he said was not the usual formula of condolence.

'I am sorry, Master,' he said in an agitated tone. 'They told me to come. Who could have predicted such a day would ever arrive!'

'Now,' said Hypereides, 'this is a hard task, my dear sir. I hope that you will make it easier for us, and prevent unpleasantness. I have brought only these men, one of them your friend and former student, so that you might be less sore of mind. It is the easier for you that we are not public officials. We have not brought upon you the head of the Boulé and the priest or priestess of Demeter. Indeed, we wished earnestly to spare you a large deputation, or any appearance for questioning by the Council, or the Assembly. You would not want a public hearing, a large scene. Consider how ugly that would be: Athens in uproar, the common people of the city wrought into anger at you. We come to tell you – just us four – that Athens finds this erection unacceptable. With the best will in the world towards you, we cannot allow this monument here.'

'"Cannot allow —"'Aristotle repeated the words as if stupefied.

'No,' said Megakles. 'This is — I am afraid — most improper. Would that we could have put a stop to it earlier! But the truth of the matter, Aristotle — and Aristotle's friends —' he nodded at the rest of us, 'the truth of the matter is that this monument cannot be permitted to stand for a day. You perhaps have misunderstood. The Kerameikos is for *citizens* of Athens and the families of citizens. You, Aristotle, are not an Athenian.'

'You know, Aristotle, you are well aware of this,' added Hypereides. 'I know you have paid the Alien Tax every year. Eighteen drakhmai — twelve for yourself and six drakhmai for your wife, as *both* were foreign.'

'You are a *metoikos*, among us as an alien, even if resident,' continued Megakles. 'Athens tolerates aliens — sometimes mistakenly, I believe, but that is my opinion. In any case, they do not have the same rights as citizens. You are a *metoikos*, allowed to reside here. You are with us but not of us. So too was your wife, a foreign woman, not of Athenian parentage. Your little girl is not a citizen's daughter. I think you have only one child, a female? Your little girl must not expect to serve Artemis as a bear at Brauron like little Athenian girls. And your wife should not have expected to be buried in the Kerameikos.'

'Indeed not!' said Eurymedon, speaking to us for the first time that morning, in his cold clear voice. 'From somewhere outlandish, was she not? Some sort of Asian person?'

'She was the daughter of Hermias of Atarneos,' said

Aristotle, gesturing towards the monument as a text wherein that information was clearly conveyed. 'Hermias was a Greek ruler, a Greek speaker, a student of Plato and a lover of philosophy –'

'Very nice, I am sure,' said Hypereides soothingly. 'But she was a foreigner as her father was. Hermias would not be allowed a monument in the Kerameikos either.'

'And did he not die in some disgraceful manner?' added Eurymedon. 'Stapled to the tympanon like a common criminal, or something of the sort, so I have heard.'

'Let us not dig up old stories or unhappy truths,' said Hypereides. 'The tyrant of Atarneos is dead, however his death befell. The point at present is that he was not and could not be an Athenian, nor could his daughter be metamorphosed into an Athenian, however legitimate she might be in Assos or Atarneos. Pythias has no right, strictly speaking, to a grave in the Kerameikos. Certainly no right at all to a public monument – to *such* a public monument – with an inscription.'

'What will Athens come to?' Megakles enquired of us. 'You must see, Athens will cease to be Athens if we allow all and sundry to stick their monuments and their outlandish names and so on here. We could have Arabs and Phoenicians and all sorts. Once you start that sort of thing, there is no going back.'

'But – we are Greeks!' protested Aristotle.

'I have a suggestion – if I may presume,' said Euphorbos. 'You could put up any monument to anybody in Peiraieus. They have all sorts there now – even Phoenicians and people of Karthago with awkward inscriptions in their gibberish, and their triangle goddess! It is quite amusing to see them.'

'Euphorbos speaks beside the point,' said Eurymedon, more coldly than ever. 'We could not countenance *this* particular monument – even in Peiraieus. For, there is further offence in *this* monument. It is the more dreadful that neither you nor your friends saw at once, as you ought to have done, the offence committed.' Eurymedon drew himself up, like an orator in a prosecution, as he addressed the crowd and the circumambient air – almost, one felt, the monument itself. Neither he nor Megakles answered Aristotle directly.

'This – this uncouth *thing*,' continued Eurymedon, contorting his lips with distaste and chagrin, 'this *thing* is not only illicit but blasphemous. It is your wife to whom you give divine honour, really as the goddess Demeter. Blasphemous honour. You have committed blasphemy!'

'But no!' protested Aristotle. 'There is a reference to her worship of Demeter –'

'Just so,' said Eurymedon. 'As a member of the tribe of Eumolpidai, guardians of the sacred rites of Eleusis and all that pertains to Demeter, I must see to it that the religion of Eleusis is respected, as it always is in Athens. This figure is a travesty, a mockery of Demeter, executed at your command.'

'No, no!' cried Eudemos in protest. He was ignored.

'Surely *mockery* is the wrong word,' said Euphorbos. He was ignored likewise.

Gorgias said, 'It looks proper to me, and I and my family work with images of the gods.'

'We feel no need to call upon silversmiths to testify about Demeter,' said Eurymedon icily. 'We of the clan of Eumolpus guard her sacred image from all profanation. But if you need more clarification, let me summon a witness.'

The priestly Eurymedon moved his hand slightly. To our amazement, from behind the large monument to the virtuous Athenian lady there strolled the woman Antigone. She was modestly dressed, and had a diaphanous veil over her face, but her sandals were of reddened leather and a large gold bracelet shone upon her hand.

'This person – this female –' said Eurymedon, 'can tell you more.' Antigone stood still as if abashed. 'Come,' said he, 'state clearly who you are.'

'My name is Antigone – and I am a prostitute of Athens.'

'Come, now,' said Hypereides. 'No need to be frightened, Antigone. We know you are an *hetaira*. But tell these people again what you told me you overheard when you were in Aristotle's house.'

The woman parted her veil slightly, so the voice coming through her pretty lips could be heard by us.

'I heard him say – I don't wish to get anyone in trouble, gentlemen. But I heard him say – to another gentleman – that he loved his wife as Demeter.'

'There! Did you ever hear the like? This is blasphemy – flat blasphemy.' Eurymedon, now animated and triumphant, his great eyes shining, turned to the little knot of men. 'This man worships his wife as Demeter.'

'Though he uses whores,' said Megakles, in a low voice but with satisfaction.

'No!' I cried. '*I* was the gentleman who was present, on that day when this – this woman came into the room. That was the only occasion on which she visited Aristotle. She did not come to him to offer whorish favours, nor had he invited her. She came only to talk about her legal affairs. And Aristotle said no such thing as she alleges! He said his wife – she was still alive on that day, gentlemen – loved Demeter. He said Pythias was devoted to this goddess, and that he loved his wife. And he was talking to *me*, not to this woman.'

'And that was all?' asked Eurymedon.

'By all the gods, I swear there was nothing in the least improper about what he said. An ugly business if the chance word of a harlot should be taken in condemnation! A harlot who – even if she weren't lying – could hardly know what a conversation could be about, when she wasn't party to it. It is hard if such as she may spread such ridiculous untruths about Aristotle, whom we know so well.'

'Gentlemen,' said Aristotle earnestly. 'You cannot for a moment seriously think that I would be so blind and stupid as to think that my wife, a mortal woman, was an immortal goddess? Look you, here on the monument.' He gestured to the text again, and we all looked at it. 'Now, *clearly,* this inscription says Pythias "lived and died". She is certainly not an immortal, not a divinity, but human. Nowhere do I indicate otherwise.'

'Well, well,' said Hypereides. 'We will let pass for the while the statement of this *hetaira* Antigone. We have the greatest respect for you, Aristotle. You may step back, woman. The chief problem at present lies with the monument itself.'

'The monument itself makes his wife look like Demeter,' said Eurymedon stubbornly. 'No one has ever seen anything like it!'

'That's right,' said Megakles. 'A woman should be presented holding some household object, or her jewellery box, perhaps, even a mirror – something suitable to her feminine weakness and to her modesty also.'

'This – this objectionable female holds the emblem of the blessed goddess!' said Eurymedon in a tone of rising indignation. 'And then there's this long pompous inscription, going on about himself – a foreigner. And saying that his wife, a mere woman, has the divine intellect or whatever nonsense he means. As for her being "much loved", nobody here knew her, as she was related to nobody at all.'

'Yes,' said Hypereides, 'I'm afraid that is certainly true, one must admit it.'

'In fact,' said Megakles, with fearless relish, 'one must admit that "Here lies an obscure foreign woman whom no Athenian knew or cared about" would be a more honest inscription.'

'Perhaps,' Euphorbos suggested, 'it would do us good to have a greater variety of inscriptions. Frank statements on tombstones would certainly enliven the Kerameikos. Even make the pious Eumolpidai more interesting!' He darted a mischievous glance at the stately Eurymedon.

'But this woman cannot be interred in the Kerameikos,' said Megakles firmly. 'Whatever the inscription,' he added.

'Gentlemen,' Hypereides pleaded. 'Let there be no unpleasantness. Nothing unseemly. We come not to insult over living or dead, but only to defend our city and its ways.' He laid his hand caressingly on Aristotle's arm. 'I am deeply sorry, my good sir, but you must be wise enough yourself to see how it must end. Nobody wishes to be unjust, or harsh even in demanding justice. We will, in a particular leniency, allow Pythias' remains to rest here.

Nobody asks you to disturb her bones. That is generosity itself, surely! But . . . this monument cannot be allowed to stand.'

'*This* monument?'

'Nor any other. When this thing goes away, put no other up in its stead. I am sorry you have been put to unnecessary expense. It is against our city's customs to honour foreigners in this manner.'

'And the sacred identity of the city and its religion should not be soiled by foreign blasphemy,' added Eurymedon.

'This monument must go!' said Megakles.

'There is no help for it,' said Hypereides gently. 'The monument *must* go. You do see that, Aristotle.'

'Yes, I suppose that –'

'Excellent!' Hypereides patted his shoulder. 'I am sorry to give you pain, O Aristotle, but I am very glad that you see reason. You hear, gentleman? Aristotle now understands, and gives consent. He agrees the monument must go. Good-day, Aristotle – and to your friends.'

Hypereides then detached himself, and rapidly moved away with big swinging strides despite his sixty years. Epikrates waved his hand, in what must have been another signal. As Hypereides strode away from the scene, another group approached: a gang of slaves under the command of a working foreman. They must have been nearby all the while, but if so they had been very quiet. Now these men advanced towards the stone like an armed phalanx, each carrying a crowbar and a large mallet, the kind men use in banging down paving stones. Some of these mallets were simply made of a huge hard stone firmly fastened to a handle.

'Good!' said Megakles. 'You are ready? Now!'

The first of the workmen lifted his mallet and struck the monument a heavy blow. The mallet bounced off the marble, taking with it a chip from the inscription.

'Oh!' cried Aristotle – involuntarily, once, as a man might cry out under torture with a terrible surprise before commanding himself to be silent. I thought at the time that it was the sound a man would make who was fatally stabbed – though later I was to know better. Euphorbos said drily, 'Well thrown!' as if he were a spectator at the games; he then stood watching the proceedings and the other watchers. Megakles looked at Aristotle with disdain while Eurymedon's eager large eyes followed the fate of the monument, most particularly of its statue. The workmen once set going paid no heed to any of us. They struck again, and again, multiple blows. Aristotle was pale, his face set. It was as if he himself, or something inside him, were being battered. After that first involuntary outcry he was silent, his face taking on a mask-like sternness. He held himself erect but I could feel him trembling slightly as I held his arm. 'We can do nothing,' I whispered to him. I was sure of that.

Epikrates giggled in his low-bred way as the hammering went on. All the other spectators stood still as if enchanted. The only exception was the strange boy Parmenion, who at the first blow had uttered a loud cry or howl – almost covering Aristotle's own exclamation. The youth then threw himself face down upon the ground and remained absolutely still, not swooning, but as if removing himself from the scene. The rest of us, however unwilling, continued watching as the men swung and swung, heavy blow after heavy blow cracking down on the monument.

The stone mallets did the most damage – deep gouges and chipping resulted. Bang! went one mallet and another would follow. Crash! It was hard to imagine that Pythias in her earthen bed below did not feel the assault. Hammers of wood and stone and thick rods of metal struck the monument as if they hated it, and were glad to destroy what was also inanimate but lovelier than they.

The inscription had been largely defaced by the time the men took their crowbars and lowered the monument – not to the ground, but holding it slantwise so that they could hit the statue while it was still erect. Many of their blows struck the bearded man, who at once lost his beard and a hand, but they aimed chiefly at the monument's vivid lady. Blows rained on the body of the lady who looked like Demeter. The top of her sheaf of wheat flew off and hit the ground. Arms and fragments of garment turned into hail and flew about in the air. At last her head was struck off, and fell upon the earth where it bounced very slightly, and lay still. The crown of gold was still visible on the ragged hair. She looked up at us as if in enquiry. Then the paviour's hammer struck at the face, with one blow, crushing the nose and rendering the features indistinct.

'Thus perishes the false image,' said Eurymedon, clearly but not loudly.

Although it was hard work, it had not taken the workmen long to do this damage to Aristotle's monument. Once the inscription was defaced and the image of the goddess gone, Eurymedon and Megakles seemed to relax slightly.

'Come up, boys, with the wagon, and take the rest away,' said Megakles eventually.

The workmen brought up a wagon, very like the first one, and by tugging and straining with ropes and crowbars got the dishonoured remnants of monument aboard. Slowly they went away from the Kerameikos. Pythias' grave was bare earth again, but bare earth with much trampling upon it, churned up and littered with chips of marble. Even now, an after-image of the monument and its lady – or goddess – seemed to hang in the empty space. A shadowy film or *eidolon,* with her sheaf of golden wheat and blue robe and the sweet divine face.

'Aristotle, we must go home,' said Theophrastos. Hipparkhos and Eudemos picked up the strange boy Parmenion and managed to get him to walk between them. His eyes were vacant as though he chose not to see anything in particular. His lot at that moment seemed easier than that of Aristotle, who was fully in his senses as he walked between the sorrowing Theophrastos and myself. We who were his friends were sad – dismayed – frightened – angry – but of the feelings of Aristotle in that hour I realise I can have only the faintest conception.

PART II

MOVEMENT OF ANIMALS

VIII

Preparing for Flight

We went wearily through the city gate and walked in the hot midday across Athens towards the blessed coolness of the Ilissos area with its trees and refreshing shade. As we came to Aristotle's house I think all of us were looking forward to the relief of having a door to close behind us. Shelter for anger, bewilderment and shame – we longed almost with the intensity of a physical thirst for the place in which we could securely rest, give voice to what we felt, and recruit our shattered spirits.

But it was not to be easy to recruit shattered spirits. As we came to the gate of Aristotle's house we saw that the entryway was barred by defilement. Sprawled upon the herm, as if it had come expressly to lounge the day away on this pillar, was a ridiculous long-limbed hairy being that looked heart-stoppingly at first glance like a man.

Theophrastos was the first to hasten bravely towards the grim sight.

'It's not a man – it's a monkey,' he announced.

We gathered about it. It certainly was a monkey, very fully displayed, supine, showing his genitals for the world to see. His virile member, propped up in imitative mockery of the priapic symbol, vastly outbraved in length and circumference the stony penis depicted on the herm. The monkey's little face was twisted into a frightful grin. Perhaps someone had also arranged that rictus, posthumously.

'Stunned on the head, I think,' said Eudemos, walking to the back of the herm. 'Killed by a blow of an axe, most likely. Splitting the skull.'

The flies busy with the skull, which had exuded some sticky matter, seemed to corroborate this diagnosis.

'It *is* a monkey,' Theophrastos repeated. 'Not just any monkey. Kallias' monkey.'

'Yes.' I recognised it. 'Though its gold chain has been taken off. Perhaps whoever did this did not want to be accused of theft of valuables.'

'The monkey was valuable in itself – costly. Who is going to tell Kallias?' asked Hipparkhos, with a groan. 'And *how* are we to clean and purify this place?'

The monkey grinned and gave no answer to these questions, though it looked curiously knowing. 'If only it could tell us who did this,' said Eudemos. 'Poor thing,' he added.

Aristotle stared at the dead creature. 'You see the inscription?' he said, pointing to the base of the herm. To it had been attached a large clay tablet, crudely incised with a nail or some such utensil to offer the following inscription which he slowly read aloud:

' "Eminent for Virtue
Given to all good works
Much loved."

'That is a parody of Pythias' inscription! *How* could
they even have known it?' He gazed as one fascinated by
the whole spectacle: the sprawling lewd monkey, the
herm shaft with its new if temporary inscription. 'Look,
the monkey is a mockery – a blasphemy – of Pythias. Or –
it is meant for me. Is it a taunt only, I wonder? Or also a
– a warning?' He swayed a little where he stood.

'Come,' said Theophrastos; seizing Aristotle by the
elbow, though in no unfriendly grip, he guided the Master
to the back of the house. 'Water – get water for washing,'
he ordered. 'Eudemos and Hipparkhos, take care of this –
this mess. Demetrios, prepare the ritual purification, and
see that the boys make proper ablutions before they go
back indoors. Stephanos, come with us.'

'You should go away,' said Theophrastos. Those were the
first words uttered on our sad return to Aristotle's
pleasant room with the books and writing desk and
familiar furnishings. We had all undergone ritual
ablutions and cleansing, but that could not remove the
images from our mind. Aristotle sank wearily into a chair.
He was pale, his face set.

'You look ill.' I was really concerned. 'Take some wine
and water.' Theophrastos had anticipated me, pouring
some drink into a beaker. He thrust it awkwardly at
Aristotle, who meekly took it and sipped. He stared
straight ahead for a while, without speaking. Whatever
he thought about Pythias, and the monument, and the

dreadful monkey, he communed inwardly with his heart. He was not prepared to speak with us about the scene we had just witnessed in the Kerameikos.

'I shall do very well,' he said at length. 'Don't look so distressed, Stephanos. That blasphemous dead animal – you both say it belongs to Kallias? A difficult business telling him. Will he want to see it?'

'He will probably want it back,' said Theophrastos. 'To bury in his back garden. He has funerals – burials, at least – for his pets, I understand. But we must admit, this is a valuable animal. I shall send a messenger, and also give orders that the monkey is to be wrapped up in a blanket meanwhile. After the slaves have worked on the herm, it will be merely a matter of ritual form to purify it again.'

'There isn't much blood on it.' I produced this feeble consolation. 'It's strange,' I added, 'this is really the first time they have risked killing a valuable animal. Otherwise, it's like the others. After all, a number of people have had a similar experience this summer. Like Alkibiades and the Mutilation of the Herms.'

'Really?' said Aristotle. 'I didn't know. I used to know everything,' he said with a sigh. It was very unlike Aristotle. Painful to see him as this tight-lipped sighing man, leaning back in his chair.

'Yes. Some people don't much want to talk about it, but you should know.' I explained about Gorgias and Eutikleides, and some of the others. I didn't present my own case and the unwanted gift of the horse's head. Aristotle listened intently.

'This is very bad.' He was silent again, brooding. 'Athens is in an edgy state, I fear. I worry most immediately about that poor lad Parmenion. He has received a succession of shocks. Please instruct Phokon to enquire after his health, and to tell Demetrios that a doctor should be sent for if necessary. If the boy seems conscious and somewhat normal, feed him some hydromel; the water quenches thirst and the honey is a sweet food.'

While Theophrastos summoned Phokon and bade him do as the Master said, Aristotle closed his eyes as if meditating. We sat with him for a while, in complete silence. He opened his eyes, and I could tell that he had been going through the scene at the cemetery.

" 'This woman cannot be interred in the Kerameikos,' " he repeated. '*Metoikos* – abominable foreigner. Oh, Pythias, what have I done! And I thought to give her a lovely monument –'

'How could they take it on themselves to destroy it like that?' I began heatedly. 'It was yours – *you* paid for it. I am not sure at all that what they did was legal –'

'It probably was not strictly legal,' Theophrastos interposed. 'But they did it, all the same. And any legal remedy they resorted to might have been even worse for us. Hypereides was not wrong about that.'

'You are right, Theophrastos,' Aristotle said. 'You are always cool and steady in judgement. And you are right also in saying I should go away. It would be better for both Athens and myself if I were out of the city for a while. I believe I must plan an excursion.'

'I am planning to go away myself,' I said. 'As you know, I have been thinking of going to seek someone, in point of fact –'

'The near male relation of the woman you think of marrying,' Aristotle snatched my sentence from me. 'Very well, we have heard of this. You are going eastward?'

'To the eastern islands.'

'Theophrastos,' said Aristotle, 'just look into the passage, would you and see if anyone is waiting to see me?'

Theophrastos threw open the door, and looked about. 'Nobody waits,' he said. 'Nobody listens.' He closed the door firmly.

'I intend,' I said, 'as you know, and as Eudemos and the others know, to go to Rhodos to look for a man from Hymettos. I will get some financial assistance for this venture, so I can just about manage it. And I am also going to take extra care of my own family, and see that they are very safely lodged during the time I am away – for that may be some while.'

'You are well advised to do so,' said Aristotle. 'I also have a good reason to go abroad for a time, Stephanos. Fortunately, I can give some respectable cover to my desire to flee. The young man Parmenion. We have long been thinking that we should try to return him to his people, have we not?'

'Yes,' said Theophrastos. 'You can see that his health is not good. I fear his mind is deeply affected.'

'One of us should really escort him,' said Aristotle. 'The boy is not fit to travel on his own or even with some group, like other young men. A friend should convey him to his home. What better friend than I? Reasonable – and opportune. Unfortunately, Theophrastos, that leaves *you* in charge, and I hope that does not subject you to undue risk. But it seems to me the brunt of their animosity falls on myself.'

'Yes. I certainly believe so,' said Theophrastos.' You must remember, however, that I am myself a *metoikos*.'

'I know that,' exclaimed Aristotle. 'Who better?' I felt slightly surprised at this open admission. I must always have known or at least suspected that Theophrastos was a foreigner, but I tended to forget it. Nobody more ardently desired to be accepted as an Athenian. He spoke his Attic Greek most precisely, and pored over Plato day and night.

'Yes,' said Theophrastos, interpreting my speaking face, although I was silent. 'It is true, Stephanos. You are the only real Athenian in the room at present. I was born in Lesbos. I *feel* Athenian, but that's not quite the same thing.'

'Lesbos! So far away.'

'Yes, Theophrastos was born in Eressos, just like Sappho,' said Aristotle. 'He doesn't seem much like lyric Sappho, does he? Nor is he the son of an Athenian. And thus he is a *metoikos*, as I am.'

'I am not in any great favour,' said Theophrastos. 'I believe, however, that I am not very important, and that it is you whom they resent.'

'I think so too,' said Aristotle. 'Which makes what I am about to say to Stephanos the more shameless. Stephanos, might we join forces? Or do you think that would be dangerous for you? The idea has crossed my mind before, I will confess. I should be going to an area very close to where you are going yourself. I am fairly used to travel across the Aegean. You have never been in a ship, I think?'

I hesitated. 'Are you sure you are well enough – in your spirits – for this style of expedition?' I asked because I felt in my secret heart that I could not endure daily to accompany a man so bowed down with grief. Aristotle understood me.

'Do not be anxious, Stephanos. A well-bred man – not to say a philosopher – does not inflict his emotions upon his friends. Fortitude – fortitude and self-restraint – will come to my aid. Perhaps I may be better for a change of scene. I have sufficient funds to make travel easier for both of us. And I know some men of importance along the way, who may give us lodging and ease our journey. But you could help me in turn. I shall need some assistance in caring for that young man, Parmenion. A great responsibility.'

I was deliberating, when he said impetuously, 'Normally, this would be delightful, but given the circumstances – the animosity directed against me – it is only fair to admit that I might be a hazardous companion.'

'I would be happy to travel with you,' I said. And I meant it. As he spoke I realised how anxious I had been feeling about making this voyage into the unknown without a companion. It would mean going across wild and dangerous waters, into regions of which I knew nothing.

'I will risk any danger in your companionship,' I added. 'Once we are out of Athens they won't bother us. A good idea, for you to go away. And send your little daughter away also.'

'I have already planned to do so,' said Aristotle gravely. 'How glad I am too that I didn't have little Pythias represented as one of the mourners on that monument.' We all thought for a moment of the repulsive idea of hammers hitting his child – even if only in effigy.

'Fortunately,' he continued, 'she will be well out of Athens very soon. I am sending her to Euboia – to my mother's country. We have an estate there. The child will be looked after, in the care of Herpyllis.'

'I too already have a plan for my family's safety,' I explained. 'I wrote to Smikrenes, the father of the girl I am to marry, you know. Wrote to him asking, in effect, if my family could stay with him while I went in pursuit of his wife's brother. It is a good deal to ask, and I still await his answer. But if it is possible, I shall pack my mother and brother off to his house before I leave.'

'So you are getting married, Stephanos?' said Theophrastos in surprise. 'I didn't know. Not to the daughter of the rich citizen Kallimakhos?'

'No such thing,' I said, not pleased to be reminded of the old arrangement that had fallen through. 'That is back in the past. But you see the beauty of my plan. Nobody – not even at present my mother – *nobody* who dwells within the walls of this city knows of my plan to marry Smikrenes' daughter – save Aristotle.'

'If I can be said to be within the walls, when I live outside them.'

'Very well. Smikrenes knows, and so does his wife and her family – but they live a rather isolated life in Hymettos, where I think they hang aloof from their neighbours, so they are unlikely to have much chance to spread it. I may drop them a hint of silence, however. But it seems unlikely that anyone in this city could know of my connection with Smikrenes, or would ever suspect that any of our family were there. And my mother and brother can be safe while I am away.'

'So you were already anxious enough to write to Smikrenes before – before today?' Aristotle, however greatly assailed by the morning's events, was still alert and shrewd. 'You had, then, some reason to fear danger before now? What was it? What happened?'

I had to explain then about the horse's head. I also expounded my theory that the series of outrages seemed to me to be conducted against supporters of Makedon, or those regarded as such.

'Dear, dear. Stephanos, I fear the only reason for your being regarded as a Makedonian supporter is your association with myself.'

'Well – my cousin Philemon fought in Alexander's army,' I reminded him. 'They – whoever they may be – have targeted a number of people. Perhaps I am too fearful where my family is concerned. Probably this is the work of a few louts, egged on by a couple of discontented citizens. Just the same, I would like to get my family out of the way. It is wrong to leave a house in the care of an unprotected woman like my mother. It won't seem too odd that they should have gone away when I am travelling. But I think I won't say much about my destination. I had rather people here in Athens – if they find out that I am away – think that I am going to one of the nearer islands and may come back fairly soon.'

After I talked it over with Aristotle and Theophrastos, this plan seemed just as good as I had thought it was. In fact, it became clearer and better as Aristotle quickly came to practicalities about hiring passage on a ship, and so on. We cheered up slightly during this discussion of the future; after we took wine together, the journey seemed certain. When I went home, however, I felt sneaky and low, because I was harbouring a scheme destructive to my mother's peace without her knowledge. I had decided I would tell her as soon as I heard from my prospective father-in-law, if his reply were favourable. That interview with Mother I did not look forward to with pleasure. My mother, Eunike, is a daughter of the true Erektheids, and they are a formidable tribe. (Some say that at the beginning the founder was nurtured by – even entwined with – snakes.) Mother was unlikely to look upon my news with any great approbation.

I did not have long to wait. In the evening the slave came back with a message from Smikrenes, though not with a letter.

'I saw the gentleman Smikrenes as you directed,' he said. 'I gave the letter to him personal. And he read it and kept me there, and they gave me food and overnight lodging, and sent me back early today. He told me he would have no letter to give to you, but only a word that I was to remember. He said as how I could remember "Yes" was the word, and "Welcome", and I was certain sure I could remember that.'

So here was the keystone to my plan for getting away – a keystone safely cut and ready. I had only to attend to the details. The first and most formidable of these details was telling my mother. This meant I first had to tell her of my intention to marry Smikrenes' daughter Philomela, and my engagement with Smikrenes. This was bad enough. She burst into tears and lamentations almost at once.

'Oh no! Stephanos, how could you! A small and unimportant man – one can tell by his horrible little name! Some little country place in Eleusis, and some thick-skinned old farmer's clumsy daughter – how could you? Oh, my child, you're throwing yourself away. Oh, my poor boy why didn't you tell me? Surely you can get out of this!'

'I didn't tell you at first because it wasn't certain,' I protested. 'And it went on, so now it is certain We will have the formal *engye* after the summer is over. I don't want to get out of it.'

'*Why* didn't you tell someone who could have given you good advice? Oh, Stephanos, you don't hold yourself of enough account. Poor boy, you are not bad-looking and certainly well-born. And manly and good – and educated too. If you had only tried hard enough you could have married the daughter of some wealthy and important man.'

She sat down heavily, and rocked to and fro in her grief. 'Oh, dear, oh dear! You keep company with foreigners too much, and don't pay attention to your own interests in Athens. There was no need to go into some muddy little village in the wilds to find a wife! And you needn't tell me her father is well-born and educated and rich and polite and delightful, for I cannot believe it!'

'He is well-born enough, a true Athenian citizen. He has a little money and his own land,' I responded. 'I won't tell you he is all those other things, because it is true, they're not appropriate. But think – his wife has a family in Hymettos, who are doing well, and her brother may be able to help us to some more money. But I have to go and find him first. He may be in Rho— I mean on one of the islands, so I am going on a journey to find him.'

'So restless, Stephanos. I cannot understand it. Always wandering. Isn't Athens good enough for you? You're like your cousin Philemon, poor boy, rushing off to Asia with Alexander, as if there were any need for him to go and get killed – or nearly – away from home. All this wandering and restlessness explains the bad marriages in our family. Look what a horrible marriage Philemon has made with that wretched girl from Thebes, a foreigner who came to

Athens with scarcely the clothes she stood up in.'

'She isn't a foreigner,' I interjected, for it would be very bad for Philemon and his children if this impression were allowed to gain ground. 'She came from Thebes, but she is true Athenian –'

But my mother's speech ran in too rapid a current for her to hear me.

'You go wandering off to Delphi in the spring with your old philosopher – for no possible reason or advantage – and now you tell me that you're going to some island to look for a man you don't know. It makes my head spin!'

'Yes, yes, Mother, but there is some advantage in *this* journey,' I said. 'And don't forget, my first long journey to Euboia saved Philemon's life, and the honour of the family. But whether you like it or not, I am afraid I must go. And that leads me to my second point – or third, perhaps.'

'Don't maunder on in that unfeeling way,' she said sharply. 'Who cares if it's your second or thirty-second point! Why will you lecture and preach on at your wretched mother?' I gathered my forces.

'While I am away,' I explained, 'away on a journey I need to take and am determined to take, you and my brother Theodoros and two of the slaves must leave this house and stay with Smikrenes.'

At this she was truly aghast. 'Oh, no, Stephanos – not my home! Don't take that away! Don't ask it of me!'

'Only for a little while. It is for your own safety and protection. I cannot leave you without a man in the house, or in a house without a man, for so long. Smikrenes can take care of you both.'

'Care! In a little muddy hut with a lot of smoke, and chickens running around the floor, I dare say, and nothing comfortable and none of my own things about me. And he'll turn Theodoros into a little drudge – his sort do that. And no neighbours to talk with. Oh no – oh no! Who would have thought my son would have brought me to this pass!' Tears coursed down her cheeks. 'Oh, Nikiarkhos, why did you die and leave me to the care of this unkind son?'

'I am *not* an unkind son,' I protested. 'I try to be a good son to you, Mother, but I am afraid that you and Theodoros cannot stay here alone while I am away. And that's final.'

This last phrase (one I remember my father was fond of) I did not care much for myself, but I found myself saying it. I left the room with dignity, leaving her to get over her weeping. The female slave came to her, looking at me as reproachfully as if I had proposed pulling the house down about all their ears. Theodoros, predictably, was easier to handle, but even he was at first quick to see the disadvantages – especially being parted from his best friend Euphranor. His was a hopeful disposition, however, and he was soon able to look forward to making a journey to the country and having some different places to explore.

The next few days were full of business, as I tried to provide for both myself and my family during my journey time. I kept a sharp eye on Mother so that she didn't gossip to the neighbours about our plans. The slaves also had to be told, but I didn't tell them precisely where they were going – they would find out in due time. I went to our family farm to see old Tamia and the even frailer Dametas, in order to arrange for them to give regular supplies of our produce to the house slaves who would be going to stay with my mother. I hoped we could pay our way, really, by dint of bringing some of our own utensils and adding regularly to the food supplies at Smikrenes' modest establishment. I did not want to be an undue burden. Both slaves were to go together from Eleusis to the farm whenever my family needed anything; the male slave was agreeable enough to walking and porterage but had a tendency to lose his grip on information, and to dally by the way, whereas the woman was no dallier and nimble enough in her wits, though not as good at carrying things. Once we got to the Eleusis area, I wished her not to tell other people precisely of our new location.

It was an unusual thing to be doing, sending my mother to live in another man's household, and that man not a relative. But I had no male relative save my cousin Philemon, who was so talkative and careless. Besides, he lived in a small house in town, and thus any visitors would be subject to the scrutiny of neighbours, and Philemon with his peculiar history and strange marriage was already sufficiently suspect. No, it had to be Smikrenes. But as we were not yet connected with this man, I ought to take special precautions for the reputation of my mother.

'Be sure you stay in the women's part of the house and do not stir except at proper times and with a female companion,' I warned her.

'As if I didn't know more of behaviour than you do, Stephanos! Oh, my child, why do you use me so? Casting me out of my own house. I'm sure I could denounce you before the Assembly or somewhere for cruelty to your parents – there's a penalty in law for that –'

'Yes there is. It is loss of citizenship. And if I were not a citizen of Athens a fine pickle we should all be in,' I retorted. 'Make the best of it, Mother. I think of you and Theodoros and your welfare always. Now, I am going to take Theodoros with me for a while on a little expedition. We are going to get a dog to add to your safety.'

I kissed her but she was only partly mollified. Theodoros, however, was in high spirits at the prospect of accompanying me to get a new dog and then taking the animal to Smikrenes' house. I took a slave as well, and a donkey so that Theodoros could ride in case his legs got tired on the way back from Eleusis. The house to which we were going first, the home of one of Philemon's friends, was in the western outskirts of Athens. Philemon, who had told me this man had high-quality dogs for sale, came with Theodoros and myself to see them.

We knew there were dogs by the din of barking set up on our approach. When we went into the yard, the bitch and her sons set up a great racket. The owner brought us a young dog, barely out of puppyhood; it first dashed at us barking as if he would like to have our heads, then ran about the yard in a fury of zeal.

We stood, our little party of Philemon, Theodoros, myself and the slave, surveying the creature. The youthful dog at its master's bidding eventually stopped running round in circles, and sat down. It looked at us, and put its tongue out.

'Big, but a well-shaped muzzle,' said Philemon critically.

'Oh, he is so nice!' said Theodoros. 'Handsome and large.'

'He is surely large for a hound, isn't he?' I asked. 'He is

still not full grown – look how large his paws are.'

'Well, this sort of dog is bred for strength as well as speed. When he wants something he goes for it, and doesn't let go. You should see one go after a rabbit! He'll pretty well feed himself, if he's allowed to hunt. And they're wonderful as watch-dogs. You see how they bark at the approach of a stranger.'

'An unusual animal,' I said critically, trying to look as if I understood the minutest points of canine breeds.

'He is that,' said the owner. 'He's a Molossian hound. I mean really, a true Molossian; his father is from Molossos, and his mother too.'

'Molossos?' exclaimed Theodoros, laughing. 'What a funny name!'

'It's not funny, it's the name of a place way out West,' the owner said.

'That's right,' said Philemon. 'Olympia, Alexander's mother, comes from there. They go in for snake-handling in Molossos – part of their religion. Weird people, but great dogs.'

'They're rare in Athens,' continued the owner, refusing to be distracted by snakes. 'Rare and valuable. *Real* Molossian hounds. Frankly, I would charge more if you weren't a cousin of Philemon. And the bitch had a large litter, and our home isn't best suited to keeping them all.'

I paid this dog-breeder what he asked, to Philemon's satisfaction. (It was a moot point if Philemon had arranged the dog-buying for our benefit, or that of his friend.) The man sent his slave for a piece of leather to make a collar, and a stout rope to tie our hound with. We couldn't trust him not to run off. Meanwhile, we needed to make ourselves known to the animal.

'Theodoros, *you* are really going to be this dog's master,' I said. 'Since I will be away, and the dog must obey someone, this will be your dog.'

Theodoros' face lighted up. 'I must call him by name,' he said. 'What is his name?'

'Doesn't have one. We call him "the second pup".'

Theodoros knelt beside the animal and put his arm around its neck. 'I will give you a name,' he said. 'I will call you "Molossos" and since your father was of Molossos, we will pretend his name was "Molossos" too. You are the son of Molossos. Molossos Molossou.'

The dog cocked his head and put his tongue out again, rather as if considering the new appellation.

'So you will come when I call you, Molossos Molossou,' said Theodoros, 'and you will run with me and we will hunt together, and you will not leave me. Promise you will come when I call you, and keep everybody in my house safe. Agreed?'

Theodoros flung his arms fully round the beast and kissed the top of its head. Molossos Molossou responded by licking his face enthusiastically.

'There!' said Theodoros. 'He really is mine now, and he is willing to come with us.'

The collar was affixed amid some growls and protests, and the strong rope. We left in a procession. Philemon with nothing, Theodoros with dog, myself with donkey, the slave with basket. A few steps beyond the gate, however, the 'second pup' seemed to realise it was leaving its parent and former companions behind, and emitted a startling howl, which set off the others inside the yard. We had a deal of business quieting him. At last he consented to trot along under pressure of our united urging. Soon, however, Philemon had to leave us and go home. Noting the diminution of our number, the dog seemed to think he had a better chance of conducting the expedition as he pleased.

The countryside held innumerable attractions for Molossos Molossou, and he took off with alarming speed over a field, dragging Theodoros after him. The slave and I ran after the pair, whereupon the donkey, not knowing what to do with so much freedom, began to stray towards a cottage garden to eat the produce. Fortunately, I headed off the ass before it did any damage, and Theodoros persuaded the hound to come back to the road. This was by no means the last foray. Most alarming was the occasion when he was attracted by a chicken in the road and chased it vigorously back home, dragging Theodoros with him into a crowd of anxious and noisy fowl.

'Molossos Molossou, I cannot have you doing this all the time,' said Theodoros, wiping his brow. 'And I cannot go on calling you "Molossos Molossou" all the time either. It's too long. I shall call you just "Moloss-Molou".'

And so the dog became "Moloss-Molou" for ever after, and we proceeded on our way to Eleusis, sometimes with the boy leading the dog, sometimes with the dog pulling the boy.

Smikrenes received the news of the dog, and the dog itself, in his usual gracious manner.

'So, this beast will eat us all out of house and home,' he pronounced.

'No, no. He's supposed to be able to hunt for what he eats. He will keep down the rats and rabbits and anything that eats your crops,' I said rashly. 'And he will be a watch-dog and a guard over all.'

'Well, could be worse. This thing's going to grow – and he's only half trained. Great gawping puppy. Your little boy will have to be responsible for him. My old dog Argos could have kept him in order, if he was alive. Now, *there* was a real guard dog!'

'But my dog is alive!' said Theodoros. Theodoros had not been best pleased at being referred to as my 'little boy', but this protest to Smikrenes was meant as a point of logic, and not as impudence. It didn't seem likely that Smikrenes would see the difference.

'Don't be pert, child. Well, let us have a look at you.' Theodoros stood squarely in front of him. 'He talks back, but he is well grown. Hope you're strong, boy. Fine manly little fellow,' added Smikrenes, sighing. 'I never had any such, only the girl. Spoilt, probably. I dare say he's been softened by city ways, though – school and games and endless playtime. Not used to work, like the country boys here are.'

'I can do anything a country boy can do,' Theodoros insisted stoutly. 'And Stephanos said I was to help you.'

'Yes. No school here but life. Don't look alarmed, boy, I won't eat you, and I'll leave some time for play. Philomela my daughter will feed you well, and you can talk to her when I am not about. But you are to mind me, hear! No running away.'

'Theodoros has never given us the least trouble,' I said, answering the child's mute appeal for defence. 'He is the prop of our household. When I am away, he is the man of it, as he knows, and must look after his mother.'

'I dare say we shall all shake down well enough,' said Smikrenes, shaking his own head as if to counteract too much good cheer in this prophecy. He agreed to take charge of Moloss-Molou until our whole party should arrive on the morrow.

Theodoros, understandably fatigued, made good use of the donkey on the way home. I knew that he was – and who could wonder at it! – daunted at the prospect of life with Smikrenes. I told him frankly that was our only resource. I also explained about Philomela, whom he would meet, as he was still young enough not to be separated from the women.

The next day we all set out again. I insisted on an early start so that not too many neighbours would see our departure. A cart, drawn by two asses, was full of household effects: pallets, blankets, clothing, pots, food, and trinkets from which my mother could not bear to part. Mother had to ride, and I could afford no more estimable conveyance. I sent the slaves on ahead so we would not be too great a procession, but we were noticeable enough with my mother in her cart surrounded by piles of stuff, and one son walking along on each side of her.

It took a terribly long time to get to Eleusis, and my mother's little wails at departing from her house, though softened by her veil and her own sense of propriety, did not add to the cheer of the expedition. It was borne in upon me forcibly, though (strangely) only at this point, that the person who might suffer the most by this arrangement for a visit would be my bride-to-be, Philomela. It is hard enough for a young woman who has the honour to be a bride to adjust to life with her mother-in-law, but Philomela, without a bridal, would have to endure my mother's chiding, disapproval, weeping and worrying. It would be too much to hope that Mother would like her, I thought. Mother was so strongly against the marriage. She might try to create a breach that could never be healed. It surprised me once I realised this that I hadn't thought of it before. But then, I had been thinking only of the family's safety.

'Don't let any stranger – not of the family – feed your dog,' I warned Theodoros. 'You must train him to accept nothing that doesn't come from your hand, or that of Mother or Philomela. He can eat what he himself catches, or he can eat what you give him – not too much. But make him learn that he must not eat what anyone else offers him. Dogs have been poisoned by spiteful people before now.'

Theodoros' eyes grew big.

'You can train him,' I said. 'You can spend a good deal of your time this summer training Moloss-Molou.'

Our journey seemed to take forever, with stops on the road for eating or relieving ourselves, searching for lost articles, or resting the donkeys, but at length we arrived at Eleusis deme and then at the home of Smikrenes. Although it was already nearly evening, I took only a couple of hours' rest and some food before returning to Athens to close up our house. Next morning I would be setting out for the sea journey to the eastern islands. I departed from Eleusis under a good moon, after a tearful farewell to Mother. She kept the donkey and cart with her; travelling at night, she pointed out, could only endanger the little vehicle. Besides, she might think of something else she wanted from home. I readily agreed, not desiring the nuisance of the cart on the way back. I said my goodbyes to her within the house, but Theodoros accompanied me to the gate.

'Take care of yourself, Stepho,' he said, in a manly way.

My departure seemed to be making us more equal. Indeed, I realised to my surprise that I did have some reliance on the intelligence and judgement of Theodoros – much more than on my cousin Philemon's at any age. But there was no getting away from the fact that Theodoros was only in his tenth year.

'Farewell, and I leave you in the care of the gods,' I said formally. I could not forbear a light warning: 'Keep a wary eye out for loutish men hanging about. I thought I saw a couple of loiterers, slaves most probably, eyeing our town house the other day – one is a big beefy fellow.'

'I will watch out,' said Theodoros readily. 'After all,' he laughed, 'we don't want pieces of animals left on us, like some people!'

'Exactly.' I didn't want to alarm the child by telling him any more. But I added, though this was really an afterthought, 'Theodoros, I know you can write. I must depend on you. In Mother's little wooden box you will find a small clay tablet with two strange names on it. Aristodamos of Naxos and Oromedon son of Daliokles, of Kos. Aristotle gave me these two addresses. If I am not actually with them these men may know where I can be found.'

'I understand,' Theodoros said. 'I'll write, I promise.'

'Write at least once, just to let me know that everything is all right,' I urged. 'And please do not omit to write if you think there is any need, or if there is any trouble. I don't put great confidence in the judgement of my cousin Philemon, but if you want money or immediate assistance you may ask him. He owes me his help, and many favours.'

'I will remember what you say,' said Theodoros,

looking serious. 'I can remember the names. Aristodamos of Naxos and Oromedon of Kos – son of Daliokles. And I will look after Mother. Don't you worry, Stephanos, my brother. Moloss-Molou will guard all of us.'

So I said my last farewell to my family and stumbled wearily back to Athens and my poor deserted house to pack up the few things I could bother to take with me on my long journey.

IX

Taking Ship for the Islands

In the first morning light I went to Aristotle's house. He was, of course, ready, with his slave Phokon to carry his bags. Young Parmenion was also prepared for travel, at least as far as his dress was concerned. The boy, pale and silent, his lips compressed, stood with head bowed as one resigned to fate. Aristotle's household, including his assistants, the teachers and the students, as well as the slaves, both men and women, had drawn up to say farewell. They stood about in the cool air, some visibly distressed, others with difficulty holding in check their desire for sleep. Young Mikon gaped in a terrific yawn, and his neighbour nudged him. But the woman slave who must be Herpyllis, she who had tended Pythias during her last days, seemed greatly moved. A female slave does not have to be veiled, and Herpyllis' headgear slipped as she attended earnestly to Aristotle's farewell, rendering her fully visible. This woman had a lovely face, slightly rounder than the perfect oval, and large grey eyes of great expressiveness; the tracks of tears were visible on her cheeks. She held little Pythias by the hand, readied for travel also, with a big basket beside them. They were to set out to Euboia as soon as the Master left. Aristotle, rising to the occasion, made a grave and simple speech:

'I am going,' he told the assembled company, 'for but a while, and I look forward to returning to you all. I am taking Parmenion back to his home, and I shall also be going on a little errand of matters of importance, about which I cannot speak at present. You will be well protected when I am away. I hope to hear of your progress in work when I get back. Above all, the work of the school must not slacken. I hope all my dear students will grow in wisdom and knowledge during our time apart. May all go well with you, and the goodwill of gods and men rest upon this house and its inhabitants.'

There was a little cheer, with some sobbing. We walked away. Aristotle kept his arm tucked in Parmenion's, to make sure he would come, and Phokon brought up the rear. Aristotle had arranged an easy departure, with asses to carry the luggage and Parmenion, and ourselves if we wished. I was glad not to have to carry my bundle all the way to Peiraieus. At least by now I had learned about the necessities of travelling, and had brought useful things in a leather bag, of some defence against the weather. Aristotle assured me that Phokon would buy water for us all when we got to the port. I hadn't thought about the difficulty of getting drinking water on board the ship. It was pleasant to have a servant to wait upon me, but awkward that he belonged to somebody else. I could not have spared one of our home servants to accompany me, and the prospect of having to feed an extra mouth along the road would have been too daunting. Naturally, Aristotle would have an attendant.

The road seemed long, for I had walked many weary stadia to and from Eleusis in recent days. I was glad to see the port, with its bustle and glow of life. Peiraieus was familiar to me: at one time I had quite haunted the place. But a port always looks different when you yourself are going on a journey. At the time when I had frequented Peiraieus a couple of years before, most of the military shipping was with Alexander at the eastern edge of the ocean, ferrying troops and supplies to the coast of Asia. But now many of these ships had returned. Some warships of the stunning new size were being repaired, or made ready to be put in dry dock. Peiraieus seemed to have more slipways than before, and more sheds to house ships and tackle. These boathouses are really quite elegant, like temples for ships, with their stone columns and wooded roofs.

Aristotle made his way confidently to a particular area of the Emporion where the merchant ships are harboured. The big merchantmen are really huge close to, and I was gazing at one of the ones with a vast number of crewmen swarming aboard her when we drew near to our more modest craft. 'I have engaged a very good ship,' Aristotle explained to me. 'Excellent captain. A vessel of sufficient size to take us and our luggage without constriction. There will be a few other passengers of course. Ah! Here it is. The *Eudaimonia* of Peiraieus.'

It seemed a good sign that the ship had such a cheerful name, although some philosophers tell us that we should seek first *Arete*, excellence or virtue, and not care about prosperity or the good spirits signified by *Eudaimonia*.

Both Aristotle and I, so I thought, could do with a little happiness.

'Stephanos, this is our good captain Aiskhines. Of Peiraieus, like the ship. He is the *kybernetes* who commands this ship, and also the *naukleros*.'

'Lucky for you,' said the captain cheerfully. 'A man who owns his ship will surely take the best care of it, and his passengers too. Rowers all hand-picked – the six best have manned ships in the wars. Experienced men.'

I looked curiously at the man on whom we were to depend, and was reassured. Aiskhines had a square capable face, and smiling brown eyes. 'A nice ship,' I said cautiously, knowing very little about ships.

'She is that, sir. A *keles*, not as big as some, but built for speed. Responds well to the rowers, and carries sail, as you see.'

It is well that I kept my countenance, for the word *keles* is well known in another context: as 'a good fast ride' or 'a fast go'. It is what a man pays the highest price for in the brothels when he wants a woman to ride him. We used to giggle a lot about the word in school. After we really knew what we were talking about, the laughter changed.

'A *keles*, yes,' I said approvingly. 'I didn't know we were taking cargo with us,' I added, with less approbation. Aiskhines and his crew were engaged in storing a lot of things on the vessel. I had not realised we were going to have to share our ship with anything but human freight.

'Oh, just a little oil – scarcely anything in the way of cargo this trip. Why, you wouldn't believe it perhaps, but this little cutter can take nearly thirty talents' weight of cargo! Very snug hold. You'll be glad of the cargo aboard, sir, for it adds ballast and stability, and prevents the ship jumping about too much on the waves. And she's a lively filly when she gets her head!'

'Where can my slave put our luggage?' Aristotle enquired.

'Come with me, sir. Right there, down in the back of the hold, but be sure it's in the dry part. Now the kitchen area is in that little galley aft, if you have kitchen stuff to leave off – but be careful. That's where the firepot is.'

I looked and saw that the roofed space at the very back of the deck was nicely tiled over, with a hole cut for the smoke to go out from a portable hearth. The firepot was sturdy, ingeniously made of multiple layers, to keep the fire safe from wind and spray. Utensils, knives and spoons and a pot or two, hung neatly on pegs, jammed in place with other pegs so they would not swing about.

'I had no idea that a ship could have a kitchen,' I said admiringly.

'Oh, there's no home like ship, sir, as you'll find. Everything you could want, handy as can be. Not like the great naval fleet that had to stop for breakfast by the little goat-trough creeks at Aigospotamoi. Because they stopped they got caught by the Spartan admiral Lysander. A famous defeat, Aigospotamoi. A whole navy lost for the sake of a breakfast – except for one commander who didn't beach for a meal, and saved his ships.' The captain laughed. 'Now, if they'd all had kitchens, there'd have been no loss. But it's true, you can't feed men in a *trieres*, with nearly two hundred mouths. But *we* can eat when we like. Mind you, doing the Kyklades run we can probably hop on an island for the night and you can dine on dry land, as landsmen prefer. But we could cook you up a fine dinner at sea.'

The captain was torn between the desire to go on praising his ship and the desire to continue attending to the cargo. He and his men were evidently so busy that we begged not to interrupt him. About one sixth or so of the ship's interior was taken up with a wooden rack with rows of square holes in which to hold pots securely; the crew were packing into these the kind of long pots with a spike at the bottom that are used for shipping liquid products. The holes were partly filled with packing sand, into which the spike could be run, and then the tops of the bottles were packed about with soft twigs and some straw.

'We'll be off as soon as we've got our oil ready,' the captain explained briskly. 'A couple of other passengers and yourselves. We're carrying fresh water for ourselves and the crew – we have a large water tank in the hold.' He pointed to a gigantic pot covered thickly with pitch. 'Though you can bring your own if you fancy it. Crew are likely to go through the water supply at a great rate in this heat. Hope to get off soon before the sun has risen further up the sky. You may as well go and get something to eat before we depart.'

Thus encouraged, we left our baggage with Phokon to look after it, and climbed out again. We betook ourselves to the market area. Peiraieus has what must be the best market in the world – goods come from everywhere. There are hides from Argos and the islands; perfumes and carvings and papyrus from Egypt; pottery from the Greek colonies around Poseidonia in the West; brightly coloured cushions and carpets from Karthago and from Persia; spices from places far away; and beautiful jewellery looted from Persian lands and pawned or put up for sale. Everyone in Peiraieus seems to be trading something. Bankers set up their tables here, along the waterfront, with their scales and piles of coin and bullion, all guarded by stout and competent slaves. You could hear the quick clicking patter-patter of tiles of silver and gold falling on one another, as rich persons from home or abroad made an exchange or deposit, or took out a loan.

Just seeing all this made me feel happier, and hungry. Peiraieus specialises in tripe, and also other organs. I looked for the list of official prices and was glad to see that costs had not gone up. The list offered mouthwatering delicacies. I hesitated between tripe and a stew of pigs' trotters (while being coaxed by the hot-meat seller to try the fried brains), but eventually settled on the tripe.

'You *are* a brave man,' exclaimed Aristotle.

'I'm hungry now,' I said, 'and these little stalls do tripe very well. You ought to try it. What about yourself, Parmenion?'

Parmenion simply looked offended, and Aristotle said, 'Well, before sailing some people are more anxious about their stomachs.'

I hadn't thought of this, but waved the consideration away. 'I'll be fine,' I said with assurance. My eye was caught by the large sign showing the exact measures to be used according to the law. In a sandstone slab bits and pieces of a man appeared in outline – an arm, a hand, a foot. I pointed this out, laughing. 'It looks as if the man is disappearing into the sand. Evaporated, even, leaving only the outline of his fragments. That would be a mystery to solve, indeed Where did he go?' I persisted in the fantasy (which perhaps first arose from my state of fatigue), partly because I saw it as my responsibility to

keep Aristotle cheerful, mentally occupied with interesting and amusing things.

It was a great relief to me that Aristotle had allowed no
signs of his mourning to escape him since we had left his
home. He was right: fortitude and philosophy had come to
his aid, as well as the natural self-restraint of a gentleman
unwilling to burden his friends. Once we started
travelling, and our minds were turned to new things, he
would resign himself, forget to recall his loss. So at the
sight of the comical sign – the man in parts disappearing
– I laughed out loud to encourage Aristotle. The tripe
seller glared, thinking I was laughing at him, which I
certainly wasn't.

The sight of the foot, suspended in stone in mid-air,
reminded me of my own feet. My sandals were worn
down, although they were the toughest kind with
hobnails in the soles. The pause in Peiraieus gave me time
to buy a sturdy new pair. 'At least,' I said to our company,
'I shall be walking on a piece of Attika all the time. I shall
feel better with Athenian footwear on.' I also felt better
because the shoemaker kindly allowed me to wash my
legs and feet, as I was thick with dust from toes to knees.

As we headed back to our little ship, I dawdled behind
Aristotle and Parmenion, looking at the fine goods for
sale. I was annoyed by an urchin wearing a hood like
someone who is ill; the boy kept trying to make me buy
oregano or fennel. In attempting to evade the little fellow,
who made me curiously uneasy, I bumped into a slow-
moving woman. I apologised before I realised that this
female was only a slave. Then I noticed that she was lame,
and could walk only haltingly. Yet, most strangely, she
was carrying a dog in her arms. 'Here,' I said, handing her

a hemi-obol. I hurried after Aristotle, but the woman came thumping after me with her uneven tread.

When we drew near the ship we could see that it was almost ready to depart. Two unknown men, obviously not sailors but passengers, were already on board her. We stood and gazed at our ship, a little deeper in the water now as it rode with the oil jars in its hold.

'Won't be long – come on board!' the captain called to us. He and one of his sailors were critically inspecting the sail, which they then proceeded to furl, stowing the mast within the ship, running all the length of it under the rowers' thwarts. 'We don't use sail till we're out on open water,' he explained, 'and not then unless the wind is right for it. Still, you catch a good wind, you cut down on the time. Anybody want to go to Delos?' he added jokingly.

The woman with the dog drew up to us.

'Oh please, good sirs, take me with you! I wish to go – I *need* to go – to Delos. I have some money. I can pay my way! Passage for me and my poor dear little dog here. It's a cripple, deary me! – just like me. Can hardly walk. But we both need to get to Delos.' The lame dog in her arms whined. It looked neither young nor healthy.

'What is your name and who is your mistress? Should you not be travelling with her?' Phokon asked. 'And where is your mistress?' added the captain.

'Oh, sirs, my name is Doris, and my mistress is Kardaka. She has gone to her mother's family home on the island for the summer. She left me to close up the house in Peiraieus. But she wants me to meet her in Delos. Rheneia, actually. Greater Delos. That's why I have the money to go. But I must take this dog, and not every boat has room for a dog.'

'Why do you carry this dog about?' I asked bluntly. 'It is not that small a dog, and you are obviously crippled.'

She flushed.

'Yes, I am quite lame,' she admitted. 'But the dog is, too – he wouldn't get about at all, hardly, without me. This dog is the dearest thing to me. I have looked after him all his life. And now he has got lame and not too well the mistress said she would give him to me outright if I would take care of him. But we need to meet her in the island next to Delos, and I can pay for my passage.'

'Can't be doing with dogs running around the ship!' exclaimed the captain.

'Oh, please! Sirs, please! Let me take the dog, I beg of you. I can put him in a basket of some kind – there are basket sellers hereabouts. And we can sit at the very back. I'll pay extra for the dog.'

'Well,' said Aristotle, 'I suppose we can do one act of kindness.'

'It's not too kind if we're not paying for it,' I reminded him.

'Can you get a basket without delay, woman, for that there dog?' demanded the captain. 'For we need to set off – the day is advancing.'

The woman succeeded in cajoling a basket with a lid out of one of the neighbouring shops for a very low price. In this the dog was forcibly and duly incarcerated. The basket was lowered into the well of the boat, the dog whining and sniffling, and the poor limping slavewoman was helped aboard by two of the crew. We all followed. Our own party was by far the most numerous: Aristotle, myself, young Parmenion and Phokon. The power of numbers was such that we forced the two men of business travelling with us to make room. One of these was an insignificant, partly bald little fellow of the sort that one can see everywhere every day. He had a kind of shawl to keep sun off his neck, and a number of small parcels. I tried to help him, but he said 'Let my things alone!' in a grumpy voice, and then heaped the little bundles about him suspiciously, as if he suspected us of wanting to steal them.

'One cannot tell in a boat full of *dogs* what may happen to one's things,' he said in peevish tones, casting a baleful look at the lame slavewoman and her unfortunate pet. 'It's not what I'm used to, I'm happy to say. Never.'

This genial fellow then huddled in his shawl, although the weather was so warm, and seemed disinclined for conversation. The other man was much more forthcoming. As we moved our own bundles about (suddenly we all seemed to have a great many), this man explained that his name was Miltiades, that he had done the run to Sounion often before, and thought that at least that leg of the trip should go smoothly, given the weather conditions. Certain men always seem to know more about the weather than other people, even somehow to own it, as if it came from their own manufactory.

'We are slightly delayed,' said Captain Aiskhines. 'But we'll use all our oarsmen in getting out of harbour and down to Sounion. Passengers, I beg you to settle yourselves.'

We sat down and arranged ourselves comfortably. Then we had to move again because we were in the way of the oarsmen, who seemed to have multiplied greatly. It is not easy for passengers to distribute themselves, as of course the oarsmen come first – they have to be where they are.

The oarsmen were handsome fellows enough, and sinewy. Brown as earth, they all went naked, each man sitting on his own leather cushion on the bench, oar in hand. The oar was fitted through a round hole in the boat's side, but the hole had a leather bag tightly fitted in it, to prevent it from admitting spray. The men sat facing backwards, looking to the stern, but the captain and a keelsman faced forward.

While the oars were readied, we had leisure to look about us. 'Only think,' I said to Aristotle, anxious to divert his thoughts. 'Only think of all that this harbour has seen. As I have read, and heard also, long ago in the time of Sokrates and Alkibiades there were a hundred triremes crowded together – here – ready to depart for Sikilia. And all the relatives and friends of these thousands of men came crowding to the shore too. What a vast crowd it must have been! Music played, and the whole crowd said their prayers in unison – what a heart-stirring moment! And the captains, led by Alkibiades, poured upon the waters libations from goblets of gold and silver.'

The captain frowned. 'It's not great good luck to talk about the Sikilian Expedition,' he announced. I was embarrassed. Of course I ought to have remembered that famous Expedition had ended in defeat and loss. It made sense that seafarers did not want to hear about disaster. Now a helper on shore untied the rope that bound our ship, and the first sailor hauled in the anchor. The captain then burned a pinch of incense on the little altar at the back of the boat. He poured a libation of wine into the sea, not like an Alkibiades from a golden goblet, but from an ordinary earthen beaker.

'We're off! In the name of Zeus Protector and Saviour,

of Poseidon and all the gods. Wait for the *keleusma*, men! Six oars through the harbour. One-two-and *three*!' The captain chanted the *keleusma*, the beat that gave the rhythm to the oarsmen.

'Here we go!' said Aristotle. 'Bid farewell to your city, Stephanos.'

'Your first time at sea, young man?' asked Miltiades. 'You should enjoy it, even if this is a small ship. On big ships like the *triereis*, of course, it's wonderful – a multitude of rowers. And there is a boatswain who does nothing but chant the beat – even pipers to give the time.'

Even if we had only a relatively small ship, it was exciting to move out into the harbour, threading our way through other shipping. I admired the exactness with which the captain foresaw how the oars must be handled or idled in order to swing, to change direction, to make a manoeuvre. We swung out into the gulf, with a dipping of oars and the plash of waves and the voice keeping time – the first time I had heard that peculiar rhythmic sound, or set of sounds. Gulls screamed overhead, sailors on other ships called out friendly or obscene remarks, and the land began to slip away. In no time at all we were in the gulf and out of the harbour. It was a startling view. Aigina, just ahead, looked very big, a conical island that it seemed hard not to bump into.

'Look west, Stephanos, and you will see the Peloponnesos,' said Aristotle. Facing backwards like the rowers and craning my neck I could see a great deal of land with many hills, and towering above it one startling triangular peak.

'That peak – that is Akrokorinthos,' Aristotle explained. 'Almost directly behind us is Korinthos itself.'

'Oh, I see,' I said. I was almost disappointed. When Aristotle had once gone by sea to Korinthos on my behalf on a dangerous winter journey, I had been deeply impressed. But now it didn't seem so distant; I began fully to realise that you could indeed get to Korinthos by boat, and it was not extremely far away.

The oarsmen moved to their task with deliberate speed, and the wind and currents favoured us. We were moving – and moving not slowly along the coast of Attika. The sun shone brightly on the water. Soon it was hot, though not as hot as it would be on land.

'Rig 'em up some shade, boys,' advised the captain. Nimbly two of the rowers put up a light framework on which they spread cloths, attached by tabs of material to the poles of the airy scaffolding. We had a shelter from the beating sun, a small tent roof where we sat on the deck.

'All the conveniences of home,' said the captain. 'By the way, you will find it most convenient, gentleman, to do your pissing – and if possible your shitting too – over the side. We could rig up the latrine, but it makes a drag on the ship, and there aren't any ladies aboard at the moment. We've also got a serviceable pot, but that has to be emptied each time. As for that there dog –' he looked at the slavewoman – 'you've got to clean up his messes. Understood?'

She nodded mutely. We shared some of our water with her; Phokon had seen to it that we had purchased a good supply of fresh drinking-water in skin bottles at the port. Phokon also offered us a few flat loaves of barley and some olives, as we watched Attika go by. I declined, as my own tripes were still dealing with the Peiraieus tripe. I enjoyed the view in a fatigued and stupefied way. The sun and the rowing lulled my senses and I was content to sit and stare.

Bay and inlet and headland, there it was – Attika; stadia and stadia of Attika, stretching in its long peninsula, the sweet green Middle Land with its vegetable gardens, its fields of grain, its olive groves and its vineyards. The sun and the scenery were making me contented and sleepy; perhaps the tripe I had eaten had its share in this effect. But principally it was the reaction to having taken so little sleep in the recent strenuous days. Now I lay on the ship, half in sun and half in shade, and let the world slip by me, lulled by the rhythm of oars as we coasted along in sight of our shore. Aristotle need not have worried, I thought drowsily, I was not the kind to get seasick. Instead, I felt a sense of profound relief at having got away from my home and the past, and the worries and pains that had occupied us so much in the last month. I tried to dismiss from my mind the less pleasant images that rose in it occasionally: a horse's decaying head, a swinging heavy mallet, a dead monkey sprawled and grinning.

All day green Attika slipped past us. Only one thin strip of sunset glow was left on the western horizon, when we arrived at Sounion. Above us towered the great temple, visible by torchlight even in this growing darkness, a sight in white and blue and gold. We got into the gentle bay at the foot of its cliff on the western side and nestled there, sleeping on board. When we awoke in the morning at the first gleams of coming light, Poseidon's bright temple was the first thing we saw. There was nothing between it and the eastern horizon, and the sun appeared to rise through the glowing temple.

'Here we make our sacrifice to Poseidon,' said the

captain briskly. 'As you will want to do before a long journey. And we have a few more passengers to pick up. But I hope we will be under way to Delos this morning. So be quick about your prayers.'

We could not properly get to the great shrine by the shortest route, which would be to ascend directly by the little cliff up to the Propylaia, the entryway to the temple; we walked, as we were supposed to do, the long winding marble path, stopping at the Temple of Athena of Sounion to pay our respects before proceeding to the great and beautiful structure dedicated to the god of the sea. I had seen before this most beautiful temple, commissioned by Perikles after the old one had been ruined by the Persian invasion. It is built of our own marble of Attika.

I had not really visited Sounion since I was a boy. This time, I noticed how heavily fortified the place was. As this was the first citadel of Attika to be encountered by comers from the East, with more mature eyes I could comprehend its strategic importance. The Makedonian forces had taken it over in recent years; they had strengthened the fortifications, and put several soldiers about to keep watch.

'If it isn't patrolled, Sounion can be a terrible place for pirates,' our captain remarked. 'The ship-sheds need to be protected as well as the port. Many vessels stop here.'

'Yes – including the grain ships on their way from Euboia.' Aristotle sighed unexpectedly.

'Mind you don't try to buy nothing from the sellers around this place,' said the captain. 'They're terrible sharp, the people of Sounion, and they go their own way. They often set runaway slaves free. I dare say the new government'll put a stop to those tricks.'

We walked on upwards to the wonderful temple, where

we could see the great frieze of the contest of the Lapiths and Centaurs, and the feats of Theseus, the daring adventurer and prince of Attika who had slain the dreadful Minotaur in Krete, and returned triumphant home again. Within, the astonishing bronze statue of Poseidon commanded our attention. We made some offerings and uttered our prayers, as a group. I made a promise to the divine ruler of the sea to put up a votive tablet at Sounion if my voyage went well. (I didn't define for myself and the god clearly what 'going well' would mean, which was a mistake – you need to be clear about such things.) The whole area of the *temenos* was full of votive offerings to Poseidon, from the most gigantic kouroi in marble, dedicatory statues of young men, to little clay plaques of the feeblest kind. I resisted all the sellers trying to offer us plaques of Poseidon or miniature statues, and we strolled about looking from this vantage point. Just offshore there were only a few little uninteresting islands. Westward, whence we had come, we could just make out the lumpy shape of Aigina. Eastward was the blue horizon a-dazzle with early sun, the great blank to which I was travelling.

'I have promised a votive offering to Poseidon,' I said to one of the sailors as we marched downward again. 'But he's not one of my favourite gods, I have to say. Earthquakes and tempests – and the big empty sea.'

'O sir, don't say such a thing!' The *nautes* looked shocked. 'You will bring us ill fortune! You tempt divine power and risk the success of your own voyage. How can you say such things of the great and good god! He who provides us with the road that connects man and man – and gives the great abundance of fish of all kinds for humans to eat! Oh, please take back these words! Go back to the temple and utter good words about the King of the ancient Waters.'

I felt a trifle alarmed myself, now I thought of it. Hastily I returned (the sailor trotting along to make sure I did so), and found some formulas in my tired brain. 'I honour and adore the great and good King of the Sea in his infinite depth and great majesty. And I humbly pray to him for good success when venturing upon the deep, his realm for ever. And I promise, most solemnly, a votive offering if I return alive, as well as the special offering promised before if my journey goes well.'

With this, Poseidon and the sailor had to content themselves. The day was advancing, and we needed to move smartly down the path, against the flow of ascending visitors. When we got to the landing stage, we found other passengers waiting to board our ship. The grumpy and uncommunicative man had, happily, left us for good at Sounion, but bright-faced Miltiades was rejoining us, having purchased water and fresh provisions. Another gentleman, younger than Miltiades, presumably also a man of business, joined us here, a very handsome man with an air of authority and a beautifully straight nose. With great elegance of manner, he introduced himself as Philokhoros of the deme of Akharneia. Philokhoros of the straight nose and elegant bearing had a slave-boy with him, a slender young fellow of about Parmenion's age but not his growth. This youth, whose name we were told was 'Sosios', looked nervous at being on the water, and cast a dismal look at the land when at last (so it seems from a ship) it began to slip away from us.

There was also a new party of a different kind, a domestic group that stood to one side. An old man, a hooded woman and a little girl. They seemed respectable, indeed of the better class, though not ostentatiously or out of measure well-to-do; their clothes were carefully mended in places. The little girl was pale and thin, and stooped over. You could see her breathing, and she coughed several times as she stood there, holding her mother's hand and looking about her as well as she could in her circumstances.

'This is Hermippos of Laurion,' explained Captain Aiskhines. 'With his daughter and his little grand-daughter, as well as their female slave. Now we shall have to put the latrine up,' he advised his men.

The old man stood erect and spoke formal greetings to us with great gravity.

'We travel far,' he explained, 'we are pursuing our route as far as the island of Kos.' He gave commands to a short thin slavewoman who bustled in with their belongings. Two seamen gave their attention to rigging up a latrine on the left side of the boat not far from the galley. This little contraption was made to overhang the side of the boat: you stepped in from the deck, but then you were sitting straight above the ocean and your offering plopped directly into the deep. In fact, the women and children for whose benefit this was put up were hardly the chief beneficiaries, as each preferred to utilise the pot, having someone shield her with a cloak during the operaton of necessity.

The latrine was not the only addition to the proprieties.

''Fraid we must gird up, boys!' the captain said, and the men, grumbling only slightly, fastened loincloths about themselves.

'At least it keeps your bum and balls from splinters,'

said the sailor who had spoken to me of Poseidon.
'Trouble is, cloth gets soaked with salt. Either splinters or
in a pickle – that's the fate of our members!'

When we all had got aboard, with still more bundles
and belongings, the ship now seemed a tight fit. As well
as our own party – the slave Phokon, the schoolboy
Parmenion, myself and Aristotle – we still had with us
from Peiraieus the businessman Miltiades and the little
lame slavewoman with her wretched dog. Now we had the
new man Philokhoros with his nervous slave of whom he
seemed irritatingly fond, always stroking his hair. And we
had this new family, with the sickly-looking little girl,
another female slave and two adults – one of them a
woman of the most respectable class. That was
troublesome, as we all had to make a kind of unofficial
women's quarters of one side of the vessel. It doesn't
matter with slavewomen – they don't require a *gynaikon*
– but naturally we men are not supposed to hob-nob with
wives and daughters of the respectable classes. Of course,
the little girl had some of the freedom of the very young;
she seemed to be only six or seven years old. But she was
rightly bidden to stay close to her mother.

'Wasn't prepared for this number of passengers,'
growled Miltiades, though not with the extremest ill
nature. 'We could have done without that limping lady's
maid there and her pathetic beast.' I felt inclined to agree,
though the advent of this female was our fault.

'No cause to worry,' said the captain. 'My men are light,
though they're lively, and we didn't take half the cargo we
could have, on purpose to accommodate you all. We really
should have some *more* weight on board. Raise the sail,
men!'

'Pity,' said Miltiades, more amiably, 'I could accommodate you once I get to Paros and Naxos, for I am in the marble way of business, and marble would supply weight enough. But I shouldn't have thought of this cutter as a cargo ship.'

'She's surely built for speed, the *Eudaimonia*,' said the captain. He looked fondly at the mast which had again been raised, the sail now bellying out in the wind. 'But she's a terrific carrier. A bit of ballast in a ship makes it go better when the sea gets high. Cast off, men. We're off! In the name of Poseidon and all the gods!'

So with a quick libation we swung out of the good harbour of Sounion, and the rowers were soon manoeuvring us beyond the cape, the sail pulling us impatiently onward. Seeing the temple in the sun stirred me like a song – a sad song, for the temple was getting smaller.

'Now if we turned left after rounding this point,' said Aristotle, 'we would get to Euboia.' He added in firm tones, 'Eastward is where our journey lies. How do you find yourself, Parmenion?'

'Very well,' said Parmenion, with cool indifference. At least he was now awake, mentally as well as physically, for he seemed to look about him and to gaze almost hopefully eastward.

I could not answer as Parmenion had done. I suddenly stopped feeling very well. The ship was now in a very different kind of water, it seemed to me, from what we had experienced yesterday along the coast. After we left the shelter of the headland we were in big deep water manifesting the most amazing activity. The little ship moved in a different way, now falling, now rising, at the same time shifting side to side. The rhythm of the oars,

slower now, but steady, was in conflict sometimes with
the rhythm of the waves, and not just the waves I could
see but big internal swellings of water within the sea that
seemed to match internal swellings in myself. If I looked
at the prow or the mast swaying against the horizon I felt
dizzy. Soon I was overtaken by my sensations. Trying to
choose a post where I would be least annoying to others,
I leaned over the side and cast my offering into the sea. It
was the sincerest sort of offering to Poseidon, given with
heartfelt desire. Soon I had nothing more to yield, and yet
could not stop retching.

'Fetches them that way, often,' said the sailor nearest
me, pulling his oar steadily. I gathered that the
slavewoman who had come with the party from Laurion
was similarly overcome. But it was shaming that the feeble
little girl seemed unaffected, and even though the lame
Doris, sitting beside her dog, uttered moans as the ship
lunged, she did not devote her attention to the side of the
ship as I was doing.

'Are you all right, Stephanos?' It was Aristotle, peering
anxiously at me. His hair and beard were shaken by the
wind.

'Certainly,' I said haughtily – or as haughtily as one can
under these circumstances. 'Must have been something I
ate in Sounion.'

'Don't worry, most people are a little seasick at first,'
said Aristotle. 'It goes off.'

'Some say as swallowing a mouth of seawater helps,'
suggested Phokon.

'Already tried it,' I mumbled. And I had, inadvertently,
taken in a large mouthful of seawater from a passing
wave.

'You'll feel better soon,' Aristotle reiterated, helplessly. This sounded like nonsense. But I was passing into a calm indifference to my fate. Indeed, had someone announced to me that I would die within the next hour it would have seemed like news not of the first importance. The wind being from the west, and no land to interrupt it, we sped along faster and encountered more waves. I gazed fascinated at the running of the sea, the marble hardness of the top of the water and the ripples and white foam from the oars breaking and casting the water away and the boiling white tips of the waves and the strange patterns swirling in the lacy aftermath of the lively foam – all before my eyes like a dream or nightmare that will never end save with blessed death that comes to all . . .

'Hold on to him, Phokon!' Aristotle commanded. And Phokon grasped me firmly lest I slip over the side as I was retching my poor heart out once again.

At last I was somewhat better, and could lie back in the boat again, shivering and looking at the blue sky. I took water from a cup (not to contaminate the water-skin). The little girl looked at me with pitying eyes.

'You are *very* poorly,' she said. My performance had evidently impressed her. 'I'm poorly sometimes too.'

'Tush, Philokleia, don't bother the gentleman,' said her grandfather.

'Not a bother,' I said weakly.

'It's true, you know, Father,' said the child's mother. 'For you know sometimes we have not been able to keep a thing down her. I am glad this sea doesn't seem to bother her. Indeed, Philokleia has not been coughing as much since we came upon the water, I think?'

'Possibly,' said grandfather Hermippos.

'I am sorry to hear that the little girl is sickly,' said Aristotle. 'What precisely may be the matter?'

'She has trouble fetching enough breath at times,' said the grandfather. 'Her breathing is laboured, and she hangs down her head with the effort to get air. Her breath makes strange noises in her chest, and she coughs a good deal.'

'And when Philokleia has one of the worst spasms, then she will puke.' The mother seemed so interested in the little girl's case that she omitted the formality of her veiled state. Indeed, with all of us so cheek-by-jowl the strictness of a woman's quarters was harder to maintain. 'Sir' — she turned her veiled head to Aristotle — 'are you a doctor? Can you do something for her perhaps?'

'I am a physician in a sense, though not a public practitioner,' said Aristotle. 'Does the child cough blood?'

'Oh, no.'

'And is the coughing and the labour in getting breath worse in certain seasons?'

'Indeed, yes. When the summer comes and the dust flies around Laurion, or in the winter when the worst of the rains and fogs come. When the smoke from the smelters blows over us.'

'Then there is reason for much hope,' said Aristotle. 'This is an asthma, and the condition might be cured or at least alleviated by change of air and water. You are going to Kos?'

'Precisely so,' said the old man. 'On the child's account. We hope the island of Hippokrates and the doctors there may do something for her.'

'You could hardly do better,' said Aristotle. 'And perhaps the young lady is hungry right now, and would do us the honour of sharing some of our provisions? Are you hungry, my child?'

'Oh yes, I am,' said little Philokleia with confidence, and she deigned to take a barley cake from Aristotle's hand. 'Say "thank you" to the gentleman,' her mother commanded, but Philokleia had already said 'thank you' like a perfectly well-bred child. She ate the flat barley loaf with visible pleasure, though she declined anything else at present. Aristotle and Phokon and Parmenion regaled themselves on barley loaves, cheese, olives and some dried fruit. The sight of other people eating made me feel less than sturdy. I tried to distract myself, but it was hard to know where to look. The flapping sail, the moving mast, the rising and falling waters – all of these were productive of unease. I felt some slight mean satisfaction in finding that the boy Sosios belonging to the newcomer Philokhoros was seized with internal distraction and misery as I had been before.

The others ate – all those who cared to – and sat about in postures of relaxation, in so far as our cramped quarters would allow it. In a calmer moment the sailors rigged us up our awning again to protect against the midday sun, and we flew along, our hair and cloaks (and, in the case of the lady, her veil) blowing in the breeze. Doris' dog now yapped every now and then to let us know it was alive, though it seemed at first to have been astounded by its change of condition. Doris promised to muzzle it, tying its jaws together so it could not bark but only whine. She pitied the animal as she did so, and sat beside it, throwing it a word now and then.

'Going well,' said the sailor. 'The wind favours us. Look, to the south you can see the islands.'

I looked drearily but could descry only the faintest smudges of blue against the lighter blue of sky.

'We're lucky in the wind,' said the captain. 'This time of year you can get the choppy Etesian winds, or even a sudden fierce Boreas, roaring like a bear out of the north –'

'Really?' the grandfatherly Hermippos exclaimed. 'I should have thought the wind from the north was for winter. Surely this is the best season for travelling by sea?'

'Not saying it isn't – though the best month is last month. The Etesiai rule the dog-days. Now, on land you'd welcome such a wind as a cooling breeze, but at sea the north-west winds can stir up the waters something fearful, chopping up the waves so you cannot land. Not uncommon in the Kyklades in summer. Just occasional, there's a hot wind from the south, from Africa – I've known it to bring sand with it and fling it on the water and the ships.'

'Yet,' said Aristotle, 'I have travelled these waters before, and we seem to be making good time at present, with little to complain of. Calm sea, good breeze and pleasant day.'

'Right,' said the sailor. 'Our good captain here, he makes wise use of both rowers and sail. Saves the rowers. And he gives us proper breaks too.'

It was true. Two rowers were off at any given time, save when coming into or leaving a port. These two usually slept or at least lay full-length in the hold. As the working rowers were each at their oar and had to use energy and breath for their rowing, they could join in conversation only in short bursts. They were not held back by any shyness, it struck me. And they were not subservient to the captain or to us. For all this talk of calm sea and pleasant breeze, I lay there in a stupor, with the water boiling and rioting below my head.

As evening approached we made landfall of a kind – an island or islet heaving into our view.

'There's where we'll spend the night,' said the captain. 'We can beach the boat when we've caught our supper. Now boys, fish!'

The two sailors at the back put up their oars. One reached for a net and the other for a fishing hook. Soon they were using all their skill to get the fish out of the sea and into our boat, encouraged by the other rowers, who grinned and expressed envy or disparagement. I gathered the men took it in turns to engage in this pastime which also meant supper. The two sailors were crafty at the work, and we arrived in the small deserted harbourage with enough creatures of the deep to feed us all. Not that I was going to need very much feeding, but I was delighted to step on solid ground again. So was the slavewoman's dog, which was allowed to run – or rather to limp – around a bit, attached to the end of a long rope, which the stumbling Doris faithfully held.

'Here's the oil, men,' said the captain, tossing his sailors a jar of oil for ablutions, and the sailors took their strigils and scraped away the dirt, sea spray and salt sweat of their day. They romped about a bit as they did so, laughing. It was like being in a gymnasium. (The women were made to sit aside and not look.) Clean and refreshed, these sailors quickly created a fire from their well-defended firepot, and used their neat galley to cook us all a meal of fresh seafood. We sat on land, on pieces of cloth strewn about the beach and boulders, and took our meal – or at least the others did – in relative comfort. The night was mild, and the shore sandy enough to make for easy sleeping.

The next day went as that first day had done, although now I was much better and able to sit up and converse, and even to begin to eat like other people. Again the sailors (a different pair) went a-fishing over the boat's side, and again we landed on an island for dinner and a night's free lodging. I was hungry by this time and took full advantage of the fish the men had caught. As I looked at my sea bass with its row of sharp teeth and its reproachful grilled eye, I thought: 'This morning this fish intended to eat with those teeth, and not to be eaten'. Had I fallen into the ocean when I was sick, this sharp-toothed creature could have eaten me. It seemed strange that I had won.

'You see,' said the sailor to me – the one who had spoken to me at Sounion – 'you see the beneficence of Poseidon to us!'

'You would pay a fortune for such a fish dinner in Athens,' chimed in his rowing companion. 'The area around Peiraieus is nearly fished out. Poor little tiddlers in the markets at high prices.'

'And think,' continued the first sailor, 'how much harder it is to find food on a land journey, and how easy here. The gods are gracious. This is a good life, the life on the sea, for free men.'

'You are all free men,' I observed. It was plain that, though stripped for action, none of them carried any of the badges of slavery. Nor did the captain insult or beat them. Moreover, they could not have used the oil and strigils had they not been free, slaves being forbidden to engage in gymnasium exercises or to cleanse themselves in that noble manner.

'Certainly we are free!' exclaimed my friend of Poseidon's temple, with some indignation. 'I worked for the navy – we were manning the ships for Alexander when he transported all those troops to Asia. We are free Athenian citizens, who fight for their country.'

'But you did not fight as a soldier,' I mused.

'No, sir. We are all poor men. You must know you can be a soldier for Athens only if you can afford your own sword, shield and helmet – it's too expensive for many men. We sailors can work with our own bodies merely – and an oar costs three drakhmai.'

'Not so cheap, neither,' his mate stuck in. 'Three days' complete pay. If you get paid. And of course in the navy you work for half-pay and don't get paid off till the end – *if* you're still alive.'

'But it's possible to buy your oar,' said the first sailor. 'It was our volunteering to row and fight against Persia that saved Athens – and made it impossible to deny us our full place as citizens. Where would Athens be without her naval power? And it is a good life, for any man curious to see the world and not wishful to live his life in the clay of the field.'

'How strange,' I responded, really struck by this. I had always thought of rowing as the condemnation of the poorest of men, a bitter, tough job which anyone would avoid who could. 'You have such a hard life at sea, too,' I mused. 'I should think you would soon get enough of it. Like Odysseus, who was glad to walk into the hinterland until he found people who could not recognise what an oar was and thought it was a winnowing fan.'

'I know the *Odyssey*, too,' said my sailor. 'And I think that is a ridiculous tacked-on story about King Odysseus. What would *he* ever need a winnowing fan for? He's not going to work like a peasant on the threshing-floor, separating the grain from the chaff. No, he was a king, the ruler of Ithaka. As a king, he knew how to sail and row and swim. Good Odysseus was a *nautes*, like ourselves. Now, things like hoeing and winnowing are dull hard work – hard and sweaty. And you just stand there and *stand* there – you don't get anywhere. Whereas, here's me – at my oar I pull and off I go!'

'An interesting view,' said Aristotle.

'Always somewhere to go, always something to explore. New things to see. And it's good exercise,' the sailor added, turning to me. 'Sir, you should try it some time on this voyage for the fun of the thing. We sailors, we're the backbone of Athens now, for we make it possible for all the rest of you to send and receive goods. Here we've got not only yourselves – all of you wanting to get somewhere – but we have the cargo of olive oil. So the rich people of Mykonos, Delos and Rheneia can sop their greens in the best oil of Attika!'

'There is truth in that,' said Aristotle. 'It may be that such wide commerce is going to be of increasing importance. The opening of the navy to the poorer citizens has made many more men skilled in seamanship. The bad thing is that it takes them away from their country, and from settled living on the land. Your work is hard, but I dare say you will never find yourselves workless.'

'Aye, I'm bringing up my son the same,' said the *nautes*. 'War or peace, he should do well enough. Now that

Alexander has disbanded most of his big war fleet, there's more than enough really big ships going begging. It's possible to fit one up and start a passenger and freight service, carrying three or four hundreds of people in one ship, all the way from Syrakousai in Sikilia, say, to Byzantion. In a few years, mark my words, we'll have a shipping service for travel the like of which you've never seen before. Best for my son to stay independent. I'm hoping him and me can get a boat of our own. Even a small boat gets passengers. You don't have to have one of those great hulks that carries hundreds of people, or many talents' weight of goods. People will always have reasons to move across the waters.'

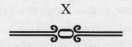

X

Delos

The next day was much like that first day on the ocean, and I was less and less disturbed by the motion of the boat. Again we plunged through the waves and stopped at an island, where we ate outdoors and slept on the ground beneath the stars. I was curiously reminded of my childhood, and how happy I was when the hot weather came and the whole family moved outside to the yard, or up to the roof, to sleep. That was when my father was alive, and even before the birth of Theodoros, when my father was merry and would tell stories as we lay in the dark. Now I was a man, travelling far from my family, but those were the same stars, brighter and more luminous here than in Athens.

'We're making good progress,' the captain told us all. 'Winds and currents have favoured us. To oars, men, and here's for the taverns of Mykonos and the girls of Rheneia!'

I took a short turn at rowing, just to have something

novel to do, when we were in what the sailor told me was 'a mild patch' of sea. I still got my oar stuck in the wave from time to time (to the amusement of the sailors) as well as hitting my knee and then, strangely, my chin, with the handle of the oar. Yet I began to see the attraction of contributing to the motion, and at least I did not commit the major crime of a rower and lose an oar. All morning, we rowed while the wind was wrong; later the sail bellied above us, but it had to be taken in. At dusk we were still in a waste of waters.

'Make a push,' the captain said. 'Safe enough from rocks hereabouts, and the moon will help us – take spells, lads, and we'll push on till morning.'

So we did not land anywhere, but went on and on through the darkness. Not an absolute darkness, for the moon rose eventually and stayed with us for a long time, throwing her white track upon the sea. When you got used to her light, it was almost like day. Beside her shone another of the heavens' great wanderers, bright above us, seeking its reflection in the waters. It glowed amid thousands of gold and silver stars. We went on climbing hills of water, up and down, some of us sleeping and some of us watching. The sailors took it in turns to sleep; each pair would fall into slumber almost as soon as they set down the oars and lay down. The little girl lay quiet in her mother's lap and Miltiades snored, but Aristotle and I watched with pleasure the great calm and blazing beauty of the sky.

When morning dawned the view had changed. The great golden sun cautiously began to show itself, first as a thin silver and then as a gold bar, and then the eastern clouds were streaked with light and burst into radiance.

And within that light I saw in the distance, but not a far distance, what seemed a host of islands, all rimmed and flowing with gold. The new light bursting out of the East poured over these islands, and they, like happy isles in some ancient tale, almost sang in the morning of their refreshed and golden beauty. It was as if one were always going to come home here, and had always been home here, and there could be no place more welcoming.

'The first of the Kyklades,' said the captain cheerfully. 'Fine sight, eh? The big one to the left is Andros, then you can make out Tenos just beyond, and Syros to your right. All these islands of the Kyklades, the Big Circle, are like pieces of a great wheel going around Delos. We'll keep Syros on the right as we head for Delos.'

'Can there be anything more lovely?' I said to Aristotle, as we watched the sun rise together. 'It is as if everything were gold, including the sky itself.'

'Yes – the fine effect of colour, which is the manifestation of light. Such a sight as this,' he added thoughtfully, 'proves my theory that many great objects in nature, perhaps all, are not solid and indivisible but transparent.'

'What do you mean?'

'Well, you know that the sky or the sea are not one colour. Each changes all the time – that is the work of light on them. What we want to see, what our eyes search for, is the visible, which we know only as colour of some kind – or as darkness, deprivation of visibility. The eye searches for the visible, and hates being confronted with the invisible only, with impenetrable and indivisible darkness. Colour is bestowed by light. Water and air are not coloured in themselves, but they let the light through.

Or they let the light happen, because fire or something like it is present within the transparent object. Objects, which are diaphanous, make themselves actual through light.'

I was dazed by this. 'You mean that the sky is not blue but has blueness as a result of the light?'

'Quite so – and certainly the sky is not always blue. Look at it now!'

And indeed the sky was white and gold and crimson at that moment.

'Air, like water, is the splendid medium of colour, the great transparency. We live in a transparent world, Stephanos, constantly changing, mutable in manifestations of constant light – though whether light is just the emanation from something else, like the sun, or whether it is a function or activity within things, I am not at all sure. But I tend to believe that light is not enclosed in any body, not even the sun. I am most inclined to believe that there is a divine fire in the universe, in which all living things share. After all, in so far as we are living beings we retain an original heat.'

Hearing him changed my sense of being, disconcertingly. It was as if I now saw myself within a translucent crystal. Everything seemed too changeable to be comfortable – nothing solid but all interfused with or emanating the light that made all objects change. If everything were diaphanous, a veil through which something else pierced, then all things seemed less substantial.

'I don't see,' I said hesitantly, 'how we can feel easy in such an idea of things. Why, what you say seems to take away the solidity of substance. Your world is shifting and restless. It is hard to see exactly, hard to measure and define, if everything keeps changing.'

'Good, Stephanos. It *is* hard to see exactly. Yet we are creatures who *must* see, who long to see, who search always for the visible – and the visible is the world of great transparencies and modulations.'

'This seems different from what you usually talk about,' I thought, remembering the catalogue of plants and animals and the good workaday shelves and tables in the Lykeion. 'All the things you talked about before, things you collect – plants and molluscs. Are they an order or a disorder?'

'Oh, an order – and a great one. There is Mind in the universe, Stephanos. I feel it – as we felt it last night watching the stars and planets, and now watching the light burst over us and all this wheel of islands coming into glorious colour. Everywhere there is Intellect – manifest both in order and energy. I told you plants and molluscs do not make ideas, nor form. We have the privilege of our own minds which participate actively in this great ordering. The mind is notable for two activities. First, it *becomes* all things – you become those islands you are looking at. That is the human mind of the individual, subject to disease and death. But Mind also is more active – it *makes* everything, makes all things as a poet makes his poem. Mind is the maker of what is. So mind or intelligence – even in you, in me, in this captain here – is like light. Light is activity making possible colours into actual energies, what we call real colours. Mind – what we call intelligence – is in essence an activity and not a *thing*. As Light is an activity and not a thing.'

My own senses and intellect were reeling from this

passionate and beautiful and very puzzling discourse taking place within the midst of the wheel of light. It was as if a prophet of Apollo, or Apollo himself, had spoken to me in some strange place in a corner of the dawn.

Fortunately, perhaps, the dawn completed itself and the sky settled into blue and the day became more normal. The sailors toiled and sweated, the little girl wanted the pot, the passengers prepared their breakfast, and the ship drove on. I had expected that the sailing would get easier as we got in among the islands, but that was not the case. 'Wind's changed!' grumbled the captain. And it had – some wind was now coming from the north, and pushing us about in an uncomfortable way. We proceeded a little more slowly and spent that night in a port at the tip of Tenos. The next day we made our way along the coast of Tenos, sitting under our awning under a hot sky. Directly under the coast of the island the going was easier, but then we broke free of Tenos and were headed for Mykonos. As we were in the open water, the wind blew ever more strongly. 'Etesian,' the captain explained resignedly. Small choppy waves fretted on top of the ocean. Seasickness became a real possibility again, and some of us succumbed. I did not – not quite. The breeze off the sea mitigated the heat a little. Then the wind became gusty, and the sailors began to mutter about a possible storm.

'Get that stuff out of the way,' said the captain with a contemptuous look at our awning. 'Can't have that flapping about like an old lady's laundry!'

We had to crouch under nothing in particular as the spray began to shoot up over the side of our little ship. The waves swelled and seemed to be coming from two directions at once.

'Oh cannot we make it to land?' implored the little girl's grandfather. 'The land seems so near us!'

'That's a landlubber for you!' said the first oarsman.

'Yes,' said the captain. 'Landsmen always think the danger lies in the waves, and safety in the shore. Whereas more often than not it's quite the other way – the shore has rocks, which are more dangerous than tempests, and the wave'll do ye no harm at all. And if you just *look* at Mykonos you'll see what I mean about rocks.'

I did. Mykonos seemed to be nothing but great brown boulders.

'They say,' said Miltiades, 'that the giants that Herakles killed are buried on Mykonos, and that the stones are their weapons. Either that, or the stones were put on the island to hold the giants down and keep them from rising again.'

The little girl wanted to hear more about Herakles and the giants, so we beguiled her and ourselves by telling the story with as many elaborations as we could. I could see the captain was troubled, principally by the lateness of the hour, when landfall seemed so treacherous. But at last, with a shout of triumph, he got us into a cove on the south coast of Mykonos, where he could rest the vessel on a sandy beach. 'We'll take you to Delos tomorrow, if the sea's right,' he said, 'and then on to somewheres for the night, but we must come back to Mykonos harbour to deliver our oil next day, before we go on.'

Provisions were slender that night. 'No good trying to fish here,' said one of the sailors. 'Too late – and the sea around Delos is bad for fish. Might as well go a-fishing in an old dry pot. Plenty of fishermen around, but running passengers is half their work.'

We slept well, however, in the ship or on the beach, unperturbed by the wind, which abated towards dawn.

In the morning we travelled the short distance to Delos, birthplace of Apollo – the short and choppy distance. We strained our eyes as we drew along the skinny brown island to catch first sight of the great Temple of Apollo and the sacred precincts of Delos. Soon we were skimming into the Sacred Harbour, with quantities of other shipping, and beyond the orchard of masts and prows we could see the marble pillars of the graceful temples.

We stepped off the boat on to the mole and walked to shore. We had to look smartly about to find how to get through the crowds. The area near the boat-landing stage was an area of markets, even a slave-market. Directly in front of us, in a temporary enclosure, a group of naked men and two naked women ran wearily around in the heat, in a perpetual circle. Thus they could be throughly inspected by prospective – and critical – purchasers. Behind this scene was a jumble of small shops, and then some grander houses. Behind these again stretched the brown and boulder-strewn hill of Kynthos. A slender river course ran down its slopes, but the stream was a mere trickle or suggestion in the heat of high summer.

'The island is not green and beautiful as I imagined,' I said to Aristotle. 'It seems harsh and brown and dry.'

'Not surprising in high summer, Stephanos. But Delos was always small and dry. Indeed, you remember in the "Hymn to Apollo" the goddess Leto herself comments on the fact when she comes there, but adds that sacrifices to her divine son will ensure sustenance for the future populace of Delos.'

'And so Artemis and Apollo were born here. But their mother wouldn't have come to Delos if she could have gone anywhere else,' said Parmenion, unexpectedly joining in the conversation. It was miraculous! Parmenion had began to speak like a rational being, as soon as we set foot on Apollo's island. I was astounded, but Aristotle replied in normal soothing tones.

'True, as the story says it was Hera's jealousy that chased Leto from place to place when she was great with Zeus' child. Only rocky Delos would receive her – some say because Delos was Leto's own sister, turned to stone and wandering in the sea.'

'And Delos was a wandering island then, but Zeus made it stable, tied to columns of adamant. There's an excellent poem by Pindar that goes something like that, but I cannot recall it,' I contributed. 'A very holy place. And holy Delos has been a part of Athens in a way, since the Delian League was founded after the Persian wars.'

'True,' said Miltiades. 'Athens was the leader of that League, and the Treasury of the Delian League was taken to Athens. You must not imagine everyone here in the Kyklades was pleased about that! Delos is a centre of the Aegean, and a port for every ship from the east, even from Thrake and the Black Sea beyond.'

'I can see by the amount of shipping here in the harbour,' I observed, 'how much commerce there must be here.'

'Indeed. The island is well furnished for men of commercial interests, not just for pilgrims. Some of the best buildings you see are *leskhes* – club houses for traders. Here we can meet with men of the Ionian coast and the islands and sell our marble. Not that trade is as good these days as it was, because of the war.'

'Come, men,' said Aiskhines. 'We make our obeisance to Apollo and then we can look for provisions and a place to rest. But who will guard the ship?'

'I will,' said Philokhoros. He cast a glance at the Sacred Harbour without too much interest, his profile exquisite against the background of temple. 'I have seen Delos before,' he explained. 'It's not a place very rich in entertainments. I'll stay by the ship. And little Sosios will keep me company.' Little Sosios the slave looked rather wistfully towards the bright buildings and the throng of people.

'Good, then,' said Aiskhines 'We shall let all off who are going ashore, and then we'll take the vessel to the other harbour at the Bay of Skardana around the point. It is less crowded. We sailors should make haste. It is decreed by long custom that sailors coming to Delos should give thanks here. And those who have made a vow and are saved from storm and wreck must whip themselves before the Horn Altar. So let's be off.'

The passengers who wished to see the temple disembarked at the Sacred Harbour, leaving Aiskhines and his men to pilot our ship around the point to the next haven. Once on land, we stopped to gape a while, and then turned left and began to wander slowly up the broad marble way, drawn to the beauties of the great Sanctuary. We passed the Propylaia, the beautiful entryway, and came upon the ancient House of the Naxians. We knew what it was, because a man of Naxos was boasting to his pilgrim companions of the ancient beauty of the place. 'Probably the original temple,' he proclaimed. 'Note the beauty and antiquity, and the pleasing design of the lovely interior colonnade. Naxos marble. Now on the north side you will see the colossal statue of Apollo, a magnificent and ancient work. *All* marble of Naxos.'

'You are patriotic today, my friend Aristodamos,' said Aristotle in a teasing and affectionate tone of voice.

The tall bearded man who had been acting as a guide whirled about and saw Aristotle. 'My friend!' he said, throwing his arms about him. 'At last you have arrived! I got your message – of course you are coming to visit me in Naxos, with all your party.'

'That would be a great honour,' said Aristotle, turning to introduce us formally – all but Miltiades who had gone his own way. At this moment the captain rejoined us, and was introduced also.

'Pleased to make your acquaintance sir,' said Aiskhines. 'Me and my men will be getting on, as we should first make an acknowledgement at the Horn Altar. We already took the boat around to the Bay of Skardana and we will meet you there later. Little harbour, nearer the Sacred Lake, the pool they call "The Hoop". Before dusk falls we'll need to find a place to doss down tonight. Would you, sir, wish to go to Rheneia? Delos lodgings are high-priced – not that they aren't bad on Mykonos too.'

'Rheneia sounds best,' said Aristotle. 'I don't think we will try to stay overnight on Delos. Expensive, as you say, and very crowded.'

'It *is* very crowded,' admitted Aristodamos. 'I have been staying with a friend whose house is packed full. I am leaving today for Naxos, so I cannot offer hospitality for this night, to my great regret. You will easily find space in Rheneia. Please promise, however, friend Aristotle, that tomorrow, and no later, you and your party will set out to visit me in Naxos.'

'That sounds agreeable,' said Aristotle. 'I accept with pleasure. All of us – my student, my friend Stephanos here, my slave and I – we shall be grateful, if you can take us in.'

'A great pleasure,' said Aristodamos. 'I live up in the hills of Naxos, so I shall send someone to the waterfront to conduct you.'

'I suppose,' I suggested, 'that Delos is so crowded because there cannot be many houses here – not since the Purification. When, in order to keep Delos and the home of holy Apollo from the plague, Athens removed all the ancestral tombs to Rheneia, and the people left Delos and had to settle in Rheneia.'

'Yes,' said Aristodamos. 'And it is forbidden to be born or to die on Delos.'

'That *does* seem hard,' I said. 'A woman may know that she is pregnant, and by taking thought avoid the place. But what man or woman can tell certainly when he or she will die? I suppose it was a necessary purity, for Apollo's sake.'

'And,' added Aristotle, with a smile, 'it is certainly a good way to keep settlers at bay. For human settlements have a great deal of birth and death in them. If Athens wanted total control, she could have found no better scheme.'

'How *do* people contrive not to die here?' I asked curiously.

Aristodamos laughed. 'Well, of course only the healthy dare to come – and most women don't stay on Delos. There are a few workshops and so on. Lots of visitors.

The only people who try to stay are traders, men in the prime of life, who can afford club-house prices at the leskhes of various associations. But if a visiting gentleman gets flushed, or pale, or has a cough, we spirit him away at once, you may believe!'

'So it is a healthy place – by law,' said Aristotle, smiling.

'Yes, you might put it like that. Excellent for the slave market! No slave-monger would dare to bring here for sale a slave in truly poor condition, for fear he or she might die on this island and get the slave merchant into terrible trouble for sacrilege. "Bought in Delos" is, you might say, a warrant of soundness. Uncommonly fine, is it not? I hope you are struck by the place?'

'Oh, yes, wonderful,' I said. I could not count on Parmenion to say anything, and he did not, though a comment from him would have been appropriate.

'You should know that the original foundation of Delos in its glory is really Naxian,' said Aristodamos. 'I know it very well. Come along with me, then, and see the beauties of the place. Here is the Stoa of the Naxians.'

I had to admit it was an impressive building, looking out over the sea. There is a colonnade on two side wings facing the sanctuary. The area in front of it is full of votive offerings.

'And here is something you will like, Stephanos,' said Aristotle. 'Here is an Athenian monument – the bronze Palm Tree dedicated by Nikias, the Athenian general, over eighty years ago. Made in Athens.'

We continued in a leisurely way, looking at the sights, strolling past the Stoa of the Naxians, to the Artemision in honour of Apollo's sister and the temple or temples of Apollo. There is an old one built in the time of Peisistratos and a new one – the Temple of the Athenians and not at all Naxian. It is very grand, made of Pentelic marble from Attika, and has seven statues and a great bronze statue of Apollo. As well as all these temples, there are numerous old and charming public buildings, the Bouleuterion of the Delians and the Prytaneion, since Delos had the appurtenances of a state.

'Now,' said Aristodamos, 'here is one of the great sights of Delos, as we turn from the sanctuary of Apollo towards the other harbour at Skardana. Here is the Avenue of Lions – all carved in Naxian marble. A sight of which you must have heard! They form a kind of guard to the "Hoop" or Sacred Lake, opposite.'

Indeed, there is what first appears an endless row of ferocious lions, to startle the visitor. These carved beasts are very ancient and very odd. They are all in the same posture but each one is different – you can see details of their ribs, their manes and tails. They roar in their silent marble power, above the stillness of the Sacred Lake, which I thought the most beautiful and moving thing in the loveliness of Delos. There are birds and the soft rustle of trees and rushes, and the gentle sound of little ripples of sweet water – so unlike the thunder of the sea-waves. And beside the lake there are real palm trees – one great and beautiful one always called 'the Tree of Leto'.

'For as you know,' said Aristodamos, 'the goddess Leto had a terrible birthing. Hera kept the goddess of childbirth from coming to her aid, so her womb would not open. Leto was in labour for nine days and nights, and she held to the palm tree in her pain, until she was delivered of the Holy Twins. Immediately the island was flooded with golden light and water and beautiful birds and flowers!'

'So the island then properly became *Delos* – that is "visible",' said Aristotle. 'You see how well that fits in with my theory about light and transparency, Stephanos. This is the visible place of the birth of invisible light. Light that makes itself known through the appearance of other things, and gives colour and what we call beauty to things of earth.'

'This island, then,' said Parmenion thoughtfully, 'should be called "the place where everything becomes clear". I wish it would!'

We were still looking at the swans and taking a cool rest under the green trees by the Sacred Lake when a well-grown young man came through the trees. His hand was held above his brow to ward off the sun and assist his eyes, as if he were looking intently for some object. His face brightened when he saw us.

'Good sirs,' he said, approaching, 'if I may be so bold as to address you. I am the slave of a lady called Kardaka, who is mistress of a poor lame slavewoman called Doris. I think one of you gentlemen is Aristotle? Of Athens?'

'I am he,' said Aristotle.

'My mistress knows you kindly urged the captain to let Doris on board your ship. She – the lady Kardaka – is very earnest in her desire to speak with you about this matter and thank you in person. As a lady cannot come searching for gentlemen, I must beg you to meet her in one of the pilgrims' rooms here. Would you be so kind?'

'Well, that was a trifle, and we have other engagements –'

'Oh sir! Please do not make me go back with a refusal!'

He spread his palms wide and looked at us in a beseeching manner. 'It will not take long, and my mistress will be so pleased. And she would likely take it out on my back if I were to fail of my errand.'

'Ah, well . . .' Aristotle arose resignedly, and I with him.

'This mistress Whoever with the unlikely name must have a terrible temper,' said Aristodamos.

'Oh, gentlemen, don't be harsh. She is a kind lady in the main, though a foreign sort – a freedwoman of part Phoenician stock, she says herself. Who knows, maybe her name is Karshadasht in her old home? But no lady likes her will crossed. Come, let me guide you – it is on the other side of the Sacred Harbour.'

The adroit slave manoeuvred us swiftly through the flux of crowds coming from the harbour and conducted us back towards to the foot of Mount Kynthos, where there were some houses and hostelries, not as grand as the temples or the leskhes on the other side near the Sanctuary. He took us into one of these low brown buildings, a hostelry of sorts. 'No need to trouble the boy or the slave,' he decided for us. 'They can take refreshment just outside, in the shade. But I shall ask you two gentlemen to come in here.' Leaving Parmenion and Phokon without, this bustling slave took us into one of the rooms evidently available (at a price) to allow travellers and persons on business the opportunity to rest and enjoy refreshment and conversation.

The room was enlivened by tapestries and cushions, and some fine cups and a wine pourer on a low table. The slave busied himself in setting up a sheet of fine fabric to divide the apartment. In a moment we understood that this was a drapery of propriety, as a tall female glided in and slipped behind the sheet. 'The lady Kardaka!' the slave announced. Propriety's divisive curtain was almost transparent, so we could still make out the femininity of this lady's bust, and the crocus-coloured wrap of silk draping over her white garments, so sweetly flowing in their soft folds that they must have been of the best linen.

'So. Sir Aristotle,' the lady Kardaka began. 'Pray, gentlemen, make yourselves at ease. I shall sit, and you do the same.' She sat upon the backless chair the attentive slave gave to her, while we too sat on similar chairs on our side of the thin partition. 'Give them something to drink, for pity's sake,' she ordered and the anxious male slave poured us wine and water, and offered sweet almonds.

'Shall I speak to them for you, madam?' queried this assiduous servant.

'No,' she replied. 'Retire to the door, and wait!' The obedient man disappeared.

'If you don't mind, gentlemen,' she said, 'I dispense with passing my words on to a slave to repeat to you, as it makes everything so slow. You should drink slow, however, it is good for the body in the middle of such a hot day. Eat a little, drink gently, and recreate.' We tried to do as she wished, as politeness demanded. 'I can see you are impatient to be off. Who can blame you? This room is warm and stuffy, while you have the beauties of Delos to see. Have you been up Mount Kynthos?'

'No, we haven't,' I replied shortly.

'You should really, once it gets cooler. The Inopos river runs down from that mountain, and how it feeds the Sacred Lake you will note. There's a fine breeze up there and you can view many islands from the top. Many, many persons go up to see the shrine of Herakles. But do wait till the sun abates a little.' She fanned herself gently with a piece of cloth.

'*So* hot,' she said. 'That is why I leave Peiraieus at this time of year. Too hot. Athens – *much* too hot. Here at least there are sea breezes. I am staying in Rheneia, as you have, I think, heard from my woman Doris. I was anxious to have my Doris come to me after she had closed up my house in town. We give you hearty thanks for your kindness to her. I hope there is some way that we can make recompense.'

'No recompense is necessary,' said Aristotle. 'It was a mere trifle. I hope you and your slave are well satisfied, and we can take our leave –'

'Sir – Oh, pray do not cut me off like that! In what have I offended?' The lady Kardaka opened her eyes so very wide that we could see them through the modest curtain. She ran her fingers through her long coiled hair. 'Gratitude is – I assure you my gratitude is *most* sincere. Anything for you, could I do it – *any thing* in the world – I would.'

This woman reminded me of someone. I thought of Antigone, the *hetaira* who came to see Aristotle and then betrayed him. But in figure, form and voice this woman was not very like Antigone. I put down her strange effect to her being part Phoenician from Karthago, as her slave had more than hinted.

'I wished,' said the woman, 'to give you some small recompense, a present, in return for your kindness to Doris. The more as I have another favour to beg of you. I understand you have a friend in Naxos and are going there soon. It is over-bold to ask gentlemen of such importance, but could you please take the ungainly but humble slavewoman Doris to that island with you? She has an errand to do for me in the hinterland of Naxos. It would be such a relief to my mind and hers if she could join your fine ship and trustworthy crew again, and be safely conveyed.'

'I am really not in the business of arranging transport for travellers in the Kyklades,' Aristotle protested.

'Oh, sir, of course it is a great piece of presumption on my part – I will not say on *ours,* for poor little Doris has as much to do with it as her lame dog.' The lady twitched her yellow mantle, shrugging it more firmly upon her shoulders. 'But you must know it is dangerous, not a little, for women to go unprotected, and our reliance on your goodness is very great. Poor Doris will leave you in Naxos. So you will not have to trouble yourself further. Her passage home is our affair.'

'Well, if that is all –' said Aristotle impatiently. He stood up. 'First thing tomorrow, at the Sacred Harbour.'

'Oh, wonderful!' The lady threw up her hands in her joy, letting her mantle slip again. 'Sir, a thousand thanks! Be assured, my poor slavewoman will meet you tomorrow morning in the Sacred Harbour. And with some little gifts for you, as well as materials she is to deliver to one of the houses on Naxos. Of course with the fare for her passage. With your good captain and crew we shall feel so safe. Oh, I am overjoyed!' The lady, shrugging on her mantle once more, arose, bowed deeply to us and glided out of the room, presumably to rejoin her slave steward who would be awaiting her without.

'Tsk, tsk, I seem to be taken as the passengers' steward and friend,' said Aristotle. 'All I can say is, it will not be a great inconvenience. If the slavewoman turns in time, then she goes — and if not, not.'

'There's something odd about these people,' I said.

'They're partly foreign, and I think that always seems odd to you. But must confess, I should not care to mingle with them.'

'I doubt if this Kardaka is any better than she should be. Although I don't think there are brothels on Delos the Holy and Pure!'

'No,' said Aristotle. 'You remember, Philokhoros said there wasn't much in the way of entertainment on this island.'

We wound our way leisurely out of the precinct of lodging houses and towards the path that leads up to Mount Kynthos. Although both Delphi and Delos are sacred to Apollo, most of Delos is as unlike mountainous Delphi as possible, being very flat and almost at sea level. There is only one high place, the hill Kynthos. (Ridiculous to call it a mountain!) I was eager to see the shrine of Herakles and to take in the view, so I persuaded Aristotle and Parmenion to go up with me; Phokon came with us. It is a short climb past a few pretty shrines and little temples to a breathtaking view. Even Parmenion seemed impressed.

'Look! You can see the whole harbour and the temple and everything,' he said, stopping and staring back. This grand view of the whole sacred site made it much easier to understand than it was on first entering the precincts. I could at last see where individual buildings and places were in relation to the others. We could see Rheneia; it has a few trees, and little homesteads, and looks much more like a normal place than did Delos. Turning about I saw many islands around us.

'You are standing at the centre point of the Circle of the Kyklades,' said Aristotle. 'Over there is Paros. Yonder, directly south-east, right in front of you, is Naxos.'

It was very satisfying to be at the still centre of this system of golden islands all wheeling about us. Delos, formerly a wanderer among islands, slipping hither and thither, like a planet in the sky, is now the still centre of the wheel, an ordering point in the midst of a serene order. We lingered, exclaiming at various sights, until we had had enough and trooped down again. The sun was descending the western sky, and if we were going anywhere, even Rheneia, we had to do so by water.

Because of the Avenue of the Lions we were confident of the direction to the other harbour of Skardana, which we had picked out from the height. The modest Inopos runs out of the lake again and into this delightful little harbour, a perfect semicircle surrounded by tight warehouses and good houses belonging to (presumably very healthy) merchants. You cannot see the great Temple of Apollo from here. Skardana seemed nicely normal, with ordinary shops around it. The small beast market is located here, so as not to disturb the sacred precinct with cackling and bellowing. There is a small ancillary slave-market (chiefly for nurses, old women, and so on). Unsold slaves are most commonly not housed in Delos, but put back on board a ship or ferried to a depot in Rheneia or Mykonos; by this time the slave merchants had packed up their merchandise and gone off. Except for a few forlorn sellers of wilting vegetables, nothing much was going on around the harbour.

The prudent Delians had built a mole or quay at Skardena, to prevent crowding of their rather stony beach. This useful structure extends a good way out into the water, on the right side of the harbour; it is covered with large flat stones at the top. We looked for our ship and spotted it away at the far end, moored with its prow to the causeway, not very close to any of the other ships.

We hailed her, but no one answered. Because of the well-built mole, we could walk out and scramble aboard the vessel without difficulty, once Phokon had pulled a rope to make the boat come closer to the mooring-place. But nobody was on board.

'That's odd,' I said. 'I thought Philokhoros was going to be here.'

'No sign of either him nor his slave,' said Phokon, looking in the hold amid the shipped oars, the mast and sail, and some ropes.

'Hey, look at this!' Parmenion cried from the stern. We rushed aft. 'Look – the galley!' He pointed. The tiles of the galley were smeared with crimson blood. Some splashes of blood had stained the wooden structure of the boat itself. More blood than on the head of a dead horse, or on a little monkey skull.

'Murder!' screamed Parmenion. He turned very white, and his body went stiff. Then his eyes rolled up in his head; slowly, he collapsed.

'Throw some water on him, please, Phokon,' said Aristotle. 'I think it is just a faint, not an epilepsy. Tell me if he starts foaming or convulsing.'

'Poor boy, he was getting better, too,' I said.

The shout of 'Murder!' had not gone unheard. Men from a neighbouring boat started to come towards us. And at the same moment, Miltiades appeared.

'Oh, no!' he cried. 'Murder on the sacred island! It is

forbidden to die here! This is terrible – it is a blasphemy! How could you do it, how could you? We shall all be subjected to dreadful penalties!'

XI

Blood at Delos, Flesh at Mykonos

'We don't know that any human being has died here,' said Aristotle. 'Let us look at the evidence.' But Miltiades did not stay to listen.

'I must tell the authorities!' he said, rushing off. Undeterred by Miltiades' precipitous departure, undistracted even by Parmenion's faint, Aristotle calmly proceeded to inspect the galley and the area around it.

'I don't see any signs of a bloody struggle. You must admit it would be very difficult to kill a grown man in this little galley. It's barely big enough to crouch in, certainly not a space for two men fighting. What other signs can we see?' He picked up the small stove. 'Now, what's this I find?' Laughing, he waved a feather above his head.

'Man is "an unfeathered biped", as Plato says. The entities that were killed here today were plumed. See what I found hiding under the stove – an innocent feather. Ah, this place was used for a sacrifice, and this knife *did* cut –

but it was a sacrifice of birds. Chickens – cocks, presumably – sacrificed earlier today. Most likely by some pious sailors.' He laughed again in his relief. Then his face became more sombre.

'But it is true that the blood has been spread around to *look* like murder. See, here. This is where the first blood fell, but instead of lying in drops it has been deliberately smeared around the galley and the deck area. With a sponge, I suppose, squeezed to create drops of blood at appropriate points – at the edge, for example. Made to look as if there were a murder aboard, and a body dropped into the sea.'

'And here,' I pointed out, 'some of Philokhoros' baggage has been smeared with blood too and then thrown under the thwart. As if it had escaped notice when the body was rolled overboard.'

'A nice touch,' said Aristotle. 'It begins to look more like a plot. Had whoever set this scene stolen the baggage or thrown it overboard, anybody looking at the ship might have decided that Philokhoros merely went off on his own, taking his luggage with him. The bloody bag seems got up to make the circumstances look more suspicious.'

'The boy's coming to,' announced Phokon.

'Good. But – oh, the vexation. Now we certainly have to find Philokhoros. I hope both he and his slave are alive and in health, but I have to admit they are not here.'

Aiskhines' broad friendly face, wrinkled with concern, appeared looking down at us over the edge of his ship.

'What is this?' our captain demanded. 'I heard people saying there was a murdered man on a ship from Peiraieus.'

'How quickly word gets out. Remarkable,' said Aristotle drily. 'I believe, good Aiskhines, that no one has been murdered, though some birds have been sacrificed. And their blood has been spread around to look *as if* a murder has happened. Now, have you seen either the slave-boy or Philokhoros since we left the ship?'

'Yes. I came back after going to the Altar. I was anxious to see to the *Eudaimonia,* and be sure it was well moored. Philokhoros was aboard, well and hearty, but worried, he said, because his slave-boy had run off. He thought Sosios must have gone to see the sights. But he asked me to go after the lad, since I knew my way around Delos better and I could identify him.'

'There was no blood spread on the ship then?'

'No – certainly not. I passed by the galley at that time, and I should surely have noticed.'

'I take it you couldn't find the boy.'

'Too true. So I came back to beg the gentleman to search for himself. Now *he*'s gone too, without a word. Strange. I don't usually lose passengers, certainly not in this manner.'

'Are you the captain of this ship?' A man loomed menacingly behind Aiskhines, a man fully dressed in contrast to the skimpy wear of our captain. A man who looked as if authority had sat upon his brow ever since he came of age. 'I am a magistrate of Delos,' he announced almost unnecessarily. 'And I must take you into custody to answer questions about a murder committed here. Disgraceful! I warn you, captain, it will go hard with you, for this is not only a killing but a blasphemy –'

'How do you do?' said Aristotle addressing him from the ship. 'I am glad to meet you, citizen magistrate. The man whose ear you are holding is a citizen of Athens, and is totally innocent of any wrongdoing.'

'Who are you?' enquired the magistrate ungraciously.

'I am Aristotle, a philosopher who dwells in Athens. I am on an embassy for Alexander's deputy, who I know will be obliged to you for any assistance you can render. It is clear to me that no murder whatever took place here. The blood comes from the sacrifice of chickens. An alarm was raised unnecessarily.'

The magistrate breathed deeply. 'I should be glad to think that was the case,' he said in milder tones.

'See for yourself –' Aristotle waved the feather. 'This feather was found under the stove. Blood for a sacrifice has been later smeared about, perhaps accidentally. But I have every reason to believe that no man has been killed. A slave-boy has gone missing – the owner told our captain to look for him. The captain has just returned – meanwhile the slave's owner (an adult citizen) has gone off, probably on his own lawful occasions. But if you could question the neighbouring sailors as to whether they have seen anything, it might be of great help.'

Reluctantly, the magistrate agreed to help to that extent. I could see that he would have preferred either to clap us all into chains, or to go away and do nothing more. This man was not made for complicated exertions. But at Aristotle's prompting, he questioned the sailors on the nearest vessels. One crew was disappointing: they had just come, and had seen nothing until we arrived But two sailors mending nets on a small fishing craft nearby were willing to speak.

'Saw some men aboard – sailors seemingly,' they said. As to what they looked like or whether the sailors on our

ship might have been our own, they were unclear. One of
them said he thought the men had 'a Phoenician look'
(leaving us to puzzle what that might be).

'I suppose,' said Aristotle, 'somebody might have
borrowed this nice tiled galley for a sacrifice. Did you see
a gentleman go off the ship – before then or after?'

The first fisherman was at a stand, but asked a
neighbour in another boat; this man was helpful.

'Yes,' he said calmly, disregarding the magistrate's
scowls. 'I reckon I saw a gentleman leave the ship, in
company with a couple other gentleman.'

'Were they fighting? Quarrelling?'

'Nothing of that sort.'

'When was this?'

'When the sun was still quite high in the sky. The
sacrifice, that must've been done later, when I put out for
a short space. I came back, since I thought I had a passenger as wanted taking to Rheneia, but they didn't show.'

'Well,' said Aristotle, sitting on a thwart and fitting his
fingertips together, 'we have this much to deal with:
Philokhoros tells the captain his boy is gone. Philokhoros
then has the ship to himself for a while. Two other
gentlemen come and conduct him off – without the boy.
Now, the beauty of Delos is that it is so small, and is
surrounded by water. It's not like another place, where a
man can unobtrusively move away on foot or on a donkey.
If Philokhoros is not in Delos, he has certainly gone to
some neighbouring island. To do that, he'd need a boat. So
– if the magistrate would encourage these fine citizens to
help us? They live here, they own small ships, and they or
their acquaintance would recognise and be able to identify
any particular craft.'

And so it proved. One of the fisherman's associates who carried passengers to and from the Sacred Harbour recalled seeing the tall stranger with the beautiful nose, accompanied by two less significant gentlemen, leaving the Sacred Harbour at midday, 'in Nearkhos' boat'. Nearkhos belonged to Mykonos, and his small vessel was not used for long journeys; it was their considered opinion that anyone leaving Delos with Nearkhos must be going to Mykonos.

'An unusually sound deduction,' said Aristotle. 'I suggest we follow it up without loss of time. Good Aiskhines, ready your ship and your men and take us at once to Mykonos harbour. I know you wish to unload your cargo of oil, and there Stephanos and I shall search for Philokhoros. Meanwhile, if the magistrate here would post a notice about the boy Sosios, we shall have done our duty in that direction. And I am sure, sir, that you must be glad to find that your problem has apparently departed from Delos, and that our ship will follow.'

Aristotle was certainly discerning. I thought the magistrate would insist on accompanying us to Mykonos, and make a nuisance of himself with suspicions and questioning. But this dignified personage, so uncomfortably covered with fine hot clothes, and so sorely fatigued with his unusual efforts, was as happy as Aristotle suggested at the prospect of his troubles vanishing to another island. Aiskhines called his men together with the utmost rapidity, and we sailed, our galley and some of the planking still dirty red. Two sailors worked at cleaning it as we went. Parmenion, improved but still silent, lay with his back propped against a thwart, out of the sun. The only other passengers were Aristotle, myself and Phokon.

We worked our way through a slightly choppy sea to the harbour at stony Mykonos. There the crew of the *Eudaimonia* could at last unload their cargo of oil. As their purchasers came down to the dock to receive it, Aristotle and I put our questions to these and other men on the waterfront, eliciting unsatisfactory responses. The number of visitors who had come to Mykonos from Delos during the day seemed phenomenal. Everyone we addressed wanted payment for answering our queries. Not only that, they wanted to bring brothers and cousins and uncles to get paid for answering questions too. Helpful information was lacking. Aristotle decided to cut this procedure short.

'Where,' he asked suddenly, 'is the nearest brothel?'

There was laughter, but ready response. 'The nearest one for respectable men is up there,' said one of the sailors. 'It's the White-Armed Sea-Nymph.'

'I don't want the most respectable one,' said Aristotle rather crossly.

'Well, then,' said the sailor, with great merriment, 'you want the sign of the Naumakhia, with its female keeper Lysis.'

'That is, if you care for pigs,' said his friend. 'You'll nose it – it's got pigpens round it, on the way up that hill.'

With succinct thanks, Aristotle gathered up myself and Phokon, leaving the sailors in charge of the ship – and of Parmenion. We were glad of some directions offered to us by Aiskhines as we worked our way uphill. The town proved labyrinthine and puzzling. 'That's often the case with these island towns,' said Aristotle. 'In some moods they're happy to receive visitors and commerce and in other moods all they can think of is pirates and how to outfox them.'

We found the place readily enough, even in this squalid maze. Like every place in Mykonos it was walled about with the rough local stones supplied in such plenty by the hillsides. Beside the door was a scratched sketch of a sea fight, bearing the name 'Naumakhia'. Crude as the picture was, you could see it was of two ships grappling together, one crew of men with heavy weapons already forcing their way into the enemy vessel. There was an undeniable odour of pig.

Without knocking, Aristotle marched in and we followed. We seemed to fill the place – a low-roofed rather dusty house, with small rooms. The scent of pig grew and blossomed, incessant and familiar.

'Who are you?' A woman of square build with a round face came towards us. She was not very old, but her skin was winkled and grimy. 'Have you an appointment of any kind?' she asked in mincing tones out of keeping with her grimy appearance.

'Alas, no,' said Aristotle. 'We have come looking for a friend who we fear has delayed here too long.'

She cackled. 'Oh, a lot stays for a while longer than they thought,' she replied.

'Perhaps some do. Some may stay for a great deal longer, I fear. But that's neither here nor there. We'll pick up our friend, whose ship is waiting, and be on our way.'

'You seem very cocksure, Citizen Whatnot from Wherever! Who's to say we have any of your fine friends here? We're –'

'Stop! Hush!' I said. 'I hear something.' And I did hear a sound like a low hum or groan.

'Pigs grunting. They do that,' explained the woman contemptuously.

'No – come on!' Acting on impulse I led the way to the back premises, where we were confronted by two contiguous pigpens; or more properly one gigantic pigpen in two parts. The outer wall or perimeter was strongly made of stones (the universal local material). The wall between the two pens was a fence of wood, with a gate in it. In the slightly larger pen, the more eligible residence, partially shaded by a short thatched roof weighted down by stones, two pigs were at home. Although the weather was dry, these animals had been given water to drink and to roll around in, as well as all the slops and sour porridge from the house, and the area was certainly very mucky. Two enormous pigs – boar and sow – glared at us.

These two balls of flesh had been digging in the dirt with their long round snouts, but now they ran back and forth and made a great rumpus. A man stuck his frowsy head out of a little window that looked into this salubrious courtyard and yelled 'Shut up!' Somebody else cursed in a language I did not know. The pigs, undeterred, kept up a great grunting. I moved cautiously around the side of this pen to the next one, the less luxurious residence totally lacking in shade. This enclosure had one inhabitant. Tied neck and heels with a gag in his mouth was our unfortunate travelling companion Philokhoros. His eyes pleaded with me over his nearly invisible fine nose.

'You get out of that-there, or I'll set the pigs on you!' the woman threatened. This was no light menace. I had rather she had said 'dogs' – for dogs you can fight off, but once a pig gets you down you are in trouble. They say pigs will eat you, dead or alive – they're not particular.

'Phokon!' commanded Aristotle.

I did not wait for Phokon, however, as we were not at leisure. I climbed into Philokhoros' filthy pigpen (having first cast off my clothes and sandals). It was like stepping into a bog. The pigs next door were incensed at this invasion of their territory. I could hear their grunts of rage and see their little red eyes glaring fiercely at me, the intruder. They galloped over to me as if to run me down with their sharp hooves, but were fortunately held back by the partition. I saw, however, that the gate in this railing was ingeniously arranged so as to be opened from outside the pen, by a string. It would certainly be possible for a keeper at any moment to admit the angry porkers into the second pen. This fact by no means increased my equanimity or good humour. I grabbed the hapless and bound Philokhoros. I had no knife to cut his bonds with, so I had to treat him as a package, and get him over the stone wall somehow. He helped as much as he could, scrabbling with his poor bound hands and feet, but it was a difficult job; perhaps I could not have accomplished it if Phokon had not stepped in (likewise naked) to my aid. The two of us heaved the grunting Philokhoros over the edge, and started to get over ourselves, just as the lady of the house made good her threat to open the gate of the first pen and let the animals into the second one. They charged around with considerable vigour, hoping to get at us. Happily, we were able to flip over the stone wall just as they made their entry.

Both Phokon and I were dripping with sweat and each of us stank like twenty pigs.

'Well done!' Aristotle clapped his hands, as at a theatre piece. 'Not a pretty scene, but heroic. How do you find yourself now, Philokhoros? Can we get his bonds off?'

Phokon found a rusty implement propped against the wall of a lean-to, and slowly sawed through the ropes that bound Philokhoros. The gentleman's clothes were indescribably filthy and it is better not to imagine what he smelt like. I removed the gag, and he coughed and panted. I expected him to rise to his feet, but he fell back with a groan.

'He won't be able to walk at first, you've got to chafe his legs and get him in better plight,' said Aristotle. 'By the Twelve Gods! He smells abominable! Can we get upwind of him – and the pigs?'

Obviously, we could not depart until we could get Philokhoros into working order. Aristotle tenderly held my clothes and Phokon's to keep them out of the muck that had ruined poor Philokhoros' habiliments.

'We need to find some clothing for this poor fellow,' he said. 'Hey, Mistress! Lysis – if that's your name' – thus he addressed the woman, who was glowering at our success.

'You're in serious trouble for what has happened here. We have friends who are waiting for us outside – we have already consulted the magistrate in Delos about this missing person. It could go very hard with you. I urge you to step smartly and help us. Assist us to carry this man into the cleaner courtyard where we can sluice him – and these other two – with water from your well. And find some clean clothes for this gentleman you have wrongfully imprisoned. At once!'

Cowed, now that her pigs had failed to put an end to our troublemaking, Lysis reluctantly led the way to the small courtyard with the well in it, keeping up a running grumble the while: 'Well-fancy-that-I-don't-know-what-

the-world-is-coming-to.   Peaceful   householders!
Intruders and spies. Nuff-to make-a-body-sick.'

Living in the vicinity of her pigs was enough to make a
body sick, but I didn't say so. We obtained the blessed
water and I was sluiced down, then Phokon, and then the
trembling Philokhoros. The establishment supplied a thin
piece of linen with holes in it for towelling, and I was dry
enough to put on my own clothes once more. Phokon was
soon in a better plight too.

'Now, Madam Pigwoman, where are clothes for this ill-
treated gentleman?'

'Ain't got no clothes. You think I'm an old-clothes
shop, you come to the wrong place.'

'What about the other men who are here – customers
or whatever?'

'Nobody here.'

'There was a man, who shouted at us out of the
window,' I reminded her.

'Just my steward. Having a rest.'

'Perhaps. And perhaps not. An idea occurs to me.'
Before I could divine what he intended, Aristotle darted
into the house, and across the hall – myself following.
'First I'll just have a look,' he said. Rapidly he flung open
the three doors in the passageways, and peered briskly
into each room, checking up on the landlady's statement
regarding current custom. At last he went confidently
into the one remaining chamber, the little room round the
corner, the one looked out on the pigpen. It had nothing
in it but a bed, and there were two heads at the top of the
bed. Without greeting, Aristotle snatched from the foot of
the bed a pile of clothes. At this, the man with the scruffy
frowsy head (who smelt quite ripe himself) roused

himself, raised that head, and began furious and then anguished protestations. His companion muttered something (I didn't catch what, but undoubtedly not complimentary). Aristotle disregarded these objurgations, and turned back with his prize.

'I'm in no mood for conversation. Here you are, Philokhoros. Sorry they don't smell better, but it's the best this hostelry affords.'

The woman screeched in wrath. 'Thieves! Give those straight back! You've no right!'

'I fear it is you who must compensate the unfortunate steward and his dear friend.' Aristotle remained calm. 'As it is really *my* friend who deserves compensation, we will take these clothes in partial payment. You owe him replacement for the garments you have ruined.'

'Don't owe nothing,' she muttered, so low that Aristotle was not obliged to hear her.

'But I must say,' he continued, 'I admire your generous conception of time off for your servants – if that man is really your steward. Happily, the clothes are those of a free person. Get dressed –' he handed his find to Philokhoros – 'and cast the stinking clothes out into the yard.'

Behind us the man in the bedroom still bellowed his rage, and his opinion as to what ought to be our future fate. But evidently he was too modest or too frightened to come and look for us – or else he was restrained by his bed-companion. The landlady subsided into spluttering.

Once Philokhoros was arrayed sufficiently to meet the claims of respectability (if not of elegance), I hoped we would go. Aristotle, however, looking at the rescued man, demanded a drink of water for him. The woman set up a renewed screeching about how much we had cost her.

'We will ask this gentleman how much damage you inflicted on him, a free citizen, and what claims he wishes to pursue in law,' said Aristotle coldly. 'If you cooperate with us, that will be taken as a sign that your complicity in this horrid affair was unwitting or unwilling. Otherwise, we must naturally think you are the chief agent. Or your husband.'

'I – I ain't the chief! And I got no husband!' The woman started to pour water into her cracked cups and began to whimper. 'Respectable widow woman.'

'Really? And really a widow?'

'Well, the same as. My husband left for somewheres a year or two back, he's probably died.' She handed us each some water, and plunked herself down on a stool. 'About yesterday – I did not do anything! Just what the two gentlemen as was with him – his friends, like – said. They said to keep him safe till they came again. *They* put him in the fix he was in, "for his own sake" they said. I thought just 'cause they didn't want the gentleman wandering off, while he was in his cups.'

She looked at us with eyes of elaborate innocence; any child could have seen through this lie.

'That you are not the chief agent in this bad action, that I can believe,' said Aristotle. 'That alone, at the moment. Explain, good sir. Did this woman threaten your life?'

'Oh, I did not! Sir, tell them I didn't!' The woman looked pleadingly at Philokhoros.

'Well, she threatened me with the pigs. And pigs could end one's life,' said Philokhoros. 'But I admit, it's not a story to go down as well in a lawcourt as if ruffians say they have a big sharp knife and will stick it in your ribs.'

'But – what happened to you? You were on board the *Eudaimonia*. And then what?'

'Well, I had a short nap, and woke to find my slave-boy gone off. So I asked the captain to find him. And then two men came to me and said the boy had been decoyed to a brothel here in Mykonos, and they would take me to him so I could buy him back. I suspected extortion, but nothing else, really. We left the ship and walked back round the beach to the Sacred Harbour, and took a ship to Mykonos. But then – when I got to Mykonos harbour – they fed me strong wine. It must have been *very* strong, such as I am not used to. Though it tasted fine. And then they brought me to this place, and we started looking through the rooms, and they offered me more wine, and then – I believe they banged me on the head, for I know I was not conscious for a while.'

'And after that?'

'They tied me up, while I was not awake. And when I came to I heard them making jokes – brothel jokes. About what to do with me – you can imagine. But they told the woman to keep me here until she got further word. She was to keep me bound, and in the pigpen so I could not get free. And the two men went away.'

'Do you know who they were?'

Philokhoros hesitated before replying. 'No. No. At least, I mean I'd *like* to think I could recognise them again. But – no.'

'Yet at Delos you went off with them without question?'

'Well, I had questions, certainly, but they seemed so *sure* they knew where the boy was.'

'Did you see any sign of the boy when you got here?'

'No.'

'Is this Lysis here who calls herself a widow a slavewoman or free?'

He was surprised by the question. '*I* don't know. The men addressed her as if she were a freedwoman. Not of the highest order –'

The woman set up a screeching. 'I'll have you know I am no slave, and he's a dirty rascal who says otherwise!'

'It is a legal matter,' Aristotle said. 'If she were a slave, we could take her forthwith and have her interrogated. But if she is freedwoman, she will have to answer questions in a court of law in due course. To counsel homicide is the same as to commit homicide. If she has been a material agent in making away with the boy, or if she has counselled such making away, and even more if she has provable designs against the life of this man, then she will face the death penalty.'

'No!' cried the woman. She was very intent now, the grumbling reluctance clean gone. 'Oh sirs, don't do this to me! *I* couldn't help it. It was a very rich man who came here at dawn today, a rich man who gave his name and some money.'

Aristotle leaned forward eagerly.

'And his name is?'

'His name is Solon. He told me to expect another party this afternoon. Meaning yourself, sir' – to Philokhoros – 'and the two friends with you. And this Solon before he left in the morning, he gave orders about the pigs and all. And there was no boy, little or big. And *no homicide!*' She was ready to shout her voice out. The veins stood out on her grimy forehead.

'Be calm, or you will do yourself an injury,' said

Aristotle. 'Can you describe this "Solon"?'

'He was a man – like all the others. But cleaner dressed and finely spoken. A good sort of figure. Not tall, really, maybe above the middle height. Not very young, but not old. He spoke like Athenian gentry, is all. That's all I know. Truly.'

'How much did Solon give you?' She blushed and hesitated. 'Come, come,' said Aristotle impatiently, 'we really need to know. It is material to the case.'

'Two hundred drakhs,' she muttered in a low voice. 'He gave one hundred and said there'd be more if he came back and found the gentleman safely stowed – I mean in the pigpen. Nothing worse than that. Just keeping him from harm, that's all.'

'Two hundred drakhs – *merely* for imprisoning someone in a pigpen?' Aristotle turned to me. 'I know prices are high in the islands but this does seem excessive, even for Mykonos. Such a handsome payment might serve as recompense for any number of activities, might it not?'

'In some towns,' I responded, 'that great a sum would pay for several murders. Getting Philokhoros away seems to have been important to whoever bought this service.'

'Yes. Whoever that may be. We need not waste time enquiring for a fellow with the name of the great lawgiver, Solon, often called "the wise man of Athens". So this new "wise man of Athens" deigns to visit this hovel.'

'Why "Solon"?' I wondered.

'Well, among other things, Stephanos, Solon is famous for dividing the populace of Athens into four classes: "the five-hundred-bushel-men" (the Aristos), then the Knights, then the Hoplites and at the bottom the Menials.

And –' with a cautious glance at Philokhoros, who was still cleaning himself – 'this mock "Solon" seems to have classified our friend here with certain domestic animals. About the man who made these arrangements – chief actor or deputy, who knows? – we are entitled to surmise only two things. He is apparently an Athenian, and not poor. Enough of this,' said Aristotle, rising. 'We must be going. Sir, I hope you are able to walk to the harbourage. You, Mistress of Pigs, we shall keep in mind. We can always have your pens searched for human remains. That will give you a pretty reputation, and a good market for your pork! I advise you to be more careful about what favours you do henceforward.'

We got up to go; Philokhoros walked in a wobbly fashion, but he was able to walk. As we made our exit I could not resist looking back at the pigpens and making a childish face at the hoggish twain who glared back at me. 'Chops!' I shouted. 'Sausages! Pig's-trotters stew! Just think!'

We left the foul place and walked gladly back to the harbour where we could savour the clean sea air in our nostrils.

'We didn't see a single girl belonging to that brothel,' I mused.

Aristotle laughed. 'They would smell dreadful. Presumably Lysis is for sale. I should think she indulges with the steward as her private treat, and rewards him with opportunity for his own pleasures. Really, the "Naumakhia" is not exactly your kind of brothel. If you look at the picture at the door, you'll see it is not clubs or swords the sailors are employing in the sea-fight. This house is not interested in girls.'

'Meaning the steward was in bed with a boy – but not Sosios.'

'No. The stewards' bed-companion was not Philokhoros' missing boy. A brothel,' Aristotle said thoughtfully, 'now, that is really a handy business for concealing other transactions. It's a place where you can get whatever you want – for a price. People running a brothel can do many favours, and not just for their ordinary carnal customers. Those pigs worry me. What an efficient way of getting rid of a corpse! If you bury a body it can be dug up. Bodies cast into seas, lakes and rivers have washed up on many banks. But what pigs have eaten stays hidden for ever.'

The good ship *Eudaimonia* took us back from Mykonos harbour to Rheneia. The ship was now without the cargo of oil, and the effect was not altogether pleasant; its new lightness encouraged it to skip and dance in the waves. On our way, Aristotle discussed with our captain Aiskhines and his crew our wish to set out for Naxos on the morrow, and our agreement to take Doris with us. Aiskhines replied that he could take us to Naxos on our way to Kos, and that if we could make our way to Delos in the morning he would collect the family with the sick daughter, as they would expect to take passage in the same ship.

I left all these arrangements to Aristotle. Aristodamos of Naxos was his friend. The short journey to Rheneia seemed to take for ever. I was chilled, and yet could take no satisfaction in wrapping my clothes about me. Try hard as we did, we had not kept our garments uncontaminated by the scent of pig. When we arrived at Rheneia, Phokon found us a lodging. The people of

Rheneia have too many visitors, for they appear slightly contemptuous of them – at least that was so in our case. Perhaps our odour had something to do with this reception.

I was tired and restless, and my sleep was strangely broken by starts and vivid dreams. You would think I would dream of the horrid pigs, but there was little of that. I remember rather a dream of great beauty; a vision of a great golden wheel slowly moving, and in the centre a sparkling dot of light. It seemed as if such a dream must have significance if only I could understand it. I awoke and felt hot, and from the dream-exaltation fell into despond. I was worrying about various things – including the poor limping slave and her limping dog, as well as the whereabouts of Philokhoros' unfortunate boy. But chiefly I wondered how I should ever complete my task and get home again.

XII

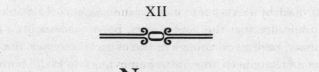

Naxos

In the morning light, the images of sleep vanished. My pleasure at dawn, was however, mitigated by the fact that my digestion was afflicted. (I put this indignity down to the drinking water in Mykonos, though it might have been the pig muck.) I could not bear to put on my old clothes again. Philokhoros, arrayed in the uncouth raiment of the brothel-keeper's steward, bought new clothes from a householder of Rheneia whose wife was a notable weaver. He gave Phokon a new tunic also. In kind acknowledgement of my helping him out of the pigpen, Philokhoros also purchased a himation for me. Although a gentleman should be chary of taking gifts, I was not too proud to accept this one.

Philokhoros, still recovering from the effects of the attack and not at all strong, decided he would stay in Rheneia, or rather go back again to Delos. He did not, he asserted, need or wish to go to Naxos, but we might all meet later in the eastern islands, some day.

'I must see if I can find that wretched boy of mine,' he said with a tired smile. 'I am concerned as to what has befallen him. Surely he has been abducted, stolen by some villains in Delos. I shall make enquiries. Perhaps there is a more sympathetic magistrate than you came upon.'

Each of the rest of us must have thought of the distinct possibility that the young slave Sosios had simply run away, having had enough of Philokhoros' caresses. But it would have been impolite to hint as much to Philokhoros, and any such notion would certainly have made life harder for the boy when retrieved. Philokhoros went with us in a small boat for the short journey from Rheneia, and we said our farewells to him in the Sacred Harbour, now in its morning ferment of activity. The day was still relatively cool and fresh, with a pleasant breeze, so the hot-food sellers could ply their trade and the slaves in the slave mart could be stirred to run round naked in their circle of display. None of these was the missing boy.

The captain and the other sailors were waiting for us by the mole at the Sacred Harbour. With them was the family group – the grandfather, his daughter and the little wheezy girl – bound for Kos. They said they would be happy to go to Naxos, as Delos was expensive, and they would find a lodging near Naxos harbour. Inevitably, Doris and her dog (basket at the ready) were awaiting us too. Doris was now encumbered with a great bundle of material which she said she must deliver to a friend or customer of her mistress Kardaka in a place called Three Villages. Standing with this familiar group – to my surprise – was Miltiades. This travelling man said genially that he had business in Naxos and was looking forward to taking another sea journey with us and our wonderful crew of the *Eudaimonia*. He seemed to have forgotten that the last time he had seen us, when we were puzzling over our bloodstained ship, he had practically accused us of murder.

We all got into the boat and settled ourselves as quickly as possible. Words were said on the subject of Doris' dog by the family party, who were anxious that their child not be incommoded by it, and also by a new passenger who eyed the animal suspiciously and ordered 'Keep that thing from barking.' Doris meekly promised to sit out of the way, and not only to put the dog in the basket but also to tie up the animal's jaws as she had done before. 'He's a very quiet dog, really,' she said. 'I can get him not to bark – when he's tied he knows he mustn't speak. He whines, just a little.' She then sat patiently beside the dog basket in the stern, having stowed her bundle of goods where it was least likely to get wet. So we left the sacred island, birthplace of Apollo. We looked back on its lovely temples as long as we could see them.

It was perhaps a good thing, in the light of our constraint regarding Miltiades, that there was a new passenger on the ship, even if he had objected to the dog. The gentleman helped conversation to become pleasant and general. He explained that he was a marble merchant, of Paros, the island next to Naxos.

'No need to go to Naxos for marble,' he boasted, 'though I do have business concerns in that other island. But everyone knows that Parian marble is the best in the world.'

I agreed that many famous temples and sculptures were made with Parian marble. I had never thought about the island itself.

'The most beautiful of the Kyklades,' he assured us. 'Such a pity you are not going to visit it. A lovely city – beautiful countryside. You could see our marble mines, which interest many visitors. The mines are very deep, and great galleries have been carved in the hills. Thousands of slaves work there – simply thousands! They cut the marble and bring it up and then it is roughly dressed in blocks, and the great white blocks are brought down to the city.'

'How do you move such heavy loads?' I asked

'Rollers – a long track of them, along which the great slabs of marble are moved by sliding. As for transport to the town, of course we have tremendous ox-carts.'

'It sounds a fine business,' I said dubiously, thinking it was rather like silver and lead mining, after all. You look at marble statues and temples and you rarely think where the stone comes from.

'Oh, it is a fine business.' He rubbed his hands together in a pleased manner. 'And Parian marble's the best! Our business increases. Of course the war made a lot of trouble and depressed trade.' (He did not add that the Kyklades had sided with the Persians, which had made for unpleasantness when the Makedonians had won.) 'But people the world over wish to have statues and other objects made of Parian marble. So our towns and cities flourish.'

'So likewise with Naxos,' said Miltiades. 'I am also in the marble business. Athens may have fine marble, but the Naxians have the best statue-works, for Naxians have been great sculptors from time immemorial.'

'You are a Naxian?'

'No, no – I am an Athenian, with connections in Naxos. Part of my business entails importing sculpture.'

'Ha! You should come to Paros – *then* you might talk about importing sculpture. Beautiful white marble. Finest workmanship. If you came, young man –' addressing me – 'you would enjoy seeing the great monument to Arkhilokhos.' Seeing my puzzled look, he added, 'You must have heard of Arkhilokhos, the great poet. Born in Paros.'

'Oh! Him,' I said recognising the name. 'The bitter-tongued poet who killed people with his cursing, and whose killer was sent packing by the Pythia at Delphi.'

'Yes – but you don't speak very appreciatively of the poet who invented iambs.'

'I thought of him as a rather biting, bitter kind of person,' I said frankly. 'I didn't know you in Paros thought so much of him.'

'Of course we are proud of our great poet,' he said stiffly. I realised I had been lacking in tact. You should never insult a man's city or its monuments or its athletes – or its poets.

'Marble,' said Miltiades, 'certainly ought to benefit this whole region. Such a demand now! It used to be that marble was just for temples – and for statues donated to the gods and placed in temples and so on. A family would give a great marble kouros, the image of a young man, sometimes in memory of a young man who had died. Soon everyone wanted such statues of gods and lovely kouroi for their own temples at home. Now all temples have many such images. But *these* days, people begin to desire some marble figures for their dwellings, too. Nowadays rich men buy marble statuary for their houses. It won't be purchased just for temples and agoras any more, you mark my words.'

'It's true, there's a demand now in private homes,' agreed the Parian. 'It may soon be the chief of the business in places like Athens. But we needn't ignore works for agoras and temples,' he added. 'Since the cities of Asia are happily free of the Persians, they will want to erect proper Greek buildings. *New* agoras, new temples, with fine statues. All marble. And they will get marble from Paros, and their new statues from the workshop of Naxos and Paros – even Athens.'

'True,' said Miltiades. 'There will likewise be a constant need for reliable transport. Now, friend,' and he turned to our captain Aiskhines, 'I have a proposition to make to you. I have, as it turns out, reason to look over a statue in Naxos and – if I approve it – to send this image to Delos. That's a short hop, you'll agree. But I need a reliable and careful crew who could pack the statue up intelligently and not damage it in any way. If you and your men felt like taking the job on tomorrow, I would offer double pay. Just a quick run to Delos. And then the packing and unpacking to consider. What do you say?'

'Well,' said Aiskhines, 'my men are tired and they will be wanting a rest in Naxos before we head off to Kos. The voyage to Kos is much more arduous than hopping from Sounion to Delos. Sir –' turning to Aristotle – 'I don't know how long you intend to stay on Naxos. We have promised to take your party all the way to Kos, so we shall certainly wait for you in the port of Naxos. The wait, I take it, will not be long.'

'I don't expect we shall stay a long while with Aristodamos, no,' said Aristotle. 'About three days, I should think. A couple of our party are not feeling very well.' He looked at myself and Parmenion as he spoke. 'A restful time in a beautiful house with friends would probably be good for us. We must allow time for getting to and from Aristodamos' house in the hills, too. On the fourth day after we set out for the house we should be able to meet you in the port of Naxos to continue our voyage.'

'Take the job, captain,' urged the most lively of the sailors, the one who so praised Poseidon and the life at sea. 'It seems we will be waiting in Naxos – so why not do a little extra work for such a lot of money? Does the gentleman realise how much it could cost to carry this statue?' He looked at Miltiades anxiously. 'That's two drakmai a day each for ten rowers minimum. Which is twenty drakhs right there – plus the captain's fee.'

'Oh, yes, I am well aware of the costs,' said Miltiades. 'Once I get to the workshop in Naxos I can readily pay – a little in advance and the whole at the end. Since it is only to Delos, the sea journey should take but a day. Less, really.'

'Ah, but there's the getting back to Naxos to be taken into account,' objected Aiskhines.

'That's right. So there is,' agreed Miltiades genially. 'We'll say, hire for two days at least, then.'

With this arrangement in prospect, the sailors seemed cheerful and skimmed along the billows in very good style. The wind favoured us, and the sail made light work for the rowers. Doris' dog was by now accustomed to the ship, and made less whimpering and whining. I had to use the latrine a good deal, but improved as the day progressed. We all enjoyed seeing the peaks of Naxos move closer and closer. As the westering sun touched the highest peaks, the marble hills like frozen waves gleamed in the rose of afternoon. It is very fine, the harbour of

Naxos, with a magnificent if unfinished temple at the very gateway, on an islet at the opening of the haven.

'The Temple to Apollo built by the tyrant Lygdamis, many generations ago,' explained the Parian. 'When the tyrant fell, it was unfinished and has never been finished. But it is beautiful, nevertheless. Mark the elegant columns in the Ionian manner.'

The temple remained unpainted, but the rosy light threw colours upon it, and as we rounded the headland into the harbour the sunset-tinted sky could be seen between its lovely columns. The city clusters at the foot of its Akropolis and runs up towards the height, so the town has the wedge shape which seems characteristic of these islands. Soft lights gleamed from the houses – you could tell from that alone that it was a rich place with plentiful oil. Surprising, as I had seen no olive groves on Delos or Rheneia, and only a few stunted trees in Mykonos.

Aristotle decided that it was too late in the day for us to try to get to Aristodamos' house, far in the hills, so we found a small hostelry and settled ourselves for the night, hiring a room for our party. The family of young Philokleia said they would find lodgings near to this pretty harbour, and could easily manage, as they had their own serving-woman with them. They would wait for the *Eudaimonia*; we promised not to leave for Kos without them. We had already said farewell to the Parian, and to Miltiades who was going to a marble statuary workshop. For lame Doris and her dog we found quarters with the servants of the place where we stayed. These Naxians seemed hospitable enough, much better than the people of Mykonos and Rheneia, I thought. Despite the sailors' warning against buying fish, we bought some, including octopus, and it was quickly grilled for us. I was so hungry I didn't mind feeling each individual sucker on the octopus leg as it went down. My stomach was ready to receive again. Parmenion looked almost cheerful, so it was an unusually festive meal. Aristotle wrote some letters, while our host regaled us with brave stories of the courage and prowess of the Naxians until sleep overtook us.

Early the next morning we were surprised by persons calling at our lodgings. Aristodamos, as promised, had sent someone to meet us – slaves bringing asses to convey us to his home in the hills. There was a donkey for each of the guests, including Phokon. I was impressed by this grand way of doing things. We were travelling like rich people, waited upon and made easy.

'Sirs – oh, please – what about me?'

The tiresome Doris manifested herself, right at our elbow. She was ready to travel, with her dog and her great bundle of stuffs. We could hardly repudiate her, after our promise (however grudging) to her mistress Kardaka. Once she explained about her errand to Three Villages, Aristodamos' men said that she could come with them as far as Aristodamos' house, and the rest of her way was a walking distance. Of course, we had to make Phokon share his animal with Doris, while one of Aristodamos' slaves was a porter for Doris' bundle. We tried to get the lame dog to run alongside, but the slow and complaining little beast was too great a nuisance; he had to be packed into his light basket, and rendered portable.

As we left the city and went up and up, I realised that the walk into the hills might be quite arduous, so even I was glad of the conveyance. When we got fairly into the countryside, the peaks towered above us. Some of these peaks were bitten into by the marble-seekers; great gashes and pits showed white as temples against the blue sky.

The road was demanding and at times hard going but I was greatly pleased to see valleys and plains and fields all around me, as well as hills everywhere, and many growing things. For the first time since we left Sounion, I felt I was back on land. Delos, Mykonos and Rheneia seemed tiny dry uncomfortable little points in the midst of the ocean, but in Naxos I could forget I was on an island. I expressed these feelings to Aristotle.

'It is such a pleasure,' I exclaimed, 'to see cultivated land, the sort of place where human beings can really live. There are barley fields here, and olive groves, many olives. And look! Vineyards! True vineyards with flourishing vines, stretching on and on. What a welcome sight.'

'You might have guessed there would be vineyards, Stephanos,' said Aristotle teasingly, 'had you but remembered the story of Ariadne.'

'Ariadne was abandoned by Theseus in Naxos,' I responded promptly. 'Which was unfair, as without Ariadne he would not have conquered the Minotaur of Krete and set the Athenians free.'

'Quite so. But there you are. Theseus left her – an impatient youth he seems, and one imagines they had some slight tiff. Poor Ariadne! She wakes up, looks for her lover – there he is, gone! She looks out to sea and at last spies his ship sailing westwards. He is going home to Athens, without her. Forgetting all his promises.'

'He should have made no promises,' said Parmenion, unexpectedly vocal. 'Then he wouldn't have broken his word. He broke another word too, forgetting his promise to his father. So he left the black sail on his ship, forgetting to put the white one in its place – and his poor father Aigeus, watching at Sounion for his return, thought his son was dead and plunged into the sea.'

'Yes. Another instance of the tiresome thoughtlessness of Theseus and his inability to look into the essence of a promise,' said Aristotle, laughing. 'But let us consider the story of Ariadne. Abandoned in Naxos. Of course she cries her eyes out. How she laments for her faithless lover! What words she says to empty air, fruitless reproaches to the absent one. But she is rapidly consoled. For lo! Comes the god of wine and jollity, his eyes alight. Wearing (we may fancy) his customary garb of skins of leopards, he comes in a rapid chariot, drawn likewise by those useful animals. He sees Ariadne – her problem is solved! She has a new lover to replace Theseus. Gold for bronze. A god in place of a man.'

'Dionysos came to Naxos, yes,' I mused. 'Dionysos, the god of passion, delight, and of wine.'

'So – if we are inclined to the poetic, Stephanos, you and I may imagine, in the midst of this hilly landscape, gleaming with marble and green with vegetation, the Dionysian train. The clash of cymbals, the piping of flutes. Satyrs dancing in the shade as the beautiful youth advances. Ariadne's eyes glow as she gazes on this divine phenomenon. Seized with the ecstasy of the god, she gives herself to him, and they are united.'

'You are rhapsodic, Aristotle,' I laughed.

'I got carried away by Dionysos. Ariadne was certainly

too passionate for Theseus, so she was better off. But my point – a mild one – is merely that any island with such a strong association with Dionysos, god of wine, *must* have vineyards, and not a few.'

Thus we beguiled ourselves and our servants as we made our way to Aristodamos' house. We were very glad to get off our sullen mounts. But here another problem arose. As she dismounted, the crippled Doris twisted her foot – her good foot. She cried out in pain.

'Oh! I can hardly walk. I should set out for Three Villages with the fabric – what will my mistress say?' she keened. The dog, aroused by her sorrow and anxiety, did his best to second her in a passion of whining, and when she took off his muzzle gave voice to what was in his heart in a series of indignant barks. Aristodamos, who had come out to greet us, was the beneficiary of all this racket. He solved the problem easily by asking Doris to stay in his house in the servants' quarters until she was recovered, and he pushed her off into the care of a little old woman who came blinking into the sunlight.

Aristodamos had a beautiful house, with marble statuary and smooth floors. His many rooms offered fine accommodations for us all. We were offered a wash, and water was brought to us in well-wrought vessels. Then we were invited outside to sit in the shade of the orchard until the last of the day should cool.

'Time for dinner,' said Aristodamos. 'It is but a simple meal out of doors tonight. I must apologise for a certain lack of service. I had promised – before I knew you were coming, mind! – I had promised my slaves that they could go to the cook's wedding party this evening and tomorrow. Promises even to slaves or children are solemn things. And I like to keep on the good side of my cook. He's a free citizen of these parts, and he invited all the household.'

With the assistance of his housekeeper, Aristodamos arranged tables and chairs for us; amid sighs and exclamations of pleasure we sat down under the trees, to be regaled on olives and other light edibles, and some cool wine-and-water in delightful cups. The waning afternoon was yet warm, but a hill breeze refreshed the day. As the sun slowly descended, the world was still and calm; long shadows were cast by the olive grove and by the apple trees around us. Most of the trees had given their fruit crop earlier in the summer, but some grew in the shade of the hill and their late apples were now the proper colour for eating. A scent of ripeness wound through the air. Bees and some wasps blundered about the fallen fruit.

'This is obviously an old orchard,' said Aristotle.

'It is so – and that is an ancestral olive grove.' Aristodamos was pleased to speak of his homestead. 'My family has lived here since before historical records began – but we can prove that I am at least the tenth generation in this house. Of course we have made alterations and improvements. Our family planted the trees and the place is called "Apple Place" because of us.'

'It is so wonderful to me, so refreshing,' I said sincerely, 'to be again in a dwelling with fields and trees, a proper home. And this is even more impressive because it is so old.'

'Ha. You like old things?' Aristodamos got up from his seat. 'Let me show you something truly old – the finest or at least most unusual feature of this orchard.'

He led the way through the trees a short distance. 'There!' he said, pointing.

I saw an enormous shape, the shape of a man lying down, his head lower than his feet. The great body was dappled by the shadows of the apple leaves. 'Come closer and look at it.' So we pressed on and stood over the man, a gigantic statue resting on the earth. I could make out the legs clearly and the feet, and various details, but the face seemed unfinished. That might have been just because the elements had worked on it.

'What is it?'

'This statue was intended for one of those temples in Delos, so we think. Probably a statue of Apollo, not just of a kouros – see how big it is. The figure has turned grey with age, but it is of Naxos marble – from one of those hills nearby. It was worked on here, presumably. Perhaps this field was a sculptor's yard in ancient days. And then – unhappy sculptor! – it broke. You can see a deep crack in it. Once the figure broke, it could not be offered to the god in a temple, and nobody wanted it. So it was left here. An ancient image. You can see the style is much more stiff than ours is now. How old this figure is we cannot know. Our family have never known the orchard without it.'

'Most distinguished,' said Aristotle. 'An ancient broken Apollo in your orchard.'

'But he looks,' Parmenion pointed out, 'like a man who has been sleeping in the orchard, taking a rest in the shade.' I thought exactly the same thing.

Pleased with this exhibition of an uncommon feature of his property, the charmingly hospitable Aristodamos led the way back to our chairs and refreshments. The cicadas abated their shrill cry, a breeze of evening advanced, and the sun set in glorious colour tinting the marble peaks. We retired early and slept well.

The next day was spent in delightful freedom, sleeping as long as we liked, and walking about in the fresh air (except for Doris, who neither worked nor walked but sat with her feet up). The servants were still at the wedding, but Aristodamos decided we must have a proper dinner.

'Perhaps it's a good thing that your friend's lame servant is here; she can help my old housekeeper, the only servant left at home to mind the house's business. At least she has learned something from my excellent cook. And if tonight is simple, we will make up for it tomorrow.'

Despite the apology, the meal was my idea of splendid. We were served as we reclined on beautiful couches in the most proper manner, and the food was excellent. I particularly enjoyed succulent young kid prepared in a most delicious sauce. Dishes were served and taken away by the old housekeeper and her new assistant, the humbly apologetic and acutely limping Doris, who was more use in cleaning pots and dishes in the kitchen than in running to and fro.

'I hope she doesn't break anything,' said Aristotle fretfully, and asked Phokon to help. But it was not Doris who broke a dish. It was a sweet evening with only one slight accident to mar it. Aristodamos was talking instructively about the history of Naxos.

'You see,' he explained, 'my family were closely involved, like other leading families of Naxos, with the affairs of Delos and the creation of the sacred site, long before Athens really thought of Delos at all. By our family's reckoning, we were on Delos long before we came to Naxos, and I am the fifteenth generation of our family to be associated with Delos. Exiles from Delos in a sense though we may be, we regard ourselves as Delians as well as Naxians. Many of the earliest beautiful buildings on Delos were erected through our efforts.'

We murmured our appreciation.

'So,' I said, 'this island is old, if you can go back ten or even fifteen generations –'

'That is nothing, Stephanos. Men have lived here in Naxos for uncounted time – probably as long as the Egyptians lived in their country. Objects from that deep time come up when we plough the fields, or build new moles in our harbours – or try to bury our dead. Look at this, for instance.'

He rose and brought back from a cabinet a white marble statue-like thing – very strange indeed. A thin, rather short figure of marble stone with a pointed head, featureless save for a triangular nose and thin arms crossed around its middle. If you looked closer you could see a pubes scratched on the surface. A figure of a woman, but not really a statue, not a good statue.

'Sometimes we speculate that this might be a goddess to the Old People,' he remarked.

'Surely not,' I said. 'We know that goddesses must be *beautiful*. This is simply odd.'

'But of great historical interest, Stephanos,' urged Aristotle.

'And look at this – how long we have ornamented our pottery.' Aristodamos picked up a fat little vase from the corner table. It was a light sandy brown, painted in swirling dark brown, the bulging figure and big eyes and rolling writhing rhythmic tentacles –

'An octopus,' I said.

'Lovely,' said Aristotle, taking the vase.

'Not *lovely*,' said I. 'An octopus is edible, but it's not pretty. Anyway, I think this one in the painting has the wrong number of legs.' I reached for the fat vase again – and dropped it. It shattered on the floor. There was a collective in-drawing of breath, while I wished that I myself could simply fall and shatter on the floor.

'Oh no! How terrible!' I cried. 'I don't know how that came to happen. Please let me pay for it –'

Aristodamos hushed me, and sent for the housekeeper to sweep up the fragments.

'It doesn't have a price,' he said. 'It came out of the earth of Naxos. And there must be many more in the earth, gifts from the people of old.'

Feeling as badly as I did about this episode, I was extremely anxious to retire to bed, and we all went off at the earliest opportunity. Doris was sent to sleep with the old housekeeper, with the dog beside her. Phokon was kept by Aristotle as a body servant, not to intrude upon the currently all-female servants' quarters.

I woke up quite late, as I think we all did. The sun was fairly high in the sky when I was told by Phokon that Aristodamos had ordered a cool drink and some light refreshment to be served in the orchard. Despite last night's great dinner I was in a humour for breakfast, and joined the others with pleasure. Doris, stumbling along, helped to serve us some bread, her face creased with anxious concern lest she drop it. She had brought her pet with her, in its container.

It was most agreeable in the orchard, under the shade of the apple trees. I nearly went to sleep again.

'The bees' buzzing is very soothing,' I remarked. 'There are no bees at sea.'

'There is a great deal of buzzing,' Aristotle agreed, 'but it's not just the bees. There seem to be a quantity of flies around today.'

'Some carrion or other,' said Aristodamos, unconcerned. 'Won't somebody let that dog out of his basket and stop his whining? He needs to run about – has to do the necessary, I suppose.'

With embarrassed apologies, Doris unfastened the dog basket and also released the animal from its muzzle. The dog leaped out, tore about, and then ran through the orchard. Suddenly it set up an announcement of barks and whines. It came running back to us and seemed to urge us to follow him.

'If it found a bone,' said Aristodamos, 'you'd think this creature would take it and say nothing.'

We trooped along to the place where the stone god lay. Now somebody else lay there too. Somebody else, with his head down and feet up, extended supine. Looking like a man taking his ease in a shady orchard at midday, fallen into a pleasant nap. But this was no sweet summer sleep. Nor was this new figure another marble god. Aiskhines. Captain Aiskhines. The flies were right. He was certainly dead.

'Ye gods!' I cried. 'How is he here? Did he come here to die?' I think I had an absurd momentary feeling that Aiskhines had come here to die because he wasn't allowed to do it in sacred Delos.

'Came here to be killed, by the look of it,' said Aristotle. 'See, Stephanos – see, Aristodamos! Our captain has been stabbed, cleanly with a knife. One good thrust alone –' He bent down to examine the body closely. 'Yes. Gone straight to the heart, I should think. Very little blood. And the knife –' he groped around in the earth and leaves, and shook out the garments of the captain. 'The knife that did it is not here.'

'This is terrible! On our property, too,' said Aristodamos. 'Who can have done this thing? Why – now – what? We must tell the authorities. Get someone from the town of Naxos! What city, what deme, does this dead person belong to?'

'He is of Peiraieus,' said Aristotle. 'Quick! I want to look at your kitchens.'

Aristotle ran back to the house and we all followed. The kitchen area was a pleasant place and remarkably clean. 'Let's look at your knives,' Aristotle commanded. Aristodamos pointed to a container. We found small knives in that. Some big knives were hanging up on pegs at the wall, in handy readiness. 'None of them is bloody,' said Aristotle. 'Remarkably fine condition. Your staff is obviously excellent at cleaning.'

'There is a kind of sand or grit that we have in Naxos that excels in polishing of all kinds –' Aristodamos was beginning to explain.

'Quite. Well, I cannot see any signs of blood, even where the blade meets the haft. Though one of these large kitchen knives could have done the job. Unfortunate Captain Aiskhines! But what was he doing here?'

'His poor crew,' I said. 'They will want to take the body home to Peiraieus.'

'So they will when they know about it. They must be questioned. But why *was* Aiskhines here? We need to find out. Had he come seeking us at Aristodamos' house?

Likely – but *why* would he undertake that arduous walk, if that is what he did?' Aristotle paused a moment. 'Let us say he knew something he wanted to tell us. We must find out from the sailors, as soon as we can.'

'Those sailors have a double loss,' I reminded him. 'Their leader and their livelihood! The ship belongs to the captain, not to them. They cannot stay in Naxos. The ship must at once be returned to his next of kin.'

'A point well taken,' said Aristotle, 'It makes it the less likely that any of the sailors would be moved to kill him.'

'But – who did kill this man?' asked Aristodamos. 'A horrible deed has been done. We need to find the murderer. Why was this captain killed? Was he carrying money upon him?'

'I don't know. He isn't now. It's a good idea, to say he was killed for money. If only,' Aristotle continued with unusual wistfulness, 'if only he had been found in a deserted area, or down by the port – near a tavern, or –'

'Well, we're not near the port,' said Aristodamos. 'And I cannot see us ferrying a body down the mountainside to the harbour, like a doll.'

'I dare say not.'

'What a blessing for my servants that they were out last night,' Aristodamos continued. 'They cannot be witnesses, so they won't have to be tortured. Oh, but my poor nearly blind housekeeper – she was here!'

The woman's face went ashen and she collapsed in a heap. 'Oh, master, don't let them torture me,' she begged. 'I did nothing, I swear it – I am as innocent as the babe just born.'

'I believe it,' said Aristodamos. 'But that's the law. Slaves cannot give evidence without being tortured first.

And then,' Aristodamos went on, 'there's this lame Doris, whose dog discovered the body. And your Phokon as well.'

Doris now collapsed in a heap and tried to take hold of Aristodamos' knee. She burst out crying.

'Oh, no-o. Oh, gods, why did I accept a ride to this horrid dwelling! What an ill fate! Demeter deliver me! Oh master, have pity on a poor crippled woman.' The two women wailed and moaned. Phokon, strong as he was, looked as if he were near doing the same.

'I simply refuse to have Phokon tortured,' said Aristotle stubbornly. 'He didn't see anything – he was with me. He's thoroughly trustworthy – I have known him for years. And you know, Aristodamos, that *I* didn't do it, and neither my friend nor my student did it.'

'We could have no kind of motive,' I said. "For we all liked this captain, and we needed him to give us our passage to Kos.'

'Again, a good point, Stephanos. We now need to find another ship, and that speedily.' Aristotle turned earnestly to Aristodamos.

'Good friend, I most heartily regret that I have brought trouble on your house. I fear that it *is* my coming that has brought this trouble, because I have reason to think that my position in the world, my safety and even my life are sought after by an enemy. It is for that reason that I have left Athens – actually fled from Athens, though with a good covering of story and business. I had no notion, however, that my staying with you could bring trouble on your household. But it may be that detaining us here and torturing my servants and so on form part of the iniquitous ones' intention. For on the very day that I met you in Delos, an apparent murder was arranged. Not unlikely that was an effort to detain me. Now there is a real killing. You are a good friend, O Aristodamos. I appeal to you. The longer I am here, the more surely my own life will be endangered. I beg you to let us go.'

'Let you go? You, Aristotle, who were always the champion of justice!'

'A less than worthy champion, for I will admit that I want to save my own life. And I am also responsible for the life of the student – as responsible as a parent. Answerable too in a different way for my friend Stephanos, whose safety I may have risked. I hope that you will be clear of danger once I have departed. As long as I am here, I fear that you and your household are in trouble.'

'What do you propose?'

'Something unorthodox. This. Let word go casually to your servants at the wedding party that they need not hurry home. They will be glad to stay – wedding parties go on for many days. Let us leave. The male slaves who conducted us hither are now all feasting with the bridegroom. Little do they know their own happiness! But I think Phokon and I can remember the route. We shall go back to Naxos harbour and there take another ship for Kos. Thus we shall be away. Once we are gone, you can "discover" the body. Perhaps it would be much the best thing for this body to be found somewhere else.'

'Do you realise what you are saying?'

'It is much to ask. But now that we are in this danger, this strategy would work best for yourself too. If the body were discovered elsewhere, it would save your house much trouble. And I promise, I could not lessen your trouble by staying here with you. Indeed, my presence would greatly add to your danger.'

'Suspicion will fall on you.'

'Assuredly it will. But if I depart quickly, nothing worse than suspicion should fall on me. I can do nothing about finding out the real murderer if I am kept in captivity – it will merely be easier for my own enemies to get at me.'

'Please – oh please! Sir! Hear my plea! Let me go with *you*, sir,' said Doris, 'and I won't say nothing about seeing you here, not ever. Oh please, sir –' and she clung to his knees.

'There's no need for you to come,' I said. 'If you go on to the Three Villages as your mistress directed, no one will suspect you of anything.'

'Oh, once the murder is out everyone in the Villages will know when I came to Naxos, and your house. You know what gossip is. All the slaves will know I was *here*. Besides –' in her agitation she pulled at the hem of Aristotle's garment – 'you're not thinking. Sir, any slave who is thought of as a witness must be tortured! Once the case goes before law, none of us will be safe. And my mistress is too far away for me to appeal to her in time.' She wept over Aristotle's feet.

'Stop that!' said Aristotle. 'If you choose to go back to the port on one of Aristodamos' donkeys, I cannot prevent you. Nor can I prevent you from buying a passage to somewhere –'

'Oh thank you! Sir, I thank you!' Doris hobbled off, her dog under her arm, to find her bundle. Almost in the instant, she was ready to depart. It took us some time longer to gather our belongings, but not much. Fear lent speed. Hastily bidding farewell, we set off on donkeys down the first of the mountainous hills, and made what felt like an agonisingly slow journey back to the port.

'Aristodamos' poor old housekeeper is in for it,' I remarked as we descended. 'As soon as the authorities find out, they will put her to the question. And under torture she will certainly talk about us.'

'She will. Unless Aristodamos thinks of something ingenious.'

XIII

Storm at Sea

I was hoping desperately to have a chance to talk with Aristotle alone. On the way down the hill, when our two mounts drew level, I thought it a good opportunity to speak with him.

'I wonder how Aristodamos will –'

He cut me off short. 'Wonder nothing, Stephanos.' There was a silence as he seemed to gather himself together. 'Say nothing about anything more weighty than the view,' he warned me. 'You don't know where there are ears to hear – passers-by, field slaves, shepherds. All have ears. We may talk of the illness of Parmenion, and how that is driving us forward in a hurry so that the sick boy can be taken to his father.' He looked solicitously at Parmenion, who had again taken on that pallid weary blanched look of former days. Like a marble kouros riding on an ass. I shivered. A marble kouros was often a commemorative gift to the gods in memory of a young man who died. I thought of the broken marble man lying so peacefully in the leaf-shadow spangled orchard . . .

It struck me after Aristotle's warning that one of the pairs of ears ready to hear was Doris. Of course she was frightened too – at the prospect of being taken for a witness. Soon too was Phokon, pressing onward, anxious to escape from Naxos. And if these two were tortured as witnesses, things would not go well with us either. Their statements would surely lead to our being returned to Athens in chains. The trial would have to take place in Athens. Two citizens of that city – no, one citizen (me) and one *metoikos* – taken to be tried for the murder of one of the citizens of Athens from Peiraieus. Or the Naxians might forget to oblige Athens in this way, and stimulate a mob to kill us on the spot. Such a solution puts an end to the tedium of legal procedures. It also cuts short the humiliation of a city guilty (however ignorantly) of harbouring murderers. Official apologies, statements of regret for killing another city's citizens in a tantrum of justice, are easy to manufacture after the event.

At least, I thought, we were making good progress towards the port of Naxos, and might get away in time. There too we would be able to get rid of the irritating Doris, who would want to keep her mouth closed for her own sake. I hadn't quite realised the difficulties that we might run into on our arrival at the port. We had hardly been long enough to draw breath in the place than we met one of the sailors, the *nautes* who had talked to me so enthusiastically of Poseidon. I didn't know what to say, but Aristotle handled the matter as adroitly as possible. 'I am sorry,' he said, 'as I know you were going to be employed in transporting the statue. But my protégé here is becoming ill. I am anxious to take him to Kos as soon as possible. We should like to set off today.'

'Oh,' said the sailor. 'We did the statue job, easy. Didn't you see our captain? Aiskhines was determined to go up to the place in the hills to see you. I thought you would have met by now. What a pity – somehow you must have crossed in the road. I don't know how you could have missed him,' he added, 'for Aiskhines should have got to your place last night. Though it looks all uphill. Well, maybe he missed his way, not being familiar with Naxos. That's the likeliest thing.'

'What was he coming to see us about?' Aristotle enquired. I pricked up my ears: the answer could be of importance.

'I don't rightly know. We finished the job of transporting the statue to Delos in a day.' He laughed. 'That man was so fussy – just about one marble figure. Don't know why he wanted to pay so high and make so much fuss over one old statue. But we got it smartly to Delos, and the sea was favourable, so we were back again before evening. He – Aiskhines – and all of us were having a meal, sitting on the strip by the port, with lots of people going by, gossiping and looking at the harbour. And Aiskhines suddenly jumps up and says he has a message for you he forgot to deliver. So he goes off to find you. There was a moon later, so it wouldn't be hard to travel in the evening, and he had an idea where the house was.'

'How surprising! I don't really understand what the message can have been,' said Aristotle.'I fear that if Aiskhines does not come very soon, I must try to find other transport. I regret this more than words can say.

But I will pay you something handsome in recompense for not shipping us to Kos.'

And to recompense you for the loss of your captain and your employment, I thought but did *not* say.

'Sir.' Another nautical sort of man had joined the group. He was tall and rangy, deeply sunburned, with friendly large blue eyes, large and wide apart. 'I couldn't help overhearing – do you need a ship and crew to take you to Kos? For I am captain and owner of a *keles* likewise, and my crew and I are bound for Kos.'

'You are willing to take passengers on such short notice?' Aristotle's tone was a trifle sharp.

The man shrugged. 'We have no passengers at present. It would certainly suit our treasury to take someone aboard. For a fee. I won't pretend the offer is disinterested.' He laughed, and his eyes had a friendly twinkle. 'But my ship is a tight seaworthy craft, built for speed. I think you are concerned about getting there as quickly as possible. Am I right?'

'Yes. Since this young man is not well,' said Aristotle, looking at Parmenion, freshly metamorphosed again into the excuse and explanation for our journey and our haste.

'Sorry to hear it. Reason to hope – Kos is the healing island, after all. I am a native of Kos. Nikias of Kos, at your service. My ship is the *Niké*. It is good to name a boat after victory. Though it's a sort of compliment to my name too – Nikias. She skims along like a bird. Used to be named *The Swallow*. I assure you, sirs, my men are first-class rowers. And we also carry sail. As you see.'

Captain Nikias had drawn us to the quayside by his ship, and we could see the men arranging the sail about the mast, mending ropes and examining their oars.

'It will not inconvenience you? You really can leave today?'

'Certainly. We have little cargo, but we carry marketable stones, rough marble pieces, as ballast, so it won't pitch bad. We should get going smartly. The longer you wait, the more storms you run into, my experience.'

'Aristotle,' I said, 'this seems like a godsend. Let us go – and get as safely away from storms as we can.'

Aristotle, frowning, made his calculations, and then paid off the crew of the *Eudaimonia*, and told Phokon and Parmenion to board the new craft. The *Niké* looked comfortable enough, although slightly more slender than the *keles* we had been on earlier, with a much more pointed prow. 'I dare say,' said Aristotle, following my gaze, 'that this was an active warship once, and that explains the prow. The *Niké* seems well built – carries a larger sail than our other ship.'

'Built for speed. I promise you that. Once one of ships in Alexander's service. And we have a large crew. As well as myself, there is a mate to assist in navigation and management, and a boatswain to chant the *keleusma*. So we can go on without a break – even at night, if need be. And, as all of us can take an oar when necessary, we can get up much more speed than that other craft –' with a glance towards the *Eudaimonia*.

'I dare say you charge accordingly,' said Aristotle, smiling, 'but I certainly have no objection to the extra crew if it means more speed, since speed is a consideration with us. As I told you, we are anxious to take our invalid boy to Kos without delay.' He glanced at the pale Parmenion.

'Shall we prepare to cast off?'

'No – no. First we must invite the family with the sick child to come with us. That was a promise, Stephanos, and promises to gods and men – and not least to children – must be honoured.'

Phokon was sent on this errand. People hanging around the wharf side in hopes of earning a hemi-obol or two knew where the strangers lodged and promised to conduct him to their door. Meanwhile, we were arranging our own baggage ourselves, when I heard an all too familiar voice:

'One of you sailors will have to carry or catch me on account of my lame leg. And put the dog's basket in *first*.'

To my astonishment, Doris and her dog were preparing to embark also. Aristotle went hastily over to her, standing in her way so she could not easily get on board.

'Woman, I thought we were saying farewell today. I thought you wished to return to Delos. You can go back to Delos. Farewell *now*. I had not promised to carry you to Kos! Our agreement was to take you back to Naxos only.'

'Sir! Oh, I won't be any trouble! I *need* to go to Kos, too! Oh please! You know well why. I will not embarrass you and myself by talking of such matters in front of others.' She put her hand to her belly, leaving our overhearers free to imagine that she had some woman's malady which prompted her desire for Kos. 'I will be better if I can get to Kos. And you will find me *utterly* faithful. You can count on my *fidelity*. I can be entrusted with anything, sir. Always reliable. Always. If you let me go to Kos.'

'It's not really –'

'Otherwise –' Doris continued, as if she had not heard him, 'I'm so scared of what might happen! Nobody wants to die, sir, we have to consider that. I'm a poor weak creature, and when things pain me I cannot stand it. I do not want to die.'

Her whole speech struck me as remarkably clever, coming from a slave – and a woman at that, a poor limping creature to boot. Aristotle's face twitched. He understood all too well. I did too. Doris had power over us, for she could tell her interrogators that Aristotle and I had been visiting Aristodamos at the time that Aiskhines had been killed, and that we knew about the corpse. If Aristodamos had made any efforts to change the body's location, Doris' testimony would make matters much worse for him. She had managed to tell us all this in adroit secret-keeping speech. Her fear, however genuine and however great, clearly had not stupefied her wits.

'Come aboard, then,' was all Aristotle said. And Doris, with many excuses and complaints about her own clumsiness, was helped aboard by the sailors, and settled as of yore beside the whining dog in his wicker box. The family with the little girl came alongside too. Captain Nikias looked at this domestic group a little dubiously.

'You sure you wish to come aboard? I wouldn't advise it. If I were you, I'd stay here. Wait for your other ship. The seas are high and we shall pelt through the steep waves. People often have to endure great discomfort before they reach their journey's end.'

'Oh, yes, we must go. The sooner the better, now we are on our way,' said the grandfather Hermippos. The little family, with their diminutive slavewoman, were helped aboard. The child Philokleia was wheezing piteously; her grandfather claimed it was because of the dust, and the dirt of the household in which they had been staying.

'She'll be better at sea, I hope,' he said.

Indeed, the child's eyes brightened as the captain lent her his hand to help her get on the ship, and she smiled at him as we cast off. I too felt the consolation in being again in the care of a captain, a strong, reliable and attentive person who knew how to manage the ship and seas, and how to take care of us all. Harkening once more to the familiar and comforting rhythm of the *keleusma* and dipping oars, we proceeded out of the harbour of Naxos. Once more we were in what I thought of as Aristotle's world of light and colour. Sun shone upon the sea, which grew deeper and darker.

'How very deep a blue the water is now,' I said to Aristotle, really in order to say something. If we could not converse about what most concerned us, it would yet seem unnatural for us not to address each other.

'Yes. Like the hue of the Indian gemstone, the hyacinth stone,' Aristotle replied, looking likewise at the deep waves.

In silence we watched for a long while as Naxos receded. Naxos, splendid in the rich midday sun, its glowing peaks like marble waves. That lovely island, which now held so foul a secret – and an ugliness from which we were running away. We seemed always now to be fugitives, Aristotle and myself. But this was more starkly serious than the mysterious unpleasantness in Athens. Aiskhines' death was more final, the mystery of his killing more grim and urgent than mere menaces, however grotesque. Worse (from our point of view, at least), Aristotle and I were now implicated in a murder.

Suppose Aristodamos felt his safest course was to go to the magistrates and complain about us? The noble Naxian might be ready to sacrifice us to the law, and his slave housekeeper to torture. Then the woman would certainly scream out all she could about our own presence and the likelihood that the visiting strangers had killed the sailor. Neither Aristodamos nor his housekeeper, however, would be able to supply any motive for our killing our good-hearted captain. But as there was nothing to stop them from inventing motives, that was small comfort.

Worst of all, we were certainly in the way of a determined killer. The decorous functioning of the law offered us all a bare chance at life, at least. In the time it would take to transport Aristotle and myself back to Athens in chains, perhaps new information would come to light. But a man determined to slice your throat is quicker and more lethal than the law. Unlike a jury, such a man does not stop to wrangle over niceties, like a rhetorician, but goes straight to his point. Were we perhaps genuinely obnoxious to the killer? Were we just in his way? Or were we mere bystanders? Perhaps this unknown murderer's quarrel was simply with the seafaring Aiskhines.

I puzzled over the motive, but could make little headway. Either somebody in Aristodamos' house had killed our poor captain, or he was followed to the place, and to the orchard, when he came up those long hills from the port. Why was the captain in the orchard, if he was coming to speak to us? Why had he come to Aristodamos' estate at all? What – or whom – had he seen that made him wish to speak urgently to Aristotle? So anxious that he was willing to give himself the trouble and fatigue of that long uphill journey. Some man he had seen – but whom? Something he had overheard – but what? If Aiskhines' death involved some dishonest professional business on his part, such as secret trading and tax avoidance, he and criminal confederates might fall out. But that should not have involved us.

I longed to talk about all this with Aristotle, but could not. We were under great constraint. It was necessary to ensure that the new crew did not suspect anything untoward, and we also had to keep our secrets from the little family from Laurion. Aristotle and I watched Doris, and she watched us – like inimical hawks. Doris did nothing remarkable, and prosed on to the women about her aches and pains, or her need to use the pot, in a highly normal manner.

'Now gentlemen – and ladies too' – Nikias smiled at the child Philokleia – 'I must warn you that we have a long voyage ahead. We cross the Aegean here. It's not like hopping around the Kyklades. We can stop for a while in Amorgos, but it would be going out of our way to try to take anchorage in any islands after that – any islands of good size are all south of us. So after Amorgos we go straight on eastward to Kos. And *then* the wind will blow and the billows will heave, I promise you. It is a long passage for my rowing men, and they must not be disturbed by coming to your aid. They cannot hold your head over the basin while you puke! So – bear up and we shall press on. Going quick with the favouring winds we shall soon be at the end, and all our troubles over.'

We all attended to this and were internally ready to put up with whatever might befall. Certainly the ship drove on well through the waves, and the waves were great. The short interval on land in Naxos had slightly unfitted me for seagoing again, and I felt queasy the first day. I did not much care – bodily discomfort was a distraction from the anxiety that tormented me; I kept pulling my mind away from the image of Aiskhines with his throat cut.

Even when the water was calm (relatively calm), so that we could see other ships in the nearer distance, I could not really talk with any of my companions – at least about anything that mattered. I tended to brood in long reverie. I thought penitently of my mother. Dear Mother, who had always been so kind to me. Mother, who had saved my life by attentive nursing (and also by maintaining the helpful fiction that I was at death's door) at a very dangerous time a couple of years ago. Now I had sent poor Mother, the only human being on earth who loved me fully, away from her own house and into the keeping of a man not really a relative. What a shame! Suppose he abused her – Robbed her? Starved her? Suppose Smikrenes – living as a single man and a kind of widower – took a sexual fancy to her and pressed his attentions? The thought was too sickening, though it seemed absurd. But it was not absurd to question that old peasant's temper. Suppose the ill-humoured man beat my little brother? What could my mother do to prevent it? I had cast my family into danger thinking I was guarding them, and had gone off on a wild chase after someone else's heir. The only thing I had gained from this selfish journey so far was to learn what seasickness meant, and to risk severe danger from the law. How did I know that my own foolish quest had not helped to bring an unjust fate upon the unfortunate Aiskhines?

I hoped to behave better if I were allowed to go back to Athens and live in peace. I would amend my life. I would stop spending the family money so selfishly, going to brothels and buying hot food at public stands instead of going home to eat. My mother never expressed any disapproval of the brothel-going, which she must have guessed at; indeed, she probably considered it necessary for my health. But the hot-food stands were a subject of contention between us from time to time. 'A head of a household, Stephanos, does not eat out in the public markets or on the roads! A head of a household – a man who is a gentleman – comes *home* to eat. It is frugal, and means he is keeping an eye on the servants, as well as keeping company with his own family.' Yes, I would change my ways . . .

'When I get home,' I suddenly informed Aristotle, 'I mean to stop spending so much money on prostitutes, and to cut out sausages in the Agora and so on. Completely.'

'These are evidently good resolutions,' said Aristotle. 'Do not take a vow or anything of that sort, I beseech you, Stephanos. We so often feel differently once we are on shore.'

I felt put out, seeing he thought I was making these decisions under the effects of seasickness. I had adjusted to the sea by this time, even when our craft went rapidly. Some other ships had left Amorgos at the same time, and seemed inclined to race us; we encountered them sporadically, popping suddenly into view amidst the foam. Even speeding along in the midst of great waters, I was feeling quite well, in body, if not in mind. Soon, however, a change ensured that none of us could feel extremely well.

After a night in which we kept going, under a favourable wind and with half of the rowers on watch, another dawn came. This dawn was hazy and misty, with a whiteness over the sky. It felt hot and stuffy, even here on the deep sea, which was now like the colour of skimmed milk. The sun was, of course, rolling along in his usual path, but Apollo's orb was hidden by clouds and mist, so that it looked like a gold coin rather than the radiant light-giver.

'Dirty weather ahead,' said the captain. 'Up sail again and see if we can outrun it, men!'

We made good headway for a time. Then the breeze slackened, and the sail flapped disconsolately. Abruptly, before the mast could be taken down, the wind reversed itself and blew strongly from the north-east, spinning us almost completely around. Indeed, I could see that our captain Nikias had to yield to the wind to avoid our being swept broadsides. He ordered the mast to be taken off and laid in the hold, so we now went without sail, only with oars. At least we were in less danger of being blown to nothing. Suddenly there was a low mutter of thunder. It came after us – so it felt – pursued us with peal after peal. Lightning flashed. Heavy bursts of rain fell upon us. It was not possible for anyone to stay dry. Aristotle and I and the old grandfather and even Parmenion all took a hand at bailing out our poor ship as rain and waves sent water upon our craft. As we all, men and women alike, wanted our lives saved, even the women joined us – Philokleia and her mother, their old slave and even crippled Doris.

'All hands stay at oars!' the captain commanded. 'Mind the position – we don't want to be shoved upon Lektera!' The men bent at the oars, and strained anxiously to hear his signals heartily ready for any manoeuvre that would help us to elude the wildest waves.

The storm was an unyielding enemy – and the sea the greater enemy. For now, chafed by the winds which were pushing the sea from different sides, the waves grew immensely tall. We almost surrendered ourselves to the baneful ocean. The waves were now peaks like mountain tops, looming over us. It was night, but no moon or stars were to be seen. It was totally dark, darkness complete, only ceasing to be absolute deprivation of light when the bolts from heaven flew for a moment across the sky.

The sea was pitch black in the shadow of the darkness. Our ship now rode up towards the invisible heavens, now fell with a plunge into the interminable black gulf where death awaited us. Death began to seem quite welcome. The wind was behaving very strangely – winds, rather, puffing at us from all sides, so they blew about in circles bringing water up from the deeps to spray upon us – as if we needed more! The whole universe was awhirl around us, with the sky-fire leaping from time to time across the heaven, sometimes shooting at and hitting the water close by us, or so it seemed. Eventually more fire joined in the game, with odd flashes of light dancing above us, like stars but much closer. Nikias addressed these round bits of fire as the Dioskouroi, Heaven's Twins. He and the sailors said prayers aloud to them, as these peculiar balls of light flame rolled about us. Some of the sailors said this was a saving sign. Then the balls of fire disappeared, and we were left in dark rain, dark wind, dark water once more.

I had long wished for death, and yet I kept on bailing out, throwing my pathetic bucketful of water overboard as more came in. On and on, the same relentless powers, the same darkness . . . it was impossible to tell if it was still night, or if the day had continued to be as the night had been. At last I thought I felt a slackening in the violence of the waves, and the rain actually ceased to fall. This respite allowed us to advance in our work, and the water level in the hold began visibly to diminish. Now some of the sailors could be spared to help us bail, and that made us feel better than we had done for a long time. We felt better too when a thin strip of light amid the clouds promised some daylight at last.

'Captain! A ship! – North – just north!'

The youngest member of the crew drew the captain's attention to a ship in the distance to our left.

'Who knows whether that's north, you monkey,' growled one of the older men. 'No stars in the night, and we've been turning around like a scrap of bark in a cascade. Heaven knows which way we're pointing.'

'I say the monkey is right,' said Captain Nikias. 'It is north. And this *is* morning – later than dawn, but still a morning by the look of it, and therefore we know what way is east. Put up the sail, boys!'

I watched eagerly in the sluggishly growing light as we drew closer to the other vessel. Even before we got to it, it was obvious that it was a large passenger ship. Not a trireme, yet a long vessel with two complete banks of oars and a capacious hold. It was certainly big compared to our own craft. Only, as we got close to it, we could see that this big ship had suffered terribly in the storm. The sailors had not been able to ship the mast and remove the crossbar holding the sail, and this yardarm hung in splinters, with some tangled shreds of sail around it.

'Captain! We can easy go on board! Can we –'

To my suprise the captain gave the excited youth a

terrific blow across the face. It was a wonder the boy had
a jaw left. He wobbled on his feet, and his eyes stared
nearly out of his head. Yet he was well disciplined
enough to say nothing.

'Hush, you monkey!' said the captain. 'Quiet, or there's
more where that came from! Men in their business
doesn't want to be disturbed by boys' babbling or
yapping. Deciding what to do – you leave that to your
betters. Let's see what the matter is.'

We cruised with relative ease, given the still-heaving
water, and with admirable efficiency our craft drew level
and hung off beside the injured ship.

Now we could see how the mast had suffered. A
burned or scorched spot on the ship's side clearly
showed that it must have been struck by lightning. The
vessel was listing markedly, and men were bailing with
frantic haste. We could hear a low moaning from injured
passengers, though whether these were victims of
lightning bolt or falling objects or just seasickness I
could not tell.

'Shall we board and –'

'Hush, boy. Let me speak to her captain first.' Captain
Nikias hailed the other ship, and the distraught captain
came over to talk with us.

'We can assist you, probably,' said Nikias. 'Do you want
us to come on board? Many passengers injured? How
about your crew?'

'Oh, sir!' The captain of the thunderstruck ship was
visibly shaken. '*Five* men swept overboard – five good
oarsmen! And two passengers. We have about one
hundred passengers on board. Some of these are
important men, bearing messages for Alexander. So it

would be a great service if you could take them on your ship, seeing as you are undamaged. You're bound for – ?'

'For Kos,' said Captain Nikias. 'And I could. For a fee. Nowhere else than Kos, mind.'

'Should do. I think most were going to Rhodos – that's near Kos. Someone is going to what used to be Halikarnassos,' responded the captain of the damaged vessel. 'We would be glad to set them on their way,' he continued, his tone expressing a limited relief. 'They could put in a good word for me, too, and say it wasn't my fault but the storm's. We are bound to be late.'

'As I can swear, too, in your excuse,' said Nikias. 'But your ship is not in mortal danger, seemingly, though it's surely damaged. Unless – what's making her list so bad to one side?'

'Cargo of woollens and hides,' said the unfortunate captain ruefully.' Just our luck! Of course the water has saturated them.'

'Best toss them all overboard,' said Nikias curtly.

'Aye, and we've still got to patch up the vessel before we can go on. Luckily, we have our spare mast, and some cloth for a sail, though it's soaked.'

'Well, we'd best leave you to all your repair work, neighbour, and be going on. Give me a few male passengers. No women, at any price. And no more than ten. Put out the grapples men, easy, so as to go alongside.'

The two ships were held together by grappling-hooks, and there was now a scrambling among the dishevelled passengers. Several came clamouring to us swearing they were carrying important dispatches – several whose claims others seemed inclined to dispute, including the sailors belonging to the distressed ship.

'That one's no more carrying dispatches than my aunt!' one sailor said in disgust, firmly, removing a passenger who was trying to climb across to our ship. Luckily, the crying women and children made no attempt to move. But the important men were eager to escape their injured craft, and a group soon gathered; these personages were more or less decorously pushed into the *Niké*.

'And you, citizen Koriskos, are you not coming with us?' one of those who had just joined us entreated his companion, who was standing on the splintered deck of the injured boat.

'No,' said this calm citizen, steadily surveying us. 'I am quite well where I am, thank you. I and my embassy will continue on this vessel. Without paying extra. I think here we know the worst.'

'But the vessel may sink! You will drown!'

'And it may not, and I may live. Who knows what safety is?' Koriskos shrugged. 'Somehow, I think I shall get my embassy to Alexander and his generals. We shall do our best to keep dry, and to get there unbroken.'

'Well – who'd have thought it!' The new arrival turned to us, in order to have someone to whom to express his wonderment. 'That ship has been through – I cannot tell you! It must be ready to fall apart. How Koriskos can trust her I do *not* know.'

'No accounting for tastes,' said Nikias, making ready to set off again.

His men rather sullenly unhooked the grapples, while Aristotle leaned forward and spoke to the other ship: 'Good citizen Koriskos, I know you, and I knew your father. Pray, when you arrive in Asia on your embassy, remember me, Aristotle, to Alexander, and to my nephew Kallisthenes. I am Aristotle of Stageira, dweller in Athens.'

Koriskos stared. 'You there, Aristotle – the philosopher? I recollect you. How goes it with you?'

'I am travelling here, on the ship of Nikias of Kos, with my friend Stephanos of Athens and my student Parmenion. We are well enough, despite a testy night. I hope you are the same. Our captain Nikias is very able. I wish you a good journey, by all the gods, and good speed!'

Aristotle sat down again, under the grumbling of the men who were hastening to get out their oars and settle on their benches. They seemed put out, perhaps because of the extra work after a long hard night. They had suffered delay, and now an addition to their load. Our mast was put up and we went off, leaving the damaged vessel to get rid of its sodden cargo and patch itself up as best it might. The men who had joined us gave fussy thanks for their deliverance, and settled themselves. I thought they might have had more compassion for their former fellow-passengers, still stuck on the dangerous listing vessel. But then, I too was thankful that our ship was whole and sound (more or less), and that we were speeding forward to Kos once more.

'That's a relief,' said Aristotle.

'You mean that the sun's out and we're on our way.'

'Yes, that. And that I spoke to Koriskos. Now Alexander will know where we are.'

'Or where we *were*,' I pointed out.

XIV

━━━◦§◦━━━

The Healing Island

The day grew brighter, the sea a little calmer, and we made our way, not without difficulty, towards our destination.

'Got blown off a bit,' said Nikias. 'We're nearer Cape Lektera than I'd like. Dangerous rocky sort of place. See, if Kos is like a big fish, then Lektera's the tail, and we want to get to the fish's mouth, so to speak. To the new city and port of Kos near the shrine to Asklepios and so on. There was an old city, in the south-west of the island – but that was destroyed by the Spartans.'

We agreed that we wanted the port of the new city of Kos, near the Asklepion. We went on fast enough, after more bailing. The men were tired and inclined to ill-humour; I noticed they spoke in disparaging tones of the large ship. 'An old tub, warped and crazy – take everything to the bottom with her, so she will,' one sailor remarked gloomily. 'Oh well,' rejoined his companion, 'not much loss. Cargo was only wools and hides.' I felt

286

disgusted at his lack of feeling – if not for the passengers, then for the vessel's oarsmen.

'Now you see,' said Nikias, 'the advantage of *our* little cargo. Rough stones of marble. Ballast when we want 'em, and cargo if and when we like. Seawater does them no good, but no great harm either – and they don't swell up and cause trouble. I'd hate to be a shipper of grain! Hides is about the worst in a long run, it's so hard to throw 'em overboard once they've swole up. Stones, now, they're easy tossed over if need arises. And we can sell the marble without much trouble – carvers here can make it into plaques and small figures and so on.'

We sailed into the harbour of Kos eventually, for which we gave proper thanks to the gods who had seen us though our dangerous journey. The little family were especially vocal regarding their intention of going to the local shrines as soon as they could, in order to offer particular thanks to Poseidon and also to the Dioskouroi, the Heavenly Twins, who appear as rescuers in moments of crisis and had appeared to us in balls of fire aboard the *Niké*. The landing itself was easy; Kos harbour was nicely fitted up with a good mole. 'Had to be,' said Nikias, when I commented on this fact. 'Alexander used it for his fleet for a bit.'

At last the feet of myself, Aristotle, Parmenion and Phokon tasted dry land. Although we walked in a rather wobbly fashion, we gave hearty thanks to be on firm ground. The easy harbour offered a smiling prospect. The city, climbing up the gentle hills and spilling around its port, looked, at first glance, a prosperous place. Aristotle paid off the captain Nikias, adding a gift to his men for bringing us so successfully through the storm. The men still seemed contentious, however, perhaps because they feared they would not get their share of the payment. I saw them as we turned away, arguing – a couple of them quite fiercely – with Nikias.

We were too tired to go far for a residence, and took lodgings at the first place we could find. Doris insisted on coming with us. 'Just until I can get word to my mistress,' she explained. 'I want to stay with respectable folks.' The little family too was looking for lodgings with us, and we all came to the same house, one respectable enough for Doris and large enough for all of us. It was quite a nice house, really, and the garden was large enough to allow us men to sleep out of doors, in the coolness. Of course the mother and the little girl were to sleep indoors. Best of all, we told the people that Doris was acting as our slave, and she had to go to the kitchen quarters and gut fish.

The owner of the house was a fisherman at least part of the time, and he ensured a steady supply of food from the sea. So we ate well, with fresh olives and grilled fish and fresh beans and green stuff, and loaves just cooked by our landlady. They promised us better fare on the morrow, and an abundance of fruit including fresh figs and apples.

'The vegetables and fruit on Kos are justly celebrated,' said Aristotle. 'This is the best watered of these islands, known for the perfection of its air and its waters. Hence Hippokrates and others have chosen it as their centre for health. This is a centre for the service of Asklepios and it is known for the training of doctors.'

During this brief lecture the grandfather and the mother looked anxiously at the child Philokleia. She was not wheezing or coughing; I thought that Kos might

prove of benefit after all. Nikias of Kos had told us this
was the healing island. I myself felt relief and pleasure, as
if I had just recovered from an illness – really, as I had
been delivered from the sea.

'I wish I could stay here,' I said to Aristotle.
'Unfortunately I must leave this wholesome island and go
on to Rhodos to look for my prospective bride's uncle.'

'Wait until we have made some enquiries here,' he
advised.

I was anxious to talk to Aristotle alone. At last there
were no sailors about to overhear us. Doris was shaken
off, doing servant's work in the house. I recommended
that Parmenion take a rest in the orchard with Phokon to
look after him. Then Aristotle and I were able to go for a
quiet stroll in a secluded place, and at last I could repeat
to him the questions I had asked of myself: What had our
good captain Aiskhines seen – or heard – that made him
decide to come after us all the way up those hills to
Aristodamos' house? Was he really trying to speak to us?
Was it barely possible that he was bound on some other
business altogether – smuggling, for instance, or some
love intrigue – so that he just happened to find himself in
Aristodamos' garden – and to find himself dead?

'These questions,' said Aristotle, 'are the same as I have
asked myself. The sea journey gave me leisure for silent
reflection, but no answers. I think as you do, that it is
unlikely that the captain had any business in the hills of
Naxos other than what concerned ourselves. From what
the sailor said, it is likely that he saw something or
overheard a remark of importance. Perhaps some facts
just fitted together suddenly in his mind.'

'Miltiades,' I said hesitantly. 'The sailor thought it odd

that Miltiades made so much ado over shipping one not very large statue. Of course, it might be of value for its antiquity, and sailors aren't judges of art. But did Miltiades try to get our sailors out of the way for a while? And was he disappointed that they performed their task so expeditiously?'

'I agree that the part played by Miltiades is not clear. He may be just a businessman. It sticks in my mind that he was very anxious to tell the magistrate in Delos that we were involved in a murder and a disappearance. Yet he came to our ship, all smiles, the next day. Something not quite right there. Our good captain, an intelligent man, may have made some deductions of his own. It seems most probable that Aiskhines came to Aristodamos' dwelling in order to warn us of something. But he was killed before he could talk.'

'Nobody alerted the household,' I observed. 'If Aiskhines came late at night, he was an intruder and the house-dog should have barked. Or Doris' dog. But there was no noise in the night time.'

'No dog did anything in the night time,' agreed Aristotle. 'Aristodamos suspects that his own house-dog had followed one of the slaves, who is the dog's great favourite. The slave either didn't notice (which is what he will say) or he encouraged the animal to join the party (more likely). As for Doris' lame dog, she must have left it muzzled, so it physically could not bark. Hard to keep a dog from barking any other way. Even if it knows the person – if that person unexpectedly turns up on the premises late at night, a dog will bark.'

'Even if muzzled, it should have whined. Of course,' I speculated, 'perhaps it is as well we didn't awaken and investigate when Aiskhines came. An investigator might have been murdered as well.'

'Possibly so. Somewhere, Stephanos, there is a determined enemy at work. Remember the events on Delos and Mykonos. An attempt was made in Delos to prevent us from moving on, with the suspicion of foul play – the blood on the ship. Philokhoros – of whom we know next to nothing! – having caught our attention, was actually spirited away, by persons unknown, who took a great deal of trouble to inveigle him away and tie him up. His slave boy was *possibly* stolen – or possibly acted in collusion (either forced or voluntary) with the kidnappers. And Philokhoros, the unfortunate man who was nearly thrown to the pigs, must have been decoyed away – did you notice this? – just at the time we were talking to Doris' mistress.'

'I didn't like that woman,' I agreed. 'Nor do I like her slave Doris any better.'

'And now Doris seems almost part of our household. By the way, I hope you noticed how adeptly I have evaded the charge of slave-stealing, by indicating that we have *borrowed* the slave – indicating our intention to pay. I wish that dreadful Kardaka would reclaim her property! But I wonder if we'll see that lady again. Perhaps her purpose has been served. Was she a tool? But whose? And why? Yet, it is suspicious, Philokhoros' abduction and being tied up coinciding with our being tied up – metaphorically only – in the interview with Kardaka.'

'But it may just be a coincidence. After all, our interview with Kardaka wasn't actually very long. You know, we really spent much more time going up the hill Kynthos and looking at the view. And that was at my insistence – Philokhoros may have been abducted because *I* wanted to see the shrine of Herakles and the view from Kynthos. So it is my fault too, in a way.'

'If you have a fault, Stephanos,' said Aristotle, laughing, 'it is that you are somewhat too fond of strenuous uphill walks to make you the ideal companion for an old person. Philokhoros' abduction is not your fault. Philokhoros – who is he? We know only what he has told us. We do not know why he was abducted in that manner. What purpose could it possibly serve?'

'Maybe,' I suggested, 'Philokhoros has an enemy of his own who wants to finish him off?'

'Why didn't this enemy do it, then?' Aristotle retorted. 'If the murderer brought him to the brothel, he had the perfect chance for murder. Or is Philokhoros in possession of some secret – and was he secured in the pigpen so he could later be interrogated by this "Solon"? Was Philokhoros really abducted, or was he pretending – ? No, it is nonsense to think any man of birth or breeding would allow himself to be bound and tossed in the pigpen for a stratagem.'

'Now what will happen? What do you think Aristodamos will do? – has done?'

'Aristodamos,' mused Aristotle, 'is a man of exceedingly good reputation, and very ancient lineage, who has the happiness not to be overlooked by a lot of inquisitive neighbours. He had with him when we left one devoted servant, a woman terrified for her life. She would do anything to aid him and avert disaster. Aristodamos is an intelligent man.'

'Do you mean, he will give us up to justice – if he can make some sort of bargain about her?'

'Oh, do think, Stephanos! But there,' he caught himself, 'who am I to say that I am such a prophet I can certainly tell what Aristodamos will do? I know what I *think* he will have done after we left. He will take the rational way out of the difficulty, if he can. I think the body of Aiskhines will be discovered – probably by now it has been discovered – well away from Aristodamos' "Apple Place". Probably in some ravine or vale among those steep Naxian hills. Most likely we shall eventually hear that the body of Aiskhines has been transported to Athens in the *Eudaimonia* by his crew, and that these injured and puzzled sailors, along with the family of the murdered man, are demanding justice of the authorities. There will be proclamations and questions.'

'So in any case our names will come up?'

'Our names will inevitably be mentioned – if not sooner, then later. It is not unlikely that a magistrate in one of these islands will eventually get hold of us. We need to make some good local friends as quickly as possible. Also, I was not lying when I said in my farewell speech that I had an embassy for Alexander. I have already sent messages to Asia to advise some of the Makedonian leaders that I shall be near the Asian coast. Luckily, because of Parmenion's poor health, I alerted them in the spring to the possibility that either Theophrastos or I might be going to the islands, and I let them know of my departure as soon as I knew it myself. I am hoping soon to receive an official message in return, and that could protect us until we get out of the shadow of Aiskhines' murder. So –' he turned to gaze towards the town – 'after I have sent a message to advise Oromedon of Kos that we are here, let us walk into Kos town, where I can make enquiries for some other persons I know of. Then we can go to the Asklepion.'

Returning to our lodgings, Aristotle sent off his note and I invited Parmenion and Phokon to walk with us. The family from Laurion were anxious to put Philokleia under the care of a doctor, and Aristotle promised to find a good one for them. When we got into the town, we found it was not as charming as it had first appeared. A number of what had been houses were simply piles of rubble with a few fragmentary remains of walls. I pointed this out to Aristotle.

'Some were ruined by the last great earthquake, I think,' he replied. 'But the town doesn't look as cheerful as it used to, and one must admit, these look like very modern ruins. Presumably the result of severe fighting at the time Alexander took the harbour. Alexander's army is very good at using missiles to destroy buildings. It was only three years ago that he took this island. Before that, you will recall, it was a Persian safety zone. The Persian commander Memnon had escaped to Kos.' He cast a worried glance at Parmenion. 'There wasn't much fighting here,' he added reassuringly. 'It was a famous and favoured port, and the island valued as a good source of provisions. Kos did not suffer too badly, by all accounts – not as badly as it did in our war against Sparta.'

Yet it became impossible not to notice the ravages of war. In the Kyklades men had spoken of war – but veritable war itself had passed this way. We began to be accosted by beggars. Numbers of persons were encamped in Kos and its outskirts, living a ragged and precarious existence. There was much crying of children and a deal of dirt and refuse, beside the harbour and in nearby areas.

'These are surely not Koans!' Aristotle exclaimed, as we went up a gentle slope away from the smell of the worst of the ragged camps. 'I remember Kos as so enlightened and civilized, so clean –'

'No,' said a middle-aged man nearby, a tall man with a rippling beard, who had caught this exclamation. 'These people are unfortunates in flight from Asia – people who have lost their cities. Many are from ruined Halikarnassos. Look yonder.' He pointed. 'You can make out a headland from here. We see the side of the Myndos cape, that some call the Cape of Halikarnassos. That great city is – was – on the southern side. You cannot see it from here, because of the cape, and the city's harbour is masked by two little islands, but Halikarnassos is not far off.'

Certainly, I could see land, bluish and dim in the morning mist but not remote, rising on the immediate horizon. My first sight of Asia! My blood quickened. Now I was truly in another part of the world.

'Halikarnassos, a great city. Entirely destroyed. It was smitten by projectiles and its walls battered down. Its soldiers – and many inhabitants who were not soldiers – were put to the sword amid great tumult. And the whole city was set on fire.'

'Yes,' I said, 'I have heard about that.' But the young man who told the history had seemed to me then – only a few months ago! – merely a teller of exotic tales. My notion of the real was changing, or perhaps the real was changing as I looked at it, as in Aristotle's translucent and iridescent world.

Meanwhile, the man with the rippling brown beard (streaked with grey) was looking fixedly at Aristotle. 'Don't I know you?' he asked.

Aristotle gazed back. 'By the sons of Asklepios – it is Iatrokles!'

'So I am recognisable, at least, old friend – with sufficient prompting. And I know you, though we both have aged. You are Aristotle of Stageira.'

'You may claim me as that and as your friend in medicine,' said Aristotle, embracing this man cordially. 'How could I not recognise you straight away? My eyes are not as good as they once were, I fear, and my mind was elsewhere. Times have changed since we studied together the arts of medicine.' He turned to me. 'Let me introduce Stephanos of Athens. Stephanos, this is Iatrokles, one of the best doctors in Kos – which means the best in the world.'

'A practitioner in the mystery, and a searcher for truth, nothing more,' said Iatrokles. 'There is so much more to do and to know.'

The two men settled themselves on some sun-warmed steps looking down on the harbour and continued their conversation, while I hovered nearby.

'How do you get on?' asked Aristotle, when some questions as to the fates and fortunes of several acquaintances had been asked and answered. 'And what is Kos like now?'

'Well, it has suffered from the war, though less than many other places. The Persian military, when they retreated here and defended this island, allowed us doctors both to study and practise, just as the Persians had always done before. Now that Makedon has taken over, we go on now much as we did. We get a few well-off pilgrims in search of health, even now. But there are numbers of people here without a home or a city any more, and so there is a constant call for our services. To people who cannot pay.'

'That kind of patient is never difficult to find,' commented Aristotle.

'But we must regard this troublous time as an opportunity. Kos' soil is rich and produces good food – you should see the great shrine of Demeter, a day's walk from here, by the way. Wheat and vegetables. Fish of course. Kos still has what it always had – excellent and abundant food and pure water. Clean and lively air, scented by sea and pine trees. Hippokrates recommends it above all other places for restoration of physical and mental harmony.'

'So he does,' said Aristotle. 'My grandfather, who came here to study at one time, knew Hippokrates,' he added.

'My grandfather did too,' said Iatrokles, 'and not only my grandfather but my father saw him as a boy. Our family is long-lived. Indeed,' turning to me, 'you should think of staying here, young man. We Koans have a fine prospect of life. Now, in such cases as those of the wretched people without a *polis* who have come here, we can examine whether the conditions offered by Kos do indeed have curative power, and for what ailments or bodily states they work best. If we can improve the health of some of these wretches, then indeed all our claims can be justified. Also, we shall have a much clearer idea as to how to go about cures in various cases.'

'The art of medicine is indeed changing,' said Aristotle. 'For the better, I think – largely owing to Hippokrates and the school of Kos. Hippokrates taught us how to treat medicine as a separate category, and how to examine physical phenomena and record them. Once medicine was the province of one tribe alone. But now the school of Kos is admitting worthy young men who can pay to learn the skill, whether or not they come from the medical lineage. The subject can now advance, and we shall have a sufficient number of doctors.'

'*You* have no reason to complain of the old way, Aristotle, as you are a descendant of Machaon. And thus rise from the chief medical lineage,' said Iatrokles, laughing. 'And I too descend from Machaon. But my friend and partner Kleumedes is a descendant of Asklepios' other son, Podaleirios. Together we cover the whole ground – surgery and internal medicine. But the opening of the art to those possessing sufficient skill is an excellent innovation. There is far more demand than one family line could meet. Kos can become the centre of an even greater school. Of course we have the advantage of the shrine to Asklepios, which will always bring to the island those who seek cure or relief. Have you seen the Asklepion?' he asked me. 'No? Oh, you should see it – it is one of our sights, and not too far away. A pleasant walk, even in summer.'

This sounded good in my ears. The harbour area was less attractive to me because of the number of people who came to beg from arriving and departing passengers, and anyone else. I had given as much as I cared to part with.

We went back, around the harbour and past our lodging house. We continued going inland, up some gentle slopes; the road wound among groves and orchards. It felt good to be walking in the countryside again and I was glad not to be in a vessel, pitching on the waves under the hot sun. We drank from a natural spring on the way, and gave thanks to the nymphs. Certainly Kos looked as Iatrokles the ageing physician said – lush, fertile, well watered and most pleasant to the senses. Little settlements were dotted here and there, mostly farms with outbuildings.

'Some of these folk are Persian,' the Koan informed us, 'though they keep quiet and don't speak their language out of doors nor practise their religion in public these days.'

It seemed very strange to me that Persians should be allowed to remain on what was now most definitely a Greek island – even if this isle had formerly sided with Darius the Great King. For that very reason, I should have thought the Greeks and Makedonians would have ruled with a firm hand and got rid of the Persians altogether. I said as much.

'But,' said Iatrokles, 'enough of that kind was done at Halikarnassos – and elsewhere. Throwing people off their land! All Koans are against it. We argued with Alexander's generals. And, after all, Alexander's troops and navy need the port, even now the navy is so greatly reduced. Kos is wanted for repairing vessels, shipping in supplies, and for sending men home. Sick or wounded army officers come to the island for health. With so much activity here, we need a regular supply of food, for Alexander's own convenience. Forcible removal of intelligent farmers in Kos would endanger the food supply. So – it has seemed wisest to proceed by turning a blind eye to the Persian presence on their small but productive farms.'

We walked at an easy old-gentleman pace, but even so we arrived at the Asklepion in a short time. I could see the advantage of its proximity to the port. 'Even invalids – most of them – could walk here.'

'Yes,' said Iatrokles, 'and it is also easy to bring them by donkey or by cart – or by litter.'

'Just enough effort made to make the journey seem like a pilgrimage,' said Aristotle. 'I had forgotten the beauty and impressiveness of this site.'

It was a well-wooded place, with a delightful prospect. On one side you could see all the way to the sea and to Asia beyond. The whole of the centre was a great grove of cypresses, with around it a thick wood of pine trees. Short lively grass, smelling of thyme, sprang from the slopes where we entered. In the midst of the site, a temple to Apollo glimmered white and gold. Cicadas chirped their summer song; wherever there was no shade the heat moved like waves in the air.

'This is a sacred grove,' said Iatrokles, 'and the whole wood beyond is sacred too. It is forbidden to die or be born there.'

Again I felt a slight twinge of nervousness, lest I offend against the gods by dying in the wrong place. 'There are mineral springs, a little fountain and a shrine of the Nymphs. Drink of the water – it has a decided taste,' Iatrokles urged. 'There, you see the shrine of Asklepios. Until very recently indeed, there was just the great open-air shrine and altar. The altar has become more magnificent, and now we have a small temple to Asklepios.' He pointed this out, a little round structure glimmering among the trees. 'We hope,' he continued, 'to have something much bigger – or at least, there is a lot of talk about this in Kos now. For with the establishment of a really fine port, recently enlarged to accommodate great ships, as well as a flourishing city (or one that could readily be so again), we could afford to make this a first-class temple complex.'

As we walked towards the centre, Iatrokles pointed out the various spots of ground that would do for a much larger sacred precinct.

'Here we could have the building with underground rooms for the incubation of dreams,' he explained. 'As well as a truly fine temple to Asklepios. With a good road, and some organisation, we could have crowds of pilgrims. Just imagine them – see them all in white, coming up that road yonder!' Iatrokles pointed back the way we had come. 'Waving palm and olive branches, singing to divine Apollo and in praise of immortal Paieon, and in pleading to Asklepios. A holy sound, in tremulous voices. There they come – full of hope!'

We could almost see the processions of the future, coming to the magnificent temple complex, to the fountains and terraces with marble stairways, the great temple of Asklepios with its surrounding porticoes, all of which he had imagined for us.

'I tell you, we could vie with Delos,' said Iatrokles, mopping his brow. 'In fact, we are much better than Delos. For look, the site is on a slope of Mount Oromedon, which graciously gives us many springs. There are other mineral springs nearby. And we have perpetual fresh sweet water, which certainly isn't true in little Delos, a desert in the sea. Water is essential for the treatment of invalids.'

'There is truth in what you say,' said Aristotle. 'The development of the sanctuary would go hand in hand with the growth of the medical school in Kos, one feeding the other. For there would be enough wealth coming into this island to fund the teaching of medicine and to give teachers and scholars agreeable conditions. The glory of Kos would spread.'

'But it does so already,' said Iatrokles confidently. 'Many cities want Koan doctors. Some pay out of public funds for a man to come and study with us. Then he must go back and be a doctor for the city. This custom is bound to gain wide acceptance. Alexander and his chiefs all want Koan doctors to attend on themselves and even on their troops. Once all the soldiery who have been made better by Koan doctors return home, they will want doctors of Kos for themselves in time of peace.'

'So the war could work out very well for you, in the long run,' commented Aristotle, with a smile. 'This is as you say, "a beautiful site",' he added. 'I had forgotten how pure and clear and sweet the air is, smelling of pine trees. Let us acknowledge Apollo and Asklepios.'

We offered a prayer, though not a sacrifice, in the quiet afternoon, at both the Temple of Apollo and the little shrine of Asklepios. Small as it was, the interior of this shrine was covered in votive offerings, with many more legs, and arms and hands than usual, and some uncommon and rather graphic depictions of holes in the torso. I thought of the last time I had been in a shrine of Asklepios with Aristotle and the now departed Pythias, and looked anxiously at him, but he made no sign of grief. He glanced with professional curiosity at the little images.

'These with holes in their bodies must be military petitioners, people wounded in the war,' he commented. 'But I see the familiar concerns of peacetime here too – there is a complete image of a child, a little girl, offered in thanksgiving by her parents.' He gestured at the silver image; the child seemed to gaze back, round-eyed.

'That reminds me, we have in our party – or, rather, we have travelled with – a family from Athens, whose only offspring, a little girl, is sickly with what I diagnose as asthma. I rashly volunteered to find her a doctor. Could you, Iatrokles, offer your expert knowledge? The family have come intending to pay,' he added. 'But I am sorry for the tiny maiden, so if the family cannot rise to the whole fee, I shall pay the remainder.'

'Think nothing of that,' said Iatrokles. 'Of course, I shall be glad to have a look at the child. Asthma is one of the conditions the Greek doctors of Hippokrates' school have been good at defining and treating.'

We left the shrine of Asklepios, quiet among the trees, and walked back to Kos. The short excursion had given us each an appetite, even Parmenion. We were glad to take some midday food at our lodging, with Iatrokles as our guest. Out in the orchard at the back we addressed ourselves to fresh onions, cheese, olives and flat cakes. The landlady was vexed to have to tell us that Doris had suddenly gone, saying only she had instructions as to how to reunite with her mistress. We reassured the landlady, saying that Doris had our permission to depart and we were glad she was able to go home. Certainly, Doris had our permission to depart! What a great relief, I felt, not to have to see her again. Of course, this loss of a servant meant our landlady was short-handed while trying to feed new lodgers.

'It is so lovely here, I wish I could stay,' I commented. 'But I must continue my journey. I wish, however, that I could get a letter from Athens before I set out again. I would so like to hear that all is well at home before undertaking this search. We must ask at your friend

Oromedon's house. You know, Aristotle, I must set off for Rhodos – for a more difficult search than I had thought when planning it out. For I do not know Rhodos at all. How hard it is to find one unimportant person in a strange place! And I now realise that Rhodos is a great large island, much larger than Kos, and yet we have hardly seen anything of *this* island.'

'Why go to Rhodos? What are you looking for?' Iatrokles asked.

'I am looking for a particular person. His name is Philokles, son of Philokles. He is a man of Athens – Hymettos in Athens. And uncle to the woman I hope to marry.'

'Ha – skat!' Iatrokles spat an olive stone into the garden with delighted emphasis. 'I believe I know exactly the man you mean. It's no good going to Rhodos to look for him. He has been *here* – in Kos – for his health.'

'Oh!' I jumped up. 'Where is he? Let me find him at once –'

'Now sit down, young man. Don't get overheated. He's not in Kos at this particular time. He and some mistress of his have gone to Kalymnos. But they'll be back.'

'You have seen him?'

'I believe so. He is – or was – the patient of a friend of mine.'

'He is ill? Oh, that could be a dreadful misfortune. If he dies before he hears my news –'

'I don't think he's anywhere near dying,' said Iatrokles impatiently. 'And I've seen a sight of dying in my time, too. No, he had pains in his back and joints. Not thinking too much of Rhodos after all – terrible windy it is – he came over here. Easy to do with all the shipping available these days. Of course Rhodos is a goodly way from here, it's south and east of us, well beyond the Cape of Knidos. But this man Philokles of Athens came here, and then he took to living with a woman who has some money, and a place of her own.'

'A woman with a place of her own?' It seemed incredible. 'You mean a prostitute with a brothel?'

'No. Not exactly. She's a young widow. Mind, I think she was the *hetaira* of one of Alexander's naval commanders. Her friend the commander set her up with her own house and garden and slaves. So as long as the Greeks and Makedonians are in power here, nobody dares abuse her, and she was living discreetly until this young Philokles came along.'

'Well!' My head spun. I had been looking for Philomela's uncle, the brother of the bee-woman, strange but beautiful Philonike. I had been imagining this uncle as a hard-working dour type of man, labouring hard as a settler in Rhodos. And here I heard of him gallivanting about quite another island with a questionable lady.

'Really!' I was almost cross. 'I have put myself to some trouble on account of this man. I hope he turns up.'

'They're bound to turn up, as she has her place here – unless he's foolish enough to quarrel with her. He's not married, and he hasn't too much of his own, so it's handy for him to have somewhere to live. She's not poor. She has business in Kalymnos too. Sponge fishery.'

'Stephanos, the gods seem to drop your answer into your lap,' Aristotle said. 'Instead of another tedious journey, you have only to rest in charming Kos and wait for this gentleman and his light-of-love to return.'

'That does seem easy,' I admitted. 'Though we don't

know when he will come. And I had hoped to deal with a serious man. Now Philokles doesn't sound serious at all.'

'You'll find back trouble serious enough,' said Iatrokles. 'Ah – and who might this be?'

While we were talking, the family from Laurion had come out into the garden. The mother came veiled and walking slowly. But Philokleia had run over to us.

'This is your potential patient,' said Aristotle. 'This is Philokleia. And here is her grandfather – no, don't take the child away. Let me introduce you. Tell Phokon to bring the chairs here so we can all talk together.'

Once we had settled ourselves, the grandfather Hermippos, with some prompting from the child's veiled mother, gave the Koan doctor an account of the little girl's history and malady. Then Iatrokles asked the child to come over to him, placed her in front of him, and with his large gentle hands felt her chest and throat and listened to her breathing.

'She is not a bad size for her age,' he said, straightening. 'The breathing does not seem bad, though I detect the labour and unevenness of asthmatic patients. Do you cough, little one?'

'I used to,' said Philokleia. 'Not at sea, though, and not much in Kos.'

'Aha,' said Iatrokles. 'So – we progress already. You live in Attika, I know – but where?'

Before her elders could answer, the child piped up. 'We live near Laurion. It's a big place with a lot of mine works, and we live by the big mines. Not like here – the earth is all tumbled about and poor men go into the holes in the ground and stay there all day.'

'That is right,' said her grandfather. 'My interests are

largely in the mining business. I own a washery and a furnace. Laurion is a very thriving place now.'

'In the mine workings – of course!' exclaimed the doctor. 'Lead and silver mines. Lots of dust from the earth. Much of the time you would also be breathing dust and smoke from the furnaces for melting metal. Now, it seems to me that the little girl's breathing could be greatly alleviated or even cleared up by remaining in a pure air. As she seems to respond well to the sea air, let her stay here for a time. Kos would be perfect for her. Let her take regular exercise, and eat our good vegetables. And –' he gestured an order – 'bring wine to the table for us.' The red wine was instantly brought, and the doctor gazed upon it with a pleased expression. He poured a libation and then ceremonially gave each of us a drink, to mix with water as we wished.

'Hippokrates says "drink the good wines of Kos", and I myself have been endeavouring faithfully to follow that advice my life long. Let the child drink the pure water, with a *little* wine added. I have often found that such an addition clears up any impurities and enhances the good of the water. Bathe her carefully, and do not let her go about with perspiration drying on her skin, which is another source of impurity.'

'Well,' said the grandfather, 'you give us reason to hope our little one will be well soon and running about like other children. And that she will live to be a grown lady, and marry and bear many children, as her good grandmother did.'

The girl's mother said nothing, but made an impatient gesture with her foot. I suppose she did not like being reminded that her own father thought she hadn't done well in childbearing, since she had produced only one child, and that a daughter.

'Yes – yes,' said Iatrokles, smiling. 'We could all live longer lives if we were careful about what we breathed and what water we drank. And if we were less inclined to eat too much. Yes, little one, stay in Kos. You will like our island. I will tell you a Koan story, which bears out my points.'

He took the child on his lap. Sipping our wine and water as the afternoon shadows lengthened and the fresh sea-flavoured breeze sprang up, we listened as he told us the following tale:

The Tale of the Hungry Prince

'Once upon a time there was a powerful king – let us call him King of Myrmidonia. He was a widower, but still quite young, and he fell in love with a beautiful girl called Dimitroula, after the goddess Demeter whom she served faithfully. Of course the lovely girl was flattered, a little, when the King told his love and offered to marry her. But she rejected him because she was in love with a poor but honest man, who was handsome and kind. The King was furious and he swore he would fight and kill his rival, the poor man. They had a great fight in a sacred wood belonging to Demeter, and Dimitroula crept into an oak tree to watch the battle. Now, so it befell, the King did kill the poor man who would wed Dimitroula. But that unfortunate handsome poor man wounded the King, so the King died too. His only heirs were his son the Prince and the Prince's young daughter Mestra.

'Then the King's son, the Prince of Myrmidonia, who was close by, swore that he would take his revenge upon all beings who had compassed his father's killing. So this Prince in his rage went at once to the wood where his father had died, vowing to cut down all the trees within the wood in his revenge. His sword plunged into an oak tree, slipping through a knot hole in it. And the tree screamed! And the tree bled! When the tree was cut down, the Prince saw the bleeding Dimitroula, pierced by his sword and dying. Oh, but the Prince was horrified – and terrified too. He had angered the wood-sprites and the gods! He and his men fled away from that wood, but not before he was cursed by the goddess Demeter, who was determined to punish him.

'The goddess Demeter made the Prince of Myrmidonia so hungry that he could never be satisfied. Oh, he had an outrageous hunger upon him always! He felt like us before we had the olives and the onions and the flat loaves – but now we feel full. So *we* aren't hungry any more. The Prince, you see, the poor Hungry Prince – he could *never* feel full. His appetite was insatiable. He used up all his money in buying food to feed himself. You never saw the like of what went into that palace! Why, there was roast meat and boiled meat, of cows and oxen, pigs, sheep and goats. And geese and ducks and chickens. And fish from the sea. – all different kinds of fish, from the sardine to the sturgeon. And octopus and sea urchin and cabbage and lettuces. Eggs and olives and cheese of all kinds, flat and round, and herbs. Wheat loaves and barley loaves, and cakes of millet. And sesame pancakes with honey on top, and more honey cakes, and then radishes – and of course lentils. Talents worth of lentils boiled and cooked with oil and cooked with cheese, and served plain and fancy and made into puddings. And rabbit, stewed and roasted, and every kind of sauce. He had sixteen cooks, that man! Until he couldn't afford them any more.

'The Hungry Prince soon spent all the money in his own purses and boxes in the palace to buy food. I was going to say, "for his meals", but the Prince didn't have meals any more in the usual way because there was too much time in between. He just had one big meal all the time! Well, eventually even the Prince found he could not afford to go on like that. By now, he had spent all the money in his treasury. So he sold his palace furniture and his golden cups to buy food, and then he sold his bronze armour. And then he sold his carved bed and his cushions of silk tapestry made in Persia – and all his deceased wife's jewellery, which should have been given to his daughter. He even parted with his own gold-leaf crown. Then – he sold the pots and pans that weren't doing their work any more, and most of the spoons and forks and spits in his kitchen. Fifteen of his sixteen cooks departed, and he had only the youngest and poorest of cooks to work in his cool bare kitchen. Then – what did he have left to sell?'

'I don't know,' said the little girl. 'Did he sell his own arm?'

'He would have sold it if anybody had wanted to

buy such a thing. But he had something that he thought buyers would want. I told you he had a little daughter named Mestra. And he sold her!'

'Oh! That was bad,' said Philokleia.

'It was – *very* bad. The goddess wouldn't let him get away with it. So Demeter gave her friend Mestra the gift of changing her shape. Her father sold Mestra to a big landowner, who took her to the farm on his great estate. Mestra liked this not at all, and immediately turned herself into a fox. Then she ran back on her little fox legs to her father's palace and changed back again to her own shape. Next time, the Hungry Prince sold his daughter to a wealthy jeweller. The wealthy jeweller put a collar of gold around the young girl's neck, and placed Mestra on a big red horse pacing along beside his very big black horse. They trotted off away from the palace, and then they galloped along the road. The jeweller made his big costly horses go faster and faster. "Soon be home," he said to Mestra. But then he saw nothing riding beside him on the red horse but a weasel! The weasel jumped off her horse, the gold collar slid to the ground, and Mestra ran back on her little weasel legs to the palace, and changed back into her own daughter-shape again.

'So then the Hungry Prince sold his daughter to another rich man, this time to a great merchant from a land far away. He took her aboard a big black ship and told the rowers to row fast and take them out upon the deep deep sea. But on board ship, in the middle of the deep dark sea, Mestra changed into a dolphin and plunged into the waves. Then she swam back to land. When she arrived at the seashore, she changed herself into a brown-shelled turtle, and walked, in a slow turtle-y way, through the seaweed and up the sandy beach to a wood beyond the shore. In the wood she became a cunning little rat. And she scuttled back to the palace on her little rat feet. But this time, she wondered if she should change back to her daughter-shape again. She twitched her pretty little rat whiskers and peered about with her little sharp eyes to see first how things were at home.

'By now, the palace was quite dilapidated and falling apart. The only reason you'd be surprised to see a rat in it in broad daylight would be because there wasn't a crumb of food left! You must know, that deplorable Hungry Prince had eaten all the food of his neighbours and their tenants and the poor slaves. By this time everybody, high and low, had run away. So – what did he do, do you think, this Greedy Prince?'

'Eat a person?'

'Yes. But he didn't eat *another* person. He would have done so, but he couldn't eat anybody – simply because he couldn't catch them. In his feasting days, when the heaps of geese and cakes kept coming into the palace, he had got out of the habit of running, or walking, or doing anything for himself. So now – the Hungry Prince turned to and ate himself! There – what do you think of that!! He ate himself till he was all gone, and nothing but the crumbs were left.'

'Oh,' said the little girl. 'What happened to his little girl?'

'To Mestra? Oh, she cried two tears out of her

little peery eyes. She changed herself back into her daughter-shape and cried two more big tears, and ran out of the sad ruinous palace to the seashore. Then the god Poseidon came and asked her to come with live with him in a sea cave and have his children. And he promised she could enjoy living right here in Kos, except now she would live in the wet instead of the dry, along the seashore instead of inland. So she agreed, and enjoyed her life. Mestra had sponges and coral and pearls in her sea cave, and when the waves were high she danced on top of them, and admired the island of Kos and the stars above it. And she had a son by Poseidon, whose name was Eurypylos. He became the first King of Kos in ancient days. Everyone was very happy, and they forgot the Hungry Prince of Myrmidonia.'

'Wasn't that a good story, Philokleia?' her grandfather asked.

'Yes,' she said seriously. 'It was – but I don't like how the first girl died.'

'Well, don't hide too long in one tree,' advised Iatrokles.

'You are a politician, Iatrokles, as well as a moralist,' said Aristotle. '*I* see clearly the point of your philosophical tale.'

'Ah,' said Iatrokles. 'You may think you do. That is the trouble with telling you philosophers a fable. You want to make application. It is the hardest thing in the world to make application! Nor is this story my own invention. Truly. A tale of Demeter here in Kos, a story of long ago. Demeter gives us enough – enough and to spare – but the gods do not say "be piggy", do they?'

'It's a very good story, with a good moral, Philokleia,' said the grandfather. 'Though I have to say, greed is not this child's fault – she doesn't eat enough, sometimes. Our girl doesn't need warning against overeating.'

'Oh, no, I never thought *she* did,' replied Iatrokles. 'And I hope you can take time from your business in Laurion to let her stay here – or somewhere like this – for a time, and grow up a strong girl. Often, under favourable conditions, such maladies as hers wane or disappear at maturity.'

'Yours is a fable about desire,' said Aristotle. 'And like all such fables, it has something to say to everyone. I had forgotten how charming, ingenious and devious you Koans can be!'

'I thank you,' said Iatrokles, bowing as if he had received a compliment. 'I hope you all enjoy Kos, and meet none but good Koans, charming and devious as we are.'

PART III
BODY AND SOUL

XV

The Doctors

I have often thought of that quiet afternoon of story-telling, its small pleasures and its laughter. We lingered as the day cooled and shadows spread. Parmenion, who had joined us in the middle of the tale, condescended to sit on the grass and share some food. He was still aloof and his eyes wandered off. He gazed into a distance that only he could see, his eyes flickering back and forth as if he were searching for some invisible rescue party who would snatch him from despair. I saw Aristotle give Iatrokles a significant nod.

'I cannot stay with this pleasant company all day,' said Iatrokles, casting a shrewd glance at Parmenion. 'I ought to hie me to my own house and see what patients await me. It is easier for some of them to come out in the cool of the evening. Of course,' he added, 'the very ill – or the very rich – I see in their own homes.'

'Let me walk with you,' said Aristotle, 'and Stephanos too, if he will. Do you wish to come with us for a walk,

Parmenion?' Parmenion indicated he would rather stay where he was; on this occasion Aristotle seemed rather relieved than displeased at his incivility. I was happy enough to move after having sat in one spot so long. We strolled at an amiable talking pace back to the harbour and to the street on the other side where Iatrokles had his dwelling. As I suspected, Aristotle wished to take the opportunity of consulting Iatrokles about Parmenion.

'It is a double problem,' he explained. 'This boy has been longing for home – he is most anxious to know what has happened to his father. And I have had no written word or other sort of message from his father for a very long while. Because there is some real cause for concern, I could not send the boy away to the eastern islands on his own. I wished to hear myself about the condition of his father before I took him to Rhodos. There was no need to gossip about the boy's trouble in Athens, where Makedonians are not always looked upon with favour. Parmenion is related to extremely important Makedonian leaders.'

'You mean, I take it, the great Parmenion?'

'Yes. He is grandson (if on the wrong side of the blanket) to the great Parmenion. Although neither this lad nor his father is, strictly speaking, legitimate, both have been acknowledged by the rest of the family; his uncle Philotas would be his guardian if anything has happened to his father. But this boy's grandfather, Alexander's right-hand man, as well as the boy's uncle Philotas are both engaged in the wars far to the east. The boy's father, Arkhebios, is also a military man, though of much less importance. Arkhebios' mother's family are of Rhodos, where Arkhebios was also posted at the time the boy came to our school. The army sometimes finds men with local connections useful in pacifying a region. The problem is, now I cannot seem to reach Arkhebios. The boy himself fears for his father's life in these wars.'

'You know,' said Iatrokles seriously, 'this is no slight matter. Many people have disappeared in the wars, for one cause or another. But what about the boy in himself? I can tell you are not satisfied with his own health.'

'That is so,' said Aristotle. 'Frankly, I fear that, whether from worrying about his family or from some other cause, young Parmenion has become – or is becoming – insane. At moments, however, he acts like a normal person, yet at other times he is not only morose but abstracted and wandering. Melancholia seems to be claiming him – even to the extent of turning his wits so that he is unfit to go about.'

'A difficult case,' said Iatrokles. 'Melancholia in the young is a bad sign – and yet it is the young who often plunge into melancholy, who are even willing to kill themselves over some little love problem or the like. But you need to talk to my friend and partner Kleumedes, the doctor whom I admire most. He is a physician with great understanding of humours and the balances of the body – and mind. Come and let us see if Kleumedes can help you. He is a widower and we live together, and help each other out in seeing patients.'

He turned into a dwelling of modest size, but neat and very clean in appearance. It was well sited on a hill, with a view of the harbour and the sea and even of the Asian coast. The house seemed more spacious inside than it had promised without, with a pleasant courtyard and handsome main room. 'Ah – books!' said Aristotle with approval, going over to examine them.

'Kleumedes, you're wanted!' Iatrokles shouted. His speaking in such a rudely raised voice, as a man would speak to a slave, surprised me. Iatrokles perceived my reaction.

'Kleumedes is a man of many parts, but a trifle deaf. He hears better when he can look at your face, but from a distance you have to shout.' A bushy head popped round the door.

'I was just speaking about the fish,' Kleumedes explained. This new doctor had a great beard and a large head with quantities of hair, much of it grey, standing out in various directions; some seemed to be growing straight upwards. His mouth was wide and generous, and his large brown eyes looked us over curiously but without hostility.

'There's enough fish to do for two dinners,' he remarked to Iatrokles, 'but we have to grill it all now – I told the cook.' After this piece of domestic information he settled into the formality of introductions. 'Aristotle the philosopher, famous in Athens, and Stephanos of Athens – Kleumedes son of Kleumedes of Kos,' said Iatrokles. Kleumedes made suitable response in his rather rumbling voice.

'My friend Kleumedes,' Iatrokles went on, still in a loud clear tone, 'is a descendant of Hippokrates. And a descendant of Asklepios' second son, expert in curing invisible ills. Kleumedes is the best of all doctors – in the world, I think.'

'You must forgive the bias of my dear friend,' said Kleumedes. 'He means well. Hyperbole is his only fault. I am a doctor who does the best he can.'

'We want to consult you about a case,' Aristotle admitted.

'Sit down,' said Kleumedes, 'and I am all ears.' Indeed, he cupped a hand behind one of those members (very large in his case), as he sat himself opposite Aristotle. 'Proceed.'

Aristotle explained Parmenion to Kleumedes much as he had already done to Iatrokles.

'Ah,' said Kleumedes, nodding thoughtfully. 'There are two parts to young Parmenion's problem. One external and the other internal. But I fear you must find out the truth about what has *really* happened to his father before you can commence any lasting treatment. Either his father is alive or he is dead. If alive, either he is well or he isn't. Either he still has his money and position, or he has lost one or both. All of these things can be ascertained eventually, as they are facts in the real world. But the deeper problem lies in what Parmenion *thinks* is in the world. And that is harder to fathom. There can be no cure for his condition without knowledge of the truth.'

'That sounds right,' said Iatrokles. 'But the condition might be ameliorated meanwhile.'

'Yes,' said Kleumedes. 'I should like to see this young man. Bring him to me tomorrow.'

He rose rather grandly, as if once he had made up his mind there was no further use in talking to us. I was amused and a trifle annoyed at this imperious and dismissive address. There was nothing for it but for us to say farewell, and to tell the doctors that we would bring Parmenion on the morrow. We found that we were addressing only Iatrokles. Kleumedes had already left the room and gone to the inner apartment before we had got to the door. We made our farewells to Iatrokles without commenting on his friend's abrupt behaviour, which he seemed to find unremarkable.

'What a strange doctor,' I said to Aristotle, once we were well away from the house. 'He is evidently quite deaf – how sad!'

'Yes, that must make difficulties for him, in his profession,' Aristotle observed. 'He copes well with it, however. Sometimes partly deaf persons train themselves to hear remarkably well, and to read faces and gestures acutely. Whereas some people whose ears are very good don't really listen well.'

'It is good that each of these doctors has a friend to cheer him during this sad time,' I remarked. As Iatrokles was Aristotle's friend, I did not comment on what an odd household his was. Two ageing men, neither with a wife. And no children, apparently. It seemed pathetic, grown men living together in an empty house, talking about fish for dinner. Men in their twenties, and even their thirties, often fall in love with young men and boys, and there is a great deal of poetry about that passion. But greying older men could hardly have such erotic feelings about other greybeards. I reminded myself, however, that the people of Kos had endured war and straitened circumstances, so it was probably economic prudence that made these two share a life in common.

Aristotle said crisply, 'We must try to get Parmenion to talk sense to the doctor. That will be our real difficulty.'

That difficulty became evident the next day, when Aristotle, exercising his talents of persuasion, prevailed on a reluctant Parmenion to accompany us to Iatrokles' house. As we walked along the harbour way the youth's eyes flickered here and there. He looked curiously towards the shipping and then glanced away, taking flight somewhere in the sky with his unknown ideas. The lad had often appeared fairly sane during the voyage, but now he seemed both more tense and more evasive. At last he spoke out.

'You want me to see that doctor,' he said to Aristotle. 'You want to do something to me! But you haven't found my father. And you don't try to find him. I want –' He stopped.

'Yes,' said Aristotle. 'You want?'

Parmenion was silent for the rest of the way

When we entered the little house again, both Iatrokles and Kleumedes awaited us.

'Come,' said Kleumedes. 'To our special room.' This room, built on to the side of the house, appeared designed to accommodate patients. There were benches that could be turned into beds, with cushions and some coverlets neatly rolled up. There was a basket of herbs, and pottery jars emitting a pleasant smell, as of herbal mixtures and lotions. On a table a set of bright implements sat in a leather case. Hanging on the wall was something like a saw, beside something like a hatchet.

'By the gods!' I exclaimed to Kleumedes. 'I believe you cut off men's limbs with these things!'

Parmenion shuddered and stiffened; Aristotle gave me an angry glance.

'Those toys belong to Iatrokles – he's the surgeon,' laughed Kleumedes. 'He is one of the tribe of Machaon. I, on the other hand, am a descendant of gentle Podaleirios. I am a doctor – I deal in coaxing the body along, not chopping it up. Do sit down, all of you. Goodness, it is as solemn as the tombs! You are all so quiet. I shall have to hire a harp player for my patients' room – music, you know, is good for the soul and body.'

'Do you play an instrument, Parmenion?' he asked the boy, addressing him comfortably by name. Parmenion shook his head.

'Nor do I – and now I am getting hard of hearing, so I dare say I shall never learn. My lad, they tell me you are not well. Why don't you tell me about it?'

'I am all right,' said Parmenion irritably. 'Nothing can be done,' he added in a low monotone.

'No – no!' said Aristotle. 'Something can always be done.'

'It troubles you, I gather,' said Kleumedes, 'that you do not know what has happened to your father. That would trouble anyone.'

Parmenion shook his head impatiently.

'You think,' said Kleumedes, 'that instead of our fussing about *you*, we had better go and look for your father.'

'Yes,' mumbled Parmenion.

'You have to speak up, child, I fear I am a trifle deaf. What you mean is that you would search for your father if you could, but you don't know how. Is that right?'

'I would!' Parmenion shouted. 'But if he's *dead*, you fool, nobody can find him! Can they? Oh, I should have stayed at home!'

'Ah – yes,' said Kleumedes. 'You feel it was wrong to send you to school in Athens when the war meant that your father was in danger. In fact, you feel guilty about having left him in the East, as if you had done a wrong thing?' His patient nodded. 'But that was *not* a wrong thing, Parmenion – you did what your father wished you to do, and that was right. You have no cause to blame yourself.'

I wondered that Kleumedes could speak so soothingly

after Parmenion had rudely called him a fool. The boy should have been whipped or at least cuffed for such bold disrespect – and to one who was not only an older man but the friend of the boy's tutor and temporary guardian.

At least Parmenion was not encouraged into further wrongful boldness by the kind forbearance of Kleumedes. The youth now hung his head and looked wistfully down at the floor. The one good thing about this was that his eyes were not wandering in all directions as if he expected help from a platoon of cavalry that never arrived.

'It seems to me,' said Kleumedes, almost with severity, 'that someone should have done something about finding this boy's father ere now. Eh?'

'Something *has* been done,' said Aristotle. 'We – Theophrastos and I – wrote to his father and to his uncle likewise, but received no reply. At this disruptive time, however, it is not unlikely that the posts simply have not been getting through. Or, a letter may sit and gather dust in some remote spot while the man addressed is travelling many parasangs in another direction. The boy's father is Arkhebios. His grandfather would be very easy to trace – Parmenion, the general of Philip and now of Alexander. Very highly thought of. Both Philip and Alexander have loaded him with honours.'

'Aye,' said Kleumedes. 'That is the sort of person whom everybody knows and nobody knows how to get hold of. Not now when Alexander's army is marching far into the eastern hinterland. As this Arkhebios is a Makedonian by paternal descent, not truly a man of Rhodos, I suppose he was merely billeted there, or given some temporary responsibility in that island. He could well have been given a new posting.'

'Tell you the best thing,' said Iatrokles. 'Make an enquiry of one of Alexander's ships – or rather, a ship bearing his officers and messengers – when it comes into port. Such ships come regularly. I believe a ship carrying dispatches and people of importance is due to arrive from Asia very soon.'

'I had already written to members of the Makedonian command in Asia,' explained Aristotle. 'In the spring I began to write enquiries about Arkhebios, though of course couched in guarded language. One can never be utterly sure. Spies are everywhere, and some soldiers are, inquisitive by nature. If my earlier letters got through, however, some persons of importance will have known that I was probably coming eastward – though, in the event, my departure from Athens was more hurried than I could have wished. And I have written this summer, from Athens, from Peiraieus and from Naxos. I also sent word by a man on a ship we encountered before arriving in Kos. Enquiries are well under way.'

'Excellent,' said Kleumedes. 'Meanwhile – how to help this young man?' He looked at Parmenion, pondering. 'He is thin, now, thinner than is quite proper for his height. I take it you are not eating very well, my lad?'

'He has not manifested an appetite for some time,' said Aristotle. 'He often seems flushed and excited, yet there is no fever – his skin is cool. Nothing changes except that he fines down, and loses his spirits and his attention.'

'Not only so,' I added. 'He sometimes seems quite dumbstruck, thunderstruck with grief or fear or something – and yet on the voyage he was often quite like other people.'

'Very good,' said Kleumedes, nodding his bushy head.

'Things become a little clearer. Now, it seems to me the first thing to do is to get his humours into a right balance. Some become ill because they have taken in too much of meat and high food, but that is not his case – is it, Parmenion?' Parmenion shook his head, as if uninterested in this discussion.

'A good diet,' Kleumedes pondered. 'Food that is soothing, a little on the infant side, might be of use. We could study his reaction every time a new food is introduced. Let him be encouraged to sleep, but after taking some exercise. Not too great an exertion. Sleep – yes. It occurs to me – although we do not have a proper place of incubation – nothing like Epidauros – it is not unknown for a patient to stay overnight in the shrine of Asklepios. A helpful dream might be vouchsafed, and he could tell us about it.'

'No!' cried Parmenion! 'No – *no dreams!*' He rose up and flailed his right arm, brushing the air against Kleumedes as if to send back to its lair the horrible suggestion.

'Very well,' said Kleumedes. 'No dreams. Though the god is more beneficent than you seem to think. A good dream with Asklepios can sometimes put to flight the horrors of nightmares, as of waking torment. But, Parmenion –' he turned to him with a look of concern, 'your heart is stuffed with painful thought. Will you let me try to relieve you with a light herbal poultice?' He had already got up and was mixing some herbs and oils in a jar. 'This,' he explained, 'is simply to lighten feelings of oppression – it is very mild. Come now.' He smeared the verdant concoction on Parmenion's arms and chest so that he began to look green. 'Let this dry, and simply breathe it in.' The scent pervaded the room, a friendly scent. Thyme and sage and rue with other refreshing odours I did not know. Parmenion subsided and inhaled, with a bemused look.

'Good, good, we make progress,' murmured bushy Kleumedes in his rumbly voice. 'My lad, at least walk out to Asklepios' shrine and make him a small offering. The little walk will be good in itself. The air is clear and refreshing at the sacred site. You are braced up like a warrior about to rush into the fray – but at the moment there is no battle! That is terribly wearing. You need inward rest, and not to go about like a bow strung at its tightest.'

'Good advice for anyone,' Aristotle said in a low tone. I noticed suddenly how tired he himself looked. Certainly the work of looking after Parmenion was telling on him.

'Now,' said Iatrokles, 'my fellow physician will begin a disquisition upon the humours.'

'I am sure Aristotle knows all about the subject,' said Kleumedes, laughing. 'The work on the humours is one of the great achievements of doctors who follow Hippokrates. For we see the design of the whole – the body is meant to be in a full and perfect balance. All the humours are necessary to that balance. But let one get out of proportion, and at once changes occur, both physical and mental. A little too much of that essential humour the blood and the man is rash, loud, self-indulgent. A great deal too much, and he is impatient of contradiction, lords it over his fellows and dies suddenly or has a terrible fit. That is the easiest one to see, perhaps. But too much of black bile, and melancholy follows – leading to thoughts of damage and self-destruction. Often an unhappiness that has no full object and no end in sight. Or, say there is a real object of fear or of loathing – the man spends his passions and spirit on that thought alone. So he loses mental and physical strength in brooding.'

Parmenion, I noticed, appeared to be listening.

'Let Parmenion have a very good diet, but not too much at any one time,' continued Kleumedes. 'And follow Pythagoras at least in this: eat no beans! They blow the body up and give uncomfortable thoughts. In fact, that is probably good advice for all – especially if sharing sleeping quarters.'

'Thank you,' said Aristotle, laughing. He arose, and the rest of us did likewise.

'Here is a sponge, so you can sponge off the medicine,' said Kleumedes, handing the object to the boy. 'Parmenion here does not wish to look like a green man in the streets of Kos. But do you not feel the benefit of the treatment already?'

'Yes,' admitted Parmenion. 'Can I stay here?' he added.

'Good heavens, Parmenion,' expostulated Aristotle, 'we cannot ask this of your doctors. This is their home and not a place of residence for the diseased.'

'Not so hasty, friend,' said Iatrokles. 'This comes upon you as a surprise, true enough, but if you stop to think of it – might it not be a good idea? Your friend Stephanos here has other fish to catch – he must look for the man from Hymettos that he seeks. You yourself will have to search for Parmenion's father. It is too hard on Parmenion himself for you to drag him about with you. It would not be impossible for him to stay here, progressing towards a cure.'

'I should have to think long and hard about *that*,' said

Aristotle. 'It is a grave responsibility to give one's charge over to another. He is a well-born lad, and I am responsible for his safety.'

'You – and he – are safe enough,' said Kleumedes frostily. 'My Hippokratic oath binds me from making any sexual overtures to patients – and I can assure you my affections do not tend towards *boys*.' He looked smilingly at Iatrokles for confirmation before continuing his emphatic speech. 'Neither am I in danger of trying to rook money from patients, or of asking any other favour whatsoever. Nor will I let him wander about and get into danger. Remember Hippokrates' motto: "First do no harm!" I govern myself by that always.'

'And I too,' said Iatrokles. 'At least, as far as a surgeon may, who must cut sometimes in order to heal.'

'Forgive me,' said Aristotle, embarrassed, 'I meant that I did not mean to lodge the boy with others. That was not my design in coming here to you and asking for your professional help. As for your medical assistance, I am most grateful – and of course I shall pay you at the ordinary rate.' He put a couple of coins on the table. 'Not as an insult, but to keep our friendship from moulting,' he added, speaking over Iatrokles' expostulations. 'I hate being the debtor. It's a thing that makes me *ill* – so you must humour me!'

'I can readily humour you,' retorted Iatrokles, 'but only to this extent. Do you leave us this money as earnest for Parmenion's keep, and let him reside here. After all, Aristotle, you will be moving about and probably will not have Stephanos with you. You cannot leave Parmenion unsupervised at the lodging you now have. Meanwhile, he does need some medical care, to help him recover his balance. Which my friend Kleumedes knows how to bring about. There – have I produced sufficient arguments to convince a rhetorician?" ˙

Aristotle, his brow creased with thought and anxiety, turned slowly to Parmenion. Parmenion, standing, looked at him fully, giving him a rare span of real attention.

'I did not intend this – I never thought of it,' Aristotle said. 'It is always hard for me to accept an idea that was not first my own. There are some things to recommend such a change of plan. But the most important matter, Parmenion, is your own choice. Come – be perfectly sincere and frank in your response. Would you like to come back to the lodging with me, or would you yourself really like to stay here?' The boy hesitated. 'Speak just as you feel,' he added encouragingly.

'I feel – oh, of course I am grateful to you, and you are my teacher whom I must obey until my father is found. But for a while I would like – oh, yes, I want to stay here, in the doctors' house.'

'Let it be so,' said Aristotle. 'Of course, Iatrokles and Kleumedes, it must be on the understanding that you allow me to pay both for his board and his treatment. The few possessions he brought with him I will have brought over by Phokon straight away.'

And so we left – without Parmenion. Still dyed by his herbal poultice, the lad said his farewells and watched us depart, going no further than the doctors' threshold, as if the little house offered him some kind of sanctuary. Strange, for I could not see that the two doctors had offered anything we could not.

XVI

Facing Asia

Strangely relieved and yet diminished by the absence of Parmenion, we walked back from the doctors' house. We glanced curiously at the harbour in the dazzle of noon sun to see if any great ships had come in. But nothing had. Only the usual small ships were stirring. One light vessel containing a few passengers was easing its way slowly to the inner harbour among the larger ships already there; it moved like some small insect along water too glittering to look at in the rays of the sun. On our return to our lodging place, Aristotle gave Phokon orders to find and transport Parmenion's few belongings to the doctors' house.

As Phokon was setting off, another slave came from the contrary direction, walking hastily but anxiously glancing at the houses as if not too sure of his destination.

'Do you know where the great Aristotle lives?' he asked Phokon.

'This is it,' said Phokon with a grin. 'And that's my master, right there.'

Another slave, a stocky fellow who happened to be passing on the other side of the road, gave us a curious glance, but then walked quickly by. The slave we had first seen, his confidence restored, rushed up to us and said, 'Oh, sir – I speak to Aristotle, the great philosopher from Athens?'

He had picked the right man. 'Yes, boy. At least, I am Aristotle,' the philosopher replied modestly.

'I thought you must be the philosopher, because of the beard,' the young slave explained. 'The other one's too young. I am very glad to find you, for my master Oromedon of Kos, having received your message, has sent to you in return. Hoping to see you this evening. He wrote you this letter yesterday – and here it is.'

He proffered some neatly tied tablets.

'Excellent!' cried Aristotle. 'Come into the garden, Stephanos, while I read these and consult with you. We will ask our landlord to give my friend's servant something to drink while he awaits an answer.' I followed Aristotle into the garden where we sat in the shade and he looked over his letter.

'There,' he said. 'We may be as wise as each other,' and he offered me the epistle, written in a sprawling hand, extravagantly covering two and a half sides of the four waxed tablets.

Oromedon son of Daliokles to his most honoured Friend, Aristotle son of Nikomakhos, Greetings

Greatly beyond measure do I regret, dearest and wisest of friends, that I have not been in Kos to receive you at your arrival. I have but now returned from a short journey. How greatly to be regretted that I should be absent at a time when you are honouring Kos with your beloved presence. You must come and take what hospitality my humble roof can offer. What fond memories of Plato's lectures and the good days of yore the sight of you will inspire. But first I have important matters to deliver. Returning to Kos, our small ship passed a large three-banked vessel, bearing news and messengers from Alexander. And one who knew me hailed me from the deck, and let me know that this great ship bears messengers and messages of great importance, including news sent to Aristotle if he is in Kos at the present time. This great ship, having stopped in Patmos, comes south and should arrive in the harbour of Kos tomorrow evening, or the day after.

I pray you to come and dine with me tomorrow, though I cannot invite you to arrive any earlier than early evening. An unfortunate request, doubly so when it is but humble fare for which you are asked to wait. I apologise for all delay, when I shall be so rejoiced to see you. You and your friend, I trust, will be residing with me from tomorrow night.

No letters have yet come for you. If you say Yes to my invitation, as I entreat, I shall leave a message at the harbour for any and all dispatches to you or your friend to be conveyed to my house. I earnestly hope I can be of assistance to you in any enterprise you have on hand. I beg your forgiveness for the fact that you are presently lodging anywhere other than my own home. My brother-in-law has been staying with me, and he is an invalid, which has made

matters more complicated. But I hope as soon as the
morrow's evening to see you happily in residence
under my roof, if, my dear friend, there is any virtue
in the entreaties of
      your friend Oromedon son of Daliokles

'This is important!' I was impressed. 'Who knows what
Alexander's message may be?'

'Well, it is less likely to come from Alexander himself
than from some officer, or a friend – perhaps even my
wonderful nephew Kallisthenes.' Aristotle's mood had
lightened. 'It will be good to see Oromedon again. We
were students in Plato's Akademeia together – so long
ago. I must send a reply, if you do not object, Stephanos,
saying that both of us will be happy to be received by him
this evening.'

I saw no objection, and he quickly dashed off a reply.
Things seemed to be going well (save that I did not yet
have a letter from home). But the style of the Koan's letter
and of the messenger had somewhat disappointed me.

'I thought Oromedon was one of the important men of
Kos?'

'Oh yes. Son of Daliokles who was a very important
citizen indeed. I should certainly like you both to become
acquainted.'

Well, the manners of Kos might not be quite as ours.
The slave was slightly impudent, but not suave, and the
letter seemed awkward if florid. I was rather puzzled at
the man's odd reference to his brother-in-law, and his
putting Aristotle off for the sake of this other man. I
ventured to say as much.

'Dear old Oromedon would not be too formal with me,'

Aristotle responded eagerly. 'His letter may flourish a bit clumsily, as you say. But he would know he need not stand on ceremony with me, if his brother-in-law is a cripple or something, and requires special attention. I dare say Oromedon is the same delightful fellow he always was. He was always a generous party-giver in Athens – I dare say he'll offer us a first-class dinner. His slave is a bit unpolished, I grant you. But the wars in Kos would have made it harder to keep good servants, as slaves have so often been pressed into service by one side or the other.'

I tried to think about how to make my over-travelled clothes respectable enough to go to a first-class dinner. Even the new garments purchased for me in Rhenaia had been through a storm at sea. I shared this humble problem with Aristotle.

'Let us ask the house slaves here to clean a khiton for each of us,' he suggested. 'Phokon would do it, but he is out. It would probably be more polite not to arrive at Oromedon's house with all our baggage, despite his kind invitation – we can move completely later on. While we dine, the slaves can clean some more clothes for us. Now, let us go out ourselves and make the most of this beautiful day, Stephanos. As we are waiting for dispatches, I cannot do anything further about Parmenion's father at the moment. Why don't we take a leisurely walk, by the sea and not uphill? If we are to ask the slaves to do a washing, we can ask for bread and cheese and thus get out of their way for a while.'

And so we set off for a good walk along the seaside. We moved along the coast, and as we did so, even for a little distance, the coast of Asia became slightly plainer to our

vision. I could pick out a few scattered farmsteads on the
infertile cape. At last we came to a good stretch of shore;
like most Koan shores it had a profusion of round grey
pebbles, but it also had a little soft fine sand, and some low
sandstone rocks to sit on. We sat down lazily, looked at
the rock pools, and then lapsed into silence. For a long
time we had not had this kind of peace, the kind where
nobody can overhear you. Some gulls screamed overhead.
The little waves came up tranquilly and splashed along
the shore. Beyond, the sea stretched green and blue to the
far point where the blue line of coast seemed to beckon us
to come.

'Asia,' said Aristotle. 'I hope you see it some time,
Stephanos, it is very beautiful.' He sighed, and was quiet.
I was restless. After teasing a couple of crabs, I felt hot,
and the water looked refreshingly cool in its blue
transparency. The stones beneath the water were visible
and striped with slender threads of light as the light was
woven by the sea.

'Come on!' I said. Freeing myself of clothes I rushed
into the water, with the usual wonderful almost
frightening cold shock that you get when you enter the
sea on a hot day. When I was chest deep in the water,
before I could stretch out my arms to embrace the waves
and kick off for a swim, there was a sudden loud hiss. I
started as an enormous octopus swam towards me, all its
tentacles waving. It looked angry and covered the
distance amazingly quickly. Its strange mouth was
making a great noise, blowing water and air in a steamy
'Hsss – ssssht!' Stumbling on stones, I moved awkwardly
backwards through the water. The thing was chasing me
– or so it seemed – its horrible pink tentacles all alive,

stretching out, now parallel to me, now closing in on me, the tips waving and curling; I could see the powerful suckers. One fleshy obstinate strand caught on my arm and clung –

Aristotle rushed into the water and we both yelled at the creature. Slowly it let go and swam off, indignant. Its tentacles curved and undulated in the water and reappeared among the foam of the further waves.

Aristotle was laughing, the first genuine laugh I had heard from him in a long time. 'That creature nearly had you! What an amusing reversal! Octopus has Stephanos for dinner.'

I went spluttering back to the beach, coughing out some water I didn't need.

'Powerful animals, octopodes, in their way. Amazing. They belong to the category of bloodless animals: the Softs. You can see how its head is between its legs, and these legs are an extensive part, highly active, used both as feet and hands.'

'It seemed to whistle and hiss at me through its mean mouth,' I said.

'No – no. It was whistling to you – as you put it – through its tube. They have a tube to send back from the belly-sack any seawater which has got in. That is not the mouth.'

'Those horrible tentacles – I have heard that if it gets its suckers fastened along your throat an octopus can choke a man.'

'I have heard so too, but I have not known a case. Did you realise the octopus does not use all tentacles alike? As I have often said, Nature makes special parts for various activities. An animal is like a good drama, each lively part with its own function, and the parts well articulated. The octopus uses two tentacles to take in food, which it puts in its real mouth – it has an oesophagus and a very neat gut. Such interesting animals!' Aristotle perched on a warm sandstone shelf, idle in the sun, and continued giving me the benefit of all that was in his capacious mind about the octopus in general.

'Do you know, a female octopus' gut can become extremely large, overflowing with eggs like the fruit of white poplar, which she discharges into some shady chamber under the sea – like little Mestra's sea cave at the end of Iatrokles' story. Hidden treasure. And one of the male's tentacles is divided at the tip and is specially used to uncoil and touch smoothly. That is the one he uses in the sexual act. So, you see, the female octopus is not going to be torn apart or unpleasantly clamped by the suckers at the great embrace. The pair lie down together, the second fitting itself carefully on to the tentacles of the first, so that their suckers match. Wonderful creatures! Come, Stephanos, cast care aside – let us swim!'

We swam, diving and tossing lightly through the cool waves and riding on the foam. When we were tired and had enough of this, we returned to the warm rocks and let ourselves dry in the sun. We looked together across the water to the land quite close to us.

'The coast of Asia,' said Aristotle slowly. 'And not far hence the towers of our most unfortunate Halikarnassos.'

'Too bad!' I did not wish him to go on in this melancholy reminiscence, for we both knew people who had endured the fatal siege of the destroyed city. One of them was only a girl. I stretched out in the sun. Exercise had given me many hungers.

'I really need to find a brothel,' I grumbled. 'And not one like the "Naumakhia", either.'

'Oh, I don't know, Stephanos,' he retorted. 'A nice plump sucking-pig and a nice plump sailor.'

I burst out laughing – chiefly with surprise, for such talk was most unlike him. He laughed also – too loudly. When I looked at him I found that his laughter had changed to sobs. Aristotle was actually crying! I gazed at him helplessly. Painful tears slowly and against his will left his eyes and coursed down the furrows of his face. As he was naked he could not fling up a cloak or sleeve to cover his emotion.

'Forgive me,' he said, 'but I must weep. Whether it is the salt waves, like tears themselves, or the memory of Asia, I cannot now but weep. I remember and lament my lost wife. Oh, Pythias, Pythias, why did you leave me? We were once together, and now I am so lonely!' He wept. I looked away the while, embarrassed, and unwilling to grieve him with a memory of curious eyes fastened on his tears. I was very startled.

'Dear friend,' I said, once his shoulders had stopped shaking, 'I thought you were a stronger – I mean, I thought that philosophy had given you the means to quench grief.'

'No – not exactly, Stephanos. Philosophy may tell a man *why* it may do him little good to mourn, and why others will despise him for doing so. But grief cannot be held for ever within the breast. It seeks relief.'

Aristotle sat up on his rock; a few tears still coursed down his cheeks and neck and fell on his chest, on the chest hair, matted but grey. I saw him suddenly as an old man. Yet he was strong too, his chest well muscled, and he held his head erect on his strong neck, turning his countenance towards Asia.

'You don't know – you cannot know – but I feel moved to tell you,' he said slowly, 'what Asia means to me. I left Athens after Plato died. His death shook me very much – all the more as I had been an orphan early, when I first began to study with him. My father was a deeply educated man, a physician of Stageira. Our city is in Khalkidike, of old accounted part of Thrake. I am so tired of being considered simply a Makedonian! My father's family came from the island of Andros, the northernmost of the Kyklades, an island sacred to Dionysos. My mother's family came from Khalkis in Euboia, wonder-working Khalkis of the workers in bronze and copper. We were making bronze armour and other intricate things when most Athenians could barely cut and store a little grain! I still have some family land in Euboia, inherited from my mother's side. With Plato gone there was nothing to keep me in Athens. I started roving, drawing on my inheritance. It occurs to me that, having never been short of money, I've been able to do what I wanted, most of the time.'

'Some would say there are dangers in that.'

'Perhaps there are. Well, still young and still in the constant quest of philosophy, after Plato died I went to the court of Hermias of Atarneus, where other friends and former scholars of Plato had gone. I won't say that I had not some notion of pleasing King Philip, who was anxious to keep up good relations with a Greek city on a coast so largely controlled by Persia. But I remained because of Hermias himself.'

'What made him so fascinating?' I was really curious.

Aristotle seemed to hold this odd and unsuccessful character in such high regard.

'Well – how to describe him to you? A slave who was no slave in his mind. He started out as a slave indeed, a mere banker's assistant, and rose by his own abilities to an important position as the ruler of Atarneos and Assos. His native ability was very great. But he was uneducated. Therefore Plato had sent to his court two of his scholars, Erastos and Koriskos, members of such important families in Skepsis that Hermias could not ignore them. They became friends, and created a little Akademeia in Assos. Hermias, unlike the bullies who so frequently rise to power, was eager to learn.'

'Admirable,' I commented, still puzzled at the notion of a banker's slave becoming a ruler.

'Hermias had an aspiring soul, and an intellect that could grasp essentials. His court became a centre of learning. And not only that. Only think, Stephanos, the man changed his mind! This is astonishing in any human beings, especially in the powerful. Hermias modified his ideas of the ruler or dictator, and gave his little nation a constitution along the lines that we suggested. It was very exciting to see thought becoming reality. That was one of the best times in my life. It was also in Assos, amid the wonders of the Asian landscape and coast, that I decided to study all life – the living creatures. A subject not much touched upon in our books. We live in this great and beautiful world full of living creatures, and yet we understand so little about it.'

'So,' I said, encouragingly, 'that was a good thing. It explains why you are still studying the animals and so on.'

'Yes, Stephanos. It may be the interest comes to me

from both my father's and my mother's family. From my father the physician's side, the interest in living forms of bodies. From the metal-workers and designers comes this deep concern with how things are made and how they function. Study of the living material beings has been a lifelong work. Nowadays I have those adult scholars to assist me, and we have begun to make great strides. But it all began with my wandering about the rocks and sands of the coast of Asia, and going out in small boats to little islands.'

'All on your own?'

'Eventually I had one companion and fellow-worker – a little girl. She used to come to me with a basket or a pottery jar and we would go out to look for specimens. Catch things in rock pools, or watch anemones. At first, of course, I was just "amusing the child" in letting her pretend to help, but rapidly I realised she was truly observant, and had great patience. As you have guessed, this little girl was the daughter – adopted and motherless daughter – of Hermias.'

'What a strange way to take up with a woman!'

'Well, it was our way. But then came the bad time, when Hermias' position was not so sure. I took the child to safety at his request, and we settled for a while in Lesbos. It was in Lesbos also that I truly came to know Theophrastos and we began the connection that has proved so happy for me.'

'So – there you were in Lesbos, looking at tadpoles, the three of you –'

'Yes. Lesbos is very beautiful, and its coast is warm and full of wildlife. Our work kept us all happy and distracted the child from sorrow over her separation from her father.

We would watch crabs together by the day, and study the behaviour of fishes and little molluscs – and octopodes. I thought of all this when you saw the octopus today. I remember talking about octopodes with Pythias. We watched a pair mating on the sea floor in a shallow area – so beautiful, like dancers. Pythias and I used to wander along the shore and stop for a long while to watch the little crabs and sea-urchins.'

'How curious!' I was struck by a certain impropriety in all this. 'She had no other guardian?'

'Just her old nurse. But she was a sacred trust to me. Now I wish I could have the old days back again, with young Pythias on a rock beside me. Her long legs stretched out, and her hair flopping into the water as she watches the rock pool's inhabitants. Or the two of us waiting in dusk, quietly, for the rising of the moon, and counting the various night birds.'

'Did she feel no anxiety about her reputation?'

'Well, we lived quite a solitary existence for a while, and she was used to me. And then we all went to King Philip in Makedonia, at his command. He thought I could be useful in telling him about Asia, and also acting as tutor to Alexander. I should add that Alexander had a number of tutors – I was but one. King Philip perhaps wanted me under his eye. It struck me later that the reports I had sent back from Atarneos and Assos may have been too good. Maybe I praised Hermias over-much. Oh, Stephanos, I fear King Philip threw Hermias to the wolves and deliberately let the Persians have him! Hermias too knew that unless his luck took some very decided new turns, his life was threatened. But he trusted a man – a Persian, though oddly enough he was named

Mentor. And Mentor it was who betrayed him.'

'And as Hermias was a ruler,' I thought aloud, 'he could not just leave, or take evasive action by disappearing, as a common man may do if he has enemies.'

'Indeed not. And you must not think of Hermias as weak, or lacking in practical military ability. He withstood a Persian siege during the time I was with him. Under the last fatal threat, Hermias did not run away, neither did he try to injure innocent Persians to retaliate against those who injured him. In the end, the Persians captured Assos and took Hermias. That was less than a year after I had arrived in King Philip's court.'

'And Hermias met his end.'

'And Hermias met his end. I could not help him. All the rest of my life I have treasured up – a terrible treasure – every bit of information I could gather about the dreadful end of my friend. Hermias did not give way under torture, nor lead his torturers to anyone else. Among his last words were a request to his brutal captors to tell his friends that he had done nothing against the soul or unworthy of philosophy.'

I could now begin to see why Aristotle was always such an enthusiast for the former ruler of Assos, though many people others in Athens said everything denigrating they could about Hermias – who still seemed to me somewhat odd.

'And so,' I said sympathetically, 'you were left with his daughter on your hands. Who probably had nothing! No inheritance, no dowry. The Persians would have taken everything Hermias had.'

'Yes. As she was the daughter of Hermias, who had died tortured by the Persians and out of favour with the

Makedonians, nobody would be anxious to befriend her. Hermias, however, had earlier asked me to take care of her always, in case anything happened to him. She was a sacred trust.'

'Another burden for you,' I said sympathetically. 'It seems a pity the Makedonian King could not help her.'

'Philip practically ignored her existence. Better so. But you must understand, I loved her. Of course I had loved her when she was a little child, but as one feels affection for a little child. One day when she was fourteen I suddenly found myself feeling . . . something quite different. But I was determined to take no advantage of her youth and helpless state. Indeed, I do not approve of early marriage and childbearing for girls. It weakens their bodies; the babies are often unhealthy and the young women die. So I said nothing to Pythias. And I made no gesture to her that couldn't have been made by any brother before an audience of watchers.'

'But then – you married her?'

'I ardently wished to, but held back, until Pythias herself told me she wanted this and felt she was ready. She was always a reserved person, but deeply honest. And very steady.'

'An improper courtship! And one in which the lady asks the question!' I nearly laughed, but caught myself. 'I mean – you couldn't ask her father, neither of you had parents, you were drifting about together in each other's company every day – most unsuitable –'

'Well, when you put it that way I agree it was unorthodox, Stephanos,' said Aristotle stiffly. 'And it is not what I would advise others to do. No, not at all. Ours was a special case. We married – quite properly and formally – in Pella. We were of an appropriate age. Eighteen for the woman. Really, nobody should bear children before that. I was in my later thirties. I have maintained that thirty-seven is a good age for a man to beget – and that was about what I was when we started seriously on child-creation. We have always lived with the greatest propriety as man and wife – no more wanderings by the shore. Pythias has been exemplary. At the time, I registered the marriage everywhere one possibly could. My sister accepted her as my wife. Then I took Pythias in my arms – but oh, the joy is now repaid by grieving! I fear I killed her, Stephanos. I ought not to have allowed the pregnancy to proceed. I was too old for this last child – too old for child-getting.' His tears, which had dried up during his narrative, started to flow again.

'I have even published my opinion that a man should not beget children after he is fifty years old. But Pythias was so much younger, I felt it worth the risk. We hadn't had a son – and our little girl is very healthy. If only I had my Pythias back, we could go back to living in that brotherly manner, as we did when we watched the shellfish off the rocks of Lesbos.'

This seemed too odd a vision of happiness to suit with my own notions. But I knew I ought to try to comfort him.

'You have the memories,' I said lamely. 'And really, Aristotle, it has been a while since your wife died. I thought you had got over it. Or almost. Like all good philosophers, you seem in your writings to hold women of such little account, on the whole. Philosophers are supposed to excel anyway at doing away with grief, even for the death of a man. You have seemed so like your normal self on most of the journey.'

'Oh, Stephanos,' said Aristotle, 'it is hard to hold back all the time – more than flesh and blood can bear. But you are too taken with externals.' He dried his eyes, and looked away from me for a moment, out to sea. 'You must make a distinction between what men say and what they think. And between how they appear and what they are feeling. Many a man with a broken heart will smile; many a fellow who is full of rage will speak in a polite and even kindly manner.'

He got up, in the slow manner of the ageing. When he stood up, however, outlined against the sea with its deep transparency and afternoon brightness, he looked sadly heroic, like a bronze figure. He looked out again at Asia, which I now knew was a land of dreams and memories for him. Then we both scrambled into our clothes again.

'Have you observed,' Aristotle remarked conversationally, 'how soon one dries off after bathing in salt water, and how much longer it takes after being immersed in water that is sweet? The cause must be all the material in the sea – there is less actual water.' I was not pleased to find that a gull had made a target of my khiton. At the sight of the bird-shit painting my garment Aristotle laughed heartily, though I did not.

We made our way back to our lodging and put on our clean khitons in preparation for dinner. Oromedon's house was large, almost magnificent. He had a marble statue near the entrance, and a kind of floor I had never seen before, of pebbles arranged in a pattern, handsome but not comfortable to walk on. His house was certainly a contrast to the doctors' modest dwelling. Indeed, it seemed so large I was surprised that the presence of a brother-in-law could at all have incommoded him. Oromedon seemed a man accustomed to making arrangements.

'I regret,' he said courteously, 'that so far no letters have arrived for either of you. But most probably that will soon be rectified.'

'I hope so,' I said. 'I really don't think,' I added, turning to Aristotle, 'that I can leave Kos until I have heard from home.'

'It pleases me to inform you both,' said Oromedon, 'that I have sent a messenger to bring your messages from the great ship; they should arrive as soon as you have eaten. It wouldn't do, my dear Aristotle, for you to have news *before* a meal. Such a diversion is bad for the digestion. I must uphold the reputation of Kos for good medical practice.'

Aristotle, weary as he was after today's grief, was alert at the idea of news, and chafing secretly at having it withheld from him. I also ardently wished for a letter. Dinner, served only to the three of us, seemed unnecessarily elaborate and long-lasting, though we were certainly hungry enough at the outset, after our swim. Oromedon was a middle-sized man with an impressive middle-aged manner, though not a great deal to boast of in the way of looks. He had aged less gracefully than Aristotle. He was not quite bald, but his hair at the top consisted of a few strips more distressing than baldness. While he talked, he had a habit of smoothing these grey wisps along the top of his head, as if to make sure he still had something in those regions. I decided uncharitably that Oromedon's idea of being philosophical was to talk slowly in long sentences. But then, I was spoiled by Aristotle's quick way of going on.

At length the meal was done, compliments exchanged. Oromedon left the room and came back almost immediately.

'I had hoped merely to offer you letters, and to see to it myself,' he said. 'But there is an actual messenger for you, O Aristotle. He claims to be on an embassy from the very highest quarters. I would not, however, allow this person to incommode your dining hour. We have fed him in the kitchen, do not fear. But it is probable that you had best speak to him.'

'A messenger? News!' Aristotle jumped up quickly.' 'Yes, let us have the man in.'

The messenger who came into the room was a surprise. He was a well-developed man smartly dressed. Too good for a slave.

'Sir,' he said to Aristotle, 'I am sent to entreat you to come aboard the warship in the harbour, where there is one who would speak with you with a message from Alexander's officer. We beg that you will come now, even though the day waxes late.'

'But who –'

'Sir, I am a freedman, serving Peleus who is in the great army. I understand that he has a message for you – messages, both in speech and in letters. The matter is of some urgency, and Peleus begs that you will come today. We have a tender to carry you aboard the ship.'

'My friend Stephanos will come with me, in that case,' said Aristotle genially. 'He is accustomed to assisting my faltering steps.'

I wondered, doubtless open eyed (I hope not open-mouthed) at this outrageous statement.

'And good Oromedon,' Aristotle turned to his friend, 'would you like to board the vessel?'

'I shall accompany you, of course,' said Oromedon. 'You are my guest and I am responsible for your safety and pleasure. Only if you wish my presence during your conversation.'

'Three of you then. Very well,' said the freedman, bowing. 'I can lead the way, sir, if you do not mind. Time presses.'

We left the house with much less ceremony than I would have thought possible in Oromedon's deliberate, and followed the sturdy and active fellow back to the harbour mouth.

'I am sorry, Stephanos,' said Aristotle, 'to drag you off to another ship. But it suddenly struck me – I do not know this fellow or his officer, and it is sometimes foolish to go alone into you know not what company. It is always good to have a young and active man in the party.'

We two and Oromedon were soon engaged in the business of getting into the small boat, rowed by only two men, and setting off through the crowded harbour towards the area beyond, where the great ship lay at anchor. I looked back at the harbour of Kos and the houses that we knew. The waters were richly golden in the light of the sun as it slid down the sky. Suddenly we had arrived, and I was moving up a fragile-seeming ladder of rope, trying not to look down.

This vessel was so large – nothing like the friendly boats in which we had made our journey. This was a long sleek craft, wide enough in the waist to hold the ranks of oarsmen. These men were busy oiling themselves or serving cold food, while the ship lay at anchor. Evidently they had not been allowed to go ashore. We looked upon rows and rows of benches.

'Please come aft, gentlemen,' said our guide. 'There is one there who waits for you. He will explain all.'

We were shown into a small cabin with a kind of shelf for a bed and other purposes. Standing in the centre of the room was a well-muscled man of a commanding presence. His hair was cut military style, and he had a manly and military bearing.

'Sir,' exclaimed Aristotle, 'I see you are a member of the Greek army. From the look of you, you are one of those in the Makedonian brigades. We are honoured to meet an officer of Alexander's forces. I am Aristotle son of Nikomakhos for whom you have sent. This is my friend Oromedon son of Daliokles of Kos. This is my friend Stephanos son of Nikiarkhos, a man of Athens. We are told you can give us news?'

'Delighted to see you on board my ship,' said this military person, bowing. 'Peleus at your service. I have come from the interior of Asia and shall return to the southern coast. I have a commission to deliver, and will be pleased to be of use to you, Aristotle of Stageira. We should converse – Pray sit down.' We sat on the small folding stools.

'I have much to ask,' said Aristotle. 'First, and most important, I must ask about the father of the young man in my charge. Young Parmenion, whose father Arkhebios, half-brother of Philotas the brave, is in the army. Formerly posted in Rhodos, now I think fighting in Asia. My lad's even more famous grandfather is

Parmenion, long Alexander's second-in-command. Parmenion who fought with such distinction at Granikos and in the battle by Payas river near Issos town. We enquire most earnestly for the health of Arkhebios.'

Peleus frowned.

'I fear,' he said gravely, 'we do not start on the happiest of notes. I wish I had better news to relate. As for his health – Arkhebios is dead. He died in one of those mountain skirmishes when the army was pursuing Darius, and not in the main battle. His body could not be brought back. You may tell Arkhebios' son that his father was properly buried.'

'I am sorry to hear this,' Aristotle said seriously. 'We feared as much. That the boy's father is dead sufficiently explains why we have not heard from him. So I suppose we may give the lad into the care of his grandfather Parmenion?'

'This is even more difficult to say,' said Peleus. 'Hard to know how to put this. But there seems to have been some kind of disagreement between Alexander and Parmenion. Parmenion is no longer as favoured as he was. He is not the second-in-command any more. He has been told to take on the task of delivering the treasure of Persepolis to Ekbatana of the Medes, while Alexander pursues his conquests further in the East. Parmenion is even now engaged in this difficult escort duty, rather than pursuing the Persian King to his last stronghold. I fear if you wish to advance the youth you speak of, Arkhebios' son, it would *not* be a good policy to give him in charge of Parmenion at this moment.'

'Parmenion in disfavour!' Aristotle seemed much

struck. 'Hard to imagine! Parmenion has been such a strong support of both Philip and Alexander. The army seemed to depend on him – and on Philotas, too.'

'Too bad!' said Oromedon, arranging his three locks of hair carefully. 'But in many affairs men cool to each other and then warm again. Likely this will all blow over in time.'

'The army does not depend on one man,' said Peleus firmly. 'All of us serve to the best of our ability.'

'Quite so, quite so.' Aristotle's eyes went upward as if he sought inspiration in the rought planking that served as a ceiling. He scratched his beard. The boat rocked slightly.

'Our questions in this case are, sadly, answered. Thank you, however, for your candour in giving us the news which cannot be agreeable but must be heard. I wish also to ask you about my nephew Kallisthenes.'

Peleus' brow cleared. 'There I am happy to help you,' he said with a smile. 'Kallisthenes will go far. His unflagging energy and attention to detail impress everyone. He has made himself useful in many things, including the interrogations of Persian prisoners and the organisation of scouts and spies. I hear him well spoken of everywhere. Kallisthenes' ability to write truthful and yet captivating historical accounts has greatly endeared him to Alexander. The first part of his history of the campaigns of Alexander is already being copied. What an indispensable history it will be! Alexander, so I hear, is most pleased with it. And Kallisthenes has been given many favours by the Commander.'

'I expected no less,' said Aristotle, glowing. 'Kallisthenes has the most remarkable abilities, and he begins with a store of learning surprising in one so young.'

'I have even better news to report,' said the soldier Peleus encouragingly. 'You will have every opportunity of meeting your nephew, should you wish to do so. For Alexander's friend the noble Harpalos is inviting you to come and meet him within Asia, and Kallisthenes will accompany Harpalos.'

'To see Kallisthenes – and meet Harpalos?'

'Yes. My commission is to invite and entreat you to come back with our contingent to Greek Phaselis in western Asia. Not really so far. Harpalos, Alexander's Treasurer, wishes to take advantage of your proximity to consult with you personally about affairs in Athens and elsewhere. Naturally, Alexander and his ministers need to know where their resources are best deployed.'

Aristotle looked at me. I said encouragingly, 'Don't worry about myself, Aristotle, for as you know I have another personal commission to fulfil. While you are in Asia I must really wait in Kos for the man you know of to return.' I didn't want to spell out all of my affairs in front of this military Peleus. It was no concern of his. If I were a little surprised at having Aristotle spirited away from me, as it were, so suddenly, I had no business to complain. I had come to the islands on business of my own. But Aristotle hesitated, his mouth pursed in dubiety.

'I should prefer,' he said at last, 'if it could be arranged that my friend Stephanos accompany me. I have no other travelling companion on this journey – except my slave Phokon of course. Stephanos' presence would be of assistance to me.'

'No trouble in the world.' Peleus seemed confident.

'Two men are as easy to take along as one. You won't need to take your slave: you are advised not to do so, for you will have abundant servants supplied by us. But it would be suitable that you had some company for the road. Both for the way out and the way back, for it's likely to be a different group of us accompanying you back to the coast on your return.'

'If you would only come, Stephanos?' Aristotle turned to me. 'Instead of waiting in a sedentary manner in Kos, you could take advantage of the opportunity – perhaps the only one – to see something of Asia.' I hesitated. This scheme was no part of my own plans. But – it was my chance to see Asia . . .

'If it were not for the expense – and the fact that I hadn't heard from home yet,' I began.

'Pray, don't think of expense,' said Aristotle, while Peleus answered, 'Oh, there will be *no* expenses. You will travel in royal style, all paid for. Your friend is welcome to come, Aristotle. Our destination is between five and seven days' march from the coast.'

'We go by land?' Aristotle was surprised. 'I took it you meant a quick sea journey to Phaselis.'

'Not exactly. A swift journey to Halikarnassos port, and then onward by land. We are escorting supplies for several garrisons. You will see something of Asia itself, not just the sea coast – and no danger of pirates. You should arrive at Phaselis at the same time as Harpalos. Kallisthenes will be travelling with Harpalos, and is himself delighted at the prospect of a reunion. Here is his letter.' The epistle the soldier brought forth was on two small waxed tablets, tied together and backed with highly polished wood.

'A letter from Kallisthenes! I recognise his scrawl,' said Aristotle, happily seizing and perusing it instantly. 'Brief, Stephanos, but to the point. This is what it says:

> *To my most honoured uncle Aristotle son of Nikomakhos, from Kallisthenes, Greetings*
>
> *That you are well, dear uncle, is the prayer of the writer, who also wishes for your presence. By the greatest good fortune we are closer to one another now than we have been for years, and nearer than I could have hoped. I have turned back briefly to accompany Harpalos after travelling many parasangs with Alexander. I want to give you my new book. I earnestly hope you will come. Your sight will give pleasure to the eyes of your affectionate and admiring nephew.*

'Oh, it is true,' said Aristotle, clutching the tablets. 'I cannot pass up such a chance. But we must think . . . This journey – the difficulties.' Aristotle's face, which had lit up with his pleasure at hearing from Kallisthenes, became thoughtful again.

'To go by land into Asia as far as Phaselis – that is an expedition. How long do we have? And how – what is expected –'

'You need have no cares,' said Peleus. 'Nothing to worry about. No expenses as I said, and hardly anything to arrange. You will want to collect clothes and so on tonight. Don't bring too much with you. Remember, baggage impedes. We have blankets and pots, to be sure. Come aboard before dawn. I will keep our oarsmen here tonight so we can make a rapid start on the morrow. It is a very short voyage indeed to Halikarnassos – as you know.'

He ushered us out of his room again, and into the open. The setting sun burned its colours upon the waters around us as Peleus prepared to send us off.

'A brief and pleasant voyage tomorrow. Once we disembark at Halikarnassos, by the little citadel, we proceed to the camp by Mylas Gate – just a few stadia. A proper baggage train with horses and mules meets us there, and we shall be on our way. We can travel quickly, we know the road. No danger. It is cleared of Persians, and there are military posting houses along the route. Best method of travelling! You'll be surprised at how comfortable it is.'

XVII

◆

The Letter

A small train of men, animals and wagons moved in a light cloud of dust along a hot and winding road. The winding road led down a precipitous rough cliff. An onlooker – and there must have been onlookers (some hostile) in the hills – would have noticed the curious wagons and their load. They would have noted the excellence of most of the horses, the fine quality of the dust from the arable land, and the military discipline of the men. All save two. Aristotle and I moved with the weariness of civilians, not accustomed to the regular tramp-tramp of an army. We had been going for some days; at times, it felt like some weeks.

I now thought rather enviously of our past experiences of travelling by water. The most recent of our sea journeys was the short voyage from Kos to Halikarnassos. That could not take place until an unhappy errand had been fulfilled. We had gone in the middle of the night (or so it seemed by then) to break the news of the death of his

father to young Parmenion. Telling these tidings was by
no means pleasant, though Parmenion was not inclined to
scream and cry. He stood pale and stony, a statue of
misery. We had to leave him to Iatrokles and Kleumedes
to deal with. Aristotle and I then packed our few things
and left the comfortable lodging in Kos at an uncomfortably early hour. To my surprise, Oromedon joined us
in the tender that once again set out for the big ship in the
outer harbour.

'Naturally, I could not be easy unless I had seen you
off, Aristotle, and knew that you were in good hands,' he
said. 'I regret so deeply that you will not be under my
roof! Fate snatches your visit from me. But please convey
my regards to your nephew Kallisthenes. And – oh, yes –
I find a message for your young friend Stephanos here
was sent to my house last evening.' Oromedon handed
me a letter. Two rather shabby waxed tablets, battered at
the edges and bound with coarse twine. The epistle was
undoubtedly meant for me. The outer part bore a small
piece of grubby papyrus sealed to the board with pitch:

> To Stephanos son of Nikiarkhos
>   With Aristotle
>   By favour of Oromedon
> son of Daliokles of Kos

'I recognise the handwriting!' I nearly shouted.
'Theodoros! My brother, Theodoros. What a relief to my
mind, to hear from home. Forgive me but I shall open it
straight away.'

I broke the twine in a great hurry to see the letter. It
did not reward my haste.

The waxen page within was very clean and new, and incised with a few lines. First, a straggling line of salutation, large letters incised irregularly (as in the rest of this epistle), in a youthful hand:

To my dear and honoured Brother Stephanos

was followed by a line that might be found in any ordinary letter:

Greetings to you from Th and I trust you are well.

So far this was a conventional and proper opening. But no ordinary letter followed. Instead there were two lines of poetry – a quotation. This couplet was followed by the short line *Mother's love*, and then the conventional word *'Farewell'*. The whole of this puzzling epistle didn't take up a page. The other page, the facing waxed side, was a perfect blank.

'Strange,' I exclaimed. 'Aristotle, he does not write me a real letter, merely sends a quotation – from Hesiod I think. What can he be thinking of? And I shouldn't have thought Theodoros knew Hesiod. Homer, yes, he's started Homer –'

'Probably his schoolmaster quotes those lines,' Aristotle suggested, looking over my shoulder. 'Conventional schoolmaster stuff. *Works and Days*. I have often quoted those lines myself:

"Best is that man above all men who everything can know,
And next in good is humbler he who to these wise will go;

> Who cannot for himself see truth, or from another
>> hear it
> To store away in his own mind – this man is without
>> merit."'

'Yes, that sounds most likely.' Oromedon nodded sagely, having peered (uninvited) over my shoulder likewise. 'After all, how old is your little brother?'

'He is not yet ten years of age.'

'There you are, then. He wishes to write something impressive to his elder brother, and to let you know they are all going on well at home. So he sends this odd missive – a boy showing off and trying to look grown-up. But at least,' Oromedon continued, 'you have the comfort, as you set off on your brief journey, of knowing that everyone is well and that your little brother has leisure to pursue his studies.'

I read the letter again.

> *To my dear and honoured Brother Stephanos*
>> *Greetings to you from Th and I trust you are*
> *well.*
> *Who cannot for himself see truth, or from another*
>> *hear it*
> *To store away in his own mind – this man is without*
>> *merit.*
>> *Mother's love*
>> *Farewell*

'It seems almost like a joke.' I frowned. 'Theodoros should know better than to play jokes or to show off at such a time. Expensive to send such a letter all this way too, with no news – he might have said something about everyone.' I caught myself. It was impolite to grumble about something that was certainly not the fault of my company. Nor did I have reason to seem churlish to Oromedon, especially since he was such an important man in Kos.

'I thank you a thousand times for delivering this to me,' I said earnestly. 'You have gone out of your way to accommodate me and mine. Let me reimburse you for anything you have had to pay a messenger.'

Oromedon waved away any question of payment with an elegant air of finality.

The short ride in the little boat gave me time for reading and pondering Theodoros' epistle, but we were soon scrambling aboard the great ship. The three-banked vessel looked very splendid in the dawn light. Baggage was being loaded aboard, including, I saw, several great parcels of sharp spears, piles of helmets, and even parts of siege engines. Peleus and his adjutant supervised these, whilst his men inspected and stowed bags of flour and unwieldy flour mills and other humble goods. In much less time than I expected, we were waving farewell to Oromedon as our great ship set out for sea.

It was exciting to be on a vessel with such an enormous number of rowers. We plunged magnificently through the waves, the ship seeming to pass the measure of her own length with one sweep of the great oars. It felt as if there were no pause at all. The men worked miraculously together and the vessel shuddered as if with excitement at this power. The *keleusma* on such a big ship is practically deafening, unignorable; I wondered how anybody could get used to it. The speaker or singer was accompanied at one end of the ship by a piper, at the other by a heavy triangle struck at the same instant as his cry. The metallic shout and the whistle blended with the human in an unearthly concert of pure sound.

Aristotle was made uncomfortable by the sight of the rowers working together with unremitting and concentrated labour.

'But this is a mill, Stephanos!' he exclaimed. 'A giant mill, where the men are made into parts, like blind oxen and donkeys that turn a stone. How can one make citizens of people who do so?'

'Well, they get paid, and they do make us go fast,' I pointed out practically.

Indeed, the coast of Asia loomed close, rising out of a drapery of white morning mist. Kos receded rapidly. I regretted leaving its quiet hospitality and friendly doctors. And suppose my brother-in law (to be) returned to this island while I was not there? True, I had asked Iatrokles to get in touch with him, but would the doctor remember?

We proceeded parallel with the Cape of Myndos, passing an odd triangular hill and then swooping to our harbourage. Halikarnassos itself was masked by two or three low scrubby islands, and only when we passed between them could we see the magnificent harbour, and behind it the ragged edges of the broken city set on low hills. The harbour is a great semicircle; as you approach it there is a castellation on the right, and to the left a fortification and towers (ruined now) on a high and terraced hill, with an outlook over the whole harbour. The walls of this town had never been mended; they consisted largely of heaps of stone lying about. Here and there I could make out the shape of a building. One structure had notoriously been spared – by Alexander's personal order. Directly ahead of us, rising above the wrecked centre of the town, was the glittering Mausoleum, monument to the dead ruler Mausolus put up by his widow (and sister) Artemisia, twenty years before the city fell to Alexander. On top of a pyramid stands a four-horse chariot in bronze and gold, with giant statues of Mausolus and Artemisia in it. They appeared unduly smug, driving along in their splendour over the ruins of their people and their city.

The Mausoleum is just beyond the port, which was surprisingly busy. We heard the sounds of activity, the work of the hammers of smiths and the cries of vegetable sellers. A row of hopeless beggars sat in the sun – men mostly, wounded and useless. The beggars exhibited a variety of afflictions, and their appeals and groans mingled with the more vivacious cries of the hucksters. 'Pray, a small coin, sir?' 'Spare something for a poor man, I beseech.' Some said nothing, perhaps almost resigned to their fate. One pathetic man had a wen and a raw scar. Next to him sat a blind man, in a ragged and foul cloak with a kind of hood; he made no appeal, simply waggled a dirty foot to and fro, groaning occasionally and incoherently. He was too repulsive to tempt one to go near, his skin scabbed with dreadful red sores.

In what had once been a city you could see the fallen towers and stones burnt black, with a few charred beams not yet cleared away. I had heard before of the fire and the devastation from someone who was in Halikarnassos when it was taken. It was not rebuilt. Here and there would appear an apologetic group of dwellings in ill-made mud brick – humble housing that had either been spared or was thrown up after the cataclysm. You couldn't imagine this city truly recovering. Yet some poor folks were actually dwelling in the scorched ruins, as their rags showed.

'Oh, yes,' said Peleus. 'They hunt about for pickings from the ruins, largely. And there are some wells of good water in there, once they're cleansed and purified. The harbour supplies work. Queen Ada is anxious to put things back on something like the old footing. A slow business. We have assuredly clean wells with excellent water for the garrison at Mylas Gate. Also stabling for a good number of animals there. You'll see how convenient it is.'

The men, having quickly unloaded the ship, with the help of mules and carts moved the goods to the garrison station, a series of sheds, temporary houses and stables. Some soldiers and their servants were waiting to join us.

'Another shipment of arms and armour just came down from the North,' said Peleus, pleased. 'We'll add them to our load – we will be taking armaments and a few other supplies with us. Won't take us long to load up. One never goes east without taking some more supplies. Here, this is Menestor, a Theban slave. He can assist you. His Greek is perfect of course, but he knows Persian by now too.'

A diffident young man, rather grimy like most slaves but with a humble uncertain smile, came to see if we wanted anything. Attentively he offered us food and drink while we were waiting, and carefully made sure our luggage was stowed properly away. I felt uncomfortable dealing with a slave from Thebes, and remarked on this to Peleus.

'Well, you must realise there are a *lot* of Theban slaves,' he said frankly. 'Something like thirty thousand men, women, and children were made captive at the fall of that defiant city. And of course a lot of people on the mainland don't like having them, so a great proportion of them were brought over here to Asia. Quite a number serve the army, which needs many Greek-speaking porters. They are quite serviceable. That boy makes himself useful. You see how smartly the men and their attendants get things ready. We can soon set off.'

True, the preparations had gone quickly. Alexander's army and those who served it were used to efficiency. 'I am surprised at the order with which you arrange the things in the wagons,' I remarked.

'I am more surprised,' said Aristotle, 'to see wagons at all. I believe Alexander, like his father, is firmly against their use.'

'Oh, that's in warfare,' said Peleus. 'Yes Philip and Alexander like the army to move along briskly. There's no doubt wagons are slow. Having slaves to carry stuff and march with you is much faster – and of course each soldier carries his own basic supplies and weapons. You know that Alexander forbade women and children of any kind to follow the army, and the ban on wagons supported that policy. But that ban applies to an army on the march, invading and conquering. Nowadays we have settled garrisons to supply. Naturally, we use wagons and large carts, and take all sorts of heavy loads. We have a great many mules, for one thing – and tough and strong, so we can cover the ground. Let's be off!'

There were military men armed to the head and to the rear of our party, and where Aristotle and I walked in the middle there was also an armed soldier. Instead of making me feel safer, this was alarming. I suddenly realised that I had come to a region at war, or recently pacified, where armed insurrection was a possibility.

'Don't worry,' said Peleus, seeing, as it were, into my thoughts. 'This land is ours now.'

I was no longer in Attika, my native and good Attika, where our ancestors sprang out of the soil. We know it is our natural place; we belong on land that is truly ours. Sword-taken land seems another kind of thing from home land. Every step I took I felt I was going in the wrong direction, farther and farther away from my home, from my mother whom I had sworn to protect, and from my puzzling Theodoros, who was old enough to write, it seemed, but not of age to make sense.

We came to a river, which I was told was the Xanthos. Barges were lined up for our use, and with our supplies (including heaps of animal fodder) and our cargo of arms and armour we got into them and moved on down the river. The flat boats were propelled partly by the draught power of animals and partly by men rowing or pushing the craft along. We had a good view of some of the land and the trees; the breeze from the river made a welcome coolness. Too soon we had to get out and march again, at the staging post by the riverside where a host of animals and some more soldiers awaited us. Again, the cargo was put aboard wagons and carts (except for some equipment left at this post), and we set off, marching on and on. Soon we were covered with the fine dust that floated up from the arable ground, beaten into a flour by the tramp of men and animals.

Aristotle and I were offered a place to ride in a wagon,

under a linen shelter, but we refused. It was too undignified, in the presence of these soldiers to sit (like old ladies or wanton camp-followers) on top of the armour and baggage. We marched with the rest. The pace was not too hard for civilians, but it was hard in the sense that we could not stop and dally at our own sweet will. Not at all like travelling to Delphi. Although my journey to Delphi had its more frightening aspects, I remembered the meadows, and the places where we stopped to eat and look at the flowers and hear the (quarrelsome) shepherds sing. Now the songs we heard were military ditties. From the people whom we passed, silence.

We had to stop occasionally to let the animals eat and drink.

'They seem to need a lot of water,' I remarked.

'And food,' said Peleus. 'That's the difficulty of organising any kind of army expedition – keeping up with the demands not only of the men, but also of the animals. When you work the animals hard, they drink even more. We calculate how much fodder the animals will need – we cannot always rely on the land. We now have charts showing where the good wells are. An expedition like this is nothing compared to a truly major operation. I must admit, Parmenion is wonderfully able in organising transport in big operations – almost as good as Alexander himself. Now, they tell me, Parmenion, in order to transport the great Persian treasure to Ekbatana, must take twenty thousand mules and five thousand camels!'

'Ah! Five thousand camels?' said Aristotle, brightening. 'Then it is no wonder that Alexander has asked him to conduct this complex expedition. Only Parmenion could deal with it. That gives me cause to hope that there is no real falling-out between Parmenion and Alexander. Such a task might be seen as a high compliment.'

'Perhaps,' was Peleus' only reply. But Aristotle whispered to me, 'This man is not of high enough position to know the truth about generals. We must enquire of Kallisthenes, or Harpalos.'

Each night we stopped at a posting house, as promised. There was dinner every night, and we usually slept under some sort of roof, though in a place with open walls to let the air in, as it was so hot. The animals, both by night and by day, emitted a good deal of noise, and some smell. The army possessed (or had commandeered) an endless supply of donkeys and mules, most of which seemed to bray outside my bedchamber. There were numerous and very handsome horses. All these animals emitted unignorable smells.

At the posting stations they also had a few oxen for really heavy loads, but these slow beasts were used for local transport. We were, however, escorting some heavy loads of valuable equipment. I saw one wagon full of sarissas, those very long light spears favoured by Makedonians, and a cart brimming over with shining bronze helmets and corselets.

'I should have thought,' I said looking at these, 'that by now you had the Persians making this sort of thing.'

Peleus laughed.

'Yes, we have taken over all the Persian manufactories, and they are remarkably good. They have made armaments and armour for Darius and his ancestors for many ages. But, you understand, a lot of Greek generals and most Makedonians, especially the leaders, don't want to fight with anything but the best – and what they are used to. So they send back for weapons and armour from the mainland. The sarissas come from Pella or from Deon, in Makedonia.'

'And the bronze helmets and corselets are certainly from Khalkis,' said Aristotle, fingering one of these in a thoughtful and familiar way. 'Where else could you find quality like that?'

So in this military style we were marching day after day at a good pace, in company with horses, mules, asses and men, through huge brown hills which became increasingly craggy. The country is very vast: it seemed bigger than Greece. Sometimes you would see fields stretching to the horizon and then hill after great hill. When we turned south we occasionally caught a glimpse of dramatic crags and cliffs plunging seaward. The weather was hot, save when a breeze blew, which was rarely. In the fields, a few peasants toiled.

'We thought it best,' Peleus explained, 'to let some of the Persians go on growing crops. We need the food. It would not help us if the region were consumed by famine. But more of the farms are being taken over by Greek settlers, and we hope eventually to have the inland area just as Greek as the coast.'

'Do the remaining Persians not try to resist and fight you?' I asked.

He laughed. 'They have very little chance against a well-armed and organised army, I assure you. Most of them know better. Besides, here in western regions of Asia they cannot go far – we have taken over most of their animals. And a lot of the people are dead or have fled. But the peasants remaining can still grow food. We had a

good wheat harvest. Observe how fruitful this land is –
how valuable.'

It was literally fruitful, for we were now on a road
above a steep valley in which were orchards of fig and
pomegranate trees, heavy with fruit. A few women were
working sadly among the pomegranates.

'Splendid!' cried Aristotle. 'With such wealth the
Greeks can feed themselves – almost, one is tempted to
think, the world. Improved by better management, both
Egypt and Asia will give such provision that we may no
more fear famine – that great evil to mankind.'

'But I dare say Darius thought well of this land for
feeding his Persians,' I said, laughing a little on thinking
of that discomfited King. Yet I was not entirely happy to
think of all the people killed or fled who had lived a few
years ago in these prosperous homesteads and tilled the
fields.

'Well, Darius should soon be done for,' said Peleus
impatiently. 'Then we will know the real peace has begun.
It is a great pity we are still chasing Darius. He has gone
into that hinterland of mountains, a very inhospitable
region beyond the real Persia. So it will take time to dig
him out. That is where the man you were asking about –
Arkhebios – fell. In one of the many little fights among
the crags of that grim country.'

'Sad,' said Aristotle. 'One of the misfortunes of war. But
the Commander should make it up to the man's family.
And to gain such a fair country for Greece is worth even
the painful expense of lives as well as of material and time.
This war is changing the world.'

'It is wonderful,' I assented. 'But I wonder how easy the
Persian lands will be to retain? Could not the Persians

complain to the gods that we captured them unjustly, as they were not making war on us when we invaded?'

'What kind of complaint could they make to their gods, Stephanos, since in days of old they themselves were simply conquerors of all this land? Persia marched into this region, which was largely settled by Greeks. There were other peoples here before; there is a good deal of mixture in the population.

'My greatest hope, Stephanos, is that this great war and this new circumstance of having almost a new world to settle and control will bring to the Hellenes what they so badly need. Unity. Greece – or at least parts of it – is the leader among mankind in all civilised arts, and in practical matters too. Where do you find better things – from flutes and house tiles to corselets and statues? Where is there a poetry like that in the Greek language – or a language more lovely and expressive in itself? Moreover, where are there better laws, or a deeper understanding of a political constitution? Greece is the treasure-house of civilisation. But what holds her back? Simply that Greek fights Greek. Even within the same city-state there are civic quarrels, factions, even broils and bloodshed. And Athens and Sparta, two great communities, wasted their strength in fighting each other. Now in this cause all of Hellas unites – or can unite.'

'That is an amazing vision,' I said. 'I am not sure if I like it. Not if it means Athens becomes less like Athens. I shall always be an Athenian.'

'It is my belief – my prayer, if you like – that the settlement of Asia will bring about the political peace and humane stability of which the Athenian – and all other Greeks – may be capable but have not yet realised. We

could create a new Athens without its defects. The first to
benefit from the new way of things, really, are the
wretched inhabitants of this region whom you see before
you. For they will now share in the arts and letters and
political structures of the Greek world. When they have
been taught aright, and the area has been leavened with
new settlers, all the inhabitants will recognise their
benefits and blessings, and hasten to create a brighter
order. New cities will arise here, adorned with marble
council halls and high-pillared temples. Citizens will
move in an orderly way to vote in their own councils, each
a citizen of his own city, but all sharing the great idea.
Then the earth will be full of light. The light of learning
and knowledge, with good trade, good art, good medicine
– and the highest philosophic thinking about the good of
mankind and the best political structure. In that new
world, all mankind will eventually participate, and old
disunity be done away.'

He was breathless with the quick, passionate
utterance of his long speech and the rapture of his vision.
Truth to tell, I had not thought about any of this. To me,
the war against Persia had been a kind of grumbling
nuisance. For the first time I felt how it would affect my
children, and my children's children. I was not sure that
I wanted all this alteration – it was like someone giving
you too much dinner.

'I admit that it makes a change,' I said slowly.

'You will live to see it all. I have written carefully to
Kallisthenes – as he keeps such close company with
Alexander – about our civilising of Asia. All our policies
in the conquered lands should drive to this end. Oh, how
happy I am to think I shall see Kallisthenes soon! I have

missed him. You will like my nephew, Stephanos.'

'I am sure I shall,' I said, politeness masking my relative lack of interest. I could think only of my little brother Theodoros. Was he showing off? Impudent? Or merely practising his handwriting? Was his handwriting better or worse than I remembered it? I wanted to look at the letter again, but felt reluctant to discuss it.

At this point, we had to save our breath and shut off discourse lest we tumble or fall behind. We were winding down steep mountainous cliffs, turning once more towards the sea coast. It was prudent to watch one's footing, so as not to tumble straight down the rough incline on to the rocks below. Then we reached a kind of road along a beach, where sand made the going difficult.

I could scarcely believe that the journey would not go on and on, and I felt no sensation stronger than that of surprise when Peleus said we were approaching our objective, the harbour city of Phaselis. He himself seemed brighter at the thought, and regaled us with the glories of the town, including a freshwater lake. 'There is an inland town called Milyas,' he added, 'or there was, but Alexander destroyed it as he wanted to keep the passes open, without danger of attack. Phaselis is surrounded by mountains.' He laughed. 'One mountain we call "The Ladder". Our army had practically to carve steps in it – so steep! At its foot is a narrow pass on shore which is dry in calm weather but full of sea at flood tide. Alexander insisted on going over into Pamphylia in stormy weather, when the water had come in – you must believe it! Soldiers had to march in water up to their belly-buttons.'

As we were simply coming from the west, however, and the sea was ebbing, we soon marched more or less dry-shod, and gained Phaselis, with its three harbours. Phaselis was quite in tune with Aristotle's vision, for it is a handsome Greek city (if small). Its walls, temples and meeting houses were intact.

'This was one of the wise cities,' said Peleus. 'The leaders of the town came out with a gold wreath for Alexander and offered the city to him. Greek place, as you can see. An important garrison now. Alexander placed Nearkhos here to govern Lykia and Pamphylia.'

I felt at home – or almost – there in Phaselis, looking about me at the shining marble buildings in the centre of the town. Had the governor Nearkhos been there, of course we should have introduced ourselves, but we were told he was away. The streets and the Agora were full of soldiers, so Phaselis was less like a normal town than it first looked. Yet, there would be taverns here, and songs that I knew. But I was not to stay to examine the place.

We stopped, not at the central military office next to the governor's house, but at a guard post in the eastern wall of the city. Here we dropped off some of our freight, and a couple of new soldiers joined us. 'This is Diophantos, who knows his way backward and forward by now along the coast of Lykia,' said Peleus introducing this captain. 'He has charge of a platoon which will be useful to you in getting everything around and up the hill road. For it seems we must go on – a new message with orders for us.'

'Yes. So sorry to incommode you,' said Diophantos pleasantly. He was a nondescript man with a broad sunburned face and agreeable manner. 'We have had a message from Harpalos saying that if he wasn't at Phaselis by the time you got here, you and your party were to go on and meet him in the next posting station, in the direction of Side. Wait for him there.'

'Well, we must do so,' said Peleus resignedly. 'Might as well start off at once.'

We didn't start off at once, as there was a little discussion about whether we should take 'The Ladder' or the beach route. As we still had carts and some baggage, including supplies for Harpalos, everybody elected the beach. The going was squelchy and slow and we all had to put our shoulders to the carts to hoist them out of wet sand from time to time. To get to the posting station we had to climb sharply uphill. Lykia is vertical country. This next posting station east of Phaselis was, like many others, set in a wretched ruined village, as that offered good well water and the shelter of the few walls left standing. We were told to wait in a shed-like structure attached to a large expanse of broken wall. Here we had a roof thatched with leaves and brush to keep off the sun, but not much else. After the promise of marbled Phaselis, we might as well have been in the middle of nowhere.

Waiting seemed worse than walking, but we were fortunate, for the day after our arrival the scout announced a cloud of dust on the eastern road, and assured us that the party of Harpalos was approaching from Side. He proved a true prophet. Aristotle and I, in respectable clothing, were urged to meet the Treasurer and friend of Alexander as soon as he arrived. We lined up obediently, looking in the direction of the approaching storm of dust, hearing its horses' hoofbeats and beholding the looming horsemen as they emerged each from his particular cloud.

XVIII

$$\text{---} \bowtie \text{---}$$

Harpalos the Treasurer

Harpalos, first to arrive, looked down at us for a moment, not immediately dismounting from his remarkably beautiful white horse. Man and horse, even if dusty, looked finer than statues. Harpalos, sitting easily on his lovely steed, was dressed not only for riding but for war. He wore no helmet, but his red tunic was covered by a corselet of the cleanest bronze, ornamented with sculpture work in relief depicting a crowd of men looking towards the sun. Untarnished and undented, the bronze glittered in the hot rays of the day. About his neck a scarf glittered like a cobwebs with dew on it, some kind of airy Persian work. It had floated lightly behind him when he rode, and now rested in graceful folds.

'Well!' Harpalos broke into a broad smile, most pleasing to behold. His teeth were white and even, his smile no vulgar grin but the smile of a gentleman who delights in meeting a friend. 'A happy meeting! O Aristotle son of Nikomakhos, it is good in you to come this long journey to see me.' His clear grey eyes, set wide apart in his sun-bronzed face, gazed at us from above with concentrated interest.

'It is an honour to see you, O Harpalos son of Makhatas,' said Aristotle mildly. 'This is my good and trustworthy friend, a man of Athens, Stephanos son of Nikiarkhos.'

'A friend of yours is welcome, O Aristotle. For you know the good. Men, mark this day as fortunate –' turning to those cavalrymen behind him – 'for we lay eyes on one of the great men of our age, Aristotle the philosopher of Athens, who toils for the empire of knowledge and virtue.'

The men set up a dutiful murmur of applause as Harpalos wheeled his horse about. 'The two of you must share such poor shelter as I can offer. I shall let my horse take a well-earned rest.' He moved to the area set aside for the best horses, a light shed to protect them from the hot sun, and leaped off his steed. One of his men stood by to help him. I realised with a shock that this impressive man was crippled, one leg slightly withered and shorter than the other. He seemed active enough, despite his lameness, and certainly used to riding. The horse nodded peacefully as Harpalos laid a hand on its nose. The other Makedonians came up and the grooms took charge of the horses, rubbing them and feeding them grains since grazing herbage was scarce in this sunburnt place.

Harpalos strode towards us with his energetic but uneven gait; his soldiers and some servants who had arrived in a second wave were already unloading baggage. We stood at the opening of the unadorned shelter that served this station's visitors, and resumed our greetings.

'So good in you to come,' repeated Harpalos with hearty goodwill. 'Sorry not to have met you in Phaselis, but I have ridden all the way from Side.' The ride did not seem to have incommoded him. Despite his disability this man seemed youthful, full of energy. He was of course slightly older than I, a schoolfellow, as I now recalled, of Alexander – Alexander's age or just a trifle older, perhaps twenty-seven or twenty-eight. A man just arrived at his prime, and flowering in that prime. His height was in his torso and he looked less tall standing than he did sitting. But he was undeniably good looking – not as beautiful as Demetrios of Phaleron, but almost. He had the straight well-cut nose of a nobleman, and those winning frank grey eyes.

'Well, Aristotle, it is good to see you. How it brings back the days of my boyhood,' he continued. 'Do you remember the day we – Alex and I – released all the horses in the stables and put a gadfly on the rear of each? So the poor steeds, from the noblest stallion to the pitifullest knock-kneed hack, all fell to galloping in every direction over the whole world?' He turned and gave me the benefit of his smile also. 'We were bad boys at that time, you see. Oh, those were the happy days.'

'And you do not seem unhappy now,' said Aristotle, smiling. 'You have a high position. We are truly honoured in meeting you, O Harpalos.'

'And so – but why do we stay to talk in this pen!' Harpalos looked about him with disfavour. Our shed was indeed little better than a shelter for animals, though it had an impressive view of the sea below, broad and endless, burning blue and white and golden in the summer sun. 'I have asked my servants to make us a worthy room in the shade of this shanty. I did not ask you here, Aristotle – you and your friend who is so kind as to accompany you – in order to make you miserable in this poky little place. Come, we shall see what my fellows can provide for us.'

He led the way around the exterior wall. On the shadier side three men were setting up a tent on the bare ground. From a roll of material in a slender bag they quickly conjured up an elegant white structure, fluttering gently in the breeze, but apparently fixed solidly enough to the ground. And the ground was not to be bare any more, for with quick gestures the men ran about, strewing strange colourful stuffs and tapestries upon the earth, so that we were led into a miniature and quick-made palace.

'Seat yourselves,' said Harpalos, handing us each a cushion in a hospitable manner. It was most affable of him to see personally to our comfort. 'I had my fellows set it up so we shall get the breeze from the sea, without the glare. And, with my men standing guard outside, I can take off my armour.' He shrugged himself out of his handsome corselet. 'Made to my measure at my instructions,' he explained. 'A light hard bronze, so it is not inconvenient but the heat does make a difference. The scarf keeps my neck from burning.'

He clapped his hands and two servants appeared – Persian, I could guess by their appearance. He spoke to them quickly in an unknown tongue and they bowed and left the tent.

Aristotle laughed. 'You are becoming a master of languages, Harpalos. I knew a couple of Persian magi – Plato had them at the Akademeia. But the only word I could make out was "chicken".'

'Then I cannot surprise you with our meal!' Harpalos retorted. 'Too bad. But I have a better surprise for you. It will be ready by the time another party arrives, bringing one of my treasures that I am anxious to show you.'

'I shall be happy to see it.' Aristotle was polite. 'But – where is Kallisthenes? I was promised Kallisthenes would be here.'

'Yes, Kallisthenes of Olynthos. Your nephew, I believe? Our Commander's historian and adulator. Eager to see you, I promise you. He is conducting the other party I just spoke of and will be here shortly.'

'Now we are at leisure, we must congratulate you on your promotion.'

'I wouldn't call it precisely that,' Harpalos said easily. 'Something I could do for Alexander. You remember I was Treasurer before, after the death of Philip.'

'And I am glad,' said Aristotle, 'that whatever differences you and my other pupil have had in the past have been patched up.'

'Oh, well,' said Harpalos, 'all that has been widely misreported, I think. I went to Megara to help Alexander. Of course I missed the battle at Issos town. But of course you must know – I cannot fight. Not with this leg – and not with this arm.' He gazed ruefully down at this left arm and I suddenly saw that it too was withered, and the extremity of it was immobile. The hand was like a limp claw, not in use.

'As you see, young man –' he gazed at me squarely. 'That hand could grasp neither sarissa nor buckler. Alexander knows I cannot be a warrior in the field. But Alexander needs about him true men of Makedonia – nobles of his own kind, that he can trust. And he can trust

me. You know of our history of old, Aristotle. My loyalty
has been tried – and proved.'

'Yes, indeed, I know it has. Harpalos,' Aristotle
explained to me, 'was sent into exile by King Philip, who
was jealous of the loyalty of some of Alexander's men.'

'That was after King Philip's second marriage,' added
Harpalos. 'Boy! Fetch us some wine here. Yes, Philip
(though he was old enough to know better) was besotted
with his new wife and cast off Queen Olympias,
Alexander's mother, using her and even Alexander with
disgrace. Those of us who were true to Alexander were
badly treated.'

'Great men like Philip are always expecting treachery,'
remarked Aristotle.

'But the group who remained loyal to Alexander
through exile or imprisonment – these Alexander knows
he can trust. We are the Good Companions. Boy, serve
my guests in the best goblets.'

We made libation, and Harpalos stretched; he lay back
on a cushion, as one glad to be at leisure. I noticed, as he
drank his wine and rested, that there was a strong line on
his face, a furrow carved from nose to mouth, such as one
sees in those who have suffered illness or pain. It cannot
have been easy for crippled Harpalos to remain so active.
Perhaps, handsome and debonair as he seemed, he was not
free now from bodily pain.

'Bit of a journey,' he explained, as if reading my
thoughts. 'Came by ship from Damaskos, and went to
Perge and then to Side. Carrying messages from
Alexander to the governors. Philoxenos, in whose charge
the western part of Asia is laid, is busy with the fleet in the
Aegean. He can hardly be everywhere. So I do a few

errands in the West. We mustn't neglect the cities and stations in the West while we push our way East. Mind you, my own headquarters are really in Babylon. A most beautiful place – we are trying to restore it to all its glory. Even Damaskos seems now a long way westward. A busy time we're having in the East. I have good news that will surprise you!'

'Yes?' said Aristotle eagerly. We both leaned forward to hear.

Harpalos rose from his cushioned place and stood up in the middle of the tent to make his dramatic announcement.

'Darius – Darius the great King of Persia – is dead!'

'What? Really?' we exclaimed.

'Yes. I have talked with those who saw his corpse. You must know that Darius had sought shelter with his friend and loyal supporter Bessus – one of the great Persian commanders at Issos, you will remember. But Bessus, like a treacherous hound, turned against his master in his last extremity and put Darius under arrest, proclaiming himself the new King. Alexander went in swift pursuit of Darius, all the way to the Hyrkanian gates. Then with a picked band of cavalry he rushed after the fugitive Bessus. Alexander must have gone like the wind! Amazing, the distance he covered in eight days. Going over terrible country, I promise you. Anyway, the rebels had Darius with them in a cart with bars on the sides, a moving prison, with two generals to guard him. When they saw the Makedonians coming, these two generals Satibarzanes and Barsaentes knew there was no safety for them. So they stabbed Darius themselves and fled away with six hundred other horsemen, to hide in the desert.'

'And thus the Great King died,' murmured Aristotle. 'The end of the story of Darius' life.'

'And *what* an end! I tell you, the rascals in their haste to run off didn't even stab the King properly. Darius wasn't dead when they sped away! Darius was just gasping his last when our men came up. So – there is the end of the golden king. Powerful Darius, with his thousands and hundreds of thousands, his wealth and his strength. Killed pitifully, like a stuck pig in a farm cart. How much better and more honourable a death it would have been for him had he fallen at Gaugamela!'

'Extraordinary,' said Aristotle. 'History is certainly rich in the marvellous. How has Alexander conducted himself at this victory?'

'Oh, Alexander is noble. You must be proud of him, Aristotle – as one of his former tutors *and* as a Makedonian yourself. For Alexander swore to pursue and capture Bessus and all Darius' murderers. And Darius, his great opponent, Alexander has had honourably buried in Persepolis.'

'That is true greatness of mind!' exclaimed Aristotle. 'I am most heartily glad to hear it.'

'What about Bessus?' I enquired.

'Bessus? They're looking for him. Treacherous dog. I dare say they have found him by now, and I shouldn't envy him when they do. Better for him too had he fallen at Gaugamela. Hark! I think I hear the other party approaching.'

The man's hearing was excellent; shortly after, we too heard the noise not only of hooves but of wheels, and then voices. Harpalos' eyes grew bright. He rose quickly from his cushioned lair.

'Stay here,' he commanded. 'I will bring a beautiful thing to you, to delight your eyes.'

He left the tent. I could see Aristotle fidgeted to go out likewise, but our orders were clear. There was a babble of voices outside; soon I heard someone walking with haste – even running – towards our tent.

'Uncle!' A young man burst through the tent flaps and almost leaped upon Aristotle, who was already moving towards him. Without first pausing for polite sentences of greeting, the two embraced, with great affection.

'You will impress our friends by our formal manners,' Aristotle remarked. 'O Kallisthenes, I have missed you!'

'And I you! I couldn't miss a chance to see *you*. Not that I would have missed this whole expedition to Asia for anything in the world.' Kallisthenes was almost boyish. His fair hair curled along his head and down his neck. But I could see on second glance that he was older than Harpalos, a man certainly in this thirties. Aristotle's favourite nephew was tall, well-formed, thin in a manly way, in the seasoned shape of one who lives much in the open air.

Aristotle introduced us, and I was the object of a glance from those glowing deep-set eyes, disconcertingly a younger version of Aristotle's own. 'I am happy to meet a new friend,' Kallisthenes said. 'But I am sorry not to see some older friends. Theophrastos – wouldn't it be pleasant if Theophrastos was here? – Or Demetrios of Phaleron, student of both of you. Demetrios will be one of the greatest of us. How I should love to talk with Theophrastos about the plants we have discovered in Asia! I have a very carefully packed bag of flowering plants and some jars of root material for you to take back.'

Aristotle laughed. 'As if we could run them over to the next village! I tell you, young scapegrace, it took us long enough to get here.'

'It is a trouble to carry such stuff, but you will be sure to appreciate the roots – and Theophrastos will be especially happy. Harpalos and I are going to work together to create great gardens in Babylon. Theophrastos must come to see them. *And* – I have brought you my book. Boy' – to his slave – 'fetch me my box!'

'Your book is finished?' I asked politely.

'How can I finish when the story is going on?' Kallisthenes retorted. 'Of course it can't be finished at this point. I am to record all the deeds of Alexander, and Alexander isn't finished with the Persians yet. I have written the beginning. Here it is!'

Kallisthenes took from the young slave's hands a box of nicely polished wood. 'It is all written out. I was able to get good copyists, no expense spared. It needs revision of course, but it is readable. I have found a new medium to write on – the inside of sheep's hide, scraped and dried. The army eats so many sheep, there is a constant supply.'

Aristotle looked at one of the stiff sheets covered with fine brown writing. 'It should last well,' he commented. 'The material seems stronger than papyrus, and not breakable like tablets. I wonder if the Babylonians found it out before? Durable, if not as cohesive or handy as a roll.'

'No matter,' said Kallisthenes. 'It will go into rolls when it is finished. This material is cheap and ready to hand. Very good for maps and illustrations. This is only the first part. As more events take place, I write about them. So – I shall send you pieces now and then, until the whole is completed. Whenever that may be. But these first sections cover a great deal, including Tyre, Egypt, Issos. And Gaugamela, the great victory. I also offer a clear record of places we went through, the terrain, the plants and animals. I am keeping my own journal of such discoveries as those, not about Alexander but about the places.'

'Extremely valuable,' said Aristotle, taking up the book with loving hands. 'I shall treasure it always. Your philosophic writings, your natural descriptions – these I long to see also. Be observant and accurate, like a good philosopher. Keep account of the peoples too. Describe the Persian King's former subjects, their different tribes, their settlements and customs, just as you describe the animals and plants in their habitats.'

Again there was a noise outside the tent door, a most unexpected sound. Flutes! Delicate flutes, well played, astonishing in this barbarian outpost. The graceful curls of sweet sound put an end to our conversation. Harpalos poked his head through the flap.

'I promised you a treasure worth seeing,' he reminded us. 'Now you shall see it!'

We were all standing facing him when Harpalos moved into the tent, slowly to the sound of glowing music, leading by the right hand another person. A female. Ye gods, a beautiful female!

The woman who came in was slender but finely modelled, with beautiful breasts and long well-turned legs. I can say this because I could see almost all of her. She wore a clinging tunic of fine Egyptian linen, and her bosom was covered only the filmiest of fabrics –

something that shone and glowed. The lacing did not hide
the beauty of the little apples. The veil over her head was
equally filmy, a sort of immaterial idea of a veil, totally
transparent. Even this delicate integument was partly
cast back from her face. She seemed a little embarrassed
and a trifle amused also, perhaps dishevelled from just
having been kissed. Her lovely face, unveiled to our view,
showed a delicate flush. The fluctuating rosy hue, like
sunset light cast upon glowing marble, made her more
interesting than the finest statue, however brilliantly
painted.

'There!' said Harpalos with pride. 'This is one of the
wonders of the world. Pure Greek – here in the middle of
Asia. How I love Athenian art! This is my female
companion, Pythonike of Athens. These men' – he
addressed her respectfully – 'are friends of mine,
Pythonike. The most reverend one is Aristotle, of whom
you so oft have heard, and that is his friend Stephanos of
Athens.'

'Greetings, gentlemen,' she said in a clear voice, her
modesty not confounded by speaking to strange men.

'Yes, Pythonike is all mine, but she is used to meeting
company,' said Harpalos. 'I do find so boring those proper
women who cannot eat and talk with one. Pythonike,
now, she eats and converses. I adore her, and I think of her
as Perikles did of his Aspasia. Boys!' He addressed the
servants at the tent door. 'Let us eat. We are starving, I
promise you!'

There followed a most unusual meal. Unusual not only
in a woman's being one of the diners. The food was indeed
the promised chicken, but cooked in a delicious manner
with spices I do not recollect having tasted before. I could

hardly believe it was I who was dining on Eastern food, and in such fine state (for there were low tables and proper plates, as well as handsome wrought goblets). It was I, being served by Persians while reclining on soft and colourful Persian stuffs and gazing at the most beautiful woman. It was like some enchanting dream.'

'Pythonike goes about with me everywhere,' Harpalos said. 'And everyone respects her. Even Alexander knows it's hands off.'

'Our Commander,' Kallisthenes announced admiringly, 'is famous for his temperance and self-control. For when he had Darius' wife and daughter and his concubines in his power, he treated them civilly and did not rape any of them, even the servants. He has treated them as royal ladies, and put them in proper lodgings.'

'Again, he displays magnanimity,' said Aristotle, with approbation. 'This is how a man great of soul should behave.'

'True,' said Harpalos. 'But the temptation was only moderate, after all. Now, had Alexander been faced by a beautiful youth, the down just coming on his cheeks, he would have more need of his vaunted self-control.'

'But Alexander loves women too,' objected Kallisthenes.

'Yes. Everything that is lovable our Commander loves, which is most worthy of him.'

'I hope he is temperate,' Aristotle said in a worried tone.

'There speaks the tutor. Look, he is no glutton. He told Queen Ada to stop sending him sweetmeats and baked goods as if he were a boy. His tutors, he said, had taught him that hunger was the best sauce and to eat sparingly. On the march, he shared all supplies with the troops; the rougher the going, the more scrupulously he limited himself to his men's own ration of food and water. Nowadays, I admit, when he makes camp he is apt to enquire after the cooks and the bakers, and he loves to sit long at splendid dinners with his wine, talking of this and that. Of course, he's not a lad of twenty any more. And as for women – he ate up that gorgeous Persian woman, Memnon's widow, the lovely Barsinna, fast enough when she was set before him.'

'And,' said Pythonike, 'the Commander now pays court in a respectful but interesting way to the elder daughter of Darius. She might be a queen yet if she plays her game well.'

'True. But he is a man for men, and loves above all his dear Hephaistion, whom he calls his Patroklos, the dearest to him of the Good Companions.'

'Hephaistion is also a fine general,' said Kallisthenes. 'It's excellent that Alexander has so many young generals. They understand what he has in mind – and they possess great energy and fortitude.'

'That reminds me,' said Aristotle. 'I was sad to hear recently of the death of Arkhebios, the general Parmenion's son – a recognised son, though born out of wedlock. Arkhebios was the father of one of our students at the Lykeion, a young Parmenion. Now, as this boy – almost a young man – is a grandson of the general, I thought the best thing we could do for this youth is to give him into the care of great Parmenion. Or into the care of the boy's uncle, admirable Philotas, commander of cavalry. But I do not know how to reach either of them. Surely, Harpalos, you might help us.'

Kallisthenes looked grave, and put his goblet down. He

and Harpalos looked at each other, and Harpalos set aside his plate.

'You broach a difficult topic,' he said, pausing sufficiently to let us know he chose his words with care.'Parmenion has grown old in the service of the royal house of Makedon. A great general and a great man, undoubtedly. But we had best tell you frankly that he is under a cloud, and it is unlikely that cloud will be lifted.'

'I had some hint of this before,' said Aristotle. 'Hard to believe. What has gone wrong? Is there no remedy? I know great Parmenion − reliable and indefatigable. He always seemed the epitome of loyalty.'

'Loyalty . . . Hmm. It is difficult to define what "loyalty" is in all circumstances. If you are loyal to a man it's either because of crude self-interest, or because you respect yourself as well as him. And if this man behaves so as your loyalty and self-respect are in conflict? Then what? There are several factors in the fall of Parmenion from grace. In the first instance, both he and your friend Antipater lost their places in the inner core of Alexander's heart when they urged him − too emphatically − to marry and beget an heir before taking off after Darius.'

'But why should he mind that?' I was genuinely surprised. 'It is good advice. For a king to marry and leave an heir is good for him and for the country he rules.'

'Ah, yes. But that showed, you see, that Antipater and Parmenion were capable of thinking of a Makedonian world without Alexander alive in it − and this our Commander doesn't like at all. He was − and *is* − still young, with the immortality of youth. He takes great personal risks, so that one would think he had a contempt of death, but in fact he doesn't wish at all to imagine the world after his death.'

'Well, that is a minor matter,' said Kallisthenes. 'Young men often don't like old men jawing at them about marriage. And you see Antipater remains on quite good terms with Alexander.'

'Yes – as long as Antipater stays in Greece and does what Alexander tells him. But now comes a graver reason for the Commander's displeasure against Parmenion. The general has spoken too frankly to Alexander of putting an end to these conquests, now that Persepolis is taken.'

'Parmenion thought the taking of Persepolis was the end of the war! That once we killed off Darius we were all to stop, and go home for supper, as it were,' interjected Kallisthenes. 'That's because Parmenion's too *old*. He must be over seventy! He is physically a wonder, I grant you, for his age. But he is too old.'

'That may be. Parmenion has certainly displayed to the Commander that he cannot share the Commander's view of the future. That is a grave fault. The problem is the more serious as this man has undeniably given his life to Makedonian service, and so have his sons. Alexander has endeavoured to keep him fairly happy while demoting him – which is what he has done in sending him to Ekbatana, to guard the treasure. Two of Parmenion's legitimate sons are dead now, as well as your bastard Arkhebios, but Philotas is still quite powerful.'

'But it may be,' said Pythonike, unabashedly addressing a room of men, 'that Philotas will not hereafter be too friendly to Alexander. Now that his father has been tucked away as a mere caretaker of the treasure in Ekbatana and is no longer an important general.'

'Yes, we know what Philotas is like – a priggish man with a great conceit of himself.'

'He is not as priggish as you make him out,' said Pythonike. 'He has sent for his beloved from Athens – a woman called Antigone – who is travelling all the way to the veritable East to keep him company. Philotas is no youth by now: he must number some forty summers. But that shows a certain amount of youthful ardour.'

'Antigone!' Aristotle was startled. 'I wonder if this is the same woman – ? Well, well. Rather juvenile conduct on Philotas' part, certainly. It would give a handle to detractors.'

'Oh, come now,' said Harpalos. 'Be reasonable, Aristotle. This is a long war! Not every man likes Persian ladies. And some of us *fully* value the beauty of Greece.' He smiled upon Pythonike. 'But this is not the time to hand over any poor youth to the care of Philotas.'

'Harpalos is quite right,' said Kallisthenes. 'It would be putting the lad in harm's way. His father Arkhebios was picked out for a dangerous detail, with little chance of glory, live or die.'

'And you see, he died,' said Pythonike, with a gentle smile.

'Killed in one of those mountain skirmishes – his body not brought back, either.'

'I understand you, gentlemen,' said Aristotle, with a sigh. 'Though I do not know what to do with the boy. Perhaps things may take a happier turn in the future. At present I shall simply tell the young man that his grandfather and uncle are in remote and dangerous areas, and cannot wish him to come until things are more settled. I deeply regret that I cannot see Alexander myself. I hope he is not being unreasonable.'

'You must watch your words!' Kallisthenes laughed. 'We don't talk of him that way in the army, I do assure you. He is the bravest of the brave. Kingliest of kings. Fit to command all other men of war who ever lived. Never has there been a general his equal. Philip may be said to have discovered a new art of war, the phalanx with sarissas bristling. But Alexander has perfected it. Our Commander also discovered a new method of beginning battles and sieges with missiles, which rain destruction and confusion. He is invincible. There is no man like him!'

'Our Commander is fortunate in his historian,' said Harpalos, smiling at Kallisthenes. 'Isn't it true that you were the one who said that very pretty thing about the waves that subsided along the Pamphylian coast near here? That they were like the Persians prostrating themselves in homage to Alexander! Very poetical. That prettiness took very well with our leader.'

'Indeed,' said Kallisthenes, 'men in the future for many generations will long to hear of Alexander and will tell stories and make poems about him. I am happily the first narrator of his exploits, the one who is with him while history is being made. I see as it were, the great bronze statue while the metal is melted and poured and shaped and worked — I am in a position to supply the most appropriate and potent imagery, to create for readers of the far future the complete feeling of the events and these occasions.'

'It is given to few to live in such stirring times,' Aristotle said pensively. 'The reconquest of the western regions of Asia is most heroic. We have liberated Ionia, Lydia, Karia. But it is only a beginning. Now it is clear that in order to make the world safe and the Greek settlements secure, Alexander will take charge of more of Asia. He comes in the name and power of all the Greeks. Peaceful and prosperous cities, well governed and beautiful, will rise in these hills and along the great rivers. Hellenic civilisation will extend to the Euphrates and the Oxus.'

'So I do believe,' said Kallisthenes. 'Alexander will make us safe for ever from attack from Persians, or from Assyrians or any other barbarians. These crude peoples will change their nature, as our settlements take root and their world is absorbed into ours. Then, after Egypt and Asia, we must also conquer Karthago and the Phoenician dominions. That was Alkibiades' plan in the Sikilian Expedition – which he was not allowed to complete. First take all of Sikilia, then Karthago. A good idea, simply postponed.'

'In the end,' Aristotle added, 'the arts of peace shall complete what war began. Just as in the islands of the Aegean, as in Syrakousai and in Great Hellas of the far western lands – so will all the known world eventually be rendered civilised.'

'You go so fast, you philosophers,' grumbled Harpalos good-humouredly. '*You*, O Aristotle – and Kallisthenes takes his vision from you – do not have to wield the sword. Just as easy for you to say "conquer Karthago" as for me to say "Boy, fetch a cheese"! Nor do you have to pay for these expeditions. Really, you know, many Greeks in Asia – in Ionia, Lydia, Karia – were perfectly happy under the Persian Empire. Who asked to be liberated? Not they. In fact, at the beginning of the war, there were more Greeks fighting for Darius than for Alexander – if you

subtract Makedonians. After the defeat of Issos, many of
the Greek soldiers in the Persian army fled to Krete, and
there Agis of Sparta was able to raise his army to fight
against Antipater, last spring. Some Greeks – in Asia, too
– don't consider us Makedonians true Greeks, anyway.
And, after all, these barbarian lands have some good in
them.' He stretched luxuriously. 'For instance, they have
the most wonderful way of making drinks of snow that
they collect and keep from the mountain tops –
unimaginably delicious in hot weather!'

'True, I have tasted it,' agreed Kallisthenes. 'But such
things a man would disdain to call "civilisation". We need
to illumine the path, not only with law courts and cities
but also with Greek knowledge and learning.'

'And now there will be fewer boundaries to learning,'
Aristotle mused. 'Once the land is pacified and settled,
Greek travellers and scholars shall be able to pass easily
from one region to another, eastward as far as one can
imagine, and so to the southern lands also.'

'Yes,' agreed Kallisthenes. 'As we press on now into
Persia proper and the other lands that Persia owned
farther to the east, we discover more about the earth,
and more about plants and animals. We will be able
to build up our knowledge, far beyond where it was
before.'

'You philosophers may well enjoy running after
conies in the sand or trying to snatch buzzards in the
high slopes.' Harpalos grinned. 'That's not *my* idea of
pleasure. Do not forget the labour of conquest. It was
comparatively easy to take the western edge of Asia. It
may be relatively easy to hold down central Persia, with
its great cities. But beyond, there are many wild lands

that the Persians themselves conquered with difficulty. Speaking so many languages, too, it's hard to tell them they are conquered! In the hill country, enemies – even their children – can lay down jagged objects on the few and narrow roads. We call them "cavalry-stoppers", and these can halt a troop of horsemen. Horses in pain may throw themselves and their riders off precipices. So many angry tribes on their mountain tops. They may not have loved Persia, but they are not friendly towards us.'

'We will train people to learn those languages,' asserted Kallisthenes. 'I myself have found men among our troops who learn these languages well enough to interrogate prisoners. That is one of the things the Commander put me in charge of – interrogations – as well as of calculating and recording distances.'

'I drink to the success of our Commander in seeing Darius to the tomb.' Harpalos suited his action to his words. 'But now the easy part is over. Bessus fled to the wilds of Baktria, where it is extremely difficult to get at him. All sorts of princelings in rough mountain districts will pop up.'

'Some will wish to avenge Darius,' said Pythonike.

'Certainly. Unbelievably lucky for us that one of the natives killed the Great King. What a piece of good fortune that has been!'

'Alexander does seem born under a lucky star,' Pythonike observed.

'True,' said Harpalos. 'But are we under the same star? You forget, O Aristotle, that all this war-making is *costly*. It costs greatly. It costs many lives. It swallows up many years, and great labour. It costs money, too.'

'But making war against a rich empire yields profits,'
Aristotle objected. 'You captured all the wealth of Sardis
– and then of Susa. And do you not have the treasure-
store of Persepolis?'

'We do. And we already have demands upon that
wealth. People who have waited for their money need to
be paid. We have to pay off former members of the
infantry and cavalry. The Athenian cavalry was
practically useless, between ourselves, but that is by the
way. They still want silver in hand.'

'The Athenian cavalry was most valuable as a token,'
Kallisthenes commented. 'To make everybody – including
the Athenians – *think* that the Athenians were heavily
engaged in a pan-Hellenic war. We Makedonians do the
best fighting.'

'Not that we should say anything against Athens,' said
Harpalos, observing my frown. After all, I was the only
Athenian present (discounting Pythonike). 'Where
should we be without Athens – without its intelligence,
skill and leadership through the years?'

Nobody answered this question. It occurred to me, to
my chagrin, that it might be ironic.

'Our pleasant meal has nicely taken up the hot
afternoon,' observed Harpalos. 'Now I wish to talk with
Aristotle alone. Perhaps you, Kallisthenes, will escort
Pythonike outside to her waiting woman. You might like
a little stroll along the cliffs, my dear? Kallisthenes, I
count on you to take care that no one listens to us. Move
the men away from the tent, and see that all the servants
are busy somewhere else. Tell the boy to bring me a lamp
and a brazier with live coals, and then make sure he gets
out of the way.'

Pythonike obediently stood up, and Kallisthenes also. I likewise arose upon this hint, but Aristotle beckoned me to stay. I sat down while the others left.

'I can tell from your tone, Harpalos,' said Aristotle gravely, 'that you are going to ask me to do something for you. As Stephanos is my travelling companion, I would have to tell him in any case. It appears best for you to tell both of us as much as you can.'

'Hmmh,' said Harpalos. 'I cannot refuse my old tutor. Though there is one point, Aristotle, which I shall beg you to keep to yourself only.' He turned to the servant entering the tent. 'Put the lamp there, boy. And the brazier on that table. Now light the lamp. And begone. Close the tent flap.'

He turned to us as we sat there on the cushions and beautiful stuffs. The lamplight now fitfully illuminated the tent and cast a glow on the fabrics with their strange patterns.

'It is about money, is it not?' Aristotle's deep-set eyes scanned Harpalos' face, though it was not easy to see in that flickering light.

'Yes, indeed. About money. Look, Aristotle, I want you to take with you some bags of gold for me. This transporting wealth around has to be done delicately. I want you to take one bag to Kos. Do not tell Oromedon, but only the man whom I shall indicate to you. Then take the other bag to Athens, and give it to citizen Phokion or his brother. To no one else.'

'Harpalos, you cannot be serious! You expect me to carry bags of gold about? Someone could steal them! And suppose anything were to happen to me? How could I take on this responsibility? We are not travelling in great naval ships, you know. The journey back to Peiraieus is going to be arduous, in small boats –'

'Do not worry.' Harpalos smiled magnificently.'We shall arrange a naval transport for you to travel back from Kos to Peiraieus. And now there will be a three-banked ship waiting for you at Halikarnassos harbour, to get you back to Kos. No expense spared, and everything thought of. You will not yourself have to pay a penny. Neither you nor your friend Stephanos here. Have you spent anything thus far?'

'No,' Aristotle admitted, but without smiling.

'Now, my dear tutor, is it fair of you to come all this way to meet me without doing for me what *I* need done? Really such a small thing.' He laughed. 'I am not asking you to *spend* the money – I know you philosophers have trouble with that. But I need to pay for goods and services, to sustain Alexander's credit. The gold has to be kept secret – money must not fall into the wrong hands.'

Aristotle sighed resignedly. 'I can say nothing against that,' he remarked. 'And I dare say you mean that I should be discreet in giving the money to the men in question. If that is all, it can be done.'

'Discreet – exactly! And there are so few men who are trustworthy like yourself, my dear philosopher. The world is so full of thieves! You are a ruby among pebbles. Discretion is what I count upon. Today I shall give you the two bags of gold to deliver. But that is not *quite* all.'

'No?'

'I need you to go to another place, a particular spot. Go there in a small private vessel after you have arrived back in Kos. In a moment I shall write down the direction and draw a map. For your eyes only. In a hiding place, not too far from Halikarnassos, I have secreted a little store of money and other treasure. I want you to remove – discreetly – these treasures and money from that place of deposit. Take all of that with you to Athens and give it to . . . to a particular individual whose name I shall write down for your eyes alone.'

I felt greatly dismayed, and I think Aristotle did too.

'That is much more complicated,' he protested.

'True. That is why we – Alexander and I and the rest of the Good Companions – count on you, O Aristotle. You see how well your nephew is getting on. You must wish to forward his promising career. I *trust* you. And you, with your strength of intellect, will already have perceived that it is not only Persians whom we cannot trust. This wealth must fall only into the right hands.'

Harpalos opened a cloth bag and took out a thin fragment of material. 'This is a kind of bark that is strong enough for one to write on,' he commented. He took up a pin and wrote quickly, scratching into the bark. 'Come Aristotle! Here are the names – one Koan, one Athenian. And a little map. You know the geography of the coast well: an advantage. Can you make it out?' Aristotle went over to the lighted lamp, and the two bent over the piece of bark.

'Can you commit that to memory? Absolutely? Do you know where to look?'

'Yes.'

'Look at it one more time. Now I destroy it. There! It is gone!' Harpalos lit the bark with the flame of the lamp, letting it sizzle and smoke on the brazier until it was nothing but an ashen fragment. I had hopes of snatching a glance, for I have often observed that marks can survive burning, but Harpalos stirred the ashes into tiny particles of dust.

'This is a great boon,' Harpalos said joyfully, this ceremony being accomplished. 'A great relief. There is *nothing* I will not do to repay you. I task myself with doing something handsome the next time I see you – perhaps in Babylon.'

This was evidently a farewell of sorts. Alexander's Treasurer himself held open the tent flap for us (as the servants had been sent away) and we all three left his tent, where we had enjoyed such a happy dinner. Less carefree than during the little feast, we walked outside. The sun was low in the sky now, the shadows were lengthening, and the sea was a deep and silent purple.

XIX

Carrying Treasure

That night Aristotle and I slept with Peleus and Diophantos and the rest in the shed that Harpalos had so disdained. Harpalos and Pythonike shared the white tent and its cushions. Laughter and kissing (and other noises) emanated from the tent. I had to grit my teeth. It was a long time since I had had a woman. And I doubted I should ever have one like Pythonike.

In the morning we had to get off. Kallisthenes lovingly entrusted his book to us.

'Be careful in handling it,' he enjoined. 'The parchment is firm and reliable, but the ink is only cuttlefish and it would wash off if the manuscript gets wet. Wrap materials around the box and keep it in the very driest part of any ship.'

Aristotle promised, and went off to find a place for this new treasure, which I could see he valued above the bags of gold that Harpalos surreptitiously gave him. These bags were not as conspicuous as they sound, of very plain leather, and scuffed, with woollen material bulging out of them as if they were merely containers of warm clothing and fleeces.

Having a momentary opportunity to talk alone with Aristotle's nephew, I put it to use.

'You know a good deal about manuscripts and books,' I remarked to Kallisthenes.'Do you use wax tablets?'

'Who would be without them? We have quantities in our baggage train. I take a little pile with me each day, so I can jot down notes during Alexander's excursions. To capture how things looked and what the Commander said. But anything of the sort has to be copied quickly into some firmer medium.'

'Tell me,' I said. 'You work at catching spies, and you know about writings. Would it be possible to fake part of a letter on a wax tablet?'

'Yes, indeed!' he answered before I could finish. 'Tablets are famous vehicles for forgeries – letters of all kinds convey misinformation in various ways. You remember the story Herodotos tells of the secret message hidden in a letter sent in tablets? The man in Asia who warned Sparta of the coming invasion of the Persians, in a letter that seemed perfectly ordinary. Until the woman Gorgo guessed the secret and bade them look under the wax, where they found the warning inscribed on the wood itself.'

'But suppose – would it be possible to falsify just *part* of a letter on a waxed tablet? Leaving the original salutation, say, and first line, and then inserting another message?'

'Certainly. As you are Aristotle's friend, I won't ask *why* you want to forge an epistle. It would take some trouble and skill, but with a hot bar of metal, held by some kind of handle, you could melt the wax on the lower half of the page without injuring the top. It would have to be done quickly and accurately. Then, wait for the wax to cool and you can insert your own statements without losing the original lines at the top of the page.'

'Perhaps I had better show you,' I said. 'I have received a strange letter.'

I called to the slave Menestor to bring my own bag, and he did so at once. My relatively few possessions were all there – all save Theodoros' letter.

'It may have been put somewhere else.' Worried, I asked Aristotle to see if Theodoros' letter were in his bag, but no.

'Must have fallen out on the journey,' suggested Menestor.

'Yes,' said Diophantos. 'We went down some very steep paths, could have been jolted.'

'It's not important,' I said, embarrassed at the attention the matter was attracting. 'I just wanted to refer to something in my brother's letter. That's all. Doubtless it is lost, as you say.'

'Perhaps it will turn up somewhere,' said Peleus, in the usual uninterested way in which people bear the losses of others. I determined to say nothing more of the matter.

Meanwhile Aristotle had his farewells to say to Kallisthenes. He spoke in a low tone, but so earnestly I could not help overhearing.

'I feel sad to leave you. And I am worried – perhaps unduly – by some things you have said. That flattering remark to the Commander about the waves prostrating themselves – it bothers me. If you flatter a king *too* well to begin with, you can never go back. Anything less than hyperbole will seem like criticism.'

'Oh, don't worry. It was rather a joke, you know – the Persians are so ridiculous, prostrating themselves to the great man. Figure of speech. The Commander knows poetry when he hears it.'

'But does he? Alexander values the *Iliad* as a record of fact and a model of conduct. Moreover, he takes himself for Akhilleus. Remember, Kallisthenes, he *is* a king. And I know him from a boy. He is full of charm – he bewitches all who come near. And he seems – nay, he *is* – so good-humoured and generous. But he may love in the waning moon what he despises at the full. Don't rely on him. He is given to fits of rage.'

'Don't be so anxious, uncle.' Kallisthenes patted his elder relative's arm reassuringly. 'I can take care of myself. And since I have travelled with Alexander for two years now or more, I know him very well. He's not a boy any longer. Cheer up! After a year or two more of my excursions in Asia, I shall come back to Athens and publish my history to the world. Alexander will be so pleased he will doubtless award me a pension! Then you'll see me back in the Lykeion. I can help you and Theophrastos with your giant plan of collecting all the plants and animals that ever were or can be.'

With a laugh, Kallisthenes sprang to his horse. Pythonike, with a demure wave, got into her wagon with her attendant and was seen by us no more. Harpalos, preparing to mount his perfect white horse, embraced Aristotle.

'A pleasure to talk with you once more, my tutor,' he said. 'You will be hearing from me, of course, and I expect to hear from you. And from Theophrastos – perhaps he will come to Babylon and help with my gardens. You don't know, O Aristotle, how much you mean to me – as well as to Alexander. The way of reason – we shall all pursue it! And perhaps we can spread some of the civilisation and laws you so value.'

He leaped on to his horse and set off at the head of his party. His group had attached the sarissas and the helmets we had been transporting, and one of the carts. Our party, led by Peleus with Diophantos as second-in-command, now had in their train only one large cart drawn by mules, half full of rugs and tapestries in the Persian style. We set off, much less dramatically than Harpalos' entourage.

'I was very glad to meet Kallisthenes,' I said to cheer Aristotle up as we marched along. 'I know everybody must have told you this for years, but he is very striking in looks, and in bearing. And so markedly intelligent.'

'Yes,' said Aristotle. 'He is my beautiful sister's son. I think he is like my father in intellect, and a little like him in disposition.'

I chewed on this for a while. Something about this statement puzzled me.

'Aristotle,' I said, 'Kallisthenes is your *sister's* son. Now, you know you have said in your lectures and written in books that the child is all the father's, with nothing of the mother in its essential nature. The child belongs completely to the father. So your nephew Kallisthenes must be like *his* father, your sister's husband, and that man's father, and so on. He cannot resemble your own father Nikiarkhos at all! And it follows that he cannot be like you, either.'

Aristotle seemed displeased at my observation, though it was both scientific and logical.

'I never said the mother contributed nothing,' he said defensively. 'Obviously, the quality of the mother's flesh and blood affects that of the child, and her milk nourishes it. And there is something in influence – the things the mother looks at while pregnant, the way she teaches the baby –'

'But that isn't the main matter, is it?' I persisted. 'The child inherits none of its qualities from the mother, so you say. If I have a child, it will be all *mine*. It will take after my family and not its mother's.' I was thinking I would not care to have my poor son looking like Smikrenes.

'Oh, don't bother me,' said Aristotle, really quite cross. He drew me apart from the marching band. 'Cannot you see,' he said in a low tone, 'that I am quite worried. I am trying to work out what has just happened.'

'What happened?'

'It was no accident, I think, that we didn't meet Harpalos in Phaselis as was planned – or was *said* to be planned. Better for him to meet us in that out-of-the-way corner of the world, where he could have everything his own way, and shake off the people who might interfere or distract us – or overhear. Harpalos isn't the sort of person who lets things happen accidentally. He bribed me to come with the promise of meeting Kallisthenes. We meet in a wilderness. Harpalos tells us disturbing news, he makes me worry about my nephew, and *then* he asks me to do something very awkward – perhaps dangerous. A secret errand along the coast of Asia.'

'Never mind,' I said consolingly. 'We shall be taken back first to Kos. From there you can set out on your errand and do it quickly. After that, we can go back to Athens on a real naval vessel – a fast ship.'

I myself was cheered at the thought that this time I was facing the right way. Every step I now took was taking me westward, towards Kos and then home.

We arrived in Phaselis, where Peleus said we had better stop for the night at the guard post and prepare for a really long journey next day. 'I find I have to go into the city to get further orders,' he informed us with his usual frank courtesy.

'It looks as if I shall be your escort,' he continued. 'We should get to the coast without mishap. I'll put you on a three- or five-banked warship in Halikarnassos. The weather is still fine, you ought to get swiftly back to Kos. See you tomorrow,' Peleus added in pleasant farewell, as he strode away to get his orders at the central military offices near the governor's mansion.

The remaining soldiers gave us a bed-space in their quarters by the guard post, and we were up betimes. The Theban servant Menestor arrived early; ever willing to help, he assisted us in getting all our belongings well stowed. We now had a good deal to keep account of! There was a large rough homespun bag full of earth and roots that Kallisthenes had given us, and two earthenware pots with some kinds of bulbs or root material in them. There was the sacred wooden box with his manuscript *History*. And Aristotle had to worry about the two bags of 'clothes' that were really bags of gold, the coins and bricks wrapped up in fine wool so they wouldn't chink. (I knew because we had checked the bags privately ourselves.)

I looked forward to seeing Peleus again this morning.

An efficient and pleasant man, I thought, remembering how cleverly and really quickly he had brought us such a distance on our earlier eastern journey. Peleus, well organised in his thought and actions, would get us to Kos with a minimum of trouble.

We were standing ready, waiting for him, when Diophantos came up and said, 'It seems I am your captain and guide for the rest of this expedition.'

'But where is Peleus?' I asked, letting my disappointment show.

'He has an assignment elsewhere. I dare say he told you that was a possibility.'

'Yes,' I had to agree. 'He warned us before, we might go back with somebody else.'

'Well, I am the captain Somebody-else. And we have a few more goods for the load. Changing from a cart to a light wagon. Ready in a moment. Come on men. Stow all goods!'

The soldiers began hastily to take out of the cart all our other cargo, including the bags of woolly gold and Kallisthenes' box, and started to put them on board the light wagon. Meanwhile, two porters who had brought things in another mule cart approached our larger vehicle. When their turn came, the first thing these servants did was to disarrange all our packing to make room for the stuffs they had. The chief object of their care was a very large carpet or tapestry rolled around some blankets. When they had made a suitable space for this, they carried it between them, one man at each end, to our wagon and laid it near the bottom. Then they placed on top of this tube of material many new packages, and heaps of stuffs and cushions. We had to rescue our own things and find crannies again in this now-crowded wagon for our rootstocks and the precious manuscript and the bags of 'woollen clothes'. To our dismay, the two porters added at the very top of the pile a pungent horsehide.

'That won't come to harm,' they said. 'It protects the rest against rain.' Looking at this ugly object, Theban Menestor drily agreed. 'No – such things don't come to harm.'

About the wagon there was a scent of resin in the air, not unpleasant, some sort of treatment of the Persian fabrics, I supposed. It was in combat with the odour of stale sweat and withering horsemeat. The hide was unmistakably still in the shape of horse, rendered flat instead of being a solid body. 'It's like the poor ox-hide at the Bouphonia,' I remarked to Aristotle. 'Except it's not stuffed.'

'Hooves and all,' Aristotle agreed, wrinkling his nose. 'Not sufficiently cured.'

We set off with our new wagon, drawn by straining mules, and continued our march up a winding craggy path. The days were shorter now. I thought longingly of long sunny days when we had been travelling in our pretty little boat among the Kyklades. Now we were covered in dust and pestered by flies.

'That horsehide!' said the Theban slave disdainfully. 'It attracts the flies so. How it stinks! Who could want such a thing?'

'Well, there you are,' said one of the soldiers. 'We were told some general or someone had lost his horse in the battle and wanted its hide and hooves shipped home as a memento. Funny thing, isn't it? The horse coming back – when so many brave men don't come back to be buried, not so much as the skin or nails of them.'

Nothing much of note happened on the journey, save that one of the men sprained his ankle. Aristotle ran into trouble with his sandal and requested a stout cobbler's needle, saying he would repair his own footwear himself, and could do so by moonlight. I was surprised at his demeaning himself to this humble task, but the men were tired and had enough to do.

We were all glad to come to the River Xanthos, to be pulled along in barges by stout oxen on the riverbank. The men amused themselves in the shade with stories and gambling games, and enjoyed being off their feet. Disembarking from the flat boats, we struggled into marching order again, on a road that seemed always uphill. But at last it was clear we were near to Halikarnassos. Then from a hilltop I saw below the crescent of harbour that would give us a ship homeward. At last I could leave this weary march and the abominable horsehide whose stench seemed to gain remarkably in volume.

'I just hope the stinking thing doesn't affect the manuscript,' I whispered to Aristotle. 'I should not like it to smell of dead horse — though I suppose the pages are made of dead sheep.'

'No, I thought of that,' he said. 'I soaked some stout cloths in vinegar and spices a while back and wrapped it around Kallisthenes' box.'

We found the harbour area of Halikarnassos agreeably full, crowded with sailors as well as with petty merchants, vegetable sellers, and the inevitable crowd of pitiful beggars. Passengers were going and coming, including three men in white, who stood together near the ships as if expecting something.

'Here we shall enquire about your warship,' said Diophantos briskly. 'I wonder which it is.' He put his hand over his eyes and scanned the harbour. 'I am afraid,' he remarked, 'that I do not see any big naval vessel here. But I shall make enquiries at once of the soldiers and the boatmen.' Diophantos plunged into the crowd. He was back again soon, looking crestfallen.

'It is too bad!' he cried. 'There is no ship of the sort here now – the naval vessel left yesterday and another is not expected for some days. But this is vexing! I promised to have you taken to Kos as smartly as possible.'

'Yes,' I agreed, straining my eyes to look towards Kos.

'Well, sirs, good morning!' a familiar voice greeted us.

'Nikias!' I recollected this man with the kindly broad smile and weatherbeaten features. Our second captain, the one who had rescued us when we were at a loss in the port of Naxos. "Nikias, how do you do? What a strange thing, running into you like this.'

'A surprise, maybe. But not really so strange. This is a fine harbour, and almost everyone hereabouts uses it. Were you dissatisfied with Kos, then? I took you there, remember. And that other family – they came over here looking for a better air for their child. But they have had enough of it, and they're ready to go back to Kos.'

And there was that little family again. I remembered suddenly my first glimpse of them at the harbour at Sounion: the old man Hermippos, so respectable, the stolid veiled mother, the little wheezy girl Philokleia who was so much better at sea.

Aristotle and I uttered our greetings. 'The last time we really spoke with you,' Aristotle said, 'was when we listened in the orchard to the good doctor Iatrokles' tale of the Hungry Prince.'

'That was a good day,' said the grandfather. 'But we got tired of the lodgings and the beggars around Kos harbour, so we took a turn in Patmos. That didn't answer. So we took another turn at sea for the sea air. Didn't even bring our servant this time, she has a sickness in her stomach. We came on this short journey to see Halikarnassos. But it is a rather sad place, isn't it?'

'This city was all knocked down and burned,' said the child earnestly.

'Too true!' said Nikias. 'And so you see, they are anxious to go back to Kos. And some pilgrims to Asklepios was likewise minded to cross over.' He nodded at the three men waiting by their bundles. I could see now that one fellow, leaning on the arm of his friend, looked decidedly feverish, and the third man was crippled. 'They need to go to Kos for their health. I regret, we're already spoken for. And you seem to have a deal of baggage.' He looked at the soldiers unloading our wagon. 'But we could come back and collect you, gentlemen. Though we have a short crew today.'

'No,' said Diophantos firmly. 'We can commandeer the boat, by the authority of the army. I must inform you, Koan captain, that you are *compelled* to take these men back to Kos without delay.'

'Why should we not wait for another ship – an official one?' asked Aristotle. He drew Diophantos aside and explained in a low tone, 'When I sailed with this man before, I was not at all sure that he wasn't a pirate.'

'Oh,' said Diophantos impatiently, 'some of these islanders misbehave a little, but not when they have the army's eye up on them. And he did take you safely before, did he not? His is a good swift ship. Alexander's army grants you a right to this or any other seaworthy craft that we command to take you. Sorry about the want of a trireme. But – no point lingering about in Halikarnassos when we promised immediate passage to Kos.'

'But –'

'No fear – the army warrants your safety throughout. Man –' turning to Nikias – 'you are commanded to take these two gentlemen back to Kos. As for these other civilians, clodhoppers they seem, let them wait. This counts as official business. Army orders. As from the Commander.'

'Will your Commander be able to pay for a trip? That's the question!' Nikias expostulated. '*I* ain't in the army, nor the official navy! Just a humble boatman, trying to make a living. Me and my rowers, we don't work for the good of our health alone.'

'No impudence, fellow! We pay what is reasonable. These others will have to wait.' Diophantos looked scornfully at the little family and the two pilgrims.

'No!' said the grandfather. 'We already made the arrangement!'

Little Philokleia asked reasonably, 'Why cannot we all go?'

'*These* are important personages,' said Diophantos, waving towards us. 'They have their mission. No reason they should be asked to mix with who knows what sort of common people.'

'But,' said the Theban slave Menestor hesitantly, 'it is such a short trip – and would the boat not balance better with a number?'

'Possibly,' said Diophantos grudgingly. 'But officials don't have to travel with civilians and riff-raff. We also have cargo to stow. If these other folk are carrying a lot of their own baggage, it is out of the question.' He looked hard at Nikias.

'I see,' said Nikias, shrugging, 'Fortune is against me, and I yield. No, these others do not have much baggage to take aboard. Very well. You see how it is, folks.' He turned to the family from Laurion and the three nameless pilgrims, as they all stood there looking hopeful. 'You can come or stay as you will, but I am compelled to take these persons to Kos.'

'And you can take all this baggage also, as far as Kos,' said Diophantos decidedly. He and Menestor led the soldiers and the other slaves in unloading the wagon and putting most of the contents into the hold of the *Niké*. The contents included the tube of carpet, the many fine cushions and so on. I wondered whether these were just personal mementoes, booty attached by individual soldiers during the conquest and now being sent back home, or whether somebody in the army hoped to make a profit by selling a lot of such stuff.

Nikias' sailors rushed up to help – both to see that the boat was properly loaded and to receive some reward for their pains, I guessed. Some of the idlers and beggars at the seafront tried to put in their claim by offering feeble assistance, their hands held out for obols all the while. The crippled and maimed promised to work for us, and uttered appeals. The tall blind man whom I had noticed last time, the one with the terrible skin condition, uttered a low wail, and offered and asked for nothing. 'I saw him before,' I said, nodding in the direction of this poor creature. 'Too bad. I suppose he lost his sight in the war.'

'Oh, that fellow, he's surely crazy too,' volunteered one of the ragged crew of harbour rats trying to aid us. Menestor chimed in: 'He seems lunatic – leave him alone.' Certainly the blind man kept up a low muttering the way crazy people do, mixed with little moans. It seemed too bad that no one offered him ointment for his sores; I threw him a hemi-obol anyway.

Aristotle had wandered off while the men were busy loading the vessel, and disappeared into one of the little food shops. I was amused that even he could not resist the lure of the fleshpots. Meanwhile, the men busy at the loading complained vociferously about the stench of the horsehide. Some people on neighbouring boats made pointed remarks about our personal cleanliness. I myself was heartily sorry that we were going to return to Kos in company with the stinking hide. By the time Aristotle came back, wiping his mouth in a meditative manner, those around us were uttering strong hints that we should be gone with all possible speed. The feverish pilgrim appeared deeply impressed, not to say knocked out, by the smell; he and his companion decided not to go on our boat after all.

'Whyn't you take another boat, friend, too, as the stink is so troublesome?' Nikias said to the crippled man. But this determined pilgrim only murmured, 'I must get to Kos and see Asklepios!' He sat himself in the boat, uncomplaining.

'You folk are going to mind the smell, too,' said Nikias to the little family. But having got on board, they were reluctant to move.

'What happens to that hide once we get to Kos?' I asked.

'You'll be rid of it soon,' said Diophantos, looking ruefully at the dark and redolent remains. 'Officers at Kos will take it from you and send it on to the horse's owner. It will be only a short trip with this minor discomfort. I shall send this Theban slave to look after you,' he added, abruptly pushing Menestor into the boat. 'Farewell!'

'If you are a Theban,' Aristotle said conversationally, 'Menestor is an odd name. If it really *is* your name.'

'I *am* a Theban,' the youth replied steadily. 'I was captured when I was eleven years old. Menestor is the name I go by.'

I knew that Aristotle was not reconciled to the idea of enslaving free men, or children who should have grown up to be free. The scandal of the Greeks made into captives in Alexander's wars had induced Athens' chief political leader Lykourgos, just a few months ago, to make a law that no Athenian was to buy an enslaved person from one of the defeated Greek cities. Hearing about dead Thebes made me uncomfortable. It was almost a matter of luck that on the terrible day when Alexander's men captured the city, my cousin Philemon's wife had escaped from Thebes, and had thus also escaped being sold into slavery.

Our craft moved away from the harbour and into the deeper water. There were only twelve men rowing, but they were rowing hard. It was a lovely day, with just a light breeze to help the sail, and the water was beautifully still. I began to think about my future brother-in-law, and whether he had returned to Kos with his disreputable woman. I should have to look for him as soon as I got back. But – Kos wasn't growing any closer. Aristotle noticed this too.

'Why aren't we drawing closer to Kos?'

'We have to bear to the other side of the island,' Nikias said easily. 'A bad current that we need to avoid. 'Twill take us a bit longer, that's all.'

We accepted this for a long time, until we really saw that Kos was growing smaller in the distance, and turning an unfamiliar shape.

'What do you mean by this?' we asked in alarm.

'Make yourselves easy,' said Nikias. 'There is a weakness in two of the oars, and in the oar-holes, which have worn too large. We cannot pull as we should. We are just coming into an islet where we can make all right again.'

It was a very small and sandy islet, from which Kos was barely visible, partly because of other small isles in the way. The place seemed not too distant from the Asian mainland.

'We will have to get rid of this stinking thing, too,' said Nikias firmly. 'It is making the rowers ill.' He heard no objections from us – the thing had been making me feel ill as well. And the little girl, pale Philokleia, had thrown up once over the side.

'Get to it, men,' said Nikias. 'Get rid of whatever we don't need before we go ashore. Fetch some old ballast stones and anchors.'

'Right,' said the most active of the rowing men. He and the young rower opposite him, the one whom Nikias once addressed as 'monkey', rose and dived off the back of the boat. Soon they were wading about in the shallows, by a beach on which two other craft were already resting. The industrious sailors collected a pile of weights, round stones like old anchors and pieces of rough marble. These the 'monkey' dragged to in a net and handed up to the others. The pair neatly hoisted themselves back aboard over the side of the ship, dripping lightly on the cushions and fine stuffs.

'Now,' said Nikias, 'before we land – get rid of this big stinking thing.'

'Yes,' said the Theban slave Menestor, jumping up to assist, 'we can be thankful that we need it no more.'

He helped to unfurl the horrible hide, and the sailor men filled the middle of the horse's discarded skin with the round stones. Philokleia and even Aristotle turned slightly paler as the stench met us in full force. None too soon, the men dropped the oddly shaped thing so weighted into the water. We all watched. Slowly and lazily but inevitably it sank, one side a trifle faster than the other.

'That horse rides no more,' said the Theban with a laugh. 'It has run its course and served its turn.'

'Right,' said Nikias. 'Now, take heed of that long carpet, men – it needs special care.' The men grubbed down deep into the boat, dislodging all the baggage, so that we cried out in alarm. Aristotle made a leap for the manuscript box of Kallisthenes, and the rootstock. I grabbed the woolly bags of gold and a bulb pot, while Hermippos' party saved their clothes. The seedy-looking pilgrim seemed not to have anything worth saving. Soon two of Nikias' men, aided by the agile Menestor, had taken a firm grip on the long round carpet roll, and were moving this so that it lay on the top of everything else, a colourful tube. There was still a very bad smell, as if the horse were still with us, but also the faint resinous odour. We were puzzled. 'By Herakles! What an uncalled-for stench!' cried one of the two men who had hauled up the thick fabric roll. 'What's in here?'

The two men began to unwind the roll. 'Stop!' cried Nikias, running awkwardly along the top of the vessel and its contents. 'Stop! You'll damage it!' He slapped one of the two sailors a great clout across the face. But before they had quite desisted, little Philokleia, peering into the tube from her lower vantage point, was the first of our party to find out the truth.

'There's a man in there!'

'Well, yes and no,' said someone ruefully. The other sailors were already unrolling, first the rug and then within it a roll of ordinary blankets – and then we could see that indeed there was a man. Peleus. Peleus wizened and blackened, as a man will be who has been dead for many days in hot weather. Peleus, who must have been dead since before we left Phaselis

'When is a man not a man?' asked Menestor. 'When he's a corpse.'

'This is terrible!' exclaimed Nikias. 'Someone has played us a trick. However did this thing get here on my nice clean ship? Really, I am surprised – I am shocked!' He glowered at his men. 'We will find out more later about this here shocking affair. I suspect that Theban! But meanwhile, this thing won't keep, no more than the horse. Sorry – but necessity presses us.'

'You should've stopped it from stinking,' said one of the sailors to Menestor.

'Hot weather. We tried to reduce the stench,' explained Menestor. 'We covered the corpse with a mixture of vinegar with a little honey and a lot of resin. The Egyptians know how to preserve corpses for all time. But we're no Egyptians!'

'Certainly you are not,' said the seaman with disfavour, holding his nose. 'The horsehide was of use to cover up the other stink, then?'

The older sailors were wrestling distastefully with the body, while a couple of rowers took our craft out a bit further into the little bay.

'Weight it with a couple of stones,' advised Nikias.' Not just to his feet – his feet may not last. He'll be so yeasty he may bob up again.'

Quickly the men tied the stones to the feet and hands of the cadaver of the thrice-unfortunate Peleus: betrayed – then killed – now denied proper burial. Elbowing us out of the way, the men did their dire task, without putting a kindly coin in the mouth of the departed. Standing up and counting as in a *keleusma*, they flipped the dark and sticky body of Peleus into the water, stone-weighted feet first. There was a loud splash. Peleus made a hole in the sea. Through the clear water we could see his face one last time as it submerged.

'Well, now, that's a good deed done,' said Nikias.' You must all witness that this was a matter of reasonable public health. Have to get rid of stinking corpses. *I* am not responsible for bad cargo sent aboard. And now we can make for land. Beach it, men! Welcome to my island!'

XX

The Killing Island

'Welcome to this little island,' repeated Nikias, once the
Nikē's prow was fast in the sand. 'Look lively! You must all
get off this vessel while we repair it. Yes, take your precious
luggage with you. We may be here for some while.'

We had to dig for our own bundles; the sailors were in
no hurry to help us. They were more concerned with
removing all oars from the ships. The Laurion family,
alarmed, searched hurriedly for anything the little girl
might need. Only the seedy pilgrim, who had scanty
personal possessions, seemed unperturbed. I made sure to
take the bag of plants and the pots of roots. Aristotle
disembarked awkwardly as he was taking particular care
of the manuscript and the woolly bags.

'Ho, old man, do you think you can use those bags of old
clothes as bladders to float you in the sea?' one of the
sailors asked in mock concern.

'Not much good for that,' said the Theban slave, joining
in the laughter.

424

'Sir,' said Aristotle to Nikias, 'we need to conduct an enquiry into the death of the captain Peleus. How his corpse – apparently with some attempt at embalming or mummifying by this Theban here – came on our ship –'

'Oh, it's ill doing with a dead man. And this ain't Athens, my good friend. I don't see no Areopagos hereabouts. Better let things pass for a while. Make yourselves comfortable.'

We stood bemused on the sandy islet, clutching our goods and gazing about us at the three beached ships, the scrubby thorn trees, the signs of camp fires. There was a sudden sharp yapping. A little lame dog came staggering into the clearing. 'By Herakles,' I exclaimed, 'I recognise that beast!'

'I do too,' said Aristotle. 'And that lame animal bodes no good to us.'

'That creature belonged to the cook,' said one of the men. 'Not here now – we have to cook for ourselves. But the dog can stand guard, and don't eat much. Come on.'

The men hurried us to a narrow pathway through some low scrub and a couple of short trees twisted by the wind. From this place, though it was near the beach, we could not see the mainland. Neither could we now see the longed-for Kos.

'My little realm – such as it is,' said Nikias. 'We've come here before while making repairs. Not much here in the way of shelter, but it's still summer, after all. The men will cook you up some fish stew soon. Time's getting on.'

So it was. The sun was lower in the sky than I should have liked. The days were undeniably shorter now. It was an unpleasant thought that the night would come while we were stranded here in such company. I needed no instruction – not now – regarding our companions.

'Aristotle,' I said in a low tone, 'these men must be pirates.'

'I know,' he replied. 'I suspected that before. And what imbeciles we have been!'

'The Theban slave is their confederate.'

'Yes. But not only he.'

There was not much chance for private conversation, with the men obviously guarding us, and Nikias looking at us with a leering glance of superiority.

'Don't worry, Aristotle sir,' he said meaningfully to the philosopher. 'We shall have a good talk on the morrow. Mayhap we can come to some kind of agreement.'

We had to content ourselves with that. The men went fishing and started the promised fish stew. Then they insisted on taking the other travellers' bags and looking through them. There was little of value, but they adopted what they could use.

'I shall take these earrings, if you don't mind,' said the tall sailor, fishing two pair of silver earrings out of the little girl's mother's bag. The woman shut her eyes and did not reply. 'But those are *our* things!' protested Philokleia.

'Least said, soonest mended,' said the tall sailor in a jocular tone. 'I have a lady friend these baubles would certainly suit. She's sad and lonely at the moment. You wouldn't want to deprive her, would you?'

'Well, if you have a woman already,' said a gruff sailor with a big chin, 'then what about me? Don't *I* have a right to what has been brought to us here?' He looked at the woman.

'Hush, pig,' said Menestor. 'Forbidden. Meat for your masters. Do not interfere when not called upon.'

The big-chinned man subsided, scowling. But I felt for the woman and the dangerous case she was in, surrounded by rough men who had no other women on the island. If the sailors committed such an act of hubris as this man appeared to meditate, I ought to try to help her fight off an attacker. But what chance would I have against so many sailors? – as well as the Theban, for I could see that Menestor, slave though he might be, was a leading spirit.

No outrages happened that night, however; the woman slept between her father and her daughter, with Aristotle on the child's other side, and myself by Aristotle trying to keep one eye open. We awoke cooled by night breezes and stiffening in our sandy bed, but the day was fine; there was water to drink and, a little later, a flat bread cake only slightly stale.

'The oar-holes are filled in and the oars are mended,' announced Nikias. The pilgrim and the family all brightened, as if they truly believed they would be taken home after a slight delaying incident.

'Time for our promised excursion!' Nikias continued. 'Sorry, it's just these two this time,' he explained to the others, nodding at Aristotle and myself. '*Important* folks, you understand. Boy, help these masters with their luggage.'

The youth Menestor assisted with alacrity in handing all our things back into the boat. While we were both wondering whether to get in or not, two sailors pushed us into the vessel. The ship then went off, with ourselves, Menestor and Nikias, and only two oarsmen rowing – the two who had fetched the stone weights the day before.

The other sailors remained to guard the rest of our party.

'You may get to Kos yet,' Nikias said in encouraging tones. We knew he was a liar. Yet my heart gave a painful thump of yearning at the thought of arriving in Kos harbour.

'I do not like to detain you unduly,' said Nikias, 'because we have an old association. Quite friendly terms we were on, weren't we? After all, I helped you out of a fix before, when you were stuck in Naxos with no ship. So you can help me, and we will call it quits.'

Aristotle was observing him steadily, but said nothing. I asked, 'What exactly do you want?'

'Oh – *exactly* is hard to say. Our wants vary from day to day. What does Alexander want, *exactly*?' Nikias seemed disposed to be playful and philosophical. 'I want first of all to talk – now we are far enough away from that mob, we cannot be overheard. I shall ask my men to swim off a bit so you can speak freely. Off you go, men. Be dolphins for a while!

'Menestor will stay here,' he added, turning to us as the two sailors obediently dived off and swam away. 'Menestor and I are both armed, I should warn you. Menestor has a club, and both of us have good daggers. So do not think you can take advantage of the situation. You cannot.'

Menestor, with a mischievous smile, waved the thick knobbed stick of which he was possessed. I saw the dagger gleaming in a belt around his waist.

'Well, now,' said Aristotle calmly. 'What is the mighty matter that demands so much secrecy from your own crew? As you must surely be all pirates together, it cannot be the mere fact of engaging in crime that you wish to conceal. Perhaps you think there is some way of benefiting yourself and leaving them out of it.'

'Maybe,' said Nikias. 'And maybe it does you no good to try to think too much. I admit you got the better of me before – to Hades with you for a clever fellow! And a fortunate! When we were in easy sea there was at first too many boats all around us. The storm at sea was unlucky. The big ship was too big and too damaged for us to take as a prize. By Herakles, I could have strangled you when you gave the news about yourself to the passenger in the damaged ship! After that, we couldn't conveniently do our business. Too many people would know about where you were last seen, if that storm-damaged vessel chanced to come to port. And it did. I was prudent to hold off. So you escaped me then.'

'So – my guess was correct,' retorted Aristotle. 'Who commissioned you to take a particular interest in me, by the way? Who exactly paid you to kill me – and how much was the deed worth? I had deduced the piracy. Later, however, I began foolishly to doubt my suspicions. Luckily, the damaged vessel was too big and still too seaworthy for you to overrun it. I am glad that my words to my friend's son – uttered by design, to ensure our safety – had a good effect.'

'For a little time,' agreed Nikias. 'Who knows what the Fates have in store? Maybe the gods have favoured *me*. I am lucky too. The Heavenly Twins appeared to me, you remember. *Then* you had nothing much worth taking. Now – *now* you have things I really want. And something that others who work with me – never mind who they are – *really* want. So we shall all do much better than before. Speak up and tell us where the hidden treasure is.

Frankly. Let us deal quite frankly, and you shall have less trouble to endure.'

'I see,' said Aristotle. He remained silent for a good while after that.

'Well, Menestor,' said Nikias after a long, frowning silence. 'Since he seems uncommunicative, what do you say to looking at their luggage? Hey?' He picked up the bag of plants and peered into it. 'What have we here? Cabbage?'

'That's material for natural philosophy,' I said, trying to explain. 'It's only valuable to people like Aristotle and Theophrastos who are working on the history of plants and animals. These are just pieces of plants from Asia.'

'So, now – soup for supper, Menestor. Catch!' He tossed the large leather bag to the youth, who caught it by the thong around the top.

'Are they poison?'

'I don't know. Some of them may be.' I answered at random since Aristotle was not talking.

'And you really have no idea,' said Nikias admiringly, 'which are poison and which aren't? These roots and shoots might kill the cooks as well as the eaters, might they not? So – though we have need of vegetables, we shall have to forgo them. Toss them away, Menestor.'

Menestor, despite Aristotle's movement of distress, opened the mouth of the bag and tossed the contents into the ripples of a moving current, which bore them away.

'The bag itself can be useful,' said Nikias easily. 'Next item. Some more plant stuff?'

'Yes – you can see for yourself.' I wasn't disposed to inform him further, could I have done so.

'Well, and more vegetables go into the briny stew!' The

roots and bulbs were tossed away, some sinking and some floating on the foam.

'Now,' said Nikias happily, 'we shall come to more interesting materials. And I think, O Aristotle, that you are distressed by these losses of your peculiar treasures. You are not blind! From your lack of speech, old man, I fear you may be going deaf.' Nikias suddenly spoke very loudly. '*Deaf* people need optical proof. You have had optical proof. Realise this: I will indeed destroy what is not useful to me. Unless you cooperate. Or unless you persuade me that something *is* useful to me. In that case, you can beg me to take it as a gift. That's the way. See? Assist me now on one small matter and you will see how grateful I can be.'

Aristotle still said nothing, but sat like one in earnest pensive thought rather than like someone studying a retort or defence. Nikias turned to me.

'Tell this old man,' he said loudly, 'that if he wants to save any more of his precious goods he must cooperate with me. I need to know something, and I want to know it *now.*'

'What is that?' I asked after a moment, to fill in for the unspeaking Aristotle.

'Harpalos the Treasurer had an interview with you both. Harpalos wants you to go to pick up more treasure elsewhere. I want – I *need* – to know what and where it is. And I want you to tell this old philosopher there's people in Athens who will be better pleased with him if he is more reasonable.'

'I cannot help you,' I said. 'If there is anything to know, Aristotle alone knows it.'

At last Aristotle spoke. 'Stephanos knows a little,' he

said casually, 'but that little is useless without me.
Together we perhaps have some knowledge – but of
things that do not concern you.'

'And perhaps,' said Nikias, 'you feel – being a
philosopher – that you can be content with what you have
already?' He peered into the woolly bags. 'Let's see now –
Why, isn't this a pretty toy!' He picked up one of the little
tablets of gold, unwrapped it and waved it about. The
morning sunlight flashed off the bright clean metal.

'Men dig for gold. Let's dig into this fine bag again –
and look what comes out! Lots and lots of gold coins.' He
showed us some in the palm of his hand, waving them
teasingly towards us and then away, above his head. 'See,
here's a pretty coin and here's its brother – and its sisters
too!' He dropped the coins into the bag, all save one which
he flipped on the back of his hand.

'I see Darius' head. A golden *dareikos*. From Sardis,
perhaps, or most likely gold from great Persepolis. Or
does this fortunate sack breed gold on its own? Menestor,
I beg you to take the other bag, and secure it. Carefully –
and don't take your eye off these gentlemen. Better not to
wave the coins about any longer, lest our loyal dolphins
catch sight of it. They would feel aggrieved they were not
let in on this pretty secret.' The two men tied up the bags
of gold.

'Does not this sight lacerate your heart, O Aristotle?
What wealth you are in the process of losing!'

'Gold is not my chief good,' said Aristotle mildly.
'Money is not the end for which I live.'

'Well, but suppose you had a duty to perform regarding
this gold? Suppose you can no longer perform that good
deed. Suppose a shocking fact becomes known to the

powers of Makedonia and to all good citizens in Athens: old reliable Aristotle took what didn't belong to him? Bags of wealth – too much for the ageing philosopher. Pure fresh gold was seductive, and he abducted it. A prudent coward, though, this old rascal. He hides himself so cleverly he is not heard of any more. Reputation – gone for ever. Will folk *then* think gold was not your object? Will it matter what you really used to live for – or say you lived for?'

'You must deal with your own honesty or dishonesty as you see fit,' said Aristotle. 'It is clear I am not able to furnish you with a sense of the Good or any respect for Justice.'

'Well – Justice!' intervened Menestor. '*Justice* is a fine word! But who knows where Justice resides? Or if there is any such thing? Was it Justice that destroyed Thebes? Justice that put me and thirty thousand like me into slavery? Justice when Alexander and Harpalos and the others stole all that gold from the Persians? Don't prattle here about Justice!'

Aristotle looked at the Theban with a kind of sad interest. 'There is something in what you say,' he remarked. 'I should be willing to converse with you on the subject. Have you read the *Republic,* by the way?'

'"Have you read the *Republic?*"' Menestor mimicked him. 'I suppose you think slaves can sit about reading all day. But I have read it, or some of it when I was a boy –'

'Stop it!' commanded Nikias. 'Where do you think this is, a schoolroom? You are a scholar, sir, as they say –' turning to Aristotle. 'So here I suppose is something you *do* value. Menestor and I looked into this box before. It is a thing with writing on it.'

'It's a book,' said Aristotle. Nikias freed the box of its integuments and opened it. The pages of Kallisthenes' parchment manuscript were quite fresh and undamaged by the journey. The clear sepia ink was readable in the easy daylight.

'Yes, it is a book,' said Menestor in his angry mimicking tone. He picked up the first page. '*The Deeds of Alexander* – glorious Alexander? Ran around Troy – declared a son of Ammon in wilds of Egypt – great feats on the riverside. Fig-sucking prattle!'

'This is a valuable piece of history,' protested Aristotle, taking the page from Menestor. 'A great labour. And I haven't had time to read it yet.'

'Well, you might have time to read it now,' said Nikias. 'We might use it for bum-wipe and stick it down the latrine.'

'Not so good for us, if somebody tried to read our latrine,' laughed Menestor. 'If one of Alexander's loyal henchmen came peering round our camp, such disrespect to these pages would be unhealthy.'

'Pity – we're so short of bum-wipe. So, O Aristotle, what to do? I see this treasure has caught your attention. I'll make you a fair offer: you may read half of it. How's that?'

'Generous,' said Menestor.

'And the other half – well, there's too much writing in the world,' said Nikias. He snatched the top leaf from Aristotle. 'No!' cried Aristotle, trying to stay Nikias' hand. Menestor jumped up and twisted his arm until he let go. 'Aha!' Nikias threw the leaf overboard.

'*Now* we see where your treasure lies! This will make you talk!' Nikias began to throw more of the manuscript pages overboard. I could see them floating on the deep, the ink melting slowly off, yet still legible. "Alexander wrote then to Darius the following letter"; "a whip, a ball, and a chest of gold"; "In the spring Alexander broke camp . . ."; "expecting that Darius' forces would meet him . . ."; "like Akhilleus, remembering . . ."' Words jumped up and down through the water. Aristotle clenched his hands on the bench where he sat, but said nothing.

'Be reasonable, man,' said Nikias encouragingly. 'Be wise. As I've heard it said:

> "Best is that man above all men who everything can
>   know,
> And next in good is humbler he who to these wise
>   will go;
> Who cannot for himself see truth, or from another
>   hear it
> To store away in his own mind – this man is without
>   merit."

Be instructed, men. You are wise if you do what we tell you.'

'Not altogether the case, even – Was it Diophantos who repeated these verses to you?'

'Diophantos? No – What does that matter? You are simply losing more of your book. We know that Harpalos told you to go to somewhere secret to pick up more treasure. Here's the agreement.' He leaned forward and looked steadily at us. 'You two take me to the secret spot where Harpalos has stored his hoard of gold and gems. Give me all the wealth and goods we find there – and swear by all the gods to keep quiet. Then you can have the rest of the manuscript, *and* a free passage home.'

'I entirely believe I should not have to worry about paying for a passage,' said Aristotle, with a dry laugh. A gull swooped down and caught a page, then stared at the piece of writing in disappointment and dropped it back in the sea.

'You should not go about destroying books,' Aristotle continued. 'It's the act of a barbarian, not a Greek.'

'Pa-ta-pa-ta. I am Greek enough to serve my turn. Some say the Makedonians are only Greeks second-hand. Don't come high and mighty with *me*. You and your young friend. Your life is in my hands – think of it. If you won't cooperate today, we must see what can be done to get a better answer on the morrow. I'm being generous, mind that. But we're not patient men.'

Nikias turned the boat about and gave a whistling cry for his 'dolphins', who soon bobbed into view. Dripping from their swim, they grabbed the oars and returned us to the island. We were not glad to get there, nor was our reception agreeable. As soon as our feet touched ground, Nikias barked out an order and the men held us with a strong grip.

'Fetch the chains!' Nikias ordered Menestor, who obeyed at once, returning with zealous swiftness. In his hands he bore the dreadful manacles with which obstreperous slaves are kept in check. Metal locks and links were new and of good quality, stolen, I thought, from army supplies.

'Sorry,' said Nikias. 'But you have given me little choice. With so many of you on this island, I cannot have you all running around, chatting and plotting.' He looked at the rest of his guests – the family from Laurion, the pale-faced pilgrim.

'Pay no mind,' he said jovially. 'Just a little unfinished business between me and these naughty gentlemen here. They owes me, and won't give us our due. Know that as soon as they cooperate with me, we can all leave this island.'

They were obviously astonished, but nobody made any move to rescue or to remonstrate as the chains were fitted on us. Soon I wore an iron ring around the right hand, and iron rings about both ankles. A chain attached to the ankle rings made walking difficult, nor could one take long steps. In this degrading clanking costume we were obliged to follow our tormentor, who conducted us with mock ceremony to a side of the island away from the others, a small cove partly hidden from the view of our party's side of the island by a screen of thorny shrubs deformed by the winds.

'There you are,' said Nikias.'We may remember to give you food and water occasionally. Or not, as the fancy takes us. It is sometimes good for health and sanity to fast. But Menestor shall listen to what you say, in case your conversation proves interesting.'

The period of suffering began. It is true that Aristotle and I had the consolation of being together, but we could not really talk with such a perpetual listener. The little lame dog (Doris' dog, I was sure of it) romped towards us, whining as usual, but it was driven away by Menestor. The sun beat down upon our beach and made us thirsty. 'You can often come upon a rill of fresh water by quickly scraping up sand near a beach,' Aristotle informed me as he dug with manacled hands, 'but drink quickly, the water soon becomes brackish.' This proved true; our scraping was not rewarded with any great quantity of water, but it helped.

It was embarrassing to answer the calls of nature. We dug out a trough with our hands and feet, a small pit on the inland side at the furthest distance our chain would allow. I had never realised the horror of being truly a prisoner. Since I was a boy I had loved walking. As a free man I could go wheresoever my feet would carry me, taking pleasure in moving through the changing landscape. Now I was deprived of the power of movement, a power that wild animals (and even some tame ones) take for granted. I irritated my companion by walking restlessly the length of my chain. He pointed out that wasn't a good idea as it was using up bodily moisture. Water was supplied irregularly, food more rarely still.

The second and third day they let us alone except when Nikias came to bark some questions at us. We gathered that some of the sailors were occupying themselves with fishing, and others were indolent, playing gambling games and drinking what they had brought with them. The fourth day Nikias' active henchmen brought us out in front of our companions and subjected us to beating.

'Now you will learn, old teacher, what happens to stubborn students,' said Nikias jocularly. He flogged Aristotle on the shoulders with a rope. The others – the pilgrim and the little family – were made to watch.

'Tell this old man,' Nikias shouted, 'that if he promises to behave, you can all go home.'

Aristotle gritted his teeth and said nothing – made no outcry or remonstrance – and gave no information, of course.

They did not beat Aristotle very hard, I think because they feared for his health. Nikias earnestly hoped to get his hands on the secret cache, and killing Aristotle would spoil that game. For me they had less compunction. They tied me to a tree, bared my shoulders and beat me with rods, as a slave is beaten. I protested that this was hubris, and liable to the utmost prosecution of the law, as I was an Athenian citizen. But they were not in a mood to heed. Then I endeavoured to hold my peace, but I did not, and in the end – I am ashamed to remark it – I roared like a young child. People say slaves are cowardly because they cry when beaten, but I am now certain that it is easier to bear wounding in battle than this kind of contemptuous torture. Once the party were satisfied that we were experiencing punishment, they threw us down on the beach together to recover from our lashes. The dew gave a grateful coolness to our tortured skin. We recovered as best we could the next day, when we were unmolested. We were so sleepy and unconversational that Menestor gave up listening, and went off. That meant a precious chance to talk.

'That was bad,' I said. 'It can only get worse.'

'Yes,' said Aristotle, 'it probably will. But if I tell him what I know, it will mean instant death for the whole party. Whereas if we stall, something may turn in our favour.'

'You are sure they will kill us?'

'Certainly. It was very bad that they let us *see* they had the corpse of poor Peleus on board. We instantly knew too much. They did not care enough about us to deceive us – therefore we are not meant to tell a tale to the world outside. Not any of us. I cannot think of any way of inducing them to let the little family go.'

'Nikias did give them a chance,' I recollected. 'In Halikarnassos, he told the family and the pilgrims to wait or to take another ship. A sporting chance – but Fortune was not with them.'

'True. The worst thing is, Nikias is not acting on his own. As a mere pirate, he might be more persuadable. He is in the pay of someone much more powerful. A person or persons connected with Diophantos and his cohort.'

'While Peleus, we may believe, is what he seems – seemed.'

'Yes. A straightforward loyal Makedonian officer. So those playing some other game had him killed, in order, it seems, to get hold of us. *After* we met with Harpalos.'

'I believe,' I said, 'that my letter from Theodoros was largely forged – the Hesiod verses inserted to cover up what was there before. Odd that Nikias should have quoted those lines! The forgery would have been done *before* we met with Harpalos. I wanted to look at the letter again, but you remember it was lost.'

'Somewhere,' Aristotle thought aloud, 'there is mind at work. Somewhere an organisation, a structure. Nikias refers to people in *Athens* – not just Makedonians. Diophantos is a Makedonian, but he seems to have gone over to this other invisible party. We may presume there are officers who are disaffected, if not from Makedon, at least from Alexander. Perhaps they simply don't favour the move eastward. Or perhaps they hope to take over, leaving Alexander enmired or perhaps killed in the distant depths of Asia beyond the far mountains.'

'It reminds me,' I said, recalling a conversation once heard in the Agora. 'There are some who want Athens to keep to herself, but there are others who would like to revive the Athenian League. Athens — or the most important citizens — would take control of the cities of Ionia and Karia and so on, and the islands. Their own empire, free of Alexander.'

'True, Stephanos. We are confronting something much harder to resolve than a simple crime. Even murder is only part of it. Whoever it is, our hidden enemy, hopes now to get the money of Harpalos, for his — or their — own purpose. Presumably someone with no love for Makedon. But yet, someone of good enough position to know Harpalos, or know about him.'

'Could the plotter be Harpalos himself?'

'Not entirely impossible. There is something of the trickster about Harpalos. Whoever is behind all this seems to be a trickster of some kind. But Harpalos could scarcely act alone. I don't see what interests he could really serve by this series of events. He serves himself pretty well already!'

'That Theban slave is mixed up in it,' I said. '*He* has no love for Makedon.'

'Indeed. And we know one important thing. The lad can read — probably at a much higher level than these seamen who are his current masters. So he could have abstracted and read your letter — and destroyed it. But he is unlikely to have been the original forger, since he was in Asia. Forgery is a skilled job, not work you'd give to someone with little opportunity to practise writing.'

I was trying in a stupid head-aching way to think what all this could mean. The sun beat dully upon the water, birds cried dull cries. Suddenly there was a commotion on the other side of the sandy island. Screams, sound of running. Menestor came bursting through the under-brush.

'Come, my lads,' he said jovially, grabbing the two of us and taking us on our clanking way. 'This is sport! And it may open your eyes and mouths!'

A terrible sight met our eyes – the poor puny pilgrim with one badly bent leg was spreadeagled on the ground, face down, and two men were standing over him with rods.

'We waited for you,' said Nikias. 'We wanted everyone to see this judgement executed. This man was caught trying to flee. We will make an example of him.'

Two of his men started beating the prostrate form in a rhythmic manner.

'Put some more into it, lads!' yelled Nikias. 'Menestor – I think this grovelling fellow's a foreigner, not a Greek. So even though you are a slave, you may have your chance. Here!' And he tossed to Menestor not a rod but a short whip. 'See what *you* can do!'

Menestor gritted his teeth with the effort and bestrode his victim. He lashed and lashed away, as if he had taken leave of his senses, his face writhing and distorted, his muscles heaving. The display of rage was terrible, like an earthquake or thunderstorm, as if Menestor himself was not in charge of it but the rage in charge of him. The man twisted and shrieked under the lashes. At last he ceased writhing, then became quite still.

'Stop!' said Nikias. He took the whip from Menestor. 'I don't want you to get into the habit of unnecessary murder, my boy. There's a right and a wrong way to do everything. Let this wretched fellow die slowly, now. Turn him face up, and we'll just leave him here. We'll let the females and the old man leave the place. But *you* can watch,' he said to Aristotle. 'You cut up animals, don't you, and observe them? This will be a nice treat for you, doctor. You will be able to tell us in the end which it was – pain, blood loss, heatstroke or thirst – that killed this fellow. No – don't go near him –' as Aristotle started towards the hapless pilgrim supine in the sand, his hands tied with ropes to tree trunks nearby. 'You must only *observe*, mind.'

Weak and shaken, still in our fetters, we had to sit on the sand and observe. Little changed. The poor man's shoulders heaved occasionally with the effort of taking breath. I kept thinking he was breathing his last, but no. On it went, on with the wearying relentlessness of life that seems to have no other purpose but itself, tiring the possessor.

To my surprise, one of the sailors came tiptoeing over to us with some water to quench our thirst.

'Good man,' said Aristotle in a mild tone, 'as you have had parents and people who love you, take this drink to that poor fellow there. Dabble his lips gently – see if he can swallow.'

Surprised, the man obeyed, still in silence. The swollen mouth took in a little water. Then a little more. 'Enough,' said Aristotle eventually, with the same gentleness as before. I could see the sailor felt some awe of him, even though he had seen him beaten two days ago.

'Let me, I entreat, sit near this man all night,' Aristotle asked. 'I can do you no harm.'

The man agreed, and let us move our iron-bound selves closer to the victim; he also allowed Aristotle to keep the water with him.

'You see,' Aristotle said to me, in quite a normal tone. 'Death is not always predictable. Life and death are mysteries. Some would have died already under this treatment. It seems to me we each have our own vital heat, and this becomes exhausted slowly or quickly. In the very old, heat has been gently drawn off, and they die easily. In others, heat fluctuates, as in violent fevers, when it is over-spent. The lung and the brain supply coolness. When these do not function, the vital heat exhausts itself more rapidly. Sustain radical heat and tempering moisture both, and Nature may restore a lease on life.' He dabbled the man's mouth with water again.

Aristotle sat serenely and solemnly watching as the pale stars came up and went down. He seemed inwardly concentrated. I ceased to be able to feel anything. Not pity. Not astonishment. Looking at the dying man, I knew that this might be my fate too, just as surely as I knew that the white light around me came from the moon above us.

Perhaps Nikias was himself somewhat awed by the terrific flogging of the hapless pilgrim, for he gave us relative peace in the next few days. On the second day he moved us away from the still-breathing pilgrim back to our lonely little cove. But on the third day (I think it was the third), a day of some wind and grey sky, Nikias came to us and announced he had had enough. He seemed more glowering and anxious than usual. The slow dying of the pilgrim was perhaps twitching his soul, rendering him strained and anxious, and the weather aroused an impatience to finish his mission before the autumn.

'You cannot sit about here in this holiday fashion,' he said angrily. 'We must soon set off. Now, join the others while we think what we are to do.' We were dragged away from our prisonous hiding place and moved to the other beach. By the 'other beach' I mean the place where the little family were, and Menestor and the other sailors.

'There are too many of you,' said Nikias, 'all giving us trouble. You need food and that is becoming a serious problem. We are running out of grain for flour – and other supplies. We must depart before the weather turns. And all this trouble because of this stubborn old fellow there!' He pointed at Aristotle. 'You tell him to give us what we want, so we can let all of you go.'

'Pray, sir,' said Hermippos to Aristotle, in a voice that did not succeed in not shaking, 'pray give them what they want.'

'Will you really let us go?' asked little Philokleia. 'Will you let *him* go?' pointing at Aristotle.

'Oh, that old man,' laughed Nikias. 'Don't worry your head about him. He'll have to go a-journeying with me.'

'I don't like you,' said the little girl. 'You are mean. You do bad things. I think,' she said to Aristotle, 'he is just like the Hungry Prince. You remember, in the story. And the gods will punish him! Maybe he will try to eat himself all up.'

'What's this?' Nikias was suddenly purple with rage. He strode up to the child. 'She's a witch! Making threats and prophecies!'

'But you *are*,' said the child. 'You are like the Hungry Prince. And the gods will punish you. After you have eaten everything, then you will eat yourself.'

'This is sorcery – I won't have it!' roared Nikias. 'Uttering curses – the little toad! A seeress possessed of a demon! She's bad luck. It is bad luck to have a woman-child aboard.'

With the child in his grasp, he moved towards the smallest of his craft where it lay lightly beached. He threw the child into the little ship and jumped in himself.

'Push off, Menestor!' he ordered. And Menestor pushed the ship away. Then Nikias took the long oar and poled himself from the back of the ship, slowly, until the craft was a little way off shore. Only a little way – about the length of four or five men. Then he made the child stand up.

'Now we shall put an end to these ravings!' he cried and laid his dagger against the child's throat.

'No!' cried Aristotle in an anguished voice, but one of the sailors clapped his hands over the old man's mouth. Aristotle was trying to run towards the boat, but we both toppled in the sand, having gone the length of our short chain.

'No, I beg of you, sir,' cried aged Hermippos. 'I implore you, give us back our child and we shall give you anything you demand – to all my estate in Laurion!'

'No!' screamed the mother. 'O, Mother Demeter! Save my Philokleia! O sir, have mercy, she is only a child, a virgin –'

'A virgin! Yes, that's a problem,' said Nikias. 'Sacrificing virgins! No, I won't do that. We can soon solve that one.' He took the horrified child and thrusting up her clothing he raped her in the daylight for all to see.

'There! There's no virgin in the case now!' he screamed. The quick bronze dagger gleamed and whizzed. A dark line appeared on the child's throat. Nikias held her body up for a minute so it did not crumple to the floor of the boat even as she was giving up the spirit and the life went out of her.

'There's one less of you!' he cried, and threw the body overboard. We all heard the splash.

There was a horrible silence. Even the mother was not crying but stood like Niobe, a statue. The old grandfather had slumped down into the sand. I could feel the excitement and perturbation of the sailors. Aristotle's breath came heaving up, as if he had been able to run for parasangs to save the child – as his mind wished to do and his body could not.

'So, there you are!' shouted Nikias, defiantly. 'That's war for you. It's happened before and will happen again to better females than her. And no more witchcraft – no nasty prophesying – no curses!'

He need not have worried. We were all beyond speech. Nikias joined the other sailors for dinner and they left our little group to ourselves for a time. The moon rose. We all just sat there staring into the sea or into space.

'Look,' said Hermippos softly. 'The child floats!' We saw a gleam of light on white clothing, showing in the moon track on the water. The body was tossing gently on the top of the waves, not far from us. At last, we dropped off to sleep, still in our sitting postures. We awoke in the middle of the night on hearing – once more – a splash. Hermippos was missing from the group on the shore. First we thought he had swum out to recover the body, but then we saw that he had gone out to make a hole in the water. That was another of us gone. When we awoke in the morning, there were two less of us. The woman was hanging from a thorn tree, turning and turning in the gentle wind.

XXI

Escape

The sequence of deaths seemed to have shocked even our captors. At least I think so, because they behaved with less hostility to us in the next few days. They let us use some of our clothing (though our bags had been adopted by the pirates). I was glad of my crumpled himation now; one needed a cloak in the nights. Of course, our enemies' work of guarding us was greatly lessened now that three of our number were gone. And a fourth, the poor pilgrim, seemed to be breathing his last, stretched on the sands where they had put him. Yet at Aristotle's dignified remonstrance and entreaty, one of the men (the same who had come to us before with water) supplied the prostrate sufferer with moisture for the lips, and even allowed Aristotle to sit by him, ministering as much as he was able, at regular intervals. Aristotle had the temerity to demand honey for his patient so he could make hydromel, and after some grumbling the sweet stuff was given him from Nikias' own supplies. I noticed that Aristotle did not use all of the honey, nor put it back in the jar, but kept some in a leather pouch under a bush, which struck me as odd treatment for honey. Nourished by the hydromel that Aristotle poured delicately through his lips a drop at a time, the man continued to breathe.

'He is not as feeble as he looked, obviously,' said Aristotle. 'Or he would have died long before this. His constitution is excellent. The man must have been of a good habit of body before he got whatever wound or distress it was that urged him to take a pilgrimage to Kos.'

'Bad luck for him,' I remarked. 'He did not get to the healing island of Kos, but to a nameless island for torture and dying.'

'That does seem to be pure chance or Fate,' said Aristotle thoughtfully. 'It is no accident that you and I are here. But it seems accident that the others are – or were – here.'

We were talking as before on our old prison-beach where we had again been led, the pirate group wanting an undisturbed mealtime. These days they gave us a longer chain so we could even stroll some distance along the beach, and separately if we wished. But customarily we sat together, as now.

'I wonder exactly how long we have been here?' I looked at the sky. 'We have been way from home a long time. I kept account of the days pretty well at first, at least until we got to Asia. But now I don't know how long we have been away. The weather is still warm but the days are shorter. The stars have changed; there is a dew in the morning. I think it must be in the month of Boedromion. The celebration of the Eleusinian Mysteries may have begun by now.'

'Boedromion. Yes. The month of Apollo the Helper. Apollo-quick-to-help. The month's name means running to a man shouting for help – only too appropriate for us. But we are dumb before our slaughterers.'

'May the time bring us assistance,' I said. 'O, Aristotle, it was in the month of Boedromion that I came to you for help. I was a man bellowing for assistance, and *you* came to my aid.'

'It is kind of you to remember that, Stephanos. What I see too clearly now is that I have led you into terrible trouble. But for knowing me, you would not be here.'

I knew that was the simple truth, and could not clearly see how to comfort him.

'It doesn't matter,' I said feebly.

'But it does. You are a young man with your life before you. You have a bride waiting for you, children yet to be born. I am old. Any man who reaches fifty must realise he is not immortal. With so much I still want to do, I judged, perhaps foolishly, that I should be given more time. But I let myself – I let *us* – drift into this danger. It comes to me now that my grief affected my judgement. I didn't notice things. I had not so much attention to give to life. Thus important signs passed me by.'

'How so?'

'I should have seen that *of course* we were going to be followed out of Athens – at least, *I* was. Someone would be anxious to know that I had gone, and where I was bound. There are large political interests at stake, not just spite. We both see that there is what we might call crudely pro-Makedon and anti-Makedon sentiment in Athens. But who is using these sentiments for their own purposes? There is a strong and intelligent antagonist at work, some individual or group with a larger design, and I am important enough to have a place in that person or persons' calculations about the future of his design. Therefore I would be watched – at very least. Probably it was always intended to get rid of me once I was far enough away. We were followed out of Athens – out of Attika, rather – perhaps by more than one watcher.'

'Who? Oh, yes, that slavewoman Doris. We talked about her before. Now we know she is assuredly connected with these pirates. Doris' dog is here, though she is not. But Doris seems too lowly – and too crippled – to be a real enemy.'

'Do not underestimate her intelligence, or her cold blood. We don't even *know* that she's really a cripple. She certainly had access to the kitchen and the knives in Aristodamos' house. Doris is the most likely murderer of our first captain. Because he came to warn us of something, he had to be disposed of then and there. Most likely there was some original plan to make sure, in any event, that on the last part of our journey we sailed with Nikias.'

'Diophantos could not have been the killer on Naxos,' I agreed. 'Whatever he may have been up to in Phaselis.'

'I firmly believe that Doris alone – though acting under orders – was the killer of our good captain Aiskhines. As we noted before, her dog did not bark in the night. Who else could keep the beast quiet?'

'Perhaps the pirates got her to this island and then killed her, too?'

'No, Stephanos. If she were buried on this islet, the dog would dig up her body. If she were dead in the sea, he would be moaning at the water's edge. The dog is not grieving. Doris was here as cook. She then went away, on some other errand, without her pet. Her job of watching us was over.'

'And other watchers on the journey?'

'Philokhoros is a puzzle. He may have been trying to do us some good. Or perhaps he was merely the agent of a rival party, and both he and Doris were seeking to do us ill, in different ways.'

'And in that case, Doris' party got rid of him. Philokhoros got thrown into a pigpen. I suppose he is still searching for Sosios, his runaway boy. It is a long time since we have seen anything of those people. Delos.'

'Yes. But almost immediately after Philokhoros was no longer with us, in Naxos, Doris the efficient agent got rid of Aiskhines and put us in care of Captain Nikias. A pirate by profession. Now Nikias has made clear his intentions on that journey. What fools we were! We should have noticed his men's peculiar alertness regarding the damaged big ship that we came across, and their disappointment that they couldn't take it. They were still indignant about it when we arrived in Kos – about that and I suppose about our walking off in good health, so they lost their fee. Mere suspicion led me to take the valuable precaution of telling an acquaintance where I was. Yet, once arrived safely in Kos, I foolishly forgot my suspicions of Nikias.'

'And in Kos,' I continued, 'we had other things to think of, including young Parmenion. Then we were led on the journey to Harpalos, so you could see your nephew –'

'An interesting but costly journey that has proved to be! You remember, Nikias said some men in Athens would be glad that I was rendered more "reasonable". That statement gives me pause. It would be so much easier to negotiate with Nikias if he were acting on his own. There is no reason to doubt that he indeed has contact with someone of importance in Athens – directly, or indirectly. The centre of the plot must be Athenian.'

I arose, restlessly twitching my chain. 'Come,' I said impatiently. 'Let us walk. We have so little time before those sailors come back. They seem to have become quite confident now, leaving us alone for large periods of time.'

'I think they don't trust Menestor,' said Aristotle, getting up stiffly. 'And they don't like to risk letting any one individual among them hear our conversation. They are not so confident that they leave oars in their ships; they always take them out and guard them.'

'Except,' I responded, 'for the man who is so keen a fisherman and keeps those octopodes and so on. He is sometimes a little careless.'

'Pirates often fall out among themselves,' Aristotle observed. 'I was hoping these men might do so, but I have seen no opening.'

Unhappily we paced the seashore in the autumn light, as the sun slid down the western horizon. 'Watch out for sea-urchins,' Aristotle warned, as we crunched along the foreshore. 'Many are poisonous, and if one of the stinging spines gets into your foot you will be in pain before it works its own way out.'

'I know it from childhood,' I said feelingly.

'A number of Testacea have this system of protection, as insects have their sting.' Aristotle seemed happy talking about his animal categories once more. 'The hard matter or spine is all outside, in contrast to us mammals who have the hard matter at the centre of the body, the way modellers built figures of clay upon a hard core. The little sea-urchin has the best defence system of all shell-fish. A fine palisade of stakes. Interesting – no creature is without some strength. The cuttlefish, our Sepia, can confuse its enemies by the dark ink it squirts when frightened, evidently with the same involuntary ease as men urinate under the same circumstances. Interesting creatures.'

We moved cautiously along the tide-dampened beach, looking at the detritus that the sea spume leaves. Worm-casts and bivalves. Empty shells and strips of seaweed. Little stones and some small pieces of pottery, even some little pieces of once-valuable glass, polished hard by the sea. A large piece of painted pottery, laced with worm holes. A rotten piece of planking. An oar, broken at the handle . . .

'An oar!' I seized it and on an impulse hid it under my cloak. That cloak was already disreputable and dirty from our outdoor sleeping but it had not gone into holes yet, so the oar was momentarily safe from sight.

'An oar,' repeated Aristotle. 'An important but fragile object. If we think of any escape, we must try for it soon. Not long hence, the pirates will decide to go off this island and they will take me – us – with them. They were shocked by their own killings, I think, and then decided to await the poor pilgrim's natural death and then bury him. But this island is too full of bodies. They yearn to depart. They will finish the poor man's dying for him and take us away. They will hope to get me to talk on the mainland, near where they imagine Harpalos' hoard must be.'

It occurred to me that Aristotle was optimistic in talking of the pirates taking 'us'. So much more likely that it would be Aristotle alone who would be taken off in a boat, while I made one of the bodies buried in the sands of this islet. The prospect made me more alert.

'We must get free enough of movement to seize a ship,' I said firmly. 'And then we can use this oar to take our-selves off. To be sure, they would be after us right away –'

'My plan includes taking one of these vessels,' said Aristotle, 'The second smallest, if we can. Not the very smallest.' Neither of us wanted to say we could not bear the smallest ship as it was the site of the worst of the murders. We never spoke of that event.

'That smallest ship is the one that the fisherman-sailor uses all the time for fishing, anyway,' I remarked. 'It has his tackle in it, and he keeps live fish and octopodes there also. In a net like a bag hung over the side, so that if he needs a meal he can take one without going fishing again.'

'Yes. That figures also in my plan,' said Aristotle. 'You and I – we couldn't handle the largest ship at all. The second ship handles well in the water, I've noticed. We might just about get it to move. It seems a forlorn project, but let me explain my plan. You must promise not to be hungry, for it entails a night of fasting.'

He told me the details of it as the sunset colours began to spread across the sky.

The pirates had not eaten their main meal yet, and we had been able to smell the stew cooking all the time we were in conversation. We started back down the track, in the direction of the main camp, though of course we couldn't go there in our bonds. One of the men could be heard advancing, bearing some food for us. It was only some tired bread, and thin soup abstracted from the beginnings of the rich stew.

'Thank you,' said Aristotle politely. 'But, no. I should feel better if we were able to share of the dish you are all going to eat. I can smell it.'

Menestor — for it was he — laughed loudly. 'So — you now suspect us of poisoning you, do you? Let me tell you, we're not done with you yet, old secret-keeper. Nikias knows a trick worth two of that. But for tonight — !' The Theban slave uncoupled our chains from their mooring.

'You can trot along to the camp,' he said. 'A little exercise will do your old bones good. There you can see this fish stew you hanker after. Beg for a fish, like a pet duck! Though now you two look like two asses, being driven, or two naughty steeds. Holla!'

Laughing at this image, he drove us like a charioteer in playful hurry to the place where the men were gathered around the fire.

Aristotle went slowly, after Menestor tied the end of the chain. The philosopher circled about the cooking-pot peering into it: 'Aha,' he muttered, as some old gentlemen do in the kitchen. 'Here we have crayfish and some white fish, and some shellfish mixed together. I suppose it's very hot — ' and he stretched his hand over the pot to feel the steam.

'Dainty, aren't we?' said Nikias. 'Never mind, since you're becoming peevish about eating your own meals, you can mess from the common plate. I don't mind, this once.'

'There's fish enough,' said the fisherman with his mouth full. This was the man who kept octopodes and crayfish and other things in a net bag. 'Now we have to cook for ourselves all the time, but the food's good.'

Aristotle and I were helped with platefuls in the coarse

wooden dishes (each a slightly hollowed piece of tree).We were given a reasonable amount, and the fish smelt so good it was a little difficult not to be tempted. Following Aristotle's lead, I pretended to touch my stew, munched at nothing with my eyes on the sky, and tipped some surreptitiously into the sand. The lame dog came in for his share.

Nothing happened for a long time after this. We sat quietly. The men, replete, belched and dozed. Then Menestor got up in a hurry and ran frantically into the bushes. Unpleasant sounds ensued. This was followed by a similar fast trot on the part of another pirate, who seemed in even more dire straits. The place began to smell really bad. Tipped off by Aristotle, I stumbled off into the bushes, dragging the chain, and did a good imitation of sickness. So much excrement from both ends was now lying about in the retired spot in the bushes that it would not be easy for anyone to swear I had not been ill. Aristotle promptly followed suit. Nobody thought to secure our chains again. The little dog had gone off already – to be sick somewhere on its own, I surmised. Inwardly I hoped it choked to death on its vomit. Time passed numbered by groans and upheavals. The men then snored uneasily in unpleasant sleep, wakening to be sick once more.

Aristotle and I watched the sky impatiently. At last the thin stripe of silvery light was followed by a firmer indication of a dawn. 'Now,' Aristotle whispered and, picking up our chains, we moved off to the place where the boats were beached. The men had shipped and guarded the oars but Aristotle found one left by the careless fisherman in the smallest vessel. I had my almost-good oar with me under my cloak. Furiously I pushed at the middle-sized ship, and heard with relief its crunching slide back into the water. We hopped aboard, unhandily, as we had to carry a weight of chain. Aristotle had paused to pick up the bag of fishes danging from the end of the smallest boat. The philosopher also had to arrange some other property where he thought it would do the most good.

'Off!' I said in an urgent but low voice, and we cast off. We were not best equipped for an expedition by sea. Although I had practised for fun with the men in our island-hopping days, I was the least skilful rower that could be found – except for Aristotle. But we had a strong will to succeed and strove mightily at our oars.

I had hoped that our departure might go unnoted, but that was too good to expect. We made enough noise and splashing to arouse even the sleepy and sickly pirates. The two strongest and youngest, the sailors who had gone out with us and Nikias that first day, came running (staggering, rather) down the beach.

'Ho!' they shouted. 'Come back, you! We'll make you sorry you tried such a trick!'

'Just going for some fresh air,' Aristotle explained in his usual calm and reasonable tone.

'We're coming to get you! You'll be sorry!' they cried, but not as loudly or ferociously as they might have done before their dinner. In the dawn light we could see them clearly – the tall sailor and the other one – as they prepared to come and get us. For the sake of speed they simply dived in and swam out to us, not stopping to release one of their own boats. Of course, these were Nikias' 'dolphins'.

'Are you ready?' Aristotle asked me. I was excited rather than ready, but we got our ammunition where we wanted it and kept the boat from rocking too hard.

'Ho – won't you suffer for this! But it will be better if you give up – now!' cried the tall sailor, who was the first to reach our craft. He grabbed the boat firmly. We could see his face below us as he was about to board. Aristotle was not attending. He was reaching into a net. Then quickly and cleverly he scooped out the largest octopus among the captives and splatted it against the face and throat of this man, who was still in the water and just about to rise from it. The octopus threw about its tentacles and wrapped itself around the face, head and neck of the would-be boarder. He screamed but his scream was muffled by the octopus which had given him a new face.

Meanwhile, despite my flailing about with the oar as a weapon, the second man had swung his feet over. I made sure our cavalry-stoppers were laid just where he was going to step. He put his foot down on a sea-urchin and then on another. He let out a yelp and then a yell. 'Ai! Ai – ee!' He was just distracted enough to allow me to hit him on the head, then to push at his knees and toss him overboard. The victim of sea-urchins wasn't much help to his companion, who was still crying for liberation from the terrified octopus. Aristotle let fly a volley of sea creatures at the pair in the water, wrapping more octopodes around them and loosening upon them some terrified cuttlefish, which made a nice discharge of sepia. Then we pushed with our oars and went off as rapidly as we could.

This was not very rapidly. We were awkward and

uneven rowers, and even had we been good there were only two of us. We were not used to keeping time. I called out a *keleusma*. The broken end of the oar handle cut into my hand, and my hamstrings strained. My weak shoulder (the one that had been thrown out as a result of a fall in the mountains) began to protest. I can only imagine what Aristotle must have felt, a man by no means in his youth, troubled with sciatica and quite unaccustomed to such efforts. Yet he laboured at his oar, uncomplaining. The good thing was that we could see a distance between us and the islet. We tried to calculate a course and make for the mainland, but although we could see this shore dimly, it now seemed an enormous distance away.

'A sail! A large vessel under sail!' Aristotle was first to spy this phenomenon. A vessel with many rowers was almost bearing down upon us. I wondered if it were possible to avoid it – it might not be friendly. But the ship came relentlessly on, despite our best efforts, and it gained on us steadily. 'That's no merchant vessel,' I said, watching it. 'She moves too rapidly.'

Aristotle had to give up and gasp; leaning on his oar, he watched the ship's swift advance upon us. 'Either this brings friends of the pirates, come to see how they are,' he wheezed, 'and we are lost. Or it is a normal government ship, and we may be saved.'

As the ship came on, we could see it bore all the earmarks of a smart and well-disciplined naval vessel. It was a trireme, well painted and moving at speed. At last, we could make out the individual oarsmen.

'We have to cry out so they don't run us over,' said Aristotle. 'They're too close.' He let out a call. Just then we were able to make out the faces of the little group of men standing at the prow of the ship, scanning the water. As one of them, presumably the captain, replied to Aristotle's hail, I recognised the man standing next to him.

'Philokhoros!' I exclaimed in amazement.

And it was Philokhoros. The oars stopped at his command. He was visibly giving orders at a terrific rate, and telling the captain how to attach our vessel to theirs.

'We're sending two men to help you,' Philokhoros yelled.

'You have to send a *file* with them!' Aristotle yelled back. 'We are in chains. Most inconvenient. A file, please!'

After some active searching in the naval ship to find a file (the ship's carpentry store yielded one), two active sailors boarded our fishy ship. After freeing us from our chains, they helped us to grab hold of a rope thrown from the large vessel, so we could be swung quickly up and aboard the trireme.

'At last I find you!' cried Philokhoros, joyfully embracing us. He kissed each of us on both cheeks. Tears came to his eye. 'I have sought you so long,' he explained. 'And I failed — oh, terribly, stupidly failed! — in my mission. I was supposed to take care of you. I promised Antipater himself I would do so. But my boy — my beautiful boy! How could I fail to search for him?'

'And,' said Aristotle, a trifle drily, 'you were a private gentleman, not someone anybody could order about, like a soldier in the army. You were free to use your time as you deemed best.'

'Exactly. Not that I didn't fully intend to act for Antipater. My being a private gentleman was a distinct advantage to the very task he wished me to perform. But there I was, so foolishly trapped in Mykonos, to my shame. And I still needed to look for poor lost Sosios. Only for a little while.'

'So you tried to come back to us? Picked up the scent again, as it were?'

'Yes. Resigned at last to the loss of my poor boy, I indeed started looking for you. At last I got to Kos and picked up the story of your travel to Asia. Your failure to return left me alarmed. I went to Halikarnassos with this ship. At the military post there we first heard that the man who conducted you to Phaselis, one Peleus, had disappeared. Unnerving, as you can imagine. But then I got your message – the word you left with a tripe-and-pickled-fish-seller in the harbour at Halikarnassos. Though I was not entirely sure what to make of it. But we set out to search for a sailor-captain called Nikias.'

'I shall be delighted,' said Aristotle, 'to hear your side of our story. But not now. We have to go and save a life. A poor pilgrim, hideously abused by the pirates, lies on the point of death on a little islet not far from here. They committed a terrible murder before our eyes, such as will darken your own eyes to hear. The islet is full of dead bodies and living pirates. They have held us prisoner for an unknown length of time. Rescue the pilgrim – punish the pirates! And perhaps I can also recover the remains of Kallisthenes' manuscript.'

The ship went eagerly on at our direction. It took no time at all to arrive at the island. It seemed to take longer to beach the immense craft. I don't know what I had expected would happen then – simply, I suppose, that the leading men on the trireme would take the pirates into custody and we could all go away. But the clearing was deserted. Of course the pirates had had sufficient time to see the ship from afar. Had they gone already? Yet surely we should have seen their ships as we advanced upon the islet? Curtly selecting a gang of armed mariners to comb the island, the naval captain ordered the others to stay in the vessel, ready for instant departure. 'Take 'em alive, if you can,' ordered Philokhoros, who seemed to have unusual powers given him on this expedition.

With Aristotle and myself acting as guides, we all hurried to the other side of the island. To our surprise we found the criminal group – or most of them – at the beach where Aristotle and I had been held captive. I suppose all these men had been somewhat sluggish because of their induced illness. They had not been able to give chase to us, or to make an expeditious departure once they knew we had got away. Their two remaining ships they must have picked up and moved across the narrow island, hoping to depart unseen, out of view of the warship. The smallest pirate *keles* was upon the water already. The largest, the *Niké* itself, was beached still but ready to depart; its prow rested on the sand, but the stern swayed on the light waves of the shallows. Men were loading objects into her: they nearly dropped a familiar handsome wooden box. Among the objects successfully carried aboard was the body of the unfortunate pilgrim. The pirates ashore were frantically yelling to their fellows at sea urging them to speed away. Our trireme's captain ordered one of his men to run back to the naval vessel and tell it to give chase to the pirates' small ship. The rest of us continued to advance through the thorn bushes to the cove.

'Enemy approach!' yelled Nikias, one of the group by the *Niké*. He brandished a sword. Most of the pirates were armed. But when they saw our party advancing the pirate sailors tried to flee by jumping into their boat. They were a little less agile than usual; not only did they have the spoils of war to pack aboard, but they were also trying to handle both weapons and oars.

We rushed up to them. The men of the trireme – the captain, Philokhoros, and a select party – were well armed. We should have let these men deal with the enemy, but we were carried away. I think I felt blood-lust for the first time. Aristotle, stimulated by the sight of the container of Kallisthenes' precious manuscript, lost his discretion. 'Stop! Stop! Give me that box!' he shouted. With great vigour he ran splashing through the shallow sandy water up to the ship, his hands outstretched. He thus ran directly into danger: one of the pirate sailors, a big man, grabbed him by the hand and held a javelin to his throat. This man called to one of his mates to assist him and they seized Aristotle and dragged him aboard the ship. A useful hostage, Aristotle was a captive once more.

I had forgotten that I was not armed at all, and the pirates were. In my enthusiasm I overstepped the mark, grabbing the boat to stop it from leaving. I felt only that I must prevent them from carrying off Aristotle. I did distract the big man, who turned towards me his attention and his javelin (actually a cut-off spear with a heavy point). Had he succeeded in putting that point through my throat as he intended, I should have looked my last upon the light then and there. But I wrestled with him and his arm skidded, as it were, so that he thrust his weapon deeply into my left shoulder. I could even hear the noise it made, grinding at the side of the bone.

There was a hot sharp pain. I felt as all of me were pierced through. I lost my footing and dropped into the shallow water, which was now a confusion of legs and feet and oars and sandy splashings. Near me I saw, or sensed, a man, or parts of a live man – an arm, a hand, a foot – a man appearing and disappearing into the churning sand. An incomplete man in his death throes. I was able to move out of the way a little, crawling like a crab on my good arm and hand. The presence of the javelin as an attachment was inconvenient. I worked at getting it out of my body. All I could hear were shouts. Curses – groans – cries. A splash! A wooden box flew away from the boat, hurled into the deep. Another splash. Aristotle jumping – or falling – into the water. I don't now how it may be in a real military battle, but I expect it is something like that, a vigorous and deadly confusion. Although the captain of the trireme and Philokhoros too had wanted to take the leading pirates alive, our enemies were putting up a desperate fight. It was obvious that they (rightly) had no belief that mercy might be accorded them.

More cries. A lesser splash near me. Someone had dropped a sword. I grabbed it with my good hand – at first just to take control of it so that I should not cut me, rather than for any higher purpose. I struggled to my feet, desiring just not to be drowned in the trampling. Still holding the sword, I saw a confusion of bodies around the *Niké*. I saw Aristotle, saturated and dripping, scrambling to his feet with a piece of seaweed on his head. The others were all occupied in fighting.

Two of the pirate men had ceased to struggle. I was

thinking that it must be nearly over. But it was not. Menestor loomed, angry and like one invincible, over the fray. Having seized a superior foothold (standing on a dead body within the boat) he raised his sword and slashed violently down on one of our naval party, a man who was just about to kill Nikias. With a dreadful cry and groan, our man fell to the Theban's blow. Menestor looked hungrily about for another enemy.

Given this respite, Nikias suddenly jumped overboard, landing almost next to me. He held a sword and he was glaring at Aristotle, who stood there, harmless, unarmed, and dripping.

'You! Old man – *you* are the cause of all my trouble!' he shouted in rapid angry cry. 'By the gods, you shall not outlive this day either! I take you to Hades with me – and now!'

His sword was about to descend on the unarmed philosopher. But I was not unarmed, through the mercy of Fortune and the help of the gods. I struck just once – clumsily but effectively – at the man's neck. Nikias dropped with an expression of great surprise. He was not yet dead – I saw recognition in his eyes as he realised what had happened. Blood gushed out of the side of his throat. I tried to pull my sword loose. I remembered that someone once told me that a sword sticks near the bone, and I found this to be true The blade had bitten into his neck bone and was reluctant to let go. My strength was not great, and my own pain and the weakness from the javelin wound were so severe that I began to crumble. I might have submerged again had I not been caught by Philokhoros.

By the time I revived, the thing was over. Menestor

was the last of the enemy party to die: he had killed one of our men and seriously injured another. Our enemies had been hampered by fighting in a confined space, and striking each other. The little ship was full of dead bodies; a good deal of water had got into it and now surged back and forth over the bottom of the vessel – water that looked red, so much blood had been mixed with it. Six pirates lay dead within the vessel, and three on the beach. And Menestor. At the orders of the trireme captain, our rescuers made sure that each pirate in the ship was dead before being tossed overboard, and then that all other contents were taken out of the ship.

This wealth in this ship, Nikias' hoard, included most of the gold he had taken from us, as well as things that we did not recognise, such as some finely chased silver cups, presumably from another expedition. Lodged beneath one of the thwarts under a rower's bench, a gold object glinted through the bloody water. Not a coin, but a gold knucklebone. This I kept to myself. I carefully thrust it to the bottom of my scuffed leather bag as soon as I found that piece of baggage.

To their credit, the men of Philokhoros' group did not linger now over their new-found treasure. Following the order of their commander, a group of them got into the bloody boat and seized the oars with professional skill. They went off at a brisk pace to overtake their mates in the large ship pursuing the departing pirate craft. That little ship, which first delayed by watching the beginning of the fight, had made off in great haste when the trireme was visibly in pursuit. The great ship of war had now nearly caught up with the small vessel. As we gazed, two figures on the retreating pirate ship rose up, tall and black against the sky, and then dived off the end of it. I could not see their faces, but I knew these were Nikias' 'dolphins'. Dolphins swimming home in their element, escaping the fate that awaited the others.

'Don't worry,' said Philokhoros. 'Our men will get them. They are done for.'

Philokhoros was now in command of the group on land, as our captain had gone off in the small boat to support the trireme. He efficiently took charge of the remaining contingent of the rescue party. At his orders they lined up the bodies neatly on the beach, including Nikias, and Menestor who looked angry and brave even in death, and terribly young. I gazed on the dead face of Nikias whom I had killed, remembering his cheerful glance, and how glad we had been to see him the first time we met him. This man had been living – breathing – planning – talking – but a very short time ago. Now I had put a stop to all of that. It seemed almost unthinkable, but the fact lay there calmly on the sand.

'Ho – look here!' one of the sailors announced, pausing over a corpse. 'This one is not dead!'

'Oh!' I said. 'How could we have forgotten? That is the poor pilgrim – so terribly beaten, and left for dead.'

'He wasn't dead,' said Philokhoros. 'Likely they were taking him along with them as a hostage.'

'Give me some water,' said Aristotle. He went over to the man and gave him some moisture on the lips. To our surprise, a weak voice spoke out of the body that had seemed corpse-like for a long time.

'Are they gone?'

'Yes,' said Aristotle. 'All gone. Except that some of them need to be buried right here. And we need to set up a little hospital for the wounded – for you, and my friend Stephanos here.'

Aristotle attended to my wound, making Philokhoros find some wine and vinegar to wash it with. He also attended to the injured sailors, including the one whose right arm had been badly hacked with Menestor's sword.

'Burials next,' said Philokhoros. 'Best to be tidy. Minimum of rites and prayers, but at least it will keep the beach clean. See if there are any others.'

His crew began to dig in the sandy soil, except for two men who were sent on a tour of inspection. 'May I come with you?' Aristotle asked this pair. 'I have an idea as to where we may find another body – one I badly want to find,' he added. His idea was right. They came back shortly, with the remains of the child Philokleia. Her poor little body was badly nibbled by fish, but still recognisable.

'I thought,' said Aristotle, 'that her corpse would have drifted into that side current, and been held against the snag further down. And so it has proved. Let us give her a decent burial, and in honour to the dead atone for our failure to preserve her alive.'

And so it was. Philokleia was buried, not with the ugly pirates but in her own place, where we also interred the remains of her mother. We all said prayers over the site. Aristotle placed in the child's mouth as a fee for Kharon the most beautiful silver coin in the bags of Harpalos.

Harpalos' money (or most of it) had been recovered. Our plants were of course gone, and the box of Kallisthenes proved unfindable. Perhaps it had been weighted with stones so if lost it would sink for ever, buried in the depth of the sea. The trireme had soon returned, towing the pirates' small ship. The naval men had killed the pirates on board her, and recovered property. But the two 'dolphins' had escaped. 'Perhaps Poseidon will take them himself,' said the captain. He assembled us and all of the things taken from the pirates, and we set out for Kos in the big confident ship, leaving at last the island of bloodshed and woe.

XXII

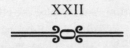

Healing and Light

I know little of that short journey to Kos. I fell into a kind of stupor for a while, and then became aware of being most disagreeably affected by the movement of the boat underneath me. When I did awaken, everything appeared larger than normal, curiously bright or curiously dark. The sound of the *keleusma* battered my soul. It seemed better to go to sleep. I was very hot, and sometimes quite cold. Rats gnawed at my left shoulder and chest; I kept trying to beat them off, and they turned into an octopus that hissed and dug its giant tooth into me. Then a small child in a cowl came and waved the herbs he carried at the sea-creature, and it went away. I knew who this cowled figure was – Telesophoros, helper of Asklepios. I slept. When I awakened, I was in a bed and nothing was moving, for which I was grateful. It was obviously daytime. I tried to get up and found that I had a large mound of cloth on my left side. I tried to tear it off, as if it were fetters.

'Hssh – it's all right.' Aristotle's face appeared, looming

large above my bed. 'You were wounded, you know – those are bandages. You are in Iatrokles' house, under excellent care.'

'Who takes my name?' asked the physician, stepping into my view. 'You are doing well, young man, you have an excellent constitution. But despite the efforts of our friend here' – nodding at Aristotle – 'your wound was not clean. Sandy, I call it. So we had to clean it out again, going in deeply. Then we wanted you to sleep, and regain strength.'

'Aristotle did try to wash the wound,' I said, defending him, 'but we were not in the best place to do that.'

'You are fortunate,' said Iatrokles. 'You will probably always feel the effects of it, but you are very lucky. Had your enemy struck slightly to your right, just a very little distance further into the torso, his spear point would have rammed through the heart or lung. There would have been nothing any doctor could do. And if he had in hand a good sarissa – !'

'I suppose,' Aristotle speculated, 'the man who struck you was hampered by fighting at close quarters. A spear or javelin works best at some distance. He would have been a better fighter with more room.'

'You sound sorry for him!' I snapped.

'No, not at all. You saved my life, Stephanos. I am deeply grateful – your debtor for all time, as I can never really repay such a gift. I have nothing to give that could –'

'I'd like some soup,' I declared.

'Hungry?' asked Iatrokles. 'A good symptom. It is long enough since you had the wound – three days. I think a little soup would be in order.'

'Three days!' I was surprised at losing time in that

spendthrift fashion. But when I drank the soup I soon fell heavily into sleep again. Yet the next day I stayed awake longer, and by the fifth day I declared myself well, and got out of bed. Aristotle looked greatly relieved when I was able to join him in the front of the house, dressed properly, though still with the great bandage.

'Thanks be to the gods you are going to be all right. It would have been a dreadful exchange if your life had been given for mine, a young for an old. I don't know how I could have lived with that.'

'We should sacrifice a cock to Asklepios,' I said. 'I am grateful to my doctors. But I would like to think I knew exactly what has been happening to me – to us – and I don't. I notice you are not staying with Oromedon. Is that just because I am here?'

'That is my excuse.' Aristotle's look darkened. 'Certainly I am not staying with Oromedon. It is quite comfortable here, and my slave Phokon is here now also. Tomorrow Philokhoros will join us, and we shall endeavour to piece together some of these events. But you and I should have a talk first.'

While I was reluctantly preparing in my foggy mind for a discussion, Iatrokles entered the room. He extended an object to me. A battered pair of wooden tablets.

'This will make you feel better, I hope. A letter from Athens, by way of Naxos. I asked at the harbour for all letters to you or to Aristotle to be sent here, and a messenger just brought this.'

The letter bore on the outside the superscription of address to me in care of Aristodamos of Naxos. It had been forwarded to Kos. I opened the tablets and read the writing on the wax:

> *To my dear and honoured Brother Stephanos*
> *Greetings to you from Th and I trust you are well.*
> *We were attacked in Smikrenes' house but all are*
> *well.*
> *Thrasymakhos' men. Moloss bravest and best. Smik*
> *to law*
> *Philemon very brave we guard.*
> > *Mother's love now to Phi Come soon*
> > *Farewell*

I read this over twice before I fully took it in. With a violent twinge of heart I realised what it told me – that my own hapless family, the dear ones left behind, had been attacked. Even on that peaceful farm near Eleusis.

'Look at this!' I forced the letter under Aristotle's nose. 'I have to go home at once! My family is in danger. Thrasymakhos – that pompous unsmiling man! – *he* is the source of trouble. I suspected it was his slaves I glimpsed running away, after the horse's head was deposited on my herm. But I wasn't sure. Now I know. Agents of outrages – which were plotted by Thrasymakhos.'

'Among others, most probably – not alone.'

'And that other letter *was* a forgery of my brother's real letter, with some parts left as they were. See here!'

'Ah-ah.' Aristotle studied the new document intently. 'The real letter sent by Theodoros. That young man will go far. He had the wit to send the same letter twice – once to the address you had given him in Naxos and again to the address in Kos. And this epistle tells us how and where the other letter was tampered with. The forgery took place in the Aegean, most likely in Kos – not in Athens.'

'Had I only got the real letter in time,' I groaned, 'I should have headed straight back home, and not gone flitting about Asia and looking for trouble.'

'But you did not get the real letter in time. Someone took great care that you should not. Nor did they wish you not to receive any letter at all, in case anxiety over your family caused you to decline further ventures eastward. In that case, I too might not have remained in Kos, nor gone to Asia.'

'Oromedon,' I said. 'Oromedon gave me a false letter. Or rather, it had been the real letter, but got altered. Kallisthenes told me it is quite easy to do that – you can even forge just part of a message, if you have the right smooth iron and a good steady hand.'

'Precisely. Now you deduce that our friend in Naxos is honest and our friend in Kos is not.'

'But the letter – the forged letter,' I puzzled on. 'It doesn't sound like Oromedon's pompous style. Would he have the wit to quote Hesiod? I can say nothing of the handwriting, for the hand was imitating that of Theodoros, but the manner of the letter was not like Oromedon. Could it be Diophantos? Or Menestor?'

'You are perspicacious. Not Oromedon's style – true. Someone other than Oromedon forged the letter, though presumably Oromedon knew the forgery had taken place. You remember how anxious he was to act as a soothing interpreter?'

'I suppose it is unlikely that Diophantos or Menestor would have been called upon just to forge a letter. And Nikias quoted to us those lines of Hesiod – which he must have heard recited by someone else recently.'

'Exactly. No reason he should have known of the

forged letter, but he had recently been in company with the the Hesiod-quoter. And he let out, before he thought, that it wasn't Diophantos who had recited those verses to him, but another. We know something else now, too. An actively hostile agency in Athens has something to do with Thrasymakhos. A well-born man with good connections, some say an orator. Not a lout. Yet his servants were harrying your family in Eleusis.'

'This is terrible! How can I know that my family are all right! – for the time when this letter was sent is now some weeks ago.'

'Theodoros' real letter,' Aristotle observed, 'indicates that Smikrenes has sworn out a charge against the servants of Thrasymakhos. That should put a sufficient stop to them at least for a while. It ought to occur to Philemon to do so as well. A pity your cousin has not written to you –'

'Philemon was never one for writing letters,' I said. 'Not even when he was in exile and Aunt Eudoxia was so worried. He hates writing. And Smikrenes isn't much better. I am surprised – and pleased – that my future father-in-law has sufficient Athenian spirit to prosecute a law case. But I think he dislikes letters and documents because he writes badly.'

'Well then, you must cultivate Theodoros, who seems a boy of unusual intelligence. Theodoros has covered the main points. At least, to him his dog is a main point. Let us hope that your enemy – and mine – is a rational being who knows he has overreached himself in this unnecessary attack upon Smikrenes' house. But we now have evidence that we did not possess before. Let me see if I can make it out.'

He propped his chin in his hands and stared into space for a little time.

'I seem to see Athens before me in its deep divisions,' he said after a while. 'We know that here are pro-Makedon and anti-Makedon parties. There are divisions even within these divisions – between the democrats, who want a continuation or expansion of the rule of the people, and the oligarkhs, who want to go back to the rule of a few very rich and very well-born men.

'Many of the poorer sort actually prefer Makedonian rule, seeing it as a means of checking the aspirations of the wealthy and powerful. Some of these are vociferous supporters of Makedon, arousing the ire of certain Aristos. Some of the older and wealthier families see any favour to Makedon as treachery, and as an impediment to their elevation. But of course there are many rich and powerful people who prosper under Alexander and quite like Makedonian rule – as long as it remains indirect.'

'Athens will always be independent!' I interjected indignantly. 'Athens must remain free!'

'I agree with you, Stephanos. But what do we mean by "free"? A city, a society, is held together by the spirit of the whole. By its *constitution*, which organises it and gives it life – as an animal has a constitution which permits all its parts to function well and the entity to survive and thrive. Iatrokles says you have "an excellent constitution". So does Athens. In a man's physical body, part is unlikely to fight against part and ruin its constitution, but that is very likely to happen in the artificial body of the city-state. *Who* among all these men is going to be free to do what he wills? Difficult times we live in.' He drew his chair closer to mine. 'Now, together let us reconstruct the strange events of the summer.'

'First,' I said, 'fragments of animals are left on the herms or doorways of people sympathetic to Makedon.'

'True. But what gave someone the idea? At the festival of the Bouphonia, attended by so many whom we know, an animal is ceremonially killed and parts of it adorn our city. Soon after, as you say, fragments of animals insultingly desecrate the entryways of many houses. Including, at last, my own.'

'And mine!' I reminded Aristotle of the hideous episode of the horse's head.

'You ought, Stephanos,' he teased, 'to consider that the Black Demeter of Arkadia has as her emblem a horse's head. In some regions it might be a compliment, I suppose.'

'Kallias' poor monkey was cut up for your benefit,' I retorted. 'Do you see that as a compliment? Poor Kallias, so fond of his animal – he surely had nothing to do with slaughtering it that way.'

'No, no. I imagine Kallias still mourns his lost monkey. Kallias is fond of the new world and the new ways, which foster trade and bring in plenty of money. *He* is not against Makedon.'

'I can scarcely imagine Thrasymakhos, however anti-Makedonian, cutting up pieces of animals,' I remarked.

'Not exactly. But Thrasymakhos is important. And – good heavens, we must call in the boy Parmenion! How could I not have seen into this before? That unfortunate lad – we must talk to him.'

He sent Phokon immediately to fetch young Parmenion, who came at once. But with him came

Kleumedes, defensively standing by the boy as if to take his part against us.

'Now,' said Aristotle, 'we have some important questions to ask —'

'*Now*,' said Kleumedes sternly, looking over his bushy beard at Aristotle and not smiling, '*we* have something important to say. I have long wished to have the opportunity to speak with you, O Aristotle, and shall do so now you are free from anxiety over Stephanos. In your absence Parmenion and I have had many chances to talk. The youth has things to say to you that should have been said before. And for that I hold *you* responsible, not this lad.' Kleumedes turned to Parmenion, who was shifting from foot to foot. He was pale and nervous, but he held his head up and looked at Aristotle, who rose to his feet.

'Speak, Parmenion,' said Kleumedes encouragingly.

'Kleumedes blames you, but *I* understand,' the boy said. 'And it was partly my own fault, because I let him bully me and also deceive me —'

'Oh, by the gods! How could I have been so blind?' Aristotle cried. 'I see it all now. My poor boy — tormented, and under my own roof at the Lykeion. How blind I have been!'

'Tell him how it was,' said Kleumedes. 'Why don't we all sit down?' he added.

They all sat down around me, Parmenion too. He raised his head and looked Aristotle in the eye, directly but not defiantly. He seemed less anxious than he had in the old days; staying with the doctors must have done him some good.

'Please,' said Aristotle, 'tell me everything, my dear Parmenion. But I believe I can guess some of the truth that you tried to keep from me. You were trying to protect me, was it not so?' The boy nodded. 'Then you were brave, but ill-rewarded. And your tormentor is – must have been – Thrasymakhos' son, young Mikon.'

'Yes,' said Parmenion. 'That is so. But it only got really bad when you were away in Delphi. Mikon teased me and he tortured me, and he got some others to do so too. I accused him of being a spy on you, O Aristotle, and so he was. I caught him going through your private writings. But he called me "Makedonian bastard" – you see, he knew my parents were not married properly according to some of the laws. Indeed, my father's parents, too – Arkhebios was not quite – but great Parmenion always acknowledged him. And my uncle is Philotas, whose fame is glorious.'

'Yes. Very brave man, your father,' said Aristotle gruffly. 'And Philotas too.'

'Mikon told me that if I told on him, he would see to it that my father was punished – tortured and killed – for treason. Mikon said it would be easy for him to get Arkhebios killed, for many on Rhodos resented him. Then Mikon would tell me he found out through Thrasymakhos and his high-placed friends that my father had been removed from Rhodos and sent into Asia. Later, he told me that wasn't right, that he found my father had been secretly imprisoned in Rhodos, along with my mother's family, for disloyalty. Then he said he wasn't sure. Sometimes he told me he heard my father was dead, and that he had been executed by the soldiers in Asia – at Alexander's orders. But he wasn't certain and would keep looking into it. In a way, it is easier to talk about this now – now that I know that my father is truly dead. I can do nothing more to save him. And you are still sure that he died in the war?'

'Yes,' Aristotle affirmed. 'We have heard from more than one source. Your father died in one of those skirmishes that the brave advance guard get into. I have it on good authority that he was properly buried. His death is, alas, not deniable.'

'At least now I *know*. But *then* – I didn't know if my father were dead or alive. Or how I could help him!'

'No wonder this anxiety was too much for you in the end. But Mikon seemed to be in your company with your free will –'

'He told me I needed him to protect myself, since if he stopped being my friend *his* father – the respected Thrasymakhos – would see that I was punished, too. As I was not a citizen of Athens I could be beaten or killed. And he said that his own father might get angry at *you*, O Aristotle, and punish you as a foreigner who committed acts in his thinking and speaking which were pernicious to the state. But then Mikon said we – he and I – must both keep an eye on you and prevent you from doing wrong, so you didn't get into trouble.'

'How amazing,' I said 'A boy to do all that! And he seemed so cheerful and light-hearted. Such an engaging little fellow, really.'

'Mikon really is cheerful,' said Parmenion. 'He is richer than the other boys, and they look up to him. But it pleases him also to be important in secret ways. Mikon liked being a spy. But he is also truly interested in learning – he loves thinking of the great books cataloguing all the animals and plants. He did enjoy the studies, you know, cutting up animals and things.'

'What a viper I have nourished,' Aristotle groaned. 'How pleased I was when Thrasymakhos brought Mikon to my school! – Thinking it a sign that the old breaches were healing and that I could bring together both pro-Makedon and anti-Makedon citizens. The boy himself, so intelligent – he seemed to have real abilities in natural philosophy. Even Theophrastos and Eudemos saw nothing wrong in him. And they are both good judges of character.'

'I suppose,' I said, 'we don't expect complicated crimes from children. But Mikon was a good child, in a way. He was working to please his father. Mikon must have found out about the monument for Pythias that you planned –'

Parmenion blushed. 'That was *me*. We knew there was to be a monument, you mentioned it, but Mikon made me look in your private writings myself to see if I could find anything more. And I found who was making it, and passed on to him a copy of the inscription that was to go on Pythias' tomb.'

'Ah, it becomes clear,' I said, thinking as I spoke. 'Thus Thrasymakhos knew in advance about the monument for Pythias – and its inscription. So he was able to organise Megakles and Hypereides and the rest who came and committed the dramatic destruction. And thus they knew ahead of time how to write a parody of your inscription and set it by Kallias' monkey.'

'It was all my fault!' exclaimed the boy wretchedly.

'No, the fault was essentially my own,' said Aristotle. 'First, for not having read correctly the state of Athens at the time, and my situation. Second, for my folly in trying to get on good terms with Hypereides. It was certainly entirely my own fault that I saw that sour Epikrates and gave the seductive Antigone an excuse to visit me.'

'But that was *my* fault!' I exclaimed. 'In a conversation in the Agora I said that Epikrates and Hypereides ought to ask your advice. That probably gave them the idea of initiating the contact, so that Antigone herself could be set to entrap you.'

'Which she was successful in doing. All she had to do was to catch some phrase that would allow her to claim she had heard me speaking blasphemously. What a liar she is! But I gave her sufficient opening.' Aristotle nodded sadly. 'You have to realise that at that point I myself was in too much anxiety about Pythias' health to be thinking as usual. Then, when she died, I was too deep in simple grief to be capable of real thought. I sensed enmity – but did not analyse it. Little Mikon seemed sympathetic and pitying of my grief, like everyone else around me in the Lykeion. I should have realised he was a person most likely to be working against me in a hidden way. After the – the outrage at the Kerameikos – I knew simply that I was in danger as well as grief, and it would be best if everything cooled for a while in my absence.'

'Yet,' I remarked, 'you could absent yourself from Athens, but not from the danger. Parmenion, you felt safer – didn't you? – as soon as we left. You seemed better almost immediately.' The boy nodded, adding, 'Until things got bad again.'

'In fact,' I mused, 'instead of our leaving the danger, the danger followed us.'

'How true. And in the cause of preserving my own life and safety, the lives of others have been destroyed!' Aristotle lamented. 'Our first captain, the good Aiskhines – murdered on Naxos. I believe Aiskhines came to warn me about something, and as a practical man he must have had real reasons for suspicion. But once again, Parmenion, we had an enemy agent within our doors.'

'Yes. That crippled slavewoman Doris,' I interjected, relishing the chance to explain. 'Doris – who pretended to have injured her ankle, so she could remain in Aristodamos' residence and watch us. Doris, who had access to the kitchen knives in Aristodamos' house – and to the Naxian powder for efficient cleaning of cutlery. The woman who could keep her dog quiet.'

'Stephanos and I discussed this before, Parmenion, and we believe that Doris was an enemy agent sent to watch us from the day we set out from Peiraieus.'

I took up the history again, for the boy's benefit:

'There were two agents, Parmenion, aboard the *Eudaimonia*. One was Doris, the enemy's tool. The other was Philokhoros, commissioned by Antipater to look after us.'

'Oh, him,' said Parmenion. 'The man with the long nose who slobbered over his boy.'

'Precisely. Philokhoros was spotted by the enemy spy as an antagonist and temporarily put out of action once we arrived in in Delos. Decoyed away and thrown into a pigsty in Mykonos. He was not very efficient. Whereas Doris was very effective. She got rid of the captain and managed to get us aboard the craft of Nikias.'

'There may have been a third agent,' Aristotle added. 'That marble merchant Miltiades. He reacted dramatically to the bloodstains on the *Eudaimonia* at Skardana, hurrying off to betray our "murder" to the magistrate at Delos. He could himself have easily created the smears of blood in the ship. This incident, I suppose, was meant chiefly to frighten us, perhaps to detain us for a while. Though possibly there was a genuine hope we might fall truly foul of the law.'

'Miltiades followed us to Naxos,' Parmenion remembered.

'You know,' I confided, 'I thought there was something odd at the time. If he were really in the marble business, wouldn't he have picked up the offer of the other marble-man and visited Paros? At one time, I think, he sounded as if he did business in Paros, but when he got near that island he seemed to deny any interest in it. When I get back to Athens, I shall try to find if there really is a Miltiades in the marble business. Just out of curiosity. We have no legal complaint against him. But you notice, under pretext of moving a statue, he took charge of our movements by hiring the *Eudaimonia* for himself for two days.'

'That,' said Aristotle, 'might connect with why Aiskhines came to find us. Something he heard or saw in the port confirmed a suspicion already aroused by Miltiades' fuss and expenditure over moving a small statue – a job the crew performed more quickly than was probably intended. Perhaps Aiskhines overheard Miltiades conversing with some other person, and this told him enough for him to realise that there was a plot against us. Our good captain then rushed to Aristodamos' estate to warn us, and sealed his personal fate. But the enemy plan was probably always to put us – to put me – in the power of Nikias on the leg of the voyage from the Kyklades. The original plan may not have necessitated the death of the captain of the *Eudaimonia*, just his being delayed.'

'If Nikias was a pirate,' asked Parmenion, 'why did he not kill us once he got us away from Naxos?'

'He complained to us about his loss of the opportunity,' Aristotle replied. 'He was commissioned, I believe, to do away with me, and I fear with my close companions too. I think he needed to get to a place where he felt safe and unobserved, so he could dispose of the bodies. Waiting too long, he lost his chance. There was the storm – and then you remember, we stopped by that damaged ship and I spoke to a man aboard her. Nikias knew it would be dangerous to do away with us if that ship survived. Nikias himself told Stephanos and me that much. And so we got safely to Kos.'

'I do not understand any of this,' said Kleumedes. 'But I think an apology to Parmenion is in order, even as he has apologised to you. And now we shall go and leave you to your discussion – which, I must say, seems to interest you more than the plight of your pupil.'

'No, no,' said Parmenion. 'This is really interesting to me. I went on that voyage, too, I was among those people, and I need to know the truth.'

'So you do,' said Aristotle. 'You have my sincere apology for the pain I have allowed you to endure. That my lack of care was inadvertent does not excuse it. We shall have a serious talk, the two of us – and soon. But now, Stephanos and I need to talk.'

'We will leave you, then,' said Kleumedes. 'But I too desire a serious talk with you, O Aristotle, and soon.' And he left the room with Parmenion.

'So we got safely to Kos,' I repeated. 'But we were not truly safe in Kos. Someone's slave was looking for us. Then Oromedon behaved so oddly. And it was from his hands I got the forged letter.'

'Indeed. Oromedon's behaviour is suspicious. He knows I have arrived in Kos, but he does not invite me to be his guest straight away. He writes that pompous epistle explaining that he has someone else staying with him, a brother-in-law. Now, who is this "brother-in-law"? Oromedon is long a widower, and he never used to allude to members of his wife's family. I could be wrong, but he has no sister that I am aware of. He used the phrase, I believe, to disguise a connection with someone who was not supposed to meet us – or, rather, someone whom we were not to meet.'

'It cannot have been Thrasymakhos – he is too staid and important to turn up in an island in the East without a slow progress and a lot of fanfare.'

'No – not Thrasymakhos, who I fancy has remained snugly in Athens. But a leading spirit, mightier and more ingenious than Thrasymakhos, may have been travelling too. Think, Stephanos – whom did we meet on Delos?'

'I cannot remember – except your friend Aristodamos who guided us around, and a lot of pilgrims, and that pompous lazy magistrate. Oh, and that chatty slave and his mistress, that funny woman with the Phoenician name. Kardaka.'

'Yes. You said at the time that there was something odd about them. O Stephanos, had I been in my normal frame of mind . . . All should have been detected then and there! You and I were deflected from the scene of action while Philokhoros was being spirited away. We were guided by the ingratiating slave – who seemed to disappear immediately (probably he was an ancillary in the plot against Philokhoros). We were taken to see that woman who gave us some kind of feeble story as to why she had to see us, simply to ask for a passage for Doris. And this expensive lady was herself one of the wonders of Delos! I believe she was not a woman at all.'

'Not a woman? Kardaka?'

'The entity we were taught to call "Kardaka" was or claimed to be the *mistress of Doris*. Thus, we do have a firm line tying Doris (whom we know to be an enemy and murderess) both to Nikias and to this questionable person. *When* was Philokhoros enticed to travel towards the pigs of Mykonos? While we were spending time rather foolishly talking with Doris' "mistress". The more I look back on that scene, the more clearly I see that someone really enjoyed playing a role. There is this element in the whole terrible series of events, Stephanos, which puzzles me more than most things about it. The comedy, the irony. The work of an ironist or jokesmith.'

'Nikias certainly has a joking side.'

'Which shows that jokers can be dangerous. Nikias did indeed have a joking side, and he committed the foulest of murders. But he is not the dazzling central jester of the plot. You yourself gave me a hint, when you said the outrages at people's doorways reminded you of Alkibiades. I sense behind the plot someone of great and devious intelligence. And an oddly light-hearted quality. Playful in a strange way.'

'Playful? Yes, that reminds me. I have something to show you.' I got up and moved about my room. 'I had almost forgotten, in my stupor. I'd intended to show you, when we were alone.' I took out from my stuffed leather bag the shiny object I had discovered under the thwarts of Nikias' ship. A gold knucklebone.

'I know only one person who has a gold knucklebone – a pair of them. Euphorbos. I saw him playing with them when he was talking in the Agora. And after the battle of the islet was over, I found this thing shining where it had got caught in the planking of the *Niké*.'

Aristotle took the golden object and examined it closely. 'You think this is his?'

'Yes. When I saw it through the bloody water swilling around that wretched ship, the memory of Euphorbos came at once to my mind. Though my mind was hazy then because of the pain. And if this gold toy does belong to Euphorbos that would mean –' I could feel myself wrinkling my brow in an effort to work it out clearly – 'it would mean there really was a connection between him and Nikias. Euphorbos would have been a passenger on the *Niké*, some time before – but not long before – our accursed trip from Halikarnassos to that dreadful island!'

'Excellent, Stephanos! So we clearly have an actor for the part of our new Alkibiades.'

'Alkibiades lived in history. He is dead now.'

'True. But I think we have another candidate for a similar role.' Aristotle began to play, unconsciously, with the shiny knucklebone. 'Someone tall, but not too tall, with fine features and complexion. Who could dress to advantage in woman's clothes. Someone able to sustain the part – the comic part – of a Phoenician pseudo-lady with spirit and success. Intelligent enough even to preserve the right female forms of words. So many would fail at that. I had begun to think before now, Stephanos, that the lady Kardaka was a gentleman.'

I thought back to the hot day in Delos, the strange interview with the fine lady in yellow silk speaking in her odd accent through the gauzy curtain. 'I'm not comfortable doing business with ladies, and I don't know how to deal with foreigners. It's not impossible,' I had to admit.

'Consider, Stephanos. The chief mover, in this plot – against ourselves, Athens, and certainly Alexander – would be a well-born Athenian. A leader in the oligarchic revolt. A citizen probably closely associated with Thrasymakhos, but far beyond Thrasymakhos in ability, and a good deal younger. Not only an aristocrat, but capable and versatile. This Alkibiades-person should be good-looking, sympathetic, light-hearted, apparently at times even trivial, a good mimic. Also shrewd, hypocritical, and far-seeing.'

'You are describing Euphorbos! And you really believe that when we were talking to Kardaka, we were talking to Euphorbos all the time?'

'I now think so. Though it was a good performance, and should have won any actor an extra purse in the Panathenia. Kardaka of Karthago was supposed to come from Peireaeius, and Euphorbos knows Peiraeius quite well and has observed the shrines of the goddess of Karthago, the triangle-goddess, which he mentioned. Such a performance is also free of risk. Suppose Euphorbos were discovered to be masking as a female of Karthago, or at least of Punic antecedents in this way – what then? Why, everyone would laugh and say only that teasing Euphorbos would have his joke. Nobody would ever believe such a jest was connected to real plots, or real death.'

'So – Nikias must have been a creature of Euphorbos?'

'Nikias' whole career was not based on Euphorbos – of course not. Nikias was a criminal in his own right. But

Euphorbos saw how to use him. The gold knucklebone entitles us to surmise also that Euphorbos was very close by –'

'Yes, if he were Oromedon's guest, his "brother-in-law", he was nearby. And he could have been the forger of Theodoros' letter, which he obtained while in Oromedon's house.'

'Alas, these are all suspicions, Stephanos. We have no proof. But if I am right, he was closer even than that. Why, Stephanos, you and I actually saw this man again, our ironist and joker, in Halikarnassos.'

'We did?' I was genuinely puzzled. 'Well I did not –'

'Oh yes, you commented on him. The blind man with the dreadful skin affliction. When I went into that food shop, I did two things. I left word (cryptically) for any messenger sent by Alexander or Antipater who might be looking for us. And I asked the landlord and other customers if they knew whether the poor blind man were a native of Halikarnassos and who he was. They did not know him, he had only recently come to the harbour. So I thought at the time that this strange beggar was there for a reason. Though I didn't then connect him with Euphorbos, of course. This beggar wore an excellent disguise: people get enough of beggars in ports, and feel particular aversion to someone with such terrible sores. He looked most repellent – to anybody but a doctor! Casting a doctor's eye on him, I thought the sores not quite real.'

'It is I who am blind,' I said in disgust. 'I myself have used a similar trick, in the past. And that disguise he chose fits in with the kind of joke put into Theodoros' letter. "Who cannot for himself see truth" – showing *I* was the blind man, not he.'

'And I am blind, too. For much good my observation in Halikarnassos did me.' Aristotle spoke ruefully. 'Only later did I realise this beggar was of similar height and even shape to Kardaka, though no longer female. At the time, I thought this "blind man" at the harbour was probably a spy for the government. Quite separately, I suspected Nikias, but not enough. I myself was totally deceived by Diophantos too, blinded by a sense of safety inspired by military command.'

'But we did not know *then* – in Halikarnassos – that Nikias was connected to Doris,' I said, trying to work it out. 'When we got to that dreadful islet and saw the crippled dog – I hope it died of dysentery! – we knew Doris must have been with Nikias. Between the time we last saw her in Kos and the time we got to the wretched isle ourselves.'

'Yes. And by now Kos may have given Doris a miraculous "recovery" from her lameness. I am all too confident that Doris is not the late lamented Doris, but alive and well, working as somebody's agent somewhere in the world. In communication with her good mistress "Kardaka" of Peiraieus – a personage better known to us, I believe, as Euphorbos of Athens.'

'But it was Diophantos who killed Peleus in Phaselis, and insisted on putting us in the care of Nikias. Hard to believe that an army man like Diophantos would do such things.'

'These events indicate that the party or parties working towards a new Athenian Empire without allegiance to Alexander must have some strong supporters within Alexander's army. Including numerous Makedonians who don't want to press on to the farthest East. And then

– so much money! People who get their hands on money can do more than just buy fine linens and perfume. They can command arms – assassins – spies – troops of fighting men – loyalty itself! The further off Alexander goes, the easier it is for many, even in the army, to believe – even to wish – that he will not return. The joker at the heart of these events, we may well believe, is on good terms with such disaffected persons, and actively capable of creating liaisons with them.'

'A truly ambitious man might see a good opportunity for picking up solid power as well as gold bars. It is tempting to take charge of the Greek cities of Western Asia, and all their riches.'

'Precisely, Stephanos. Again, remember Alkibiades – how he tried to use political events to suit himself? He was handsome and generous and pleasure-loving! So people discounted his ability, his ambition, and the potential extent of his treachery. He betrayed his own country in what he saw as his own interests. Yet he was entertaining. A wonderful companion at a symposium! A man of such intellect and attractiveness, he dazzles us even today when we meet him in the pages of Plato or Thoukydides! All our Euphorbos lacks is a Plato to give an account of him. Dear me, here is Philokhoros.'

Philokhoros indeed appeared, looking important and serious, not at all like a man who had been thrown into a pigpen. After hearing our profuse thanks to him for saving our lives, he wished to be informed about everything we knew, so we told him of the voyage to Kos, the trip into Asia, and our being carried to the dreadful island. Aristotle did not tell him certain things, I noticed; for instance, he mentioned the gold in the woolly bags but said nothing to Philokhoros about Harpalos' hidden hoard of secret wealth.

'And now,' I complained, 'everything is left in an unsatisfactory state. What can we do? First, do we warn Harpalos? After all, it was because we were carrying his money that we were so extremely attractive to bad persons. Especially the captain of that platoon that took us from Phaselis. They marched along with the decaying body of their commander concealed in a carpet, the stench covered by a nauseous horsehide. Aristotle, you looked so strange when Nikias threw the horsehide overboard!'

'Because,' Aristotle explained, 'I had sewn a message in the horsehide, and few gold coins, thinking it might get to the general who allegedly once owned the horse and wanted the hide. Though I now think that high-ranking horse-lover was a mere fiction. When the stinking thing went overboard, that means of tracing us vanished.'

'I knew nothing of that idea of yours. Had you told the "dolphins" of the gold coins, they would have recovered even the stinking hide,' I remarked. 'Diophantos was behind the horsehide trick. What can be done about that man?'

'Diophantos is definitely an officer gone to the bad,' agreed Aristotle. 'Dangerous. We were not, however, meant to see the contents of the carpet when we did — that was the carelessness of Nikias' men. Our seeing that corpse increased Nikias' problems in dealing with us, and also rendered the unwanted additional passengers a more serious liability. I wonder if Diophantos knows that Nikias and his gang are dead?'

'This is all very important and quite serious,' said Philokhoros, looking important and serious himself.

'Those who commissioned me are anxious to know the state of affairs both in Athens and in Asia, and to detect any disaffection in the armed forces. It had already come to notice that some orders were being countermanded, that some equipment was taken without strict authority. At the same time, in an enemy country in the middle of a war, it is important not to make open and large accusations and stir things up. So agents are sent out to find the truth – myself among them. Though my primary purpose on this occasion was to look after you, Aristotle, and see if anyone dogged your steps.'

'You were ideal for the role. Not only young and intelligent but Athenian. No Makedonian, you could escape odium on that score. Yet you had not lived in Athens and would not be recognised.'

'Just so. Now, from what you have said, there appears to be a plot extending to the army itself. The further Alexander is away from them, the more chance there is of naughty business in Western Asia. There is no time to be lost in confronting this Diophantos and bringing him down. I shall go to Asia myself. I shall soon find out if Diophantos already knows about the fate of Nikias, and if so who told him. But I shall indicate that – before they were killed – Nikias and the Theban slave both *confessed* to the murder of Peleus as well as to the abduction of Aristotle, and *fully* implicated Diophantos.'

'You must be careful!' I exclaimed.

'Yes,' added Aristotle. 'Be careful that none of this redounds on yourself. And I would rather not have it put about that I was *abducted* – like a feeble girl, an heiress or something. It is only Justice, Philokhoros, to point out that such tremendous greed might not have arisen were it not for Harpalos' and Alexander's new money. All that money washing around Asia is a great stimulative to the appetite for wealth and power – in many men. I except the Theban slave Menestor. He was moved not by lust for gold but by a desire for revenge. A twisted honour.'

'Too bad I could not have interrogated that Theban. Your concern is well meant, but don't worry about me,' said Philokhoros loftily. 'I shall never be decoyed or deceived again, and now they have no handle on my affections with which to gain control of me. Dear, I wonder where my poor little Sosios is! I'll sift this matter quickly, never fear.'

'How will you find out the truth?' I asked in my ignorance.

'The whole platoon will be put to the question individually, before being executed. They all need to be got rid of,' said Philokhoros easily. 'Don't worry. We shall learn everything in short order. The prospect of torture works wonders. Most people will tell you whatever you want to know, sooner rather than later. After a certain point of pain, most men prefer to settle for an easy death without undergoing the trouble of further questioning.

'I had better set about it at once,' he added, rising. 'If I can discover and put down such a plot within the army, my own repute will rise with the Makedonian powers.' He left amid our protestations of gratitude for his gallant rescue of us from the pirates.

'You gave him rather an edited version,' I exclaimed. 'You said nothing of my forged letter, for example. You entirely omitted Harpalos' map and secreted treasure. You never mentioned Euphorbos.'

'The writ of a man like Philokhoros,' said Aristotle

drily, 'cannot extend to a man like Euphorbos. At present, either Harpalos or Euphorbos is able to squash a Philokhoros like a bedbug. This is a matter where the utmost tact and care are required. We cannot act against Euphorbos.'

'Not when we *know* what he has done? And now Diophantos may implicate him.'

'Even if Diophantos under torture were to incriminate Euphorbos – if the officer knew so much – think how easy it is for Euphorbos to defend himself. He was never in Asia, he will say. This is all the fantasy of a desperate prisoner, incoherent outcries under torture, quite possibly the confection of some kind of blackmail by the upstart Philokhoros. He himself, citizen Euphorbos, was spending the last weeks of summer quietly with friends in the Athenian countryside, and he can produce witnesses to that effect – and so on. And we, Stephanos – we do *not* know what Euphorbos has done.'

'I suppose not.' I had to agree, but unhappily.

'We have no evidence. We have merely intelligent speculations. Probabilities. But what could we point to? Only slender threads of connection – a crippled dog, people quoting Hesiod, and a glittering childish toy. *I* am convinced by the evidence of the knucklebone – but what is a single knucklebone, even if of gold? A rare toy, to be sure, but we cannot swear that no one else in the world has such a thing! Should such a preposterous case be brought to court, it would be laughed away. We have no real evidence at all.'

'That is very disappointing,' I said. 'In the other cases of murder and crime which we have worked on together, you always found the evidence and the solution; the criminal was fully revealed. Could you use Harpalos somehow?'

'I am very sorry to disappoint you. Even sorrier to disappoint myself. But I urge you never to utter to other Athenians your suspicions of Euphorbos, at least as long as things remain as they presently are. And leave Harpalos out of it. He is too powerful altogether. He himself is devious. There is no need for someone like Philokhoros, however well intentioned, to know much about Harpalos, or his hidden treasure – or his vexing commission.'

'What are you going to do about the hidden treasure?'

'I shall certainly now *not* fulfil Harpalos' vexing commission. It is a burden to me that I know where hidden treasure is supposed to be, though a relief not to have to touch it. I must write to Harpalos, in guarded terms, telling him what has happened. And I must warn him too!'

'Warn Harpalos – of Diophantos – or Philokhoros?'

'No. Bedbugs, Stephanos! Harpalos' danger comes from himself. Sly from boyhood, he loves to play his own game and seek his advantage. Charming but not trustworthy. Alexander has fallen out with him before. He will certainly do so again if he suspects Harpalos is playing fast and loose with what Alexander naturally regards as *his* money. The best thing I can do about that treasure is to inform Antipater that it is where I know it is.'

'At least if somebody else hasn't go to it. You remember its location still?'

'The most I shall tell you, Stephanos, is that it is not a thousand parasangs from the coast of Knidos. I hsall give to Antipater the contents of both the woolly bags, and the information about Harpalos' hidden treasure. Certainly I shall not entangle myself by delivering this money to persons in Kos or Athens! They may simply be members of another conspiracy. But all I shall indicate to Antipater is that Harpalos tried to entrust all of this, including the hidden portion, to my care, out of concern for safety. He wished to make sure that there was enough money not only to pay troops in Western Asia but to cover expenses in Greece. Antipater will be well pleased. This way, Harpalos comes off well. He and his associates merely lose the money – but he keeps Alexander's good will. Because I taught Harpalos in his childhood, I have a soft spot for him – perhaps stupidly. I still could not wish him to run into Alexander's wrath.'

'But Harpalos and Alexander are friends,' I commented.

'Alexander has a very bad temper when aroused; he has demonstrated this from his childhood. He does not even consider it right to stop and think when he is in a passion. I fear now for the fate of Philotas, since great Parmenion has unexpectedly fallen from favour. We must certainly not send our young Parmenion to Asia.' He sighed. 'I cannot help feeling that it would be better for Kallisthenes if he could come home now – though Kallisthenes would not agree with me. And I have lost his beautiful manuscript.'

'At any rate it was but a copy,' I said comfortingly. 'He still has the original. At least we do know what happened to the book. There is so much else we do not know! We do not know where Doris is now, though she should be brought to her just reward. Nor do we know what happened to Philokhoros' slave Sosios. We can't be sure if he were murdered or not. But consider the strange plotters' string of murders – the lives lost.' I counted on my fingers:

'First, Aiskhines, the good captain. Second, Peleus, the efficient officer. Third, the little girl, Philokleia – that was terrible! And her mother and grandfather too may be accounted victims of Nikias. And one of our rescuers was killed. That is *six* innocent lives gone – three of these undoubtedly murder of the most terrible kind!'

'Seven,' said Aristotle gloomily. 'I count *seven* lives lost. At least I am not responsible for the first of the murders that we know of. The boy who died after the Bouphonia – do you remember him?'

'The vulgar child of the fisher-people? The bull-faced boy strutting about saying "I'm Alexander!" That was supposed to have been a sort of accident. Or – do you think he was killed for insulting Mikon?'

'Not just for that. But the boy expressed his admiration for Alexander – the popular belief that the new power means the subjection of people like us and Thrasymakhos and his friends. Admiration for Alexander growing among the poorer sort displeases such men. The boy was heartily punished for his little vaunt – killed as a sacrifice, but also as an animal. The use of the antique bronze axe – there again I seem to get a whiff of our joker.'

'Yet we can do nothing about Euphorbos?'

'*Nothing* – as things stand. The best way to handle Euphorbos now would be to find ways of harassing him with private lawsuits. That would tie the man to Athens, perpetually defending his property in civil courts. I might hint as much to Antipater. But as for bringing a charge of murder – impossible! First, who would bring a case? The lowly relations of Aiskhines? Nobody has any proof –

except ourselves. And they are no proofs, but a heap of surmises that would sound ridiculously feeble. Harangue against Euphorbos in the Areopagos? Absurd. To fail in bringing such a charge – that would be to fail indeed. These are dangerous times, Stephanos. Men lose all objection to injustice when they stand either to gain greatly or to lose their own lives.'

With this I could not be truly content, but I could do nothing more. I put my mind upon my own recovery, and was soon well enough to visit Asklepios' shrine myself. Not only I but the amazingly resilient pilgrim was able to give thanks to great Paieon, to Hygieia and to the kindly healer for recovery. Iatrokles offered many suggestions as to diet and simple exercise to restore the use of my shoulder and arm. Heartily sorry as the good doctor was for what we had been through, Iatrokles seemed almost as horrified by the fact that Aristotle had used his medical knowledge to poison the pirates' fish stew with honey (obtained as a remedy) which had been fermented and mixed in with animal and human dung and some very rotten shellfish. Concentrating on the task of getting well enough to go home, I had practically forgotten why I had come in the first place. I was surprised when one fine morning Iatrokles told me that Philokles wanted to see me.

'He's brought his *hetaira* with him,' Iatrokles said with some disapproval. 'I hope I am tolerant of young people's behaviour, but I don't want to lose the last of my respectable paying patients in Kos on the grounds that disorderly persons frequent our house.'

Well wrapped up in my himation (as there was a sea

wind blowing and my wound felt the chill) I met Philokles
and his woman in the garden. Philokles was well-knit and
personable, not in his first youth but still able to look
quite like a young man, with his curling hair and large
green eyes. I could see a decided resemblance to my
Philomela, though his hair was not the same colour. The
girl (or woman, rather) with him was well dressed and
decidedly self-possessed, even at meeting an unknown
gentleman. Philokles was unembarrassed.

'This is Nanno,' he said proudly. 'We are living
together in Kos. I am sorry we weren't here when you
came, but we were in Kalymnos. Nanno comes from a
sponge-fisher's family, and she has a good share of a
sponge-fishing business herself.'

'I congratulate you,' I said to this improper but
businesslike lady.

'Yes,' she said simply. 'I can always pick out the good
divers.'

'Now, Stephanos of Athens, I understand,' Philokles
began, 'that you want to marry my sister's daughter. But
you want something for her out of my father's estate – is
that right?'

I felt unable to object to discussing family business
with him in the presence of this strange woman, so I had
to reply.

'If I could have some legal share in the honey business
of the Hymettos farm,' I said, 'however you wish it tied up
for Philomela and our children, then I could go ahead with
a much easier mind.'

'Oh, I have no problem with that,' said Philokles easily.
'Let me in for a consideration. If you will attend to the sale
of the honey, I should be glad of some arrangement with

you. I don't intend to go back to Hymettos! Not now. I like the weather *here*. I don't have to strain my back in the cold fields, nor go climbing up steep slopes to peer into beehives and get stung. My sister is a remarkable woman. Let her work at producing, and you at selling.'

'My idea exactly,' I said. 'But of course it is *your* inheritance. Your claim will be respected –'

'I am sure,' he said, 'as long as the farm doesn't go to that lazy parasite Dropides, I shall be satisfied. I wish my niece very well. We'll get documents written up in Kos. Mind, if I have children, legitimate or not, I expect them to get a share, and I shall write that in.'

'Your heir,' I felt compelled to point out, 'your legitimate son, is entitled to the whole estate.'

'But that means marrying the daughter of an Athenian citizen and living in Athens. I am well as I am. Don't worry that I mean to come back and repossess the farm or anything. Highly unlikely. Give me a share of the proceeds, and I shall be content.'

Nanno appeared pleased, if not surprised, when Philokles registered his lack of interest in going back to Athens.

'It *is* highly unlikely,' said she, waving an elegant arm, with a gold and cornelian bracelet that looked very well on it. 'Cold hillsides don't suit my Philokles. If he wants business, why there's the sponges. Philokles has everything he could want, right here in the islands. We have a charming home. You must come and see us.'

It was astonishing to me to see a man – an Athenian citizen who would soon be related to me – give up Athens, citizenship, family lands, legitimate nuptials and lawful offspring. Philokles seemed perfectly happy with the

arrangement. He could live on Nanno, evidently. It struck
me that he and Dropides had more in common than either
could ever suppose.

Certainly I was fortunate, for Philokles was as good as
his word. Within three days I was in possession of
handsome legal writings, well attested. I wanted at least
one witness to be an Athenian citizen – and found this
useful citizen (not, as Nikias had supposed, a barbarian at
all) in the person of our recovering pilgrim. This man's
soundness of mind might have been questioned, for he
professed to have forgotten almost everything that
transpired on the island. My wound was mending, and the
way was now cleared for Philomela and myself to set up a
life together.

Once more I got on board a ship. It was no longer
summer, and there were long clouds streaking an
autumnal sky. We had put off sailing until it was almost
too late, and equinoctial gales threatened us. Fortunately,
we were on a fast transport and a big one – no light *keles*
but an impressive naval vessel with four banks of oars and
a *keleusma* that gave me a serious headache at first. I say
'we' had put off sailing, for Aristotle had refused to go
anywhere until I was well again.

This time our party did not include Parmenion. The lad
had announced to Kleumedes and Iatrokles his strong
desire to become a doctor. 'I will stay here,' he said firmly
to Aristotle. 'I shall live in Kos and learn to be a physician.
Now I have no father, and you tell me it is dangerous at
present to seek Philotas. But I have Kleumedes and
Iatrokles who want me to stay. They will be friends to me
and teach me. When I am with them I am well, and can
make others so.' I was surprised at the power the lad had

acquired, remembering the shrinking white-faced boy I had once known. Aristotle agreed wholeheartedly, almost meekly, for Kleumedes had expressed to him very frankly his disapproval of the way in which Parmenion's real troubles had gone unnoticed in the Lykeion.

So our travelling group consisted only of Aristotle, myself and Phokon. We had no less baggage than on our trip from Athens – more, indeed. Aristotle had purchased a mysterious stone chest which he had ordered sent over from Halikarnassos to Kos, and this object (wrapped up and extremely heavy) had to be put on the ship with us.

As we left the island and harbour of Kos I thought not just of the past, but of the days to come. A future when, as Iatrokles hoped, the great temple and treatment centre would be built, and Parmenion would be a doctor to many pilgrims in search of health. I left these lovely regions with some regret and some good memories – despite everything that had passed – of sunny days of sailing among the islands. The sun still gave us glimpses of the transparent world, and the sun and moon and wandering stars gave us light as we went on our way over the deep and wide sea.

Epilogue

Aristotle and I returned safely to Athens – for which I personally gave many thank-offerings to various deities. I could not, however, decide in relation to my vow whether my voyage had been successful or not. It had a successful issue for myself, in that I had found Philokles and got what I wanted. But the cost in human life of our expedition seemed very great. I went, however, as bound by oath, on a special journey to Sounion to give to Poseidon both a thank-offering for my return and an additional one for the success of my journey. Yet I do not think what we experienced on that journey was at all included in my original prayer.

Athens now seemed more peaceful. The outrages involving parts of animals had ceased. Aristotle was politely treated. There was no more talk of putting him on trial for blasphemy, or anything of that kind. On the whole, civility prevailed. Indeed, some wholesome fear seemed to have filtered through: perhaps news of the

death of the pirates, more likely of the harsh fates of
Diophantos and his platoon. At any rate, people invited
the philosopher out to dinner, just as before, and the work
of the Lykeion went on.

As for myself, immediately on my arrival I sought out
my family. At last I heard – and at length, from many
competing narrators – of the attack on Smikrenes'
holding. Two men had been lurking around, had done
some minor damage to the crops in the further field, and
had tried to entice the dog to take food from them. These
intruders were run off, but Theodoros had at once sent for
his cousin Philemon. Philemon arrived in cavalry style 'on
a horse' as Theodoros said in awed tones. (The horse of
course was borrowed.) Philemon threw himself into
turning the house and farm into a fortress, and supplied
Smikrenes and Theodoros with weapons of army quality
(also borrowed, from fellow-veterans who were personal
friends of his).

In the dark of night, the two men with others had come
back. They burned a small barn or goat-shed, yelled loud
insults, and, still hallooing, tried to knock the house door
down. One man looking for an easy entrance went on the
roof, where he was surprised by Philemon. Theodoros
loosed Moloss-Molou at just the right moment, while
Geta worked at putting the fire out. Meanwhile, my
mother and Philomela, as instructed by Philemon, set up
an irregular cacophony of shouts and banging of metal
frying pans and things. They made as much noise as
women at the mourning of Adonis. They also threw
stones: missiles collected the day before by Theodoros
and Smikrenes, directed by Philemon. This was the point
at which a certain friendship between my mother and

Philomela was cemented. My fiancée had gained, as Theodoros wrote, 'Mother's love'.

Meanwhile Philemon wounded the roof-climber and made him confess who he was, and that he and his fellows belonged to Thrasymakhos. Moloss-Molou got a good bite or two of another fellow. Smikrenes, searching for more intruders, ran about the farm holding both a pitch-fork and a shortened spear, like a man running mad. He nicked one intruder in the buttock with his pitchfork, but did not bring him down. Eventually the dog-bitten fellow and his auxiliaries gave up and ran away. Theodoros was very excited that he had been able to stand in the doorway holding a light sword, but language failed him when he tried to describe the virtues of Moloss-Molou.

Once I returned to Athens, Thrasymakhos backed down, and there was no need for Smikrenes to pursue his lawsuit. Thrasymakhos assured Smikrenes and myself that the slaves involved in the attack against the Eleusis farm and its inhabitants had been severely flogged and sold. Upon discreet enquiry, this appeared to be true. It seemed to be quite safe to take Theodoros and my mother back to their home in Athens.

I made other discreet enquiries also, and could find no trace of Miltiades among the marble merchants of Athens. Neither, apparently, had anyone in Peiraieus known of the foreign woman Kardaka. A few residents remembered a little lame slavewoman who used to appear in the district. I also heard in Peiraeius that Aiskhines' body had been brought back to Athens, after being discovered in a ravine in rural Naxos, where the unfortunate man must have been attacked by night bandits. His sister's husband now ran his shipping business.

One dull and drizzling evening Aristotle surprised me by coming to my door and asking me to accompany him to do one special thing. We went at midnight, that rainy autumn night, to the Kerameikos – myself and Aristotle, Theophrastos and Demetrios of Phaleron. The others were armed with picks and shovels. I kept watch for them, while they quickly and quietly dug up the remains (much altered) of Pythias, daughter of Hermias and wife to Aristotle. They enfolded her bones in a large blanket and silently took them back to Aristotle's home. There I saw that the Master of the Lykeion had caused the stone chest he had brought back from Kos to be set up in his garden. It was an ornate chest, with four *erotes* on the one side, well carved in stone, and on the other a forceful rendition of Medusa with her snaky hair. The remains of Pythias he deposited in this stone coffin, muttering softly formulas of prayer and snatches of poetic song as he himself laid them in that depository. 'This is the best kind of sarcophagus,' he said. 'It eats flesh hygienically and leaves the bones. That is how they treat bodies of the well-born in Asia. I would not let my Pythias rest longer in that despised soil of the dirty Kerameikos, where she wasn't wanted. Now she shall stay with me, or go with me wherever I go.'

My reappearance in Athens caused surprise and relief, and some happiness, especially to my mother who had never quite adjusted to Eleusis. My mother and Smikrenes had not got on well at first, even though all business between them had to be conducted (as propriety dictated) by intermediaries. I fear Philomela had a bad time of it for some weeks at the beginning of their visit. But the attack on Smikrenes' house had given them all a common cause. Moloss-Molou the valiant was now a prime favourite with everyone, and Theodoros was respected even by Smikrenes. It was a source of happiness to me that Mother and Philomela now got on well, and my dear parent had ceased to regret – at least, had ceased loudly to lament – my forthcoming marriage.

It was not such a source of happiness to me that my brother Theodoros – the intelligent Theodoros – had conceived a great admiration for his cousin Philemon, whom he regarded as a pillar of strength and a model of military resourcefulness. (Of course, Theodoros had no way of knowing how I had once saved Philemon's household when under attack, and it would seem boastful to tell him outright.) But I resolved that Theodoros should admire his elder brother at least as much as his cousin Philemon.

My own concerns – including persuading everyone in Hymettos to understand the new arrangement – engrossed my mind. The year of my marriage was to be very lively and busy, if complicated by the puzzling affairs of Demeter at Eleusis. But of that another time. One image connected with the activities of that strange summer when great Darius died still haunts my memory. I saw Euphorbos from time to time during the following autumn and winter – in the distance, for the most part. He did become the defendant in several lawsuits, just as Aristotle had predicted, only civil cases, but sufficient to keep a man at home instead of wandering abroad. I earnestly tried to keep clear of him, knowing (or believing) that this man was the fount of my suffering. Euphorbos might, so I thought, nurse malevolence towards me; after all, his plans had not truly succeeded, and many of his agents had suffered, even though he himself remained unharmed and unquestioned. But one evening in the following spring I saw Euphorbos unexpectedly at close quarters, almost running into him in the street. He was coming away from a party, staggering, a little flushed with drinking as fashionable young men are after a symposium. But in the moonlight and the torchlight I could see him clearly. He was wreathed in violets and swayed with joy, like Dionysos himself. It was hard to think harshly at that moment of a man who looked so like a god.